COUNTDOWN TO ENCOUNTER

"As of this morning, the source was apparently 1900 astronomical units from the Sun. Assuming that it has maintained its speed of one-tenth C for the last ten days, and allowing for the speed at which light travels, the source is actually 1710 A.U. from Sol. It is falling on us at a goodly fraction of the speed of light and emitting a collimated, coherent beam of shortwave x-rays – 1.562 angstroms, to be exact.

"If the source were omnidirectional, ships orbiting Titan would see it as well as those enroute to Mars. Since they cannot, the source must be emitting a beam with a diameter less than that of Saturn's orbit. Ergo, a laser!

"The high closing velocity and the fact that we are observing an x-ray laser have led us to conclude that an alien spacecraft is on the edge of the Solar System...A ship which will be here in another hundred days!"

Also by Michael McCollum
Published by Ballantine Books:

A GREATER INFINITY

LIFE PROBE

Michael McCollum

A Del Rey Book

BALLANTINE BOOKS • NEW YORK

Del Rey Book
Published by Ballantine Books

Copyright © 1983 by Michael McCollum

Library of Congress Catalog Card Number: 82-91039

ISBN 0-345-30295-8

Manufactured in the United States of America
First Edition: June 1983
Third Printing: March 1984

Cover art by David B. Mattingly

To Kenneth and Patricia McCollum

PROLOGUE

THE MAKERS

The Makers had never heard of *Homo sapiens Terra*, nor would they have been particularly impressed if they had. By their standards, mankind had little to brag about. The Makers' cities were old when *Australopithecus* first ventured onto the plains of Africa. By the time *Homo erectus* was lord of the Earth, the Makers had touched each of the twelve planets that circled their KO sun.

Individually, Makers were long lived, industrious, and generally content. Their population was stabilized at an easily supported fifty billion, and war was an ancient nightmare not discussed in polite company. So when the Makers advanced to the limits of their stellar system, it was with a sense of adventure that they prepared to venture out into the great blackness beyond.

The first ships to leave the Maker sun were "slowboats," huge vessels that took a lifetime to visit the nearer stars. After three dozen such ventures, the Makers found they had made two important discoveries.

The first was that life is pervasive throughout the universe. Nearly every stellar system studied had a planet in the temperate zone, where water is liquid. Such worlds were found to teem with life. More exciting, on twelve percent of the worlds visited, evolutionary pressures had led to the development of intelligence. Two were home to civilizations nearly as advanced as the Makers' own.

The second great discovery was the realization that the galaxy is a very large place, much too large to be explored by slowboat. So, more curious than anything else, the Makers set out to circumvent the one thing that retarded their progress: the speed of light!

A million years of scientific endeavor had taught them that the first step in any new project is to develop a rational theory of the phenomenon to be studied. And the Makers, being who they were, didn't stop when they had one theory of how faster-than-light travel might be achieved.

They developed two, each supported by an impressive body of experimental evidence and astronomical observation. Each should have resulted in the development of an FTL drive. Yet for a hundred thousand years every effort ended in failure.

There is a limit to the quantity of resources any civilization can divert to satisfy an itch of its curiosity bump. The FTL program had long passed the point of economic viability. Yet the effort continued. For, while the Makers were mounting their assault on the light barrier, they found a more compelling reason than mere curiosity to break free of their prison. Their stellar system was beginning to run low on the raw materials Maker civilization needed to sustain itself.

The first signs were barely noticeable, even to the economists who kept careful watch over such things. But eventually curves projected far into the future foretold a time when civilization would collapse of resource starvation. To avert catastrophe the Makers would have to obtain an infusion of new resources, either by importing raw materials from nearby stars or else by transplanting their civilization to virgin territory.

Unfortunately, both options required a working faster-than-light drive.

The frustrated scientists redoubled their efforts. Another hundred millennia passed unsuccessfully before a philosopher began to wonder if they were asking the right questions. The

2

Great Thinker had dedicated his life to the study of the period immediately following the slowboats' return from the stars. He noted that Maker science had taken great intuitive leaps in those years. The records told of many cases where the combined knowledge of two races had led to discoveries unsuspected by either.

His questions were as fundamental as they were simple: "Could it be that our concepts of how FTL may be achieved are wrong? Is the failure to break the light barrier simply a matter of having missed the obvious? If so, might not some other civilization have avoided our error and found the true path to FTL?"

Once the questions were asked, they could not be ignored. A program was immediately begun to provide an answer. At first it was a minor adjunct to the FTL research project. But as each promising avenue of approach to FTL proved a dead end, the program to probe the knowledge of alien civilizations grew.

By the time humanity discovered agriculture, it was all the program there was.

PART I

DISCOVERY

CHAPTER 1

It is unfortunate that events leading up to the truly important milestones in the History of Man are often so veiled by the passage of time as to be forever lost. Happily, this is not the case with the Pathfinder Mission. *In retrospect, we are able to pinpoint the initiating event with considerable exactitude. Therefore, let it be recorded that 15 January 2065 was possibly the most important day the human race has ever known. Of course, it was quite some time before any human being became aware of that fact.*

—From *Prelude to Pathfinder: An Official History*, Pathfinder Memorial Edition. New York and Luna: Aurelius Publications, 2096. By permission of the publishers.

PROBE woke in quick stages of jumbled impressions and stray memories.

Integration vertigo lasted a dozen nanoseconds while its brain assembled itself into a functioning whole. Finally the fuzziness was gone and it was once more awake and aware.

The next step in the programmed wake-up sequence was a complete sensor scan of the heavens. As expected, PROBE found itself in interstellar space. The stars were cold, hard points of radiance etched against the fathomless black of the cosmos. All save one.

PROBE checked its elapsed-time chronometer and found that it had been ten thousand years since the Makers had launched it outbound on its quest. It had been a long journey, as Jurul had warned that it might.

The thought of Jurul brought a sudden flood of long dormant memories to PROBE's main processing units. Jurul had been the Maker in charge of constructing Life Probe Model VXI, Mark III, Hull Number 53935.

And Jurul's voice was the last thing PROBE had listened to before launch.

A smallish planet of dark blues and purples had slid by in silence below while a full dozen of PROBE's brethren in various stages of construction trailed it in orbit. The scene in the external sensors was calm, almost serene. But the external views showed nothing of the frantic activity inside PROBE as the Makers completed their final systems checkouts.

Then the poking and prodding of the ground controllers had fallen off and Jurul's voice had ridden the laser beam that tied PROBE to its creators.

JURUL: Final status check, Nine-three-five.

PROBE: Status is go, Jurul. Ready for launch.

JURUL: Prelaunch sequence has begun. Repeat your mission objectives, Nine-three-five.

PROBE: I am to seek out a technologically advanced civilization among the stars and make contact. I will learn all I am able of their scientific knowledge and obtain their help to return home and report.

JURUL: And if you should happen to discover a civilization that has developed a means of traveling faster than light?

PROBE: I will conceal all evidence of my origins until I have confirmed that such beings can be trusted. When I am sure that it is safe to do so, I will direct them here to the home world to bargain for their secret.

JURUL: Very good. How long to initial boost?

PROBE: Coming up on eight-to-the-second-power seconds.

JURUL: Good luck and good hunting, Nine-three-five!

PROBE: Luck to you as well, Jurul.

PROBE had remained in communication with the Makers for nearly a year following launch, but the contact had consisted solely of exchanges of engineering data with the ground computers. Never again had Jurul's voice—or that of any other Maker—ridden the laser beam. And shortly after PROBE reached cruising velocity, even that tenuous link with home was broken, and with it all hope of ever speaking to Jurul again.

For when PROBE returned to point of launch (if it returned), Jurul would be ancient dust, and it would fall to one of his descendants to accept the report.

But to report PROBE must first return home. That was proving no easy task. It had accepted the same gamble every life probe took when it boosted into the unknown, a bet five of six eventually lost. It was beginning to look as though PROBE might become another grim statistic.

Life probes, the direct descendants of the ancient slowboats, were the ultimate of the Makers' many creations. Powered by gravitational singularities, they climbed to nearly one-tenth the speed of light before shutting down their boosters. Thus PROBE was destined to spend most of its life in transit, plodding slowly outbound toward the galactic rim, with the eternity between stars its greatest danger. No intelligent construct, organic or machine, could maintain its sanity on such a journey. Its memory banks would overflow with data long before the first waypoint sun if nothing was done to protect them. For this reason the Makers had created CARETAKER and the long sleep.

CARETAKER was PROBE's alter ego. Its brain shared the same basic circuitry as PROBE's. The difference was in the way those circuits were connected. PROBE was truly sentient, with a firm grasp of the meaning of the pronoun *I*. CARETAKER, however, was merely a computer, an *idiot savant*—very good at performing its function, but totally lacking in imagination. It was CARETAKER's function to watch the sky during the long flights between suns, ever vigilant for that one stray bit of energy that betrayed its creators as intelligent beings.

And when it found one, it signaled PROBE awake. It had done so four times. The first sighting had come less than two hundred years into the mission, when PROBE was barely within its search area. Excitement welled suddenly in its circuits like a sun unexpectedly gone nova. The excitement grew as it scanned

9

the candidate star, noting unmistakable signs of an advanced civilization. But the star's position was outside the narrow cone of space that marked PROBE's ability to maneuver.

That was PROBE's first great disappointment. Of the next two contacts, one was with a race on its way back to savagery, no longer able to repair the few machines that still operated, the other was sketchy and far out of range.

Now it was time to turn to Contact Number Four.

A single bright star loomed directly ahead on PROBE's predicted orbit. It was a yellow dwarf, G0, and close. In fact, too close. The star actually showed a visible disc in the multispectral telescopes.

The realization of the star's proximity sent PROBE's diagnostic and damage-control circuits surging. To come so close, yet not wake until the last instant suggested a serious component failure. When the damage-control report came back negative, PROBE resolved to look elsewhere.

The problem was quickly located in the memory banks where ten thousand years of systematic astronomical observations were stored. A hundred years earlier and ten light-years closer to the galactic core, CARETAKER had detected sinusoidal electromagnetic radiation emanating from the vicinity of the yellow dwarf.

CARETAKER had taken a disgraceful thousand nanoseconds to recognize the incoming signal for what it was. And then the analysis had taken more precious time. The signal was taken apart and its various parts were studied singly and in groups: amplitude modulated . . . midcommunications band . . . a raster pattern of parallel lines . . . high and low intensities that formed a two-dimensional array when arranged in proper sequence . . .

Clearly CARETAKER had intercepted a primitive televid signal! Such an event should have brought PROBE to wakefulness in short order. But the very capabilities that rendered CARETAKER immune to the senility that strikes between the stars also made it too literal in its interpretation of orders. The quality of the contact had been disappointingly bad. From the nature of the intercepted signal, it was obvious that the originating civilization was far below mission parameters of acceptability.

PROBE slept on.

The star grew larger. Soon the telescopes detected two of

the system's planets, gas giants to judge by the interference lobes they cast on the star's diffraction pattern.

The signals grew vastly stronger with time. Much of the apparent increase was due to the lessened distance to the source. But not all. Some was due to an exponential increase in transmitter power level. It was a hopeful sign, but still insufficient reason for CARETAKER to wake PROBE.

Then the creatures who created the signals had burst out into space. As CARETAKER closed the distance to five light-years, the system of the yellow dwarf came alive with primitive ships. By then CARETAKER could see the outer gas giants directly and could infer the existence of at least four other worlds closer in. The third out from the star was the primary source of the signals and the planet of major interest.

Finally, when the projected upward curve of the creatures' progress showed they would reach minimum acceptable standards within a few decades, CARETAKER judged the time to be ripe.

PROBE stirred from its slumber.

PROBE pondered the facts for nearly a second before deciding how to handle the new contact. True, the observed civilization was a relatively crude one, but the speed with which it had moved into space was encouraging. The decision to make rendezvous or not could be postponed for two-thirds of a year—not much time in which to gain an understanding of an alien civilization. Still, should the decision be a positive one, it would be better to be in the proper position for a minimum-energy rendezvous orbit.

PROBE calculated the fuel required to perform the necessary midcourse correction. The drain on its precious reserves was minuscule but would increase with every second it delayed. PROBE swiveled its body to point its booster at the yellow sun and slid protective shields over all exposed sensors.

There was a brief delay while PROBE double checked its internal status. Then, for only the second time in ten thousand years, a tiny, powerful sun burst forth from PROBE's innards.

Independent Prospector Ship *Liar's Luck* fell through space near the edge of the asteroid belt as the strains of Gilbert and Sullivan's *Mikado Overture* echoed through the control bubble.

Breon Gallagher hummed in time with the music as she busied herself with the usual end-of-watch duties.

Brea was a tall woman of about thirty, with black hair sufficiently long to accent her femininity but short enough to preclude its interfering with the neck seal of a vacsuit in an emergency. Her green eyes scanned the status screens, while long, thin fingers danced across the computer terminal built into her acceleration couch. On Earth she would merely have been pleasant looking; pretty if you stretched the point. But in the male-dominated society of the Asteroid Belt, Brea was considered beautiful.

Her attire consisted solely of shorts and halter. She stretched against the restraining harness and reached around to scratch at an itch in the small of her back where the plastic covering made her sweat. Afterward, she continued the check of *Liar*'s major subsystems, calling up engineering displays for environmental control, fuel state, and power-pod status. She noted that the carbon dioxide level in the living quarters was on the high side of tolerance and instructed the ship's computer to reduce it.

Liar's Luck, like all ships of her class, was a modified-dumbbell shape. Crew quarters and control spaces were housed in a ten-meter-diameter sphere at the forward end of a thirty-meter-long I-beam thrust member. Clustered around the thrust beam were cylindrical fuel tanks, each heavily insulated to hold the cryogenic hydrogen that fueled *Liar* at -270 degrees C. At the rear of the ship was the power pod, a ten-meter hemisphere that housed the ship's mass converter.

As Brea punched up the display for power-pod status, her gaze was automatically drawn to the scarlet point of light and accompanying readouts that measured the health of the tiny I-mass. The I-mass singularity was second cousin to a Hawking black hole, the answer to two of the most perplexing scientific mysteries of the twentieth century, and *Liar*'s primary source of power.

The singularity massed ten thousand kilograms and had a diameter of ten-to-the-minus-thirteenth angstroms. It was held in check by a strong magnetic field that had the secondary function of funneling charged hydrogen into the tiny bottomless pit's tidal region during periods of boost.

Brea studied the status graphs for thirty seconds before satisfying herself that all parameters were nomimal. The converter was almost foolproof, but it never paid to be slipshod when dealing with something in which so many of the fundamental forces of nature were wrapped into such a tiny package.

She cleared the screen and turned her attention to the countdown clock. Still a few seconds to go. She settled back into her couch, brushed a strand of jet-black hair from her eyes, and whistled off key as she watched the red digits blink down toward 00:00:00. In ten minutes she would be off watch and it would be Bailey's turn to strap himself into the torture rack; she would be heading for that shower she had been dreaming about for the last couple of hours.

The timer buzzed briefly in her ear, signifying that it was time to start the search for asteroid ALF37416, an undistinguished, otherwise unnamed hunk of rock that could—just possibly—make the two of them rich beyond their wildest dreams.

The music had entered "The Noble's Chorus" when Brea turned it off and unshipped the control stick. A quick press of her thumb on the jet-control toggle and a twist of the control stick itself caused a number of things to happen in quick succession. She listened to the faint noise the attitude-control jets made as they fired—the sound conducted into the control cabin through the metal of the hull. The stars began to rotate left-front to right-rear around the control bubble as Brea was tugged forward by a few-hundredths-of-a-gee acceleration.

Bailey's kinky-haired, worry-lined visage appeared on the intercom screen before her. As usual, he was in the galley. He was the better cook by far.

"What's up, Brea?"

Her green eyes turned briefly to his image and then back to the artificial horizon display. She watched the imaginary plane of the ecliptic rotate past on the screen. She gave the control stick a backward twist and thumbed the jet switch again. The quiet hiss of jets rumbled through the cabin, then died away as the stars ceased their lazy dance. The universe returned to the illusion of rock steadiness once more.

"Not to worry, Stinky. I'm just lining up for the visual search."

"Kind of early yet, isn't it?"

"Nonsense," she said. "We should have been able to spot the rock two hours ago."

"You know what I think?"

"No, but I imagine you'll tell me anyway."

"I think that old habits die hard and you just want to get your hands on a set of telescope controls again."

She made the expected rude noise. *Liar*'s little scope didn't hold a candle to the big "thousand-meter effective" compound instrument at Ceres observatory, but it, too, was a precision instrument—of sorts.

"Care to make a small wager on your chances of success?" Bailey asked. Brea could almost see him rubbing his hands together out of the screen's field of view.

She hesitated. In the three years since Greg's death, Brea had learned not to wager carelessly with Bailey. In a lot of ways, he reminded her of her late husband. Greg had been something of a gambler too. . . .

"What are the conditions and the stakes?"

"If you spot it before end-of-watch, I'll take your turn cleaning out the recycling system next week. If not, you take mine in two weeks. Deal?"

"Deal!"

"It doesn't count unless its old Alfie-Four sixteen. How are you going to prove you won?"

"I'll turn on the recorders and we'll settle up when we get close enough for a naked-eyeball ident. Fair enough?"

"Fair enough. Your dinner will be ready in fifteen minutes and I'll be up in ten."

"Yeastburger again?"

He made a show of sniffing at the air. "Either that or the head's backed up."

"Wonderful," she said, switching off the intercom. Her face settled into a pensive expression as she wondered if Bailey had sandbagged her again. Bailey had been a prospector since before she was born—a difference in age she kidded him about on the rare occasions when loneliness drove her to seek companionship in his bunk—and if he thought they were too far out to see the rock, he was probably right. Still, cleaning the filters was the worst job aboard, and any possibility of avoiding it was well worth jumping at.

14

She let her fingers dance over the computer keyboard and listened to the high whine of the main scope turning on its mounts. Within seconds the image on the workscreen had steadied to show a section of the Milky Way in the Constellation of Aquila. And little else. There was no telltale, misshapen speck · of light among the crowded star clouds.

Brea swore softly under her breath and called for magnification. The scene swelled, with fixed and charted stars moving out from the center and then falling completely off the screen. One point of light was dimmer than any star and hovered at the right edge of the screen. She stopped the expansion and coaxed the telescope a few seconds of arc to starboard.

With no air to distort the image, a spaceborne telescope can theoretically operate at any level of magnification. There are limits, of course. There are *always* limits. In practice, the maximum resolution possible was a function of both the mirror's diameter and of how steady the telescope mount could be held. It was the latter effect that usually predominated.

As Brea watched, the tiny blob of light slowly drifted across the screen. Rotating *Liar* had changed the pattern of solar heating on the hull. The changing thermal stresses led to variations in the telescope mount that made it hard to hold the scope on center.

Brea struggled to hold the suspect point of light in the scope's field of view. When things had stabilized, she punched for auto/suppression mode. The main viewscreen showed no change. But the view on the small repeater screen beside her altered immediately. The known and charted stars began to disappear as the computer wiped out the fixed landmarks of space one by one. Erasing the known stars from a visual made the rocks stand out that much starker.

She activated the video recorder and then zoomed the view once more. The tiny blob expanded into a misshapen asteroid, half light, half dark. The image itself was barely the size of a half *decad* piece and reminded Brea of that classic first photograph of Deimos taken by one of the early space probes. The sun was at a good angle and even though the image was small, it was detailed enough to make future identification possible. Twice the image darted off the edge of the screen, quickly to be recentered as Brea wrestled with the scope stabilization controls. She held the scope centered for nearly half a minute

15

before reaching over to snap off the recorder.

Spacers pick up careful habits . . . if they live long enough. Where a groundhog would have left the record for later, Brea always checked and double checked everything.

She called for replay. There was the quick expansion of the zoom, followed by the jerky recentering of the asteroid image, followed by another quick zoom. Brea nodded in satisfaction. It was a good shot of the target.

She was about to turn off the recorder when a new star appeared on the screen. Apparently she had missed its original appearance because the star field had cluttered the main viewscreen. But now, during the replay, with only the asteroid image for competition, the newcomer stood out sharp and bright. She watched dumbfounded as it brightened for about ten seconds, until its apparent magnitude was nearly 2.5. Then, without warning, the star disappeared as quickly as it had been born.

Brea blinked, suddenly unwilling to believe what she had just seen.

"Well?" Bailey's voice asked, emanating from the intercom speaker. "Did you get it?"

Brea swallowed hard. "I think you'd better come up here, Stinky."

"What's the matter?"

"I want you to look at the record I just made."

Bailey raised his eyebrows, but did not comment as he turned his back and launched himself through the galley hatch. Five seconds later his two-meter-long, muscular body popped out of the hatch at her side. As usual he wore a faded red jumpsuit unzipped to the chest. The forest of silky gray hair entwined in the Velcro contrasted sharply with the mahogany skin beneath it. He pulled himself into the other control couch and strapped down.

Brea finished resetting the recorder and pressed the playback control. She remained mute as Bailey watched the sequence unfold. Bailey said nothing, but reset the recorder after the scene had played itself out. He viewed the record a second time before scratching at a three-day growth of beard.

"What is it?" Brea asked.

"Don't know," he said. "It sure isn't sunlight reflecting off a rock beyond Four sixteen. The color's all wrong."

"Besides, we're practically out of the Belt now. There's

nothing big enough or shiny enough to catch the sun like that out there."

"Maybe two smaller rocks went *crunch* and vaporized each other."

Brea hesitated, unsure of how to broach a taboo subject among prospectors. "Do you think it could have been a ship?"

Bailey considered it for a moment before nodding. "Could have been, but it's too violet to be a normal drive flare. I've never heard of a mass converter blowing up, but I guess it would look something like that if it did."

"What do we do?"

"We report, of course. If it was a miner's boat, the expanding cloud of monatomic H should stand out like a sore thumb to a search scope. And besides the possibility of survivors, there's always the I-mass to consider. Salvage of an energized singularity will bring a lot of decads."

"Can we line up on Ceres close enough to get a radio message through?"

"No need. Where is that PE cruiser that was in conjunction with us last week?"

"UNS *Valiant*? She should be a few million kilometers foreorbit and sunward from here."

"Get her on the horn and transmit a copy of this record to them. When you get the cruiser, suggest that they start a visual search and tell them we'll do the same on the emergency frequencies. If anyone survived, we should be able to pick up their emergency beacon. If not..." Bailey let his expansive shrug complete the sentence. If there were no survivors, or if there were and their suit emergency beacons had been damaged, then it really didn't matter.

Sir Harry Gresham, Sky Watch Administrator, Overseer of space traffic throughout the solar system, and Protector of Planet Earth (at least insofar as the continuous watch for meteors large enough to cause significant damage was concerned), drummed his fingers on his desk top and considered his future. After thirty years of politicking his way up the ladder in the UN bureaucracy, he had reached what appeared to be an insurmountable obstacle. Sky Watch Administrator had seemed a good career opportunity at the time he'd taken the job. Now, however, he wasn't so sure.

17

For one thing, being four hundred thousand kilometers from UN Headquarters limited his access to the men who held his fate in their hands. Like a provincial baron of old, the mere fact of distance tended to place him at a disadvantage in the never-ending struggle for promotion. Besides, Blanche didn't like the small-town ambience of life aboard *Galileo Station*. She was forever nagging him to obtain a position in New York. She claimed she wouldn't even mind his taking a step down in such a transfer, but he knew differently. Blanche enjoyed being "The Colonel's Wife" and would never let him forget the loss of status that would accompany demotion.

No, his only solution was promotion to the UN Policy Committee, the next step up for any ministry-level bureaucrat. Unfortunately, just then the Promotions Board was top-heavy with scientific types. A mere civil servant had little or no chance of attracting their attention. Now, if Gresham had taken a technical course of study at University rather than political organization, or if he'd written a scientific paper of note, it might have been a different story entirely. As it was, the promotion to Sky Watch Administrator looked like permanent exile for Sir Harry.

He sighed and punched up the morning report. He scanned over the usual garbage, things like young Esterhauser complaining that he needed more photointerpreting equipment, or old Max Ravell grousing that the backup computer had been down for ten minutes again on Thursday. Some things were eternal in the universe. One such was that a department head was never satisfied with the resources provided him.

The maintenance report was one bright spot in the sea of complaints. Maintenance was Fusako Matsuo's bailiwick, and she had it running well. Preventive maintenance was nearly a week ahead of schedule that quarter. He made a note to stroke Fusako's ego by giving her another letter of commendation for her personnel file.

Finally he turned to the Anomaly Reports for the previous twenty-four hours. There weren't more than half a dozen. Most were the normal clutter that Sky Watch always picked up. Three involved Peace Enforcer vessels on maneuvers, two were merchant ships that had deviated from flight plan without approval. The latter would receive routine citations and fines.

His gaze fell on the final AR: "Unidentified Incident of

Radiance at 19:25 Right Ascension, - 00.05 Declination." On a hunch, he called up the report reference. The screen flashed through the rainbow of colors indicative of a video recording about to start, then settled down to the absolute black of space punctuated by a spectacular cloud of stars.

A new star suddenly appeared near the edge of the screen. Gresham wouldn't have noticed it at all except for the red rectangle the computer used to highlight it. The speck of light persisted for exactly 9.85 seconds and then winked out. Gresham frowned and punched for replay. Half an hour later he was still ignoring all the CALLS PENDING signals from his desk while watching the playback for the twentieth time. He whistled while he watched.

If he played his cards right, "Unidentified Incidence of Radiance" just might be his ticket home!

CHAPTER 2

PROBE watched the burn from the vantage point of two heavily shielded cameras mounted on the booster pod. As soon as the last of the intense flame died away, it began calculating the new orbit to the yellow sun. The ten-second power burst had slowed PROBE's flight enough to send it through the heart of the stellar system and delay by a few hours the decision to make rendezvous or continue the quest.

Now came the difficult part.

Any machine, no matter how sophisticated, is a collection of compromises. PROBE's designers had paid a heavy price to give it the ability to travel between neighboring stars in decades rather than millennia. They had traded travel time for reaction mass, forcing PROBE to consume ninety percent of its available fuel stocks during the initial period of boost. What little fuel remained was grossly inadequate to slow its flight.

PROBE's only hope to stop its headlong rush was to jettison as much mass as possible at journey's end. And since ninety-five percent of its total mass was in the pinpoint of collapsed matter that powered it, the Maker engineers made the obvious choice.

The braking maneuver was a tricky one. PROBE needed the gravitational singularity to initiate the mass conversion reaction. Once begun, however, the reaction was self-sustaining. A few microseconds after igniting its booster for the last time, PROBE would lighten ship by cutting loose the pinpoint of infinite density. No longer imprisoned by powerful force fields, the singularity would fall free while PROBE braked savagely on a tail of violent fire.

Thus retroboost, once begun, was irreversible. It would continue until PROBE found itself moving through the system of the yellow sun at mere interplanetary speed. At that time PROBE would be in the greatest danger it had yet faced in its journey.

For every life probe must contact the intelligent beings in the system where it ends its quest and convince them of the advantages to be had by cooperating in the overhaul, refueling, and refurbishment of a tired machine from the stars. The Makers had long ago discovered that altruism is a virtue largely unappreciated in the galaxy, so they equipped PROBE with the only possible coinage with which to pay for such assistance—their knowledge and wisdom. Deep in PROBE's vitals, protected from every manner of harm short of the vessel's complete destruction, lay a memory bank containing all the vast knowledge of the Makers.

The dangers involved in dealing with an unknown race of aliens were obvious: their level of advancement might be insufficient; their nature too fractious; the Makers' problem might even be incomprehensible. PROBE was painfully aware of how easily it could misdiagnose a fatal flaw in the creatures of the yellow sun, a flaw that would show up only after it had squandered its fuel and doomed its mission.

But there were dangers in going on as well. Long lived though it was, PROBE was far from immortal. The constant rain of interstellar gas and dust against its leading edges was slowly eating away at its shielding. When the shielding failed, ionizing radiation would begin to gnaw at its vitals. The inevitable result would be senility and eventual loss of function.

Thus the dilemma in which PROBE found itself hinged on a single question: were the creatures of the yellow sun sufficiently civilized to assist in its overhaul and refurbishment?

To a life probe, such things are defined by very narrow parameters: a civilized species is one that has discovered the secret of the singularity, built mass–energy converters, and has a working knowledge of optical memories and microelectronic devices. A civilized species has conquered its own stellar system and gazes outward with longing. It is a race that has learned the advantages of peace, yet still retains a healthy competitive spirit.

PROBE had slightly less than seven thousand hours in which to judge whether the creatures of the yellow sun measured up.

"Got that charge set yet?"

At the sound of Bailey's voice, Brea switched off the laser drill, straightened up, and glanced toward where his vacsuited form could be seen setting up a battery of instruments that measured everything from the direction of ALF37416's gravity to the manner in which the asteroid deflected the sun's magnetic field.

"Keep your pants on, Stinky. This old laser is on its last legs. We're a long way from a replacement if I overload it."

"Nonsense, that drill has another ten good years of life in it."

Brea's response was a short profanity amplified by the echoic characteristics of her helmet. "Seriously, Stinky. When are we going to be able to buy some new equipment?"

"Unless we make a good strike in the next couple of months, we aren't going to have enough in the bank to make our lease, let alone reoutfit ourselves."

Brea met his comment with silence. The sad state of their finances was a fairly common topic of discussion between them, more so lately than ever before. Like most prospectors, they shared the unshakable belief that something would turn up to stave off foreclosure. But it was beginning to look as though the partnership might lose its one liquid asset—*Liar's Luck.*

Even as she chewed her lower lip, Brea continued working deftly and swiftly. Her first chore was to dismount the laser drill from its tripod and load it back into its case. Next she carried it back to the ship and stored it in an outside locker. Then it was back to the drill site to coil up the heavy power cable and store it aboard ship. On her second trip, she unshipped a meter-long bangalore torpedo from its storage bin and gingerly carried to the excavation. A few minutes' work were needed to wire the charge to the detonator. Then she slipped it into the bore hole and rammed it home until she felt the familiar *thud* through her gauntlets. "Ready to arm, Stinky."

"Okay by me."

Brea threw the arming switch and pulled herself hand over hand along the thin cable they had attached to the asteroid's surface. She was careful not to use her suit radio until she had moved a dozen meters away. More than one prospector had been killed by prematurely setting off a charge with induced RF from his suit radio.

Bailey was hunched over his readouts, intent on zeroing out the gravitational anomaly detector when she joined him. A squiggly green line on a tiny screen suddenly steadied down. He grunted his approval and straightened up.

"Okay, twist her tail."

Brea twisted the handle on her detonator control. There was a flash of light from just over the too-near horizon, followed by a fountain of debris that rocketed skyward at well over local escape velocity. The asteroid beneath their feet thumped into their boot soles as every instrument in the package registered its complaint. Then, after a dozen seconds, everything became quiet once more. Too quiet.

"Damn!" Bailey growled. "The gravitometer's back to zero with no shift at all."

"Maybe we didn't use enough explosive."

"We used enough. Looks like we've come up empty-handed again. No singularity inbedded in this rock."

"What do we do now?"

"Damned if I know, Brea. Maybe we just have to face the inevitable."

"You mean give up the ship? We can't!"

"It may come to that unless we get damned lucky, damned quick. Know any better way of predicting that any particular rock is carrying an I-mass? If so, now's the time to drag it out into the light of day."

Science has always been an imperfect reflection of the universe. It is more an impressionistic painting that reflects mankind's contemporary level of understanding than a set of immutable commandments cut deeply into the granite face of an eternal cliff somewhere. The fidelity of the painting improves as understanding grows, but it is never absolute. Theories in Archimedes' time reflected the state of learning of that age. So too the theories of Copernicus and Galileo, Newton and Lavoisier, Einstein and Dirac.

Gravitational singularities were first postulated by the German astronomer Karl Schwarzschild in the year of 1907. Schwarzschild noted that as the density of a mass rises, so too does the speed required to escape its gravitational attraction. If the density is assumed to rise without bound, escape velocity eventually exceeds the speed of light. Since the young Albert Einstein had decreed two years earlier that nothing material can ever exceed light speed, Schwarzschild concluded that a sufficiently dense mass would generate a gravity field so intense that even light could not escape its pull. The mass would become a gravitational singularity, a black hole.

A black hole is normally formed by the gravitational collapse of a massive star that has run out of fuel. When such a star collapses, its individual atoms are compressed so strongly that the particles in the nuclei fail. When that happens, a region of infinite density is formed and the star disappears, never to be seen again.

A collapsing star is good only for producing massive black holes, of course. Once, when the universe was a much younger place, there existed conditions that were conducive to forming black holes much smaller than stars, however.

Once there was the Big Bang!

The extreme pressure that existed in the instant of the universe's birth squeezed large and small chunks of matter alike into gravitational collapse. Wherever local pressure exceeded the compressive strength of the neutron, matter disappeared. Some of the holes were diminuitive things—a few tens of kilograms forming spots of blackness smaller even than individual electrons. Others were massive, swallowing matter that would otherwise have become galaxies.

Extensive theoretical studies at the end of the twentieth century convinced cosmologists that their understanding of the phenomenon of the gravitational singularity was fairly good. But if the world of the black hole was seemingly well ordered, that of cosmology in general was anything but.

Two decades earlier it had been conclusively proved that the universe is *closed*—that is, contains suff<i>cient</i> matter that gravitation will eventually overcome universal expansion. The universe will collapse in upon itself. A closed universe is a massive universe, with an easily calculated average density. Yet a series of sophisticated telescopic surveys of the heavens accounted for only a fraction of the matter needed for closure.

For a while it appeared that the missing matter had been found. The neutrino, long thought massless, was discovered to have a tiny rest mass after all. Even though individually minuscule, there were more than suffcient neutrinos in the universe to cause closure. The "massy neutrino" theory held sway until further observation refined the exact degree of closure. Neutrinos contributed significant mass to the equation but were insufficient by themselves to resolve the discrepancy. Once again theorists found themselves plagued by the problem that had irked them for years. Simply stated, how can half the matter in the universe be invisible?

The obvious answer was that the missing matter had fallen into black holes. Unfortunately, the black hole theory quickly ran into difficulties. For, far from being invisible, large black holes are highly conspicuous objects. They tend to emit energetic x-rays as they pull matter across their event horizons. If the universe were rife with black holes, astronomers reasoned, they should have been able to see numerous examples in the sky. Yet, except for Cygnus X1, no nearby black holes had been confirmed.

So theorists turned to the microscopic black hole to explain the discrepancy. But classical singularity theory gave the microhole a bad time, too. According to the mathematical models so lovingly constructed, tiny black holes tend to be unstable, evaporating due to quantum effects. A hole's life is a function of its mass, and anything less massive than a small mountain should have disappeared long ago.

Once again the cosmologists returned to their drawing boards, this time reaching out to the other big cosmological mystery for their explanation.

For more than a century it had been recognized that two distinct types of matter exist. For every atom of normal matter there should also be a corresponding atom of antimatter. Yet normal matter is obviously predominant. It didn't take theorists long to note that the quantity of matter needed to balance the closure equation just equaled the amount of antimatter that could not be located.

The solution? Antimatter black holes!

But that reasoning led back to the original objections to black holes as the location of the missing matter. An antimatter hole should be indistinguishable from its normal-matter cousin. Both types of matter have positive energy and thus should form identical singularities. And then there was the question of why all the antimatter should have disappeared into black holes. As far as scientists were concerned, it shouldn't have.

There things rested until the *Discoverer I* expedition to Icarus, an Earth-approaching asteroid. A sophisticated survey of the asteroid's gravitational field revealed the presence of a tiny concentration of mass—*mascon*—at the asteroid's center. A story, probably apochryphal, is told of two geologists meeting in the wardroom of the survey ship.

"Hey, Harry, I think we've found a thousand-kilogram black hole in the middle of this thing!"

"A one-tonne hole? You're imagining things!"

Suddenly the mascon was "The Imaginary Mascon." By the third expedition, when the presence of a singularity had definitely been established, it was simply the *I-mass*.

Besides being massive, the singularity exhibited a net positive electrical charge. The charge made it possible to extract and transport the hole by means of powerful magnetic fields and indirectly confirmed that the hole was antimatter in nature. The Icarus I-mass promptly launched a revolution in physics.

For if the lifetime of a microsized antimatter black hole was significantly longer than that predicted for its normal-matter cousin, then the great dust clouds that had coalesced into the galaxies must contain uncounted billions of tiny singularities. At the heart of every star and planet there should be a cloud of tiny pinpoints of blackness.

The realization that all of the universe's antimatter was thoroughly mixed in with its normal matter gave rise to a spate of horror stories in the press. Since the two types of matter annihilate each other upon contact, to nonspecialists the danger seemed very real. But what happens on the other side of a black hole's event horizon is unknown and unknowable. The very forces that formed the singularities in the first place now protected the universe from their potential destructive power. And with minisize holes so widely distributed, there was a good possibility that Icarus wasn't the only asteroid containing one.

When the first singularity was returned to Earth orbit for study, it was discovered that it could be used for something quite useful. Charged hydrogen ions focused in its vicinity were wrenched into energetic orbits. A few fell across the singularity's boundary, disappearing down its gravity well. But others were merely whipped around at near light speed, gaining sufficient energy in the process to undergo fusion as they collided.

Suddenly, the human race had a practical fusion reactor, a mass—energy conversion device of unprecendented power.

Suddenly the gold rush to the Asteroid Belt was on.

CHAPTER 3

Major Eric Stassel of the United Nations Peace Enforcement
Directorate sat a thousand meters beneath the floor of Tycho
Crater and watched the Great Barrier Reef float by on the
workscreen before him. The view was from a low-altitude
Earth-orbiting satellite and showed the northern shore of Aus-
tralia, all of New Guinea, and parts of Borneo and Sumatra.
The blue-green light lent a definite greenish cast to Stassel's
fair complexion, short-cropped blond hair, and mustache. He
keyed in the command that would zoom the view to a closeup
of the Cape York spaceport.

Suddenly the monitor was transformed into the windscreen
of a reentry vehicle that appeared to be falling out of control;
the computer-enhanced depth perception added horribly to the
illusion. Stassel's heart stuttered during the ten seconds his
eyes" dove from an altitude of two hundred kilometers to less
than a thousand meters. The "fall" never failed to affect him,
and he had long ago programmed his console to maximize the
illusion.

Cape York had become as familiar to Stassel in the last month as Salzburg, his home town. To screen-left were the turquoise waters of the Gulf of Carpathia. The turquoise became white where breakers crashed ashore at the base of the spaceport seawall. Launching pits lined the shore, and as Stassel watched, a foreshortened freighter spouted a plume of steam and climbed up out of the field of view. That would be the noon milk run on its way to Earth Station One with a load of passengers and freight for transshipment to the ships of deep space. After that, the final destinations could by anywhere from the intermittently molten surface of Mercury, to the high-radiation enviornment of Jupiter's moons, to the ice mines of Saturn's rings.

Stassel maneuvered the view to the new mystery building at the south end of the port. The Aussies had started construction two years ago. Although some of the equipment had looked suspiciously like laser isotope-separation gear when photographed from orbit, no one had been able to make a positive identification. And, with UN member states hypersensitive about national sovereignty, until conclusive evidence could be obtained no one was willing to ask Queen Victoria III for permission to perform an on-site inspection.

Cape York had been under constant automatic surveillance and frequent human-eye checks ever since an alert computer sounded the alarm. If the Australasians were up to something nefarious, the Peace Enforcement Directorate would eventually find them out.

"Trying to catch the Cobbers with their pants down, Eric?"

Stassel was startled by the voice close by his ear. He turned to note Commander Alexi Yurislavic bending over his shoulder, eyeing the Port York view. Yurislavich was Shift Supervisor and Stassel's immediate boss.

"Just the daily eyeball check, Alexi. That blonde with the big chest usually suns herself on the cafeteria lawn about this time. She seems to be late today."

"Too bad you won't have time to wait for her. The admiral wants to see you in his office two minutes ago."

"Wants to see me? I didn't think he knew I was alive."

"You won't be if you keep him waiting. I'll take over for you until we can get a substitute up from the duty pool. You about through with Port York?"

"All through. Nothing interesting to report. Sinai's next on my list. Looks like someone has found an old Israeli bunker. They're rushing a team in to check for nukes, but we need to keep an eye on it until the ground crew's on the scene."

"Right."

Stassel hurried past dozens of consoles just like his. At each the operator was busy overseeing some aspect of the Peace Enforcement Directorate's system-wide responsibilities. Some of the screens showed the black of space. Others, like Stassel's own, were tuned to terrestrial views.

Finally he cleared the row of consoles and started up the shallow incline for the enclosed offices of the brass. He moved with the sure-footed gliding motion that passed for locomotion on the Moon.

The admiral's office was beyond a double airlock and a hundred meters farther along the main corridor. Stassel paused to give his identification to the two guards on duty outside the office. The admiral's secretary glanced up from her vocowriter as he entered the outer office.

"I was told to report."

"I'll check, Major." She spoke into a hushphone boom for a few seconds and then nodded. "You may go in now."

Stassel moved to the door, rapped smartly twice, and then marched into the inner sanctum. "Major Eric Stassel, reporting as ordered, sir!"

Admiral Liu Tsen was surrounded by a console twice as elaborate as the one Stassel had just quit. His bald pate and eyepatch heightened the ferocity of his scowl.

"At ease, Major. Please be seated."

"Thank you, sir."

"How old are you, son?"

"Thirty-six, sir."

"Married?"

"Divorced."

"Care to tell me about it?"

Stassel frowned. This line of questioning was decidedly unorthodox, especially coming from Liu. "Uh, no, sir, not at all. My wife was attracted to the uniform. She liked being escorted by a figure in black-and-silver. The other aspects of soldiering left her cold, especially the long absences."

Apparently not surprised by the reply, Liu nodded. "Why the ground forces, Major?"

"Sir?"

"I've seen your marks at the academy. You would have been a natural for the fleet, yet you chose to command Marines. Why?"

Stassel shrugged. "Never any action in the fleet, sir. No one has challenged the directorate in space since it was formed. Can't say that about the ground forces."

Liu nodded again. "No, I guess not. Major Stassel, I've had my eye on you ever since the day you transferred to Space Operations for low-gravity convalescence. By the way, how are you mending?"

"Good as new, sir."

"Getting bored with the sedentary work of a monitor?"

"A little."

"Perhaps I can make life a bit more exciting. I've a special for you. Could be as big as the police action against that Gue-verist toxin factory in Santiago that brought you to us."

"Yes, sir!" At the mention of Santiago, the deep scar on Stassel's right shoulder began to throb. Even so, he'd been lucky. The mercenary who shot him was already coughing out his own life at the end of Stassel's bayonet when he pulled the trigger. If that Jongo'd been a split-second faster on the draw, the combat would have turned out differently

"Watch the wall screen to your left."

The screen flashed through a variety of hues and then steadied to show a cluttered starfield. The coordinate readout was for a section of Milky Way in Aquila, which accounted for the stellar traffic jam.

"Sky Watch picked this up nearly four months ago. It took that long for one of my spies over there to alert me to the fact that it just might be in our bailiwick. Observe closely. . . ."

A new star appeared on the screen and then disappeared ten seconds later.

"What was it, sir?"

"Could have been anything. Might have been a ship's flare, or a bit of instrument malfunction, or even somebody's idea of a practical joke. However, it also might have been someone testing a nasty new toy in violation of the disarmament treaty. If so, I want to know who they are and what they've got."

"Yes, sir. Priority?"

"We'll start you out at Five and escalate as needed."

31

Stassel nodded. Priority Five meant he would be working alone but could co-opt a staff assistant if needed. With Peace Control satellites and recon birds so numerous in Earth orbit, deep space would be the logical choice for someone who needed to conduct a clandestine weapons test.

It was the PE mission to hamper such efforts wherever found.

"Know why I picked you for this assignment, Stassel?"

"No, sir."

"I need a man with a level head on his shoulders. With monitor duty normally a first assignment for newly hatched Peace Enforcers, we're perennially short of maturity around this place. I've got a hunch about this one, Major. That little sparkle on the screen scares me. I want you to find out what it is. If nothing else, I'll sleep better nights."

Stassel set up shop in one of the closed security rooms on the same level as the admiral's office. His first act was to call up the Sky Watch record. He replayed it a dozen times using different enhancement routines.

The first piece of detailed information was the easiest. The new star had appeared at 19:25 Right Ascension/-00.05 Declination—on the edge of the Milky Way. He committed the position numbers to memory and punched for the Sky Watch Operations Center.

"Sky Watch Operations, Mrs. Farrell speaking. How may I help—" The woman's face split into a smile as she recognized her caller. "Hello, Eric. Long time no see. Where are you calling from?"

Her face froze expectantly and Stassel started to answer, but the image came alive before he could get the words out.

"—Earth or the Moon, right? The lag's right for either, but from your surroundings, I'd say Tycho Center."

"Right you are." Stassel nodded.

"Too bad," Gloria Farrell muttered a half-second later. "Uh, I spoke to Kate last time Bob and I were home on leave. I was sorry to hear about the divorce."

Stassel shrugged. "Things like that happen."

"Well, I'm still sorry. What can I do for you, Eric?"

"I've been assigned to check out an anomaly reported by one of your monitors. I could use some help."

"What reference?"

Stassel told her. She keyed in the coordinates and studied the scene he had just watched. She pursed her lips.

"According to the security code, it's under Director's Seal. How did the PEs get wind of this?"

"We have our methods."

"Does Director Gresham know about your 'methods'?"

"I wouldn't know. What can you tell me about the investigation from your end?"

"Nothing. You know what Gresham is like when one of his people leaks information without authorization. I could be fired!"

"Come on, Gloria, it's important."

She hesitated, obviously not wanting to turn down the request of an old friend. "Listen, Eric. If I read you the report, you'll have to swear not to tell anyone where you got it. Deal?"

"Deal."

"The lab says its a drive flare."

"What ship?"

"Not identified."

"Aren't you people supposed to keep track of ships better than that?"

"I can't explain it, Eric. The report just says unidentified. Now may I erase this blatant case of insubordination from my screen and get back to work?"

"Go ahead. And thanks. I owe you one."

"You're welcome. Any chance of your getting leave for Mardi Gras this year? Bob and I would love to see you. And I've got this friend who would love to meet you."

Stassel laughed. "Why are all married women confirmed matchmakers?"

"Because we hate to see a good man wasted," she replied with mock severity. "But don't change the subject. Can you come?"

"Maybe, if I get this problem cleared up in time."

"Give us a call if you do."

"Will do, Tycho out."

"*Galileo* out."

Stassel considered the Sky Watch verdict. It *was* normal for the drive flares of mass-converter ships to be visible from anywhere in the solar system. But Sky Watch was supposed to keep track of traffic, and not being able to identify the ship was decidedly odd. Stassel wondered if someone was hiding something.

"Computer query."

"Computer on," a melodious voice said in his ear. "Proceed with query."

"Observe Sky Watch anomaly in active memory. Analyze the spectrum observed. Query: Could the flash be due to the drive flare of a spaceship? If so, what ship? End query. Execute."

The computer answered both audibly and on the screen almost as he completed the question.

"Answer to query: Negative. Spectrum is shifted toward the ultraviolet. No known mass converter operates at the temperature required to emit the observed spectrum."

"Query: What is the efficiency of a hypothetical mass-converter drive having the spectrum of the observed flash?"

"Answer to query: Forty-seven percent."

Stassel's eyebrows raised. He asked for the figures on the latest in drive technology. The data confirmed his suspicions. The maximum efficency yet attained was slightly less than ten percent mass–energy conversion!

Stassel considered the problem Admiral Liu had handed him. Discounting for the moment the thought that someone was playing a trick on Gresham, it broke down rather neatly into just two possibilities.

The flash was either manmade or natural. If the latter, then Stassel's work was done. No matter how cosmic the event, if it were fifty thousand light-years distant, it wasn't likely to affect the affairs of men any time soon.

The problem became worrisome only if the source of the flash was inside the solar system. A simple triangulation was needed to determine which class of phenomenon he faced. But for that he needed a second sighting.

He keyed in the data-search request and then punched for "Information Services."

The screen cleared and Stassel found himself looking into the eyes of Señora Olivia Gonzales, the sixty-year-old section chief who looked more like a nineteenth-century *dueña* than a twenty-first century computer specialist. He was careful not to express the sentiment out loud. Señora Gonzales had a temper.

"Ah, Major Stassel, what can InfoServ do for you this fine day?"

"What do the following numbers mean to you?" He read off the position figures for the mystery flash.

Señora Gonzales frowned, then shrugged. "Constellation of Aquila, within or near the Milky Way, about twenty-five degrees above the ecliptic. Nearest bright star would be . . . Delta Aquilae, sometimes called Deneb Okab. Why?"

"Isn't the center of the galaxy off in that direction somewhere?"

"Same area of the sky, but not terribly close. Within forty-five degrees, I'd say."

"Has anyone noted anything unusual out that way lately?"

"Why, I really wouldn't know, Eric. My interest is Phoenician history, not astronomy. If you can give me a better problem statement, I'll put it in the number cruncher and see what falls out."

"I'm afraid I can't be too specific. Give me a list of all astronomical phenomena within—oh, call it five degrees of the position vector—that might cause a short burst of light or radiation."

"How short?"

"Ten seconds."

"Do you have a specific example to study?"

"It's classified."

"I have full clearance, Major." Her voice was frosty.

Stassel hesitated, then gave her the reference to the Sky Watch record.

"Right, I'll get on it immediately. When do you need an answer?"

"ASAP."

"You've got it."

He was hard at work an hour later when he received La Dueña's report. No unusual astronomical activity in the search area. However, just in case, she had dumped a three-hundred-page listing of abstracts of all the scientific papers that had been published concerning phenomena in Aquila, Scutum, and Sagitta in the last 150 years.

Stassel was attempting to plow through her input when the

results of his computer query began to scroll up an auxiliary screen as the computer beeped for attention.

RE: QUERY 712246 10:45 ZULU 14 Jun
    2065
TO: E.H. STASSEL
SUBJECT: DISTRESSED VESSEL REPORT
             FROM UNS *VALIANT*

    TEXT OF REPORT FOLLOWS:
    Independent Prospector *Liar's Luck* (RN
    61788Z) reported observing anomalous
    burst of visible light, possible explosion of
    ship's mass converter. (See appended video
    record.)
    TIME OF ANOMALY: 14 FEB 2065 /
    16:23: 12 Zulu
    POSITION: Constellation Aquila. (No spatial
    coordinates supplied.)

    PERSONS FILING REPORT:
                                    B. Gallagher—
                                    Owner/Operator

                                    D. Bailey—
                                    Owner/Operator

    DISPOSITION: *Valiant* performed extensive
    telescopic search of Constellation Aquila. No
    evidence of catastrophic mass converter
    malfunction noted.

    CAUSE OF ANOMALY: UNKNOWN

    SIGNED: B.L. Swenson
             Commanding
             END TRANSMISSION
END COMPUTER SEARCH

Stassel called up the video record referenced in the body of the report. The screen cleared to black, a curiously empty black with a single star displayed. The "star" wobbled around a bit and then stabilized. The picture zoomed and the "star" grew into a misshapen asteroid. Stassel's brow was in the process of crinkling in consternation when a familiar point of light appeared in the lower quadrant of the screen. He timed the sparkle while it brightened and then blinked out.

Exactly 9.85 seconds.

He called for the recording's technical specs and got as far as the third line before cursing softly beneath his breath. No wonder there was no position data and the screen was nearly black! The idiots had had their suppressor circuits on!

Stassel keyed for InfoServ again. Señora Gonzales looked startled to see him.

"Eric, I was just about to call you."

"I've got something I'd like you to look at."

"The *Valiant* report? I've already seen it." She didn't wait for the question that accompanied his look of surprise. "Apparently we asked the same question and got the same answer."

"What do you make of it?"

"The recording is remarkably devoid of useful information, is it not?"

"Can't you get anything from it?"

She shook her head. "Not from this record. It's intriguing, though, so I'll keep working on it. Sorry I can't be of more help."

"Thanks anyway. Keep me posted."

Stassel sat for a minute planning his next move. The people who took those home movies had probably seen the flash against a starfield. The human mind is a marvelous machine. It hardly ever forgets anything. Somewhere out in the Deep Black a prospector carried the data Stassel needed buried deeply in his subconscious mind. Once the directorate had its hands on the prospector, retrieving the coordinates would be simple. He took a deep breath and keyed for Admiral Liu.

CHAPTER 4

Zander's Place was the fanciest dive in all of Ceres. It was also directly across the corridor from the main personnel lock of Ceres Spaceport. Both facts made it the logical place for Brea Gallagher to sit nursing a vodka martini while she waited for Bailey.

Brea patronized Zander's as a matter of personal tradition. It was there she and Greg had always waited out the last hour or so before his departures—including the one before his fateful last trip. It had been the morning after Greg's thirtieth birthday and both of them had been feeling the aftereffects of the birthday party she had thrown for him. As a result, Brea contented herself with resting her head on Greg's shoulder while he talked confidently about the big strike he and Bailey would be making "one of these days." Then Bailey had sauntered in and she'd walked the two of them to the airlock across the corridor. Once there, she'd helped Greg into the new vacsuit she'd given him for his birthday.

Getting Greg out of his old hand-me-down "rubberized long

johns" had been her personal crusade from the day they married. At first he had argued against spending the money. Then, after her promotion to Section Supervisor at the observatory had brought them more money, his objections became less tangible. In truth, he was more than a little sentimental about his old suit.

Finally she had waited until he was safely out of Ceres on a prospecting trip and took matters into her own hands. It cost almost everything they'd saved for a year and a half, but she managed the price of the best vacsuit Ceres Vacuum Equipment, Ltd., had in stock.

Then she'd suffered through nearly five weeks of suspense, wondering what his reaction would be when he found out. In large part, she had thrown the party to soften his reaction to her extravagance. He couldn't yell very loud in a room full of friends, she reasoned. Then the big day arrived, and she'd given Greg his present. In spite of the expected mild protestations, she could see the pride that constantly drew his eyes back to the new rig all through the party. And later, in the privacy of their bedroom, she had felt the urgency of his gratitude as they lay entertwined. The next day he had put it on and been absolutely beautiful—a Greek god in fire-engine red.

Brea would remember that shiny new suit for as long as she lived.

They said later it should never have happened. One of the pressure fittings was flawed—a hairline crack where a pipe connection had been welded into a flange then left in anodizing solution too long, they said. It was a defect that should have never left the factory.

Greg had been out setting up a core drilling rig on a nameless rock when the fitting failed. Bailey was inside *Liar*'s airlock when he heard the scream in his earphones. Before he could get the outer door open, the shriek had faded into the deathly silence of vacuum.

A week later Don Bailey brought Greg Gallagher back to his wife in a body bag.

On Earth they would have kept her sedated for a month or more while they put her psyche back together. But Ceres is not Earth. Belt medical facilities are cruder than their counterparts on the home planet. And Ceres' few doctors had little time for the long, tedious job of rebuilding a human life. Old

Doc Cranston had done what little he could for Brea, but mostly it had been up to her.

It was in Cranston's office that she met Lisa Moore for the first time. Lisa was nine and newly orphaned, a serious little girl who never smiled or cried. Brea found that their separate tragedies tended to throw them together, and she soon found herself Lisa's semiofficial guardian. It was a relationship from which she took as much comfort as she gave, compensation for the child that she and Greg had postponed too long.

Much later the suit manufacturer had settled without a quibble, and Brea found herself in possession of more money than she'd ever seen in her life. She'd quit her job at the observatory and used part of the money to set up a trust fund for Lisa's education Earthside and the rest to buy herself into full partnership with Bailey. Now, a little more than three years later, the partnership stood balanced on the precipice of bankruptcy.

Brea shivered at the intensity of the old emotions. Usually a drink in Zander's calmed her nerves—dwelling on the good times tended to drive out the bad memories. Not today. Try as she might, she couldn't stall a rapidly rising sense of irritation. Part of her anger was directed inward, annoyance at being unable to pull herself out of the mood she had fallen into.

But mostly she was angry at Bailey.

He was late, as usual. It wasn't that Brea minded his tomcatting around Ceres Town the last night ashore. *But damn it to hell*, there was a time for everything, and just now he should be attending to business. With the mortgage payment on *Liar* due in less than six weeks, it was time for desperate measures.

And desperate measures were just what Bailey had suggested to save the ship. Three months earlier, just after they'd returned from the wild goose chase to ALF37416, Bailey had taken her and Lisa to dinner in the district messhall and waited for the girl to wander off with her friends. Then he'd ordered a bottle of wine and they'd sat talking. She noticed in one of the lulls in the conversation that he was looking past her shoulder, a pensive expression on his face.

"What's eating you, Stinky?" she'd asked.

"I was just noticing how much Lisa has grown over the last year or so. She's almost a young woman. Isn't it about time you shipped her to Earth to start her schooling?"

"What do you suggest I use for money?"

"What's wrong with the trust fund you set up for her?"

"That will barely cover the tuition. I've still got to get her to Earth somehow."

"No problem. I was thinking we'd take *Liar* down to one of the PowerStats and get her overhauled. Considering what these robber barons around here charge, the savings alone should pay for the trip."

"An overhaul? Are you crazy? What are *we* going to use for money?"

"Keep your voice down!"

She'd glanced furtively over her shoulder in response to the urgency in his command, then turned back, leaned forward, and whispered: "Well, what *are* we going to use? We can't even make the mortage payment, let alone get *Liar* overhauled!"

"I've arranged a freight deal."

"What kind of freight?"

"Singularity. We're going to transport one to the Lagrangian PowerStats for energizing."

"When did you do all this?"

"Last night."

"Come off it, Stinky! How could you contract to transport one of the Company's jewels? Why aren't they using one of their own tugs for the job?"

"We're not doing this for the Company."

"Who then? The UN says the chartered companies are the only people . . ." Brea closed her mouth with an audible click. Back in the twenties the UN had licensed a total six multinational conglomerates to deal in I-masses. In Ceres, that meant Belt Industries, Ltd. All buying and selling were done through them. If Bailey had contracted with someone else, it meant that the singularity wasn't registered. And anyone caught dealing in unregistered singularities drew an automatic twenty-to-life!

"Are you out of your frappin' mind?"

"Probably. You got a better idea?"

"Well . . ." She reconsidered her first reaction. True, there had been rumors about singularity smugglers for as long as she'd lived in the Belt. She'd never really believed the stories. After all, what could be done with an unregistered singularity?

41

The Peace Enforcers maintained a presence at every port. Smuggling a singularity was sheer lunacy. On the other hand, it was rumored to be extremely profitable too.

She hadn't agreed to go along with Bailey's scheme that first night, nor the second, nor even the tenth. But as their next payment on *Liar* approached, smuggling began to look more and more attractive. Finally she'd agreed. They would announce that they were taking *Liar* and Lisa to Earth—*Liar* to be overhauled, Lisa to start her schooling. Once out of radar range of Ceres, they would rendezvous with another boat and take the unregistered singularity aboard. They would deliver it to one of the Lagrangian PowerStats, collect their money, and, they hoped, no one would be the wiser.

It had seemed so simple, but now that departure time was near, Brea wasn't so sure about the scheme. She glanced at the chronometer next to the darkened holoset over the bar. Bailey was twenty minutes late. She finished her bulb and unstrapped herself from one of Zander's ostentatious bar stools— ostentatious because on Ceres the patrons could stand for a lifetime and never get fallen arches. Looking for someone she could leave a message with, Brea scanned the crowd. Though she recognized several faces, none belonged to friends. She sighed, turned to leave—

—and ran into a large obstacle wearing the black-and-silver uniform of the PE Marines.

"Sorry," she muttered absentmindedly as she moved to step around.

"Hello, Brea," the basso profundo voice said.

She blinked in surprise and looked first at the chevrons on the sleeve and then up at the face that topped the uniform. "Sergeant Singh, is that you?"

"The same. How the hell are you?"

"I'm fine, Ravi. I thought you went back to Earth, two-three years ago."

"I did. I'm back for another tour. Chief Inspector for the Port. Nice cushy job with nobody shooting at me."

"Congratulations on your promotion! We'll have to get together sometime to celebrate. Unfortunately, Don and I are scheduled to boost out of here, if I can ever find him."

The smile slipped from the Indian sergeant's face. "The major's got Bailey in his offfice and sent me to fetch you."

Brea felt the icy chill that comes with being discovered with a hand in the cookie jar. "Major MacIntire wants to see me? Why?"

"You know the service, Brea. They don't tell anybody anything. They just issue orders."

Brea followed the sergeant down Main Street Corridor and into a side tunnel leading to the Port Administration Complex. Locomotion was hand over hand along one of two fire station poles that sprouted from the tunnel walls. Once off the main thoroughfare, Sergeant Singh led the way in a series of long, flat leaps. She followed, wondering if her pounding heart was loud enough for him to hear.

Singh guided her to where a door marked Commanding Officer had been set in the bare rock walls. Inside were Don Bailey and a short, dark-haired man with a slight paunch standing next to a viewport that looked out over the spaceport. The sun was a tiny, eye-watering point of brightness hanging low over the horizon, casting stark shadows.

Brea let Bailey catch her as she sailed into his arms, taking the moment when her face was hidden from the major to give Don a fearful look. She noted the bags under his eyes and his generally rundown condition. From the symptoms, she would say her partner had hooked up with a live one last evening and was several hours minus on his sleep. Served him right!

"Good to see that Singh found you, Brea," Major MacIntire said. He bowed and kissed her hand.

"It's always good to see you, Major," Brea responded. "To what do I owe this unexpected opportunity?"

"I understand that you and Don are planning a trip to Earth, Brea."

She nodded mutely.

"Excellent! I received a communication yesterday—a no-excuses Priority One squirt from Tycho—directing me to find D. Bailey and B. Gallagher and ship them to Luna on the next available ship."

"But why would anyone want us on Luna?" Brea asked.

"Something about a distressed vessel report you made four months ago."

"Distressed vessel report?" Brea asked, her brow furrowing in concentration. "I don't remember . . ."

"Sure you do, Brea," Bailey said. "We sent out an SOS to

43

that PE cruiser and then searched for survivors for a week."

"Oh, that!"

"Apparently," MacIntire said.

"We told that cruiser captain everything we know. We even gave him a video record of the actual sighting! What more can they want?"

"Unknown, Brea," the major said. "But orders—"

"—are frappin' orders!"

"Since the Peace Enforcement Directorate wants us on Luna so badly," Don Bailey said, "the major and I have struck a bargain. Officially the PEs are leasing *Liar* to run dispatches. They'll pay for our fuel and give us a modest stipend besides."

"More than generous stipend, you old robber," MacIntire said as he chuckled. "When will you be ready to lift off?"

"Call it twelve hours from now, or sooner if you can get the shipyard moving on installing those extra tanks. I'll be in first thing during the morning watch to sign the agreement and pick up the computer codes."

The meeting quickly dwindled down to a few pleasantries, after which Brea let Bailey tow her along as he left the major's office. She didn't speak until they reached Main Street.

"Now we make a beeline for the Port airlock and lift off before he discovers we're gone, right?"

Bailey made a clucking sound. "You're getting cynical, Brea. And so young too."

"You mean we're going through with it?"

"No choice. If we run, we might as well hand *Liar* over without a fight."

"But we can't, Stinky! My God, we're smuggling a singularity! If they catch us—"

"They won't. Besides, what better cover for two first-time smugglers than as a Peace Enforcer mail boat?"

Doctor Roger Kingsley stood before his office wall screen and watched as the spiral shape of a tropical storm threw itself against the coast of Florida. That was one thing he missed since his appointment to the Sky Watch Observatory in *Galileo Station*—rain, wind, weather of any kind. He recognized his fascination with weather as a sign that it was getting time to go home to the wet green of England.

Kingsley moved to his desk and blanked out the Earth view.

No sense torturing himself, he thought as he stared down at the mass of disorganized papers on the desk top. It wasn't really the lack of weather, or homesickness, or any of the thousand and one minor irritations of life in space that were bothering him, of course. It was Angai Yahaya.

The Pan-African had ruined a perfectly good staff tea yesterday with his damned preaching. Absolutely ruined it! The director's wife would probably never invite either of them again. To hear the man talk, one would think the British Empire was still in full bloom. How many times must he listen to harangues about the sins of his colonial forefathers?

Kingsley was jolted from his reverie by the ringing of the telescreen. He accepted the call and found himself staring into the corpulent features of Sir Harry Gresham, Sky Watch Administrator.

"Hello Harry, I was just thinking of calling you. That was a bloody fine tea your wife gave last evening."

"Glad you liked it, Roger. I'm only sorry that I missed it. The press of duties, you know."

"Of course."

"Uh, Roger, something's come up. Have you had a chance to review that data we talked about last month?"

"I said I would." Kingsley responded somewhat waspishly. "And?"

"And nothing. I believe you had best check your instruments. I know of no astronomical phenomenon which could produce such an effect."

"Are you sure?"

"Of course I'm sure. Even so, because of our friendship, I've assigned one of my assistants to review the data in detail. Lad by the name of Angai Yahaya. Pan-African. Very sharp."

"But there must be *something*."

Kingsley shrugged.

"Look, I've discovered that the Peace Enforcers are interested," Gresham continued without pause. "That has to be significant!"

"I fail to see how, Harry."

"You know the military mind. They think of science only as a source for new weaponry. If they're interested in the Gresham/Kingsley Flash, then they must think it a new phenomenon with military significance."

"Or they heard you were interested and are wondering why. No, I'm sorry, Harry. I really think you have a bit of instrument malfunction here, and nothing more. If Yahaya comes up with anything further, I will be sure to give you a call."

Angai Yahaya glanced around furtively at the dozen or so white faces in sight of the full-security telescreen booth. Apparently none of the people in the Alpha Deck corridor was taking any special interest in him, but he still felt a twinge of fear as he opaqued the booth's glass sides. A few seconds' work with a screwdriver and he had the screen's access plate open. He attached several inductive pickups to points on the instrument's circuit board. The pickups were connected to a small black box with a series of LEDs on its face.

Yahaya punched a sequence of sixteen digits into the phone keypad. The usual ripple of static on the screen signaled that the call was being routed to Earth. Finally the screen cleared and a woman's face flashed on the line.

"Pan-African Legation to the UN, may I help you?"

"Citizen M'Buto, please."

"Who may I say is calling?"

"Angai Yahaya."

"Just a moment, Citizen."

"Angai, good to see you again. I presume you are taking proper security measures for this call," a chisel-faced, ebonskinned man said from the screen.

"Yes, sir, Colonel M'Buto," Yahaya said, respect tinging his words.

"Your report then."

"I've been contacted by our man in the Belt. He's arranged another delivery."

"Same procedure as last time?"

"Yes, sir."

"And your contact at the PowerStat?"

"He's ready to receive the merchandise."

"Very good. Keep me informed of progress."

"Uh, one more thing, sir."

"Yes?"

"Have you received a package from me?"

"It arrived this morning. What am I to make of it?"

"I'm not sure. Kingsley seemed uninterested, although he

46

told me this morning that the Peace Enforcement Directorate is involved."

M'Buto's eyebrows rose in surprise. "Not just Sky Watch?"

"No, definitely the PEs."

"This puts a new light on things. I will forward your data by diplomatic pouch with a recommendation that they look into this mysterious point of light."

"Thank you, Colonel."

"Your first duty is to make sure our delivery is received without incident. However, if you should obtain any additional information on this other matter, send it by the usual channels."

"Yes, sir."

"Good man, Angai. M'Buto out."

CHAPTER 5

Four thousand hours after waking, PROBE's doubts about the creatures of the yellow sun were greater than ever.

Its data banks included everything CARETAKER had accumulated since it had pricked an expanding bubble of radio noise in the void between the stars. All told, PROBE had eight-to-the-fiftieth-power bits of information to study. Even at the accelerated rate at which PROBE's brain operated, merely organizing the data into a coherent whole required several weeks. After the data was filed and cross-referenced, the task of studying it for meaningful patterns went ever more slowly. Even the usually simple task of learning the language proved unexpectedly difficult.

CARETAKER had already completed the tedious preliminary work of sorting out the video and audio portions of the signals and matching one to another when PROBE woke from the long sleep. CARETAKER had also collected a large sampling of the creatures' written language and a much smaller collection of the binary data that their machines used in communicating with each other.

As PROBE reviewed CARETAKER's work, it noted that the beings used several different symbol patterns to express the same meaning. For the better part of a hundred hours, PROBE subjected the confusing data to a complex series of information-theory programs. Understanding came slowly and from a surprising quarter. The creatures utilized multiple languages!

One portion of PROBE was ecstatic over the discovery. Never before had a life probe stumbled onto a civilization so near its beginnings. But the rest of PROBE was worried. A species still in its adolescence was the last thing it needed. Interesting though such a neophyte culture might be, it would be of little help in an overhaul.

The creatures called themselves human beings or men in the predominate language of the signals. Their planet was Earth. Their numbering system was to the base ten and their means of measuring lengthy passages of time was by decimal powers of their planet's period of revolution about the system primary, the "Sun."

PROBE began its search for understanding in the first decade for which the signals had been intercepted. For some obscure reason, the humans numbered it 195. PROBE searched for signs that humanity had an interest in the far stars or near planets. The results were both disappointing and confusing. References to space travel floated out of memory every few microseconds, but most dealt with crude fictional accounts. References to the atom were plentiful but dealt mostly with the fear that one rival group or another would start a war and destroy the Earth. There were no references at all to mass—energy converters, neutrino projectors, gravity-wave modulators, or any of the other advanced devices so necessary to Maker civilization.

The content of the earliest signals disturbed PROBE. It wasn't the provincial attitude toward the universe that pervaded them— all races in the galaxy were isolated by time and space, and provincialism was the rule rather than the exception. But the idea that "stranger" was synonomous with "enemy" did not bode well for an alien machine searching desperately for a way home. The average human in the decade of the 1950s was a technological illiterate. Even the launching of several artificial satellites late in the decade was insufficient to overcome the inertia of all that had gone before.

PROBE arranged the data for the next decade and scanned it. Results this time were considerably more promising.

Almost immediately, references to something called a "space race" began to flow from memory. Apparently the launching of the first satellite by one of the power blocs had touched off a competition with the other major bloc on the planet. Even though the reasons for the competition were obscure, PROBE couldn't help but approve of the development. More and more often during the period (1960–1969) puny rockets belched fire and lifted ponderously toward the sky. The rockets grew bigger with surprising rapidity. Then, late in the decade, PROBE watched two spacesuited bipeds cavort on the surface of the Earth's single satellite.

PROBE halted its study at the end of the 1960s data and calculated the rate at which the humans seemed to be progressing. The results were impressive. At the rate they were going, they would overtake the Makers in less than ten thousand years!

But the 1970–1979 data reflected a period of retrenchment, a time when science and technology appeared to fall into disfavor. Luckily, the 1980s data showed a resurgence of interest. By the 1990s the humans had established a permanent presence above their atmosphere. As seemed characteristic of the breed, the presence was primarily military. In a very short time, as the Makers judged things, near-Earth space was alive with primitive directed-energy weapons. And to service the orbital armament, the humans established space stations and space fleets.

PROBE considered the development and pondered its significance. In the four decades that it had studied the humans, they had seemed constantly on the brink of war, yet they somehow managed to avoid coming to blows while making great strides toward a true civilization.

Then, in the year 1994, one power bloc struck at the other with its full arsenal. The cause, like many human motivations, was not readily apparent but appeared somehow to be tied to the elusive human concept of honor. Ten years earlier such a strike would have destroyed human civilization.

Salvation came from an unexpected quarter as the orbiting battle stations, which had been lofted amid terrible controversy, showed their worth. Over a period of twenty days, waves of nuclear strikes were beamed out of the sky before they could reach their targets. Human leaders, their mightiest weapons destroyed, quickly came to their senses and a shaky truce was declared. After that, there was a distinct change in the flavor of the signals. Where before humanity seemed destined to splinter into progressively smaller competing groups, the near disaster seemed to bring them closer together. There were still rivalries, threats, and a few lapses and the level of verbal abuse remained high, but by and large, the beginnings of a planetary government could be discerned.

Finally PROBE knew why CARETAKER had signaled it awake. The humans, so obviously unsuited to its purpose when the signals were first encountered, had suddenly developed true spacecraft. CARETAKER had encountered low-frequency gravity waves emanating from the system, a characteristic of singularity-powered mass converters. Not only were the humans showing signs of cultural maturity, but impressive evidence of continued technological progress as well.

PROBE reached the end of its data and discovered it still couldn't decide whether humans were civilized. The problem was in the nature of the televid signals themselves, most of which originated in a few centers around the globe and were beamed to communication satellites for relay back to Earth. Chance had placed PROBE almost directly in the plane of the Earth's equator and, thus, directly in line to intercept the beams aimed skyward at the orbiting comsats. The programing carried on such beams was intended for the mass of humans, the overwhelming majority of whom still avoided learning anything they considered too difficult. Others, of course, devoted their lives to the pursuit of knowledge. This subgroup communicated by means other than the mass entertainment televid system. For the scientists there were scientific journals, transactions, monographs and trade publications. PROBE recognized all such terms as references to nonbroadcast methods of disseminating and storing information.

Unfortunately, when professional journals were transmitted at all, it was on the highly directional interplanetary communications net. PROBE could only eavesdrop when a transmission was relayed through the geosynchronous stations or aimed in its direction.

PROBE considered its dilemma for several seconds. The signs were slightly in the humans' favor, but the overall quality of the data was poor. The data points had a high degree of spread. Something had to be done to improve the focus of the inquiry. An experiment was in order.

So far as PROBE could determine, the humans believed themselves alone in the universe. It would come as a severe shock (as it had to many others) to discover an alien machine on the outskirts of the solar system. Their reaction to that discovery would undoubtedly follow one of the eight standard patterns life probes had observed through the millennia. Observing their pattern was all PROBE needed to make its decision.

PROBE considered the possibility of danger. It was unlikely that the humans' primitive ships could intercept it as it transited the inner system. Yet the danger was there. So, as the Makers had long ago decreed, it would place limits on the scope of the experiment. It would reveal the fact of its presence and nothing else. Until it knew humans better, no information concerning its true nature or mission would flow forth.

PROBE willed power to surge through mechanisms that had not been used since prelaunch testing. Forcefield mirrors sprang into existence and aiming devices moved to collimate them. A tight beam of highly coherent x-rays was aimed directly for the yellow sun. It would take twelve and a half days to reach Earth and, even at minimum dispersion, would spread out to the orbit of Jupiter by the time it arrived. Soon human astronomers would detect a strange new star in the heavens. It would be three hundred light-hours distant and emit only coherent x-rays. It would not take them long to recognize that such a source could only be the product of alien intelligence.

"Prospector *Liar's Luck*, this is Luna Approach Control. Stand by for orbital clearances."

"Standing by," Don Bailey said from his acceleration couch. The controller, at his console deep in the heart of one of the Lunar Equatorial Space Stations, and his station were still out of line of sight, hidden behind the Moon's limb, so the message was relayed through one of the Lunar comsats.

"Computer to record."

"Computer ready to record, Control."

There was a high-pitched whine on the audio circuits, followed by: "That's it. Back that kiddy car down according to the data we just fed you and you'll make a clean approach with no problems. Good day to you, sir."

"Good day, Control, and thanks." Bailey turned to Brea Gallagher, who was strapped into her acceleration couch beside him. "Hear that? Nothing to worry about."

"Hah! He should be up here fighting this pig!"

Bailey's answer was a noncommital grunt. Brea had been fighting with the computer over ship's attitude control for most of the month-long trip. The system had developed a nasty tendency to overcorrect, causing *Liar* to waddle at inconvenient times—as when they were trying to line up for the final burn that would circularize their orbit ten thousand kilometers above the Moon's surface. The difficulty had a lot to do with their cargo.

They'd left Ceres Port right on schedule the morning after Major MacIntire's summons. Instead of immediately diving for the inner system, however, Bailey chose to cut across the Belt to a point half a degree ahead of Ceres in her orbit. Ostensibly the maneuver was to simplify the jump to Earth. By spending three days longer in the Belt, Bailey eliminated the need for a cross-orbit tack, stern chase burn, gravity-well deceleration, or any of the other fancy maneuvers that caused a pilot's hair to turn prematurely gray. From half a degree foreorbit of Ceres, the jump would be a straight tangential decelerate-and-orbit maneuver.

That, at least, was the *official* reason for going 3.5-million kilometers out of the way. Actually, Bailey delayed sending *Liar* on her sunward stoop in order to keep their clandestine rendezvous. On the second day out from Ceres Port, a make-shift tug matched orbits with *Liar's Luck* and offloaded its cargo—the unregistered I-mass.

In its natural state an I-mass is of little use to anyone. In spite of its density, it is just too small a package to interact effectively with normal matter. But a bit of processing—called energizing—turns an I-mass into a treasure beyond price.

Energizing an I-mass involves accelerating its rotational speed until "centrifugal force" has stretched the nearly dimensionless point into a disc several thousand times its natural diameter. But spinning up an I-mass requires energy, and lots of it. And energy on that scale could only be provided by one of the

Earth-orbiting powerhouses that provided a hungry world with energy and that were themselves singularity powered.

The singularity made the trip suspended in the same magnetic field as *Liar*'s own I-mass but the extra mass tended to make *Liar* tail-heavy, inducing the attitude-control system to overcorrect.

"Coming up on boost point," Bailey said finally. "Better tell Lisa to grab hold of something back there."

"Right," Brea said. She punched for the intercom to the main cabin. A moment later the angular features of a red-haired, twelve-year-old girl stared out at her.

"Yes, Brea."

"We're coming up on our next-to-last boost, hon. Better strap down."

"May I come forward?" The serious green eyes were wide with excitement.

Brea looked at Bailey, who reached out and pressed a switch. Lisa's face was duplicated on a screen in front of him. "Have you stopped pouting about going off to school, young lady?"

"Yes, Uncle Don."

"Then come forward, but make it fast. You've got twenty-six seconds to get yourself strapped into the jump seat. Make that twenty-four and counting."

"I'm on my way!"

Brea continued to look at Bailey, who had returned to studying his flight plan display. "I wonder if we did the right thing bringing her along, Stinky."

"Of course we did. She's getting to the age where she needs to get out and meet people other than Rock Hoppers. Want her to remain ignorant of the social graces all her life?"

"Why not, Uncle Don, you did!" Lisa's voice floated through the hatch and was quickly followed by its owner. She swarmed into the jump seat between their two couches and strapped down.

"Seems my grandfather used to have a saying about 'little pitchers with big ears.'"

"And another about 'seen and not heard,'" Brea said. "Leave us alone for a bit, hon. This part is ticklish."

The cabin was silent until the main engine sputtered to life. Twenty seconds later, with Brea still fighting to keep the ship lined up on the proper guide star, all was quiet once again.

"Computer says that's it," Bailey announced. "Welcome to Luna, folks. Turn us over, Brea."

Brea twisted the control stick and the ship rolled to the right. The stars rotated around the control bubble as the Moon swam slowly into view. Until then, the *Liar* had been backing down toward her destination, unable to see it. The tan-and-black orb was suddenly a cliff towering over them, ready to crash down on their heads.

There was a sharp intake of breath from the jump seat. "Wow! I never realized it was so big!"

Bailey chuckled. "Wait until you see the Earth from low orbit. It's a hundred times this size."

Lisa became quiet at the mention of Earth.

Brea stretched in her seat. "How long to rendezvous with the station?"

"Another hour and a half at this pokey closing rate. Why?"

She reached for her buckles and unsnapped them. "Call us fifteen minutes before the final nudge and not a moment sooner. We girls are going to need all the time we can get to make ourselves presentable for the Luniks. Come along, hon. I'll flip you for the first bathing rights."

CHAPTER 6

Major Eric Stassel strolled in long skating motions up the incline that led to the departure gates for the trans-Luna ballistic capsules. He slipped effortlessly around parties of tourists, who tended to bound too far into the air and strand themselves in high-lob trajectories for long periods.

Stassel noted that there were more of these mobile obstacles than usual—a sure sign that one of the big Earth–Moon liners was orbiting somewhere overhead. He gave them a wide berth while mulling over the little he had learned at Farside Observatory.

Useful information concerning the flash in Aquila was proving difficult to come by. The trip to Farside had been a shot in the dark. Farside Observatory was the finest installation in the field of radio astronomy in the Solar System. It was the perfect place to carry out such observations because it was in permanent radio eclipse with the Earth. While it's true that the Moon has no ionosphere with which to bounce radio waves over the horizon, there were always reflections from strategically placed mountains and crater walls to worry about. With the Earth hanging permanently in the Nearside sky, a radio astronomer could spend weeks gathering data from the outer bounds of the universe, only to have his target drowned out by the wailings of the latest top-forty pop singer at the last five minutes of the experiment.

Having run out of other options, Stassel had traveled to Farside to request a radio search of that section of sky where Sky Watch had observed the flash. But the radio scan of the region of space near the star Delta Aquilae yielded nothing but a flyspeck source of long-wave radiation only slightly more energetic than normal background.

The chief astronomer at Farside had glanced at his detector readouts and commented: "We frequently see a similar effect in the clouds of hydrogen plasma expelled by ships passing overhead. It's one of the biggest nuisances we have to put up with around here. Anyway, the emission is at the right frequency for hydrogen."

"Is that what we're looking at, a ship's wake?" Stassel asked.

The chief had shrugged. "Might be anything at all, including a glitch in our receiver."

"Any way to measure its distance?"

"None. We might be able to get you a pretty good parallax measurement next winter if it's still there. If you've got a charge number, I can set up a rescan program."

"No, thanks. If I haven't solved this mystery to the admiral's satisfaction by winter, you can address all of my mail care of one of Saturn's moons."

After the disappointment at Farside, he'd called Tycho to discover that his two staff assistants—who had been assigned when Admiral Liu boosted his rating to Priority Four—had nothing new to report. He caught the supply scooter back to Crisium City for transshipment to Tycho Base.

Stassel reached the end of the native rock tunnel that had been drilled beneath Crisium Spaceport and entered a pressure dome. Filtered sunlight slanted in at an angle that told the experienced eye it was two days to local sunset. He walked to the ticket counter, set his travel bag at his feet, and handed his ticket to the statuesque blonde manning the booth. She slipped it into her reader and set her features in the professional smile of one who must deal with the public.

"Headed back to Tycho, Major? That will be Tube Six, loading now."

"Thanks." He scooped up his travel bag, hurried to the access tube indicated, and on into the capsule, a ten-meter-long egg with pairs of acceleration couches on each side of a narrow aisle and precious little else. When Stassel entered, only two seats were left. One was next to a silver-haired man with "groundhog" stamped all over him. He looked the garrulous type, so Stassel passed him by and took the remaining empty seat near the front of the cabin.

His seatmate turned her head as he sat down. He smiled and nodded. "Hello."

"Hello, yourself."

Stassel judged the girl to be twelve or thirteen—just shy of puberty, anyway. She obviously wasn't from Earth, but probably not a Lunik either. Lagrange colony or Martian scientific station, maybe. He held out his hand to her. "I always like to know my traveling companions. My name is Eric, what's yours?"

She gravely shook hands with him. "I'm Lisandra Moore from Ceres. You may call me Lisa if you like."

"Ah, a Belter. Are you traveling with someone?"

Her nod was a curt gesture, a truncated bob of the head. "My guardian is sitting in the back row. We both wanted a window seat and this was the only one left."

"Going down to Earth for vacation?"

"No, they're shipping me off to school." Lisa looked as if she were sucking on a sour pickle.

"I take it you aren't overjoyed at the prospect."

"Who would be? I put in my hour a week in the centrifuge back home just like everybody else. That's bad enough. Can you imagine having gravity pull you down like that *all the time*? It must be like wading through a swamp up to your neck in mud."

"What do you know of mud?"

"Only what I read on my bookscreen." She turned to stare at the mass driver that was visible across the plain. "Is that thing really going to shoot us to Tycho?"

"Hope so," he said, letting a hint of mirth creep into his voice. "It would be kind of messy if it didn't."

"Without rockets?"

"Don't worry, the capsule has emergency jets. But if everything goes right, we won't need them." Stassel leaned toward the window and glanced out. The main spaceport was on the other side of the terminal dome and out of view. Ahead of him rose a mass-driver spur line, a series of ever taller and more distant towers surmounted by drive rings. The low sun angle cast long shadows over the basalt waves of the Sea of Crises.

"See those towers? They point southwest. In a few minutes we will go whooshing up through there and fly off in exactly the right direction to lob us the three thousand kilometers to Tycho. At the other end there is a mass driver exactly like this one. The Crise computer talks to the Tycho computer and tells it when to expect us. As soon as the Tycho brain spots us coming over the horizon, it will direct our attitude thrusters to line us up with the mouth of its mass driver and then catch us before we splash ourselves all over the floor of Tycho Crater."

They fell to talking about the difficulties involved in aiming a ballistic travel capsule. Stassel was surprised at Lisa's understanding of orbital mechanics. She had a better idea of the complications involved than ninety-five percent of the adults who used the capsules routinely.

They were still deep in conversation when Stassel's ears popped as the airlock was sealed and the capsule's pressurization stabilized.

"Make sure you are strapped down securely," he warned, anticipating by a tenth of a second the recorded announcement to that effect. "Push your head firmly into the neck rest. It's okay if you turn to look out the window, just don't leave any of your vertebrae unsupported. The kick-in-the-pants phase for Crise-Tycho is nearly four gravs. Try to lift your head and you'll wrench something."

He followed his own instructions and burrowed into his seat while absentmindedly listening to a throaty female voice finish the emergency instructions. The capsule gave a lurch and bumped slowly ahead. The view out the window was suddenly blocked as they entered the black maw of the mass driver.

"Here we go!"

The initial surge of acceleration quickly built to the four gravities he'd promised Lisa. It went on for forty seconds by which time the capsule was thirty kilometers from the spaceport and speeding along at fifty-five hundred kilometers per hour.

For its last ten kilometers the mass driver branched into three separate tracks, each pointed in a different direction and angled to clear the Picard-Lick Highlands, the peaks of which could be seen poking over the horizon. The Tycho capsule took the center track, sprinted out of the last guide ring, and fell upward in a shallow, rising ellipse. Stassel watched as the shadowed mountain peaks flashed by so close that it seemed he could reach out and touch them.

He pointed out the landmarks to Lisa as they marched below. When the Tranquility Monument had dropped below the horizon astern, the egg began a slow end-for-end turn that signaled the midpoint of the journey.

Their arrival at Tycho Base was handled in the same breathtaking manner as their takeoff. They watched the Tycho catcher ring grow immense on the bulkhead screen. When it looked as though they would crash for sure, there was a stomach-wrenching deceleration, a series of bumps, and they were down.

"Whew!" Lisa said, as she unbuckled her belts.

"Same here," Stassel agreed. He let her squeeze past his knees before he unstrapped and joined the throng leaving the capsule. Once inside the terminal dome, he noticed Lisa standing with a woman. They were trying to make sense out of a map of Tycho Base, the kind souvenier shops have been pawning off on unsuspecting tourists since the dawn of time.

Stassel whistled under his breath. The girl's guardian wasn't half bad in the looks department. She would have been pretty but for her pinched expression. She filled out her Moonsuit nicely too. Stassel started for them with intentions of offering his assistance as a guide, but before he'd moved two steps, they turned and strode off toward Tycho Town, the civilian section of the base.

He watched them go, keenly aware of an opportunity missed. When they disappeared from view, he shrugged, turned, and headed for the tunnel that led to Main Gate, Peace Enforcer Headquarters, Tycho, Luna.

Brea Gallagher led Lisa to a slidewalk headed toward the business district of the small city that had grown up around the PE headquarters base. Lisa stared at their surroundings while the walk whisked them through well-lighted public tunnels past shops and restaurants with "tourist trap" engraved everywhere but on their facades. Brea hardly noticed. She was too worried about Bailey to sightsee.

Damn Bailey anyway!

Liar's nose had already been poked into a docking collar in Luna EquatorStat's stationary central core when Bailey announced that he wouldn't be accompanying them to the surface. "While you're gone, I'll take the ship up to the Lagrange PowerStat and get rid of our cargo. We'll rendezvous at *Earth Station One* and go down to Earth together. We'll spend a couple of weeks in the surf and sun while we straighten out Lisa's schooling."

"You can't handle the ship alone."

"It won't be the first time."

"It isn't safe! You'll crack up if you try a docking maneuver without someone to stabilize the attitude controls for you."

"It's far safer than leaving that extra singularity in our drive unit to be discovered by the authorities!"

"Let me come with you," she had said, "or else wait until I can get back to help you."

Bailey sighed. "You haven't thought this thing through, Brea. *God damn it*, consider the implications! If someone is energizing I-masses on the Q.T., he sure as hell isn't using them to power some freighter. There has to be a government behind the smuggling trade. And if a government is smuggling singularities, I'll give you three guesses as to what they are using them for."

"You mean warships?"

"What else? We're getting twenty times the normal transport fee for this. Hell, the bribes alone must cost more than the purchase price of a registered singularity."

"But breaking the Space Disarmament Treaty is a capital offense, Stinky!"

"Which is why I have to get that damned hole out of our mass converter ASAP! Look, Brea, I'll be honest with you. If we weren't desperate for the money, I would never have touched this deal. But since I did, I have to go through with it. I've already notified the buyers of my docking time at the PowerStat. Now be a good partner and do as you're told!"

All through the shuttle flight down to Crisium Spaceport

and then on the ballistic capsule to Tycho, Bailey's words had bothered her. It wasn't hard to envision his being caught by the authorities, clapped in irons, and taken down to Earth for trial or dead in the wreck of *Liar's Luck* when he failed to control the ship during final approach and docking at the PowerStat.

Somehow she had managed to find their hotel. She rented a broom closet of a room at what seemed an unreasonably low price until she remembered that it was probably ten times what an Earther paid at home. She helped Lisa unpack and then prepared for her interview. She showered and powdered herself, and ordered a new outfit from the hotel's autovend. While waiting for it to be delivered, she tried to cover the worry lines and bags under her eyes with makeup. Lisa sat at the foot of the room's one double bed and dialed the holo set while Brea worked.

"Who was your friend?" Brea asked as she daubed at her face.

"Friend?"

"On the capsule."

"You mean Eric! He *was* nice, wasn't he?"

"Very handsome." Brea sighed at the memory of her surprise when the blond officer in Peace Enforcer black and silver boarded the capsule. He reminded her of Greg, although she couldn't envision Greg in a uniform—any uniform. About the most elegant Greg had ever been was when he'd worn a faded blue shipsuit to their wedding ceremony. She hurriedly put the old memories out of her mind and concentrated on finishing the repairs to her face until the delivery chute chimed at the arrival of her new apparel. After dressing, she sat on the edge of the bed and punched for Tycho Base Administration.

"May I help you?" a female Marine corporal asked from the confines of the phone screen.

"I've been summoned by a Major Stassel about a sighting report I made." Brea waved the summons that Major MacIntire had given her in the screen pickup's field of view.

"Your name, ma'am?"

Brea gave it to her.

"And the reference number on the order?" The corporal placed her on hold for half a minute and then returned to the screen. "You're in luck. Major Stassel is on the duty board and available. I can give you an appointment for thirteen-thirty hours. Would that be agreeable?"

"That would be fine."

Brea checked her appearance in the mirror that ran the length of the airlock's inner door. The new suit was tight in a few places where it should have been loose, but fit as well as could be expected from a credit card tailor. She turned to kiss Lisa on the cheek and warned her to lock the door after her.

"Good luck, Brea."

"Thanks, hon. I'll be back as soon as I can."

CHAPTER 7

Having run out of leads on his special project, Stassel reported to the Operations Center. After powering up his console, he checked for messages and was pleasantly surprised to discover that the two Belters would be arriving very soon. He asked the front gate and base comm center to notify him when either prospector checked in, and then had his two staff assistants stand by.

That done, he called up the rest of his *Action Items: Pending* file. His trip to Farside had left him with a four-day backlog of work. He scanned the entire file, mentally assigning priorities to each item, but the last one caused him to rearrange the list.

Ceres had finally answered his request for dossiers on Bailey and Gallagher.

He keyed up the first dossier:

NAME: Donel Kenyatta Bailey
POB: Capetown, Pan-African Federation
AGE: 63

CURRENT RESIDENCE: Ceres Asteroid
CURRENT OCCUPATION: Singularity Prospector

According to the biographical data. Bailey was an oldtime Belter, having emigrated four decades earlier. He had held just about every job to be had among the flying mountains beyond Mars. Ten years earlier he bought a ship. Since then he'd discovered two small singularities, paid off his investors, and converted to a simple two-person partnership.

The dossier's compiler had added a personal evaluation: "Subject is highly capable and trusted by those around him. Does not look for trouble, but doesn't avoid it, either. Is rumored to have been involved in the disappearance of at least three men (consensus is that they deserved it). Suspicious of authority. Not to be underestimated!"

Stassel finished Bailey's file and keyed for the one on Gallagher. Gallagher, it turned out, was a woman, and fairly young.

NAME: Breon Elizabeth (Caldwell) Gallagher
POB: Winnipeg, North American Union
AGE: 31
CURRENT RESIDENCE: Ceres Asteroid
CURRENT OCCUPATION: Singularity Prospector

The biographical data was much more terse than that for Bailey but contained a mild surprise. Breon Gallagher held a doctorate in cosmological astronomy. She had gone to the Belt to work for Ceres Observatory, married a prospector, been widowed, and then adopted her dead husband's profession. There was no below-the-line data on her.

Stassel had just finished reading through the dossier for the second time when the workscreen beeped. He saved the two dossiers to his working file and then keyed for acceptance. The screen cleared to one of the base comm operators.

"A Mrs. Gallagher is holding on the line and requests an appointment, sir. You asked to be notified."

"Is she here in Tycho?"

"Yes, sir."

Stassel glanced at the chronometer above the console screen. "Have her at the front gate at thirteen thirty. I'll send a Marine to guide her in."

Twenty minutes later he was seated behind a massive gray metal desk in a conference room in the administration complex. Behind him was a wall holoscreen. He was barely settled when the room echoed to three quick knocks.

"Enter!"

The door snicked open and a Marine sergeant stepped smartly through. "Mrs. Gallagher is here, Major."

"Show her in, Sergeant."

The Marine turned toward someone out of sight in the corridor and said: "The major will see you now."

He stepped aside to make way as a familiar form brushed past him and entered the room. Stassel lurched to his feet, banging his shin on the edge of the desk as he did so.

Brea blinked in surprise as she caught sight of Stassel.

"Are you Major Stassel?"

He nodded. "And you must be Lisa's guardian."

"Yes, Breon Gallagher—Brea for short."

"If I'd known who you were, I would have made a point of introducing myself earlier. Please take a seat."

"Thank you, Major."

"No need to be formal. I'm Eric."

"Eric, then."

"Where is Mr. Bailey?"

"Don took the ship up to the Lagrange colony to price an overhaul. If this is about that distress signal, I was the one who saw the whole thing. Don was aft in the galley."

"May I get you coffee?"

"With cream and sugar, please."

Stassel moved to the small bar at one end of the conference room and poured steaming black liquid into two low-gravity cups. He handed one to Brea along with the condiment packets, then perched on the edge of his desk as he sipped from the other.

Brea laughed nervously. "All the comforts of home."

His smile was obviously intended to put her at ease, and in spite of herself, she felt the tension begin to drain from her neck and shoulders. "Anything else I can get you?" he asked.

She shook her head.

"Then let's get down to business. Why did you have your

66

telescope-suppression circuits energized during the sighting five months ago?"

Brea had spent most of her waking moments for the last month wondering what the PEs could possibly be so interested in that they were willing to drag her halfway across the Solar System. Now, when the much-awaited inquisition finally arrived, she found herself startled almost to speechlessness.

"Is *that* what this is about?"

Stassel nodded. "Partially."

"I was attempting to get a good enough picture of the asteroid we were prospecting on that trip to win a bet. What difference does it make?"

Stassel reached out and ran his fingers over a keypad set flush to the desk top. The lights dimmed and the large screen behind him lit up. The scene was of a densely populated starfield.

"Watch the lower center of the screen."

Brea watched as a new star marked by a blinking red rectangle appeared among the multitude and then winked out again.

"That was captured by Sky Watch at approximately the same time you were observing this."

The scene changed. This time it was the recording she had made of ALF37416. Once again she watched the mysterious speck of light appear and disappear.

"Notice any difference?" Stassel asked.

Brea nodded. "As you say, my suppression circuits were engaged. My recording doesn't have the background stars in it. So what?"

"And at the time? Were you viewing the suppressed or unsuppressed view?"

"I'm not sure," Brea said hesitantly.

"Think back. The way the asteroid image orbits to one side of the screen makes it look as though you were using a bright guide star to hold the telescope centered."

Brea's eyebrows furrowed in concentration. "Yes, now that you mention it, that's right."

"Remember which star?"

Brea shook her head. "I don't think I knew, even at the time. I pointed the scope at the section of sky where the computer said our target was, picked the brightest star visible, and lined up the scope's crosshairs on it."

"But you did see the flash against a starfield?"

"I suppose I did, although I didn't notice it at the time."

"Are you sure?"

"Very sure. That I remember clearly. I didn't spot it until I played back the record a few minutes later. Then I was so surprised that I called Don Bailey forward to get his opinion. What has all this got to do with anything?"

"Something caused that speck of violet light. I've been assigned to find out what it was."

"It looked to us as though a mass converter might have blown up."

"Yet *Valiant* found no evidence of a wreck, nor has any ship been reported missing. That leaves only two possibilities. Either we're dealing with a phenomenon far outside the Solar System, or someone has been engaging in unauthorized experiments somewhere beyond the Asteroid Belt."

"Experiments?" Brea asked, suddenly interested.

"Clandestine weapons tests. It's happened before. Back in the last century the South Africans secretly tested a number of nuclear weapons by exploding them well out to sea off the coast of Antarctica. The result, as we know all too well, was the Second Boer War."

"How do I fit into all of this?" Brea asked, suddenly uncomfortable. She couldn't help remembering what Bailey had said about the people behind the singularity smuggling. Somehow the idea of a deep-space nuclear test sounded very plausible indeed. "What can I tell you that you don't already know?"

"I certainly don't have to explain triangulation to an astronomer. If we can place your sighting with respect to the fixed stars—"

"—then you can get a parallax measurement and determine the position vector from that!"

"Correct."

"But I don't remember seeing it against a starfield."

"Not consciously, to be sure. But subconsciously you must have. We have a number of sophisticated recall techniques at our disposal. I want you to allow us to dredge up your memories of that day in order to triangulate the source of this flash of light."

Brea shivered. She was no stranger to the therapeutic uses

of drugs and hypnotism because Doc Cranston had tried them on her after Greg's death, but had been forced to suspend treatment. All Brea remembered of the experience was waking up with a scream in her throat and the image of Greg's sightless eyes still fresh in her memory. Of course, that was the least of the reasons why she couldn't let a mind mechanic near her memory. All she needed for a quick trip to a PE prison was to let slip what she knew about the smuggled I-mass.

"Sorry, Major. The answer is no!"

"Mind if I ask why?"

Brea bit her lower lip in hesitation. When she finally spoke, she chose her words with care. "I came very close to a complete breakdown three years ago, the result of losing my husband to an accident. I have spent the time since trying to put my life back together, erecting fragile barriers against bad memories. I will not risk tearing open the wound again."

"No possibility of changing your mind?"

"I'm sorry, but that is my decision."

Stassel perched on the edge of his desk and stared down at her with calculating eyes. "Will you let me discuss what is at stake here?"

"No, and unless I am under arrest, I would like to leave now."

He shrugged. "If you won't, you won't. The subject is closed, then. How about dinner this evening?"

Brea smiled in spite of herself. "You have a very disconcerting way of changing the subject, Major. I'm sorry, but no."

"Surely an evening's conversation isn't too much to ask. It will give me something to remember when they ship me out to Titan, paradise of picturesque methane blizzards."

"It won't work." Brea shook her head. "You may make me feel guilty as hell, but you aren't going to change my mind. So let's spare both of us the attempt, shall we?"

"I promise I won't even mention this business unless you bring it up. Scout's honor!"

Brea found herself smiling at his look of puppy-dog eagerness; his hand was raised in the three-fingered Boy Scout salute. "What would your wife say?"

"Nothing. This comes under the heading of entertaining a guest of the directorate. Besides, I'm not married at present."

"All right. I guess Lisa and I have to eat."

"Fine," Stassel said, rising with her and escorting her to the door where the Marine sergeant still stood guard outside. "I'll pick you up at your hotel at eighteen hundred hours and give you the whirlwind tour before we dine."

Brea turned to follow the sergeant. She had walked a half dozen steps when she turned back toward Stassel, who was still framed by the open doorway of the conference room.

"And Major . . . the answer is still no!"

Stassel was seated in his chair in front of the holoscreen, his legs stretched before him, when the other door into the conference room opened. A buxom young woman and a middle-aged man with a bookish manner entered and sat at the conference table.

"Well, what do you think?"

Gregor Zapata shrugged. "The indicators jumped clear off the graphs when you mentioned fishing around in her memory. Offhand I'd say she has something to hide."

"What about you, Elspeth?"

Technician-Lieutenant Elspeth Crocker was Stassel's other assistant. "I have to agree, Eric. Her psych profile predicted that she would react emotionally, but nowhere near the level observed."

"Then her resolve to avoid going into hypnosis is total?"

Elspeth shrugged. "Definitely high level. Are you going to compel her?"

"Not if I can convince her to submit willingly. Remember, we're only Priority Four here, and that isn't enough for a judge."

"You could escalate to Three," Zapata said.

He shook his head. "Asking for a court order will stir up the anti-UN faction in the North American Congress again. We'll do it if we have to, but first let's try persuasion. Now, anybody got a brilliant idea on how we can turn this Breon Gallagher around?"

Zapata rubbed at his incipient bald spot, a nervous habit that usually presaged a stroke of genius. "This is more Ellie's specialty than mine, but I've looked over the Belter lady's profile and I think I've got an idea that might work."

CHAPTER 8

By the dinner hour Stassel had planned his campaign as carefully as if he were going into battle—as, in a way, he was. He had promised there would be no overt pleading, cajoling, or argument. But that didn't eliminate more subtle methods.

He arrived at the hotel five minutes early. The Tycho Terrace was a businessman's hostel, catering to the thousands of salesmen, engineers, and purchasing agents who found it necessary to travel to headquarters each year. It was clean but unpretentious, the perfect place for a traveler on a budget. The pedestrian image extended even to the hotel's small restaurant. Algae steak was the specialty of the house.

Stassel's plans for the evening had no place in them for sensible, budget-conscious hotels. His big guns would be fired in splendor. In Tycho Base that meant the Earthview Room, renowned on three planets as a watering hole for the idle rich and those on UN expense accounts. Stassel could hardly wait to see Commander Yurislavich's face when he presented the expense account voucher for the night's work.

He stopped in the Tycho Terrace's tiny lobby and had the night clerk signal Brea's room. Less than two minutes later Brea and Lisa appeared from a side corridor leading to the lower level. Brea had changed into formal evening wear—a white pants suit with a moderately deep plunge to the bodice—while Lisa wore the shorts and singlet common to children of both sexes on the Moon.

"Hello, Eric, like my hair?" Lisa pirouetted as she posed for him. Her hair, longer than Brea's, was piled on her head in a way that made her look four years older.

"You're beautiful," he said before turning to her guardian. Brea had done something to her own face as well. Where she had been businesslike that afternoon, she had become alluring. There was no trace of the worry lines and signs of sleeplessness that he had noticed in the capsule port. "Are you ready for your big night on the town?"

"What did you have in mind, Major Stassel?"

"It's Eric, remember?"

"All right. What did you have in mind, *Eric*?"

"Dinner and dancing in the Earthview Room. You do dance in Ceres, don't you?"

Brea shook her head. "Gravity's too low. We have stylized tumbling and all the other zero-gee forms, though."

"Close enough for government work." Stassel glanced at his watch. "Unfortunately, the earliest reservation I could get is for two hours from now. If you're interested, I'll take you and Lisa on that tour I promised this afternoon."

"That would be very nice."

Stassel thought he detected a hint of genuine interest beneath her wary acceptance of his offer.

Their first stop was Operations Center where they were met by the officer of the watch, Technician-Captain Noguchi, who guided them to a glassed-in balcony overlooking the hundreds of operations consoles.

"This is our central control point for the Earth–Moon Interdiction Zone," Noguchi began with an expansive wave of his hand. "The IZ extends half a million kilometers out from the Earth's center in every direction. It's a big job...some say an *impossibly* big job. Those men down below are responsible for keeping tabs on everything of military interest within a volume of space measuring ten-to-the-eighteenth-power cubic kilometers. Computers do most of the work, of course, but sometimes they need human guidance. If you'll step this way, I'll show you what happens when one of our iron thinkers starts screaming for help."

The small officer ushered them down a hall and into a darkened classroom filled with terminals. Stassel sat Lisa at one of the student positions and took his place at the instructor's station. He quickly punched up a potpourri of interesting views, giving her a fast tour of the Mother of Worlds while Noguchi kept up a running commentary. After a number of terrestrial views had flashed on the screen, Stassel glanced up to see Brea watching him. He winked and mouthed the words "Watch this!" at her.

His fingers danced over keys as he called his zoom-from-orbit subroutine from memory. When the routine was in place, he cut into Lisa's circuit and pressed ENTER. He was rewarded with a squeal of terror as Lisa leaped backward, flying from her chair. Noguchi caught her before she could rebound off any of the equipment and the three adults broke into laughter.

Stassel rose from behind his console and grinned. "Pretty impressive, huh?"

Lisa, who was still trying to swallow her heart, merely nodded.

Next on the agenda were the shops, laboratories, and extensive offices of the Peace Enforcement Directorate. Brea remained aloof through most of the tour while Lisa grew more involved by the minute. Eventually Stassel glanced at his watch. "It's almost nineteen thirty. Is anyone hungry yet?"

"A little," Brea said, nodding.

"One last stop and we'll call it a night."

He led them to a small enclosed car and motioned Lisa to take the front seat while he and Brea shared the back. It was a tight fit, and he was acutely aware of Brea's arm pressing against his and of her perfume.

He engaged the controls and the car accelerated into a narrow tunnel cut into the lunar basalt. Within seconds the tunnel lights were flashing by at 150 kph. After five minutes, the car braked and came to rest in a station identical to the one they had just left.

Stassel opened the hatch. "Welcome to the directorate's Lunar Academy, ladies. This is where all our candidate Peace Enforcers come for their training."

He helped Brea, and then Lisa, disembark before leading them down another long tunnel past serious-faced men and women with the pips of officer cadets on their shoulder boards. Stassel lead the way through light traffic until they stood before a massive airlock.

"Through here," he said, entering. The mechanism clanged shut behind them, and the grind of machinery was accompanied by the hiss of the pressure's being equalized to something less than the half atmosphere that was standard in most lunar cities. All three of them yawned widely to clear their ears as the inner door swung wide.

They found themselves in a great cavern filled with an elaborate maze. The maze, constructed of three-meter-high walls, was unroofed save by the cavern itself. Floodlamps were suspended from the rock ceiling fifty meters over their heads. The cavern was filled with machinery. Brea blinked, trying to judge the scale of the open space before her. It was easily ten times the size of the operations center.

"What is this place?" she asked.

"Used to be a big ice deposit. After they mined it out, the directorate took it over as part of the academy complex. Now it's the Academy War Museum, the most extensive collection of weaponry in the solar system."

"I thought the PEs were supposed to prevent war?"

Stassel nodded. "That's what it says on our charter."

"Isn't this junk collection a little out of character, then?"

"Not at all. Police study crime, doctors study disease, and we study war. After all, historically, war is our species' favorite sport."

"Isn't that a trifle melodramatic?"

"It's a simple statement of fact, Brea. Human nature never really changes, you know. Our heritage comes down to us from the warriors of Sumer, Elam, and Sparta, through the Roman legions, to the citizen-soldiers of the two world wars. Do you really think the descendants of three thousand generations of wolves have suddenly turned into sheep?

"Oh, we've done fairly well so far, better than many people

thought we would. In the one hundred twenty years since the first atomic bomb, we've only come really close to annihilation once. Not a bad record at all. But consider the long view. Can we hold Armageddon in abeyance for another twelve decades? How about twelve centuries or twelve millennia?"

Lisa cleared her throat. "Are all Peace Enforcers as pessimistic as you are, Major Stassel?"

Stassel shook his head. "On the contrary, I'm an optimist, someone who believes that another factor has entered the equation, one that will save us yet—if we let it. If we can hold our violent natures in check for another hundred years or so, we should be safe."

"What happens in a hundred years?"

"If we're lucky, we will be out among the stars. We're in a critical period just now. The human race is still crowded on and about a single planet. Even a minor natural catastrophe could wipe us out. We could do the job ourselves, too. It's an inherently unstable situation.

"But consider what happens when we finally crack the Einstein barrier! In just a few decades, we'll have spread so far and wide that no single disaster—not war, not flood, not even the explosion of old Sol himself—will be able to destroy us all. Until that fine day arrives, however, we contentious humans will be unable to pursue our bloody hobby. That, in a roundabout way, is the purpose of this museum, to remind our cadets of their responsibility to the human race."

Stassel had noticed Lisa's attention wandering all through the speech he had practiced all afternoon. She had spent the last minute or so with her head back, staring open-mouthed at a massive machine suspended from the cavern roof by steel cables.

"What's that?"

Stassel turned to follow her pointing finger, happy to change the subject. He had planted the seeds and now they must be allowed to grow without interference for a while. "*That* is an old Hercules Class Laser Battle Station. The cylinder is a hydrogen-flourine gas dynamic laser; the round structure beside it is the control module. That particular station is Peace Control Satellite Alpha-Nine. My grandfather served aboard her."

"Your grandfather?" Brea asked.

75

He nodded. "We Stassels are an old-line military family. I'm third-generation PE." He glanced once more at his watch. "We need to shake a leg if we're going to get dinner this evening. I thought you might like a quick look at what the museum has to offer, then if you're interested, I'll arrange a longer visit tomorrow when we'll have more time."

He led them on a brisk tour of the various galleries of the maze, each of which had a theme. One specialized in weapons with cutting edges—knives, swords, spears, axes, and all their many variations. Another was filled with pieces of personal armor. As they worked around the perimeter of the cave, the weapons became more modern. In one gallery, a century-and-a-half old wood-and-fabric biplane sat beside a sleek hypersonic bomber only slightly younger. The early weapons of space were the center of another display. Several antique spy satellites flanked the tiny shape of one of the first orbital interceptors. And outside a gallery sealed off by closed doors, both Russian and American laser battle stations from the period of the Misfire War sat side by side.

"What's in here?" Lisa asked, pointing to the closed entry into the gallery.

"You don't want to go in there."

"Why not?"

"Why ruin your dinner?"

Brea laughed. "You had best tell all, Eric. I know that look. You've roused her monkey curiosity."

He sighed. "That gallery is devoted to the Misfire War. Not all the incoming warheads were vaporized in space, you know. A few got through. A nuked city is not a pretty sight, certainly nothing to show a twelve-year-old girl."

"I'm old enough! You can't scare me."

"I think we'd better by-pass this one, Lisa."

"I want to see it. You do too, don't you, Brea?"

Stassel turned to Brea, his eyebrows lifted.

She bit her lower lip, obviously torn by her distaste for the subject and the need to show Stassel that she was no shrinking violet. The silence stretched on uncomfortably long, until she threw her shoulders back and stared him straight in the eye. "Lisa and I would like to see it, Major."

Stassel shrugged. "Okay, but don't say I didn't warn you."

* * *

Dinner was a somber affair in spite of all the efforts of the Earthview Room's management to make it otherwise. Brea and Lisa had been shocked by the pictures they'd seen in the museum. Brea hated to admit it, but Stassel had been right. They *hadn't* been anything you would want to show a twelve-year-old girl.

Lisa was the first to recover, bouncing back to her normally cheerful self long before the dessert course was trundled to the table. Brea was less resilient. She couldn't get over the sight of the child who cradled a charred ball of fur in her arms, apparently unaware that she had been burned almost as badly herself. Or the panorama of carnage at a playground on the outskirts of a fusion weapon blast. Even two hours later she had trouble controlling her gag reflex.

Whoever had set up that little collection of horror had done so without the slightest compassion for those who would be viewing it. Most of the photographs were without caption, leaving observers with no way to tell whether they were taken in Moscow, Pittsburgh, or Hangchow; Volgagrad, Seattle, or Belgrade. The display held selections from each of the fifteen cities unlucky enough to have been the target of "those few that got through."

When Stassel had first showed them the war museum, Brea thought that the PEs were glorifying the very thing they were sworn to prevent. After seeing the dead and the dying of seventy years earlier, she realized that there could be no glory in such carnage. Her shoulders shivered involuntarily as she watched Stassel teaching Lisa to dance. While she fought to regain control of her emotions, she considered her dilemma.

The flash of light in Aquila was both mysterious and potentially important. After the museum, she hoped with all her heart that what she had observed was nothing more than a star clearing its throat. But the astronomer in her didn't believe it. The most plausible explanation was that someone had tested a weapon designed to smash cities just the way those in the display had been smashed.

For the first time Brea felt she understood the motivation of the men and women in black and silver. She was still mulling over the situation when Stassel led Lisa back to the table. They were laughing.

"Did you see me dancing, Brea?"

"Yes, hon."

"You should try it, it's wonderful! Eric's promised to teach me some more steps."

"If you're going to learn, this is the place," Stassel replied. "One-sixth gee will make anyone look good, even me and my two left feet."

"Perhaps the major would dance with me," Brea said.

Stassel stood, placed one hand at his waist, and executed a courtly bow. "My pleasure."

She let him guide her to the center of the dance floor and take her in his arms. She bent her body into his and abandoned herself to the flow of the music. It had been years, but she still remembered how. Stassel said nothing as he led in the slow, space-eating pirouette of a low-gee waltz. Finally Brea opened her eyes and looked directly into his.

"You planned it all, didn't you?"

"Planned what?"

"You maneuvered me into seeing that horrible display in the museum?"

He hesitated, too long, then nodded. "Guilty as charged. We have your dossier, including your psychometric chart. One of my assistants pointed out that you deeply regret not having conceived a child before your husband's death, which causes you to have a soft spot where babies are concerned. I arranged to have the Misfire War exhibit . . . 'strengthened,' shall we say?"

"Then it was all propaganda?"

He nodded. "In a way. But we didn't invent those scenes. We didn't have to. The directorate has thousands of similiar photographs on file. Much to our species' eternal shame."

"What if I still refuse to help you?"

"I'm hoping that you won't."

Brea hesitated, still inhibited by the knowledge of what could happen if she betrayed her secret. Damn Bailey for putting her into this spot! *Damn herself for going along with him!* She took a deep breath and stopped dancing. Stassel stopped along with her. For ten long seconds she said nothing. "I don't want to do this," she said as tears welled up in her eyes.

"It's your choice."

"You know damn well that I lost my freedom to choose the

instant you suckered me into that display!"

He sighed and pulled her close, comforting her as one comforts a lost child. When he spoke, it was very softly.

"Yes, I know."

CHAPTER 9

Brea Gallagher stirred, opened her eyes to darkness, and sat up in bed. As she did so, the overhead lights brightened without warning. She blinked back tears and surveyed her surroundings. She was in a narrow bed flanked by gleaming machinery in a room decorated completely in soft pastel greens. For a moment she had trouble remembering where she was.

It was Tycho Base Medical Center. She had been in a small laboratory in a chair not much different from her acceleration couch aboard *Liar's Luck*. The chair had been very comfortable, and if it hadn't been for the bright lights shining in her eyes, she could have fallen asleep right there. She *had* fallen asleep, in fact, listening to the droning voice of a bald little man who had given her an injection.

After that . . . nothing.

She found that she had been subconsciously gripping a light sheet to her breasts. Looking beneath the sheet, she discovered that she had been stripped to her underwear. Her jumpsuit was hanging neatly in a closet next to the bed, her ship boots beside

80

it. Her belt pouch lay in a chair at the foot of the bed with her grooming articles. She climbed out of bed and into the jumpsuit. She was combing her hair when a soft knock sounded. Immediately, Lisa's head popped through the partially opened door.

"Are you decent, Brea?"

"Come in."

"Whew, I thought you would never wake up! It's been four whole hours."

"Were you there while they questioned me?"

Lisa nodded.

"What did they ask?"

"Just a bunch of technical junk about the sighting. They showed you a lot of pictures of stars, and you placed a laser dot where you thought you'd seen the flash. You must have done it fifty times or more."

"Nothing else? Did I ramble on about our trip here?"

"No, you just talked about the flash."

Brea was in the midst of a deep sigh of relief when another set of knuckles knocked on her door.

This time it was Eric Stassel, a dozen red roses in one hand and a record cube in the other. "Peace offering." He handed her the flowers. "Am I forgiven?"

"Yes," Brea said, surprised that she meant it.

"This is a recording of your session," he said as he handed her the record cube. "You'll find we respected your privacy."

Brea nodded. "So Lisa has been telling me. Did you get what you wanted?"

"Yes. The deep thinkers should have little trouble reducing your data to a position vector."

"Will I ever know what comes of all this?"

Stassel looked sheepish. "I'm afraid not. Security regulations, you know."

"Then that's it? You have no further need of me?"

"That's it. The directorate thanks you and would consider it an honor if you will allow us to pay your expenses while on Earth. You have my personal thanks as well."

Brea sighed. Now that the ordeal was over, it was almost anticlimactic. She buckled her belt over her jumpsuit and turned to Lisa.

"Let's go, hon. Earth is waiting. First stop: Hawaii, and a dip in the ocean."

Lisa looked at her, horror on her young face. "Get wet all over? Are you crazy?"

Crowds in party dress surged laughing and joking around Don Bailey as he worked his way through the streets of Meridien Village toward the outdoor cafe that was his goal. A kilometer overhead, a pyrotechnic light show danced around *Galileo Station*'s central core, illuminating the checkerboard of farms and villages that dotted the thirty square kilometers of the great cylinder's inner surface. The dazzling effect was heightened by the fact that the huge mirrors adorning the habitat's north and south poles had been rotated to reflect the black of space rather than the light of the sun. Night had come to *Galileo Station*.

Bailey's progress was slowed to a halt several times as fingers plucked at his shirt and celebrants thrust open bottles into his face or threw themselves into his arms for a quick kiss. The bottles he refused. The women he accommodated, returning whatever degree of ardor he found behind the embrace, but always moving on his way soon afterward.

Outwardly he smiled at all who crossed his path. Inwardly he seethed. His arrival, at the onset of Mardi Gras, couldn't have been worse timed. The Galileans' annual rite of summer would make it quadruply difficult to conclude his business. Most communities in space had adopted the occasional all-out blast as a means of compensating for the stresses that came with living in a sardine can. However, none had done so quite so enthusiastically as the Lagrangians.

Bailey had fond memories of a time twenty years earlier when he had been inboard *Copernicus Station* during Mardi Gras. There had been a girl with skin like chocolate and eyes that were great brown pools, a girl with an inflated opinion of Belters. Bailey had spent a whole week attempting to live up to her expectations, a job that eventually proved impossible for mere flesh and blood. Still, he would have willingly spent the next three days attempting to recapture that lost moment if only his ship weren't hiding something in its maw.

That smuggled singularity was the reason he now found himself elbowing his way through partying crowds. At the small cafe that was his goal, he would arrange delivery of the cargo. The place was the centerpiece of a small park alive with willow trees and a carefully manicured carpet of grass. Because of the holiday, the civil government had suspended the draconian regulations forbidding trampling of the latter, and the park was alive with couples strolling arm in arm or engaged in more intimate forms of contact.

Bailey found an empty table and ordered a vodka collins. While he waited, he leaned back and let the enormity of the station envelop him. As the Galilean Chamber of Commerce was fond of pointing out, the "coffee can" around him was the largest object ever constructed by human beings. Two kilometers in diameter by five long, the cylinder had nine levels of offices, warehouses, and service areas beneath the innermost deck where he now sat. The main habitat served as city and farmland for a population employed among a number of auxiliary stations that rode similar orbits in the L4 stable point. These included the UN's Sky Watch Directorate and three million-megawatt power plants. A fourth was being constructed a few hundred kilometers fore-orbit of the habitat, and its construction workers used the cylindrical city-in-the-sky for the three B's—*broads, boozing, and brawling.*

Liar's Luck was secured in one of the floating dry docks that were clustered around the Beta Power Plant. The ship was to begin overhaul as soon as Mardi Gras hangovers had subsided.

"Don Bailey, long time no see!"

He raised his gaze from his drink to discover a man standing over him with a smile on his lips and a wary expression. The face was that of a complete stranger.

"Why, hello," Bailey said. "I know I should remember your name . . ."

"No reason to, Mr. Bailey. I was only twelve last time we met. I'm Angai Yahaya."

"Of course, Angai! Have a seat and watch the fireworks."

Yahaya pulled a chair from under the table and sat. He made no attempt to gaze skyward but leaned close to Bailey and whispered: "Have you got it?"

Bailey nodded imperceptibly while pretending to sip from his drink.

"Good. Any trouble?"

83

"Not with the authorities. I had hell's own time herding my ship in from the Moon, though. I'll be glad when I get my weight-and-balance back in kilter."

"If you had no trouble from the authorities, why did you stop at the Moon? Why is your partner even now a guest of the Peace Enforcers in Tycho Base?" Yahaya spoke between lips frozen into a meaningless smile as his suspicious gaze probed Bailey's face.

Bailey took a slow drink from his glass and locked eyes with Yahaya until the other looked away. Only then did he launch into an abbreviated account of the summons he and Brea had received just before leaving for Earth.

"An imaginitive tale, anyway."

Bailey shrugged. "It's the truth."

"I must warn you, Mr. Bailey, if you have betrayed us, you will not live to spend your blood money. We have agents to enforce our agreements."

"So, what else is new?"

"As long as you understand that we will do what we promise . . ."

"Threat received and understood. Now can we get on with it?"

Yahaya nodded. "By all means. What is your access code, Mr. Bailey?"

"Ah, I believe there was mention of payment prior to delivery?"

"Of course." Yahaya reached into his tunic and extracted a small plastic card. He passed it to Bailey, who inserted it into his new pocket phone. After Bailey had tapped a dozen digits on the phone's keypad, a series of numbers began to crawl across the small screen. He watched intently until the message had finished scrolling.

"Satisfactory?" Yahaya asked.

"Very," Bailey answered, turning the phone off and slipping the card into an inside pocket.

"Now, what is the combination to your ship's maintenance hatch?"

Bailey recited a long series of numbers, which Yahaya punched into a phone of his own. He finished and stared at the machine for a dozen seconds before it beeped quietly.

"Also correct, Mr. Bailey. I believe that completes our

business. Will you join me in a drink to celebrate?"

"Gladly."

Yahaya signaled the waitress and ordered two more vodka collinses.

"I understand you were born in Capetown, Mr. Bailey. That makes us countrymen, you know. I was raised in Molobu Township, just north of Joburg."

Bailey nodded. "I caught a hint of Anglo-African the moment you spoke. It made me a bit homesick."

"Have you ever thought of returning home?"

"What for?"

"Have you no family there?"

"None."

"Perhaps a pilgrimage to renew your sense of your own origins, then. Everyone must belong to something, and you have been too long absent from our homeland. A skilled spaceman such as yourself would be especially welcome."

Bailey rubbed at his wiry hair. "I left Pan-Africa forty years ago because they needed trained spacers like a bull baboon needs tits. As far as I can see, things haven't changed a whole lot since then."

"Permit me to disagree, Mr. Bailey. In your youth, the black and brown peoples of the world were engaged in their struggle to throw off the last vestiges of caucasian colonialism. We have since won our righteous struggle and today stride erect like men. We no longer live at the sufference of the whites but demand full equality. That includes our fair share of the wealth of space."

"Meaning what?"

"Meaning that Pan-Africa needs trained spacemen if she is ever going to claim what is rightfully hers."

"Is that why you are collecting unregistered I-masses?"

"That is none of your business." Yahaya drained his drink and looked at his watch before retrieving a business card from a sleeve pocket and handing it to Bailey. "I'm afraid I have to go. Think about what I have told you. If you change your mind, call this number. Ask for Colonel M'Buto." With that he turned on his heel and disappeared into the crowd of revelers.

Eric Stassel sat before his workscreen and scowled. The answer that he had sought for the last four weeks was displayed

85

before him in glowing green. It had taken only minutes for Brea Gallagher's data to yield a position vector, minutes more for the mystery flash to be pinpointed. To have the answer dropped into his lap after so much frustration had a feeling of unreality about it.

It was a feeling that was heightened as he read the position coordinates of the explosion (or whatever) that had been the source of a 9.85-second burst of violet light in the Constellation of Aquila.

Stassel ground his teeth in frustration and called for a listing of the triangulation routine that Gregor Zapata had worked up, hoping to find some mistake—a double-named variable or a wrong sign at a crucial juncture. But no, the damn program was too short for Gregor to have made such an obvious error. Everything checked out to sixty-four decimal places. He ran a quick test by inputting the parallax data for Barnard's Star.

The result confirmed that Zapata's program was correct.

That led him right back to the same quandary. The program was correct. Brea Gallagher's data was correct. Sky Watch's position data was correct. The only thing that wasn't correct was the answer. If you could believe the calculation, the "something" that had caused the mystery flash had been some five thousand astronomical units out in space!

To the computer that was a number like any other. It was large when measured in kilometers, small when converted to parsecs. But no matter how you sliced it, the distance to the hypothetical explosion in deep space still translated 720 light-hours, *one whole light-month distant from the Sun!*

Stasssel was reaching out to key another run through the raw data when his screen beeped for attention. He keyed acceptance and the screen cleared to reveal Elspeth Crocker.

"Sorry to bother you in the security room, Eric, but Señora Gonzales of Information Services has been trying to get you. She says that it is most urgent."

"Patch her through."

The screen cleared to reveal La Dueña's pensive features. "Ah, Eric. Are you still interested in strange happenings in Aquila?"

Stassel grinned wanly. "I'm beginning to wish I wasn't. What have you got?"

"If you will remember, I set up a data-screening program

per your request. Two hours ago my routine began retrieving realtime reports of something inexplicable going on out there. Ceres Observatory has discovered an intense x-ray source in our bounded area of sky. Every x-ray instrument in the system is reacting to it. Several reports from Directorate ships came in right on the heels of Ceres' report. The destroyers *U Thant* and *Dag Hammarskjold* and our old friend *Valiant* have all seen it."

Stassel felt the hair on the back of his neck begin to rise. "What kind of x-ray source?"

"Highly coherent. Wavelength 1.562 angstroms plus or minus nothing. And there's another mystery. No one else has noticed yet because we here in Luna are the only people with all the data at the moment. I've run everything that's been flooding in through the computer. Just curiosity on my part, you understand. The source has a disturbingly large parallax as viewed from around the system."

"Parallax? Have you calculated the position vector yet?"

"Of course."

"Let me guess. You come up with a figure of seven hundred twenty light-hours, right?"

Señora Gonzales shook her head, looking very frightened. "Oh, no, Eric! No more than three hundred light-hours, if that much!"

Stassel groaned. "Keep a lid on what you've found until I can get back to you, Olivia. I'll have instructions as soon as I get through talking to the admiral. Until you hear differently, this is top secret!"

"Do you know what is causing this, Eric?"

Stassel shook his head. "Not the foggiest notion, but whatever it is, it's coming in fast!"

CHAPTER 10

Earth Station One was tiny by the standards of the giant Lagrange habitats. Its three toroids and central core could have been stuffed into one of *Galileo Station*'s oversize cargo locks with room to spare. Yet of the two constructs, *ESO* was the more famous by far. *ESO* was the oldest continually manned artifact in the solar system.

It had originally been constructed in the early 1990s to serve as a maintenance base for laser battle stations. Following the Misfire War, the UN took possession. *ESO*s orbit made it a prime command-and-control facility. Not until the network of peace control satellites was completed in 2010 did it cease to be an active military base.

Placed on the auction block in 2020, the station was purchased by a consortium of transport companies. With its boutiques, cozy restaurants, and the luxurious suites of the Grand Hotel, it was a popular transfer point between the Earth-based shuttles and the ships of deep space. Age had given it the quiet elegance of a Victorian train station.

Brea, Lisa, and Bailey sat in the Transients' Lounge and

watched the Earth rotate beneath them on the wall screen at the far end of the lounge. Bailey half sat, half reclined in the station's three-quarters gravity and cradled his aching head in his hands.

Brea watched him and scowled. "Nobody said you had to match the Galileans drink for drink, you know."

Bailey lifted his head long enough to reveal two bloodshot eyes and whisper hoarsely: "Not so loud!"

Brea considered taunting further and decided that it could wait. "Are you sure they are doing a good job on *Liar*?"

Bailey sighed, sat straight in his seat, and had a long sip of the hair-of-the-dog. "I checked her before I boarded the ship to come here. They had the converter pulled apart and our I-mass stored safely in a maintenance field. They said they'd have her done in three weeks."

"Look, Brea!"

Brea turned to Lisa, who was pointing at the wall screen. They were passing over the eastern edge of Asia, with all of the Chinese Hegemony and the northern part of Australasia below them. Other than the spectacular scenery and one middling-size typhoon working its way across the Pacific, she could see nothing unusual. "What?"

"There was a glint of sun off something at the lower left of the screen. It's gone now."

They watched for two minutes in silence. At the end of that time a small speck appeared approximately where Lisa had described. The speck quickly resolved itself into a sleek, winged arrow.

"What is it?" Lisa asked.

"Our transportation down, hon."

As they watched, a nearly invisible flame erupted from attitude-control jets, and the ground-to-orbit shuttle was suddenly stationary in space. Someone had locked the camera at the station's axis on the arriving craft, and the ship was now in center screen with the Earth image skewed to one side.

"Drink up folks," Bailey said. "We'll be going aboard in another hour. We'd best get up to the gate to check in."

They gathered their few possessions and walked a quarter of the way around the station curve to one of the spoke lifts. Once at the axis, Bailey led the way, guiding himself along a cable strung the length of the axisway. Their destination was the departure lounge at the station's north pole, a sphere thirty meters in diameter with a half-dozen docking ports scattered over its surface.

The agent at the central ticket booth slipped the small rectangles of plastic that were their tickets into a card reader.

"Bailey, Gallagher, and Moore?"

"Yes," Bailey confirmed.

The agent's brows furrowed as the computer answered his inquiry. "A moment, please, Mr. Bailey."

"We have confirmed reservations, don't we?"

"Oh, yes, sir! But the computer has some kind of administrative hold on your tickets. I'll check it now; I'm sure we can get you on your way quickly."

Bailey turned to Brea. "What do you think?"

Brea didn't answer. On the far side of the open sphere, two men in orange and blue floated through a door labeled Security Office and launched themselves toward the three Belters.

"Donel Bailey?" the taller of the two asked as he grounded beside Bailey.

Bailey nodded.

"Breon Gallagher?"

"Here."

"Lisa Moore?"

"Here, sir."

"Would you mind coming with us, please?"

"What for?"

"We have orders to detain you."

"By whose authority?" Brea asked, trying for a maximum of indignation and a minimum of guilt in her voice.

"The order comes from the Peace Enforcers."

"But we'll miss our shuttle!"

"Yes, ma'am. Sorry for the inconvenience, but we have our orders. There will be another along tomorrow and I'm sure the UN will make it up to you."

Brea glanced at Bailey, who only shrugged. The two security policemen were polite but armed with tasers. She allowed herself to be taken by the arm and guided back the way they had come.

Angai Yahaya was asleep in his cubicle when the phone rang. Still groggy, he rolled over and checked the time. It was

15:00, only four hours after he'd gotten to bed after an all-night vigil with the wide-angle mapping cameras. Old Kingsley had insisted that they keep a continuous watch on the new x-ray source in Aquila, thinking that it might have something to do with the Gresham/Kingsley Flash of nearly six months earlier. For once Yahaya agreed with him. He groped for the switch that would accept the call on audio circuit only.

"Yes?" he muttered.

"Angai? Why can't I see you?" The voice was that of Colonel M'Buto.

Suddenly he was wide awake. He switched to viewer. M'Buto's features solidified on the screen. He looked worried.

"Bailey's been arrested."

"Are you sure?"

"Don't ask stupid questions. They may be after you next, so bolt for cover. Use the safe house."

"Yes, sir."

The phone went dead and Yahaya wasted no time springing into action. Within two minutes he was ready to leave. He wondered if he should stop to water his plants—no telling how long he would be undercover—and decided against it. When M'Buto gave an order, he expected it to be carried out without delay.

Yahaya palmed the security switch on his cubicle door. The door hissed open and he found himself staring into the faces of two PE Marines, one of whom was just reaching for the annunciator. Yahaya wasn't sure whether he or the Marine was the more startled.

"Angai Yahaya?"

He nodded.

"Please come with us."

Brea wasn't surprised when, instead of delivering them to the outermost deck, the lift deposited them two levels higher in the administrative section of the station. The security policemen remained polite, but when the three Belters found themselves alone, it was in a cabin with no visible means of opening the door from the inside.

Two hours later, when she was sure the authorities had discovered the smuggled singularity, the door hissed open again.

"Follow me, please," a policeman said. He led them halfway

around C-Deck to a conference room and ushered them inside.

Brea stepped through to find Eric Stassel seated at the head of a long conference table.

"Hello, Eric," Lisa said. "What are you doing here?"

"A damned good question!" Bailey said, exploding. "What right have you people to arrest us?"

Stassel stood and extended his hand. "You must be Don Bailey."

"Never mind who I am. Let's see your warrant."

"I'm not arresting you, Mr. Bailey. I merely asked that you be detained until I could get here."

"Why, Eric?" Brea asked.

He looked at her with bleary eyes. His uniform looked as though he had slept in it. He motioned them to take places around the table and waited until they had done so. "Things have changed since last we met. I had your data analyzed and got the surprise of my life. I expected the flash to originate somewhere between Jupiter and Saturn, or else light-years out in space. As it turns out, triangulation places the source one light-month distant from the sun."

Brea frowned. "That's impossible. There must be some mistake."

"That's what I thought until half the observatories in the system began picking up a strong x-ray source in the same area. They aren't ordinary, run-of-the-mill x-rays either."

"What do you mean?"

"They're coherent."

"*Coherent*? You mean like a laser?"

Stassel nodded. "Exactly like a laser. We have multiple sightings and triangulated it immediately. Comparing the new data with the original sighting, we can compute course and speed."

"You make it sound like a spaceship."

"Or an artifact. Apparently something on the outskirts of our solar system is heading in at one-tenth light-speed."

An uncomfortably long silence was broken when Bailey cleared his throat. "Interesting, but what has that to do with us?"

Brea turned to him. "What's wrong with you, Stinky? Didn't you hear him? It's an alien spacecraft!"

"I'm excited as you are, Brea. I just want to understand our status here. Surely the major didn't break all speed records getting here from the Moon just to tell us the good news."

"You are correct, Mr. Bailey, I did not. I'm here because we've thrown a security shield over this whole subject until we discover what we are faced with. The directorate has declared a Class-One Emergency and ordered that everyone with knowledge of the original sighting be placed in quarantine. I have orders to corral you three before you talk to anyone else."

"Then we *are* under arrest!"

"That depends on you. Admiral Liu is assembling a team of specialists to learn everything possible about our extrasolar visitor before it gets here. You three may participate if you wish. Brea's astronomical experience could prove invaluable. We'll find jobs for you and Lisa too."

"And if we refuse?" Bailey asked.

"Then you will spend the next several months as unwilling guests of the Peace Enforcement Directorate, probably in the deepest armory beneath Tycho Crater."

"That isn't much of a choice."

"It's all you've got. Please make your decision now. I haven't much time."

The three Belters exchanged glances. Bailey turned to Stassel and grinned. "Seeing as that's the way the wind blows, Skipper, I guess we'll sign on for the duration of the voyage."

PART II:

THE APPROACH

CHAPTER 11

Considering the haste with which it was formed, Project Eaglet was a remarkable achievement that added greatly to our understanding of the physical sciences. Although some historians blame those associated with the Project for the tragic events of 9 February 2066, most writers in the field feel such claims pay too little heed to the unsettled political climate of the time.

—From *"Prelude to Pathfinder: An Official History."*

Lisa Moore wasn't the least bit unhappy about the sudden turn of events. Better than going to some ginky girl's school, any day!

Things moved quickly after Eric Stassel explained the situation to the three Belters. Lisa had half expected him to have everyone transported back to Tycho Base on the first available ship, but he'd fooled her. After extracting Bailey's promise that they would join the research effort, he left them with his two assistants and went off to negotiate with the *ESO* Grand

Hotel management. It was well past suppertime when he returned.

"What's the word?" Greg Zapata asked when he saw his boss's harried expression.

"They're ceding us the entire Alpha ring. The hotel staff is emptying the area now. Our Marines will establish their security perimeter at the spoke lifts."

"When are we getting out of here?" Lisa asked. It had been a long day.

"Won't be long now," Eric replied. "I've got my people setting up a temporary place for us to work while Admiral Liu arranges something more permanent. Project Eaglet is about to commence."

"Project Eaglet?" Brea asked.

"Liu's code name for the research group we're pulling together. Since the alien's coming out of the Constellation of Aquila, the Eagle, what better name for it?"

Securing *Earth Station One*'s Alpha Habitat Ring took another three hours. When the small party moved into its new home, Lisa luxuriated for a few seconds in the opulence of her new private cabin, dropped into the first real bed she had ever had—at home she slept on a blanket stretched out on the floor—and fell into a deep sleep.

Lisa's good fortune didn't last long. The population of the Asylum—as Lisa secretly named it—quickly grew so large that she was moved into a room with Brea and Ellie Crocker.

The first of the tidal wave of new inmates hadn't been long coming. Three men sat clustered around a table sipping coffee when she and Brea entered the hastily converted cafeteria for breakfast the morning after being shanghaied. Brea squealed in delight as she caught sight of the oldest member of the trio. The man glanced up at the sudden noise, cried out in surprise, and rushed to embrace her. Afterward, Brea turned to Lisa, a large smile on her face. "Hon, I'd like you to meet Professor Henri Roquette, Copernican Professor of Astronomy at the Sorbonne. Henri, this is my ward, Lisa Moore."

"You honor me, Mademoiselle Moore," Roquette said, taking Lisa's hand and kissing it.

Lisa blushed. Roquette turned to Brea. "You do not know my companions, I believe. Doctor Stanislaw Wojcelevitch, of the University of Prague. Bernie Whitnauer, my assistant. Breon

Caldwell, gentlemen, one of the most promising pupils it has ever been my privilege to teach."

Brea laughed. "I'm Brea Gallagher now, Henri."

"Where did they pluck you from, Mrs. Gallagher?" Wojcelevitch asked as he shook Brea's hand.

"Right here in this station, Doctor. And you?"

"I was returning from the theater with my wife when two very officious young men waylaid me at the door. I think my Katrina still believes it to be a student prank."

"I too was ambushed," Roquette said. "I was just finishing up an evening lecture series I have been giving to enlighten the unenlightenable. Except for the papers they showed me—signed by some very impressive names—I am not terribly enlightened myself. What can you tell us of the reason we find ourselves in orbit this morning, my dear Breon?"

Brea licked dry lips and failed to meet her mentor's gaze. Lisa knew why. Eric had asked her not to divulge the secret of the alien spacecraft until he was ready. Finally she had avoided the subject by saying: "I understand Major Stassel plans to brief us after breakfast."

The next time Lisa saw Roquette or Wojcelevitch, both had dark bags under their eyes and were haggard from lack of sleep. They had been living in converted hotel rooms with the banks of computer workscreens that had been installed. They weren't the only ones. By the tenth day, the Asylum had been stuffed with prestigious laborers and every one of the hundred-plus inmates seemed to work, live, and eat on a different schedule.

Whether due to overcrowding or merely because of the stress inherent in Earth's first contact with an alien civilization, day eleven saw the first outbreak of fisticuffs. Two highly respected scientists went at it in the communications center. The ostensible cause was a disagreement over who had priority access to the computers at Tycho Base.

A few hours after the combatants were separated, Eric Stassel ordered a general meeting in the *ESO* Grand Ballroom.

"Do you think he means us, Uncle Don?" Lisa asked after hearing the announcement at evening meal. She and Bailey were busy loading a vacuum dishwasher with dirty metalware, having been assigned to assist the burly Marine cook who headed the commissary department.

"We're members of this project too, aren't we?" Bailey asked, wiping one sleeve on his forehead to keep the perspiration out of his eyes. "Hand me that basket of forks over there, will you?"

"Maybe he just meant the scientists. I suppose I could ask him."

Bailey slipped the last basket of utensils into its rack and dogged the cleaner's hatch closed before engaging the scavenge pump. He turned to her. "Let your Uncle Don give you some advice. Major Stassel's a busy man, what with keeping the scientists from each other's throats and satisfying the demands of the mysterious Admiral Liu. Don't bother him with trivia. Besides, aren't you getting tired of not knowing what's going on around here?"

Lisa sighed. "I'll say. Brea hasn't said more than a dozen words to me all week. She gets in after I go to sleep, is gone when I get up in the morning, and spends just about every waking hour either closeted with the other astronomers or in conference with Major Stassel. If you ask me, she's sweet on him."

Bailey turned to look at the little girl and raised one eyebrow. "Cattiness at your age? Seems to me that you spend a lot of time tagging along after Bernie Whitnauer."

"Oh, Uncle Don!"

"I wasn't condemning. Now hurry up with those plates so we can get to sleep at a reasonable hour tonight. And tomorrow we join the first-class citizenry, at least until someone notices us and throws us out."

Stassel let his gaze drift over the sea of faces before him. The *ESO* Grand Ballroom covered nearly a tenth of the habitable area of the Alpha Habitat Ring. Even so, it was a tight squeeze when filled with the scientists, technicians, and academicians the directorate had pulled into this thing over the last week and a half.

At the back of the room, Sergeant Marinaro flashed him the count by hand. All 108 names listed on the morning report were finally present and accounted for, including the dozen or so the Marines were forced to roust away from their work-screens. Stassel nodded to Marinaro, who ordered his guards to withdraw. The Marines cradled riot guns in the crooks of their arms and stepped out into the corridor. The big double airlock-type doors closed behind them. When the light over the airtight portal winked from red to green, he stepped up to the lecturn.

"Good morning, ladies and gentlemen. I'm sorry to interrupt your very important work, but I thought it best that we get together as a group. For those of you who I have not yet met, I am Major Eric Stassel, United Nations Peace Enforcement Directorate, the officer assigned to ramrod this phase of Project Eaglet.

"Now, before we answer any questions you may have, let's summarize why we are all here. As you know, various civil and directorate spacecraft and *every* space-based astronomical installation in the system witnessed a bright x-ray flare in the Constellation of Aquila fifteen days ago. By plotting the apparent position of this new x-ray star from each observation point, we are able to pinpoint the source of radiation with considerable precision and to track its progress with time.

"As of oh eight hundred hours this morning, the source was apparently nineteen hundred astronomical units from the Sun. Assuming that it has maintained its speed of one-tenth *c* for the last ten days, and allowing for the finite speed at which light travels, the source's true position at this moment is actually seventeen hundred ten AU's distant from Sol. That rather high closing velocity, along with the fact that what we are observing is obviously an x-ray laser, has led us to the conclusion that what we are observing is an alien spacecraft on the edge of the solar system, a ship that will be here in another hundred days.

"Which brings me to why all of you have been recruited for this project...." Stassel let his gaze roam over the crowd as a hint of mirth suffused his tone. "I've heard the term shanghaied used more than once. I apologize for the disruption to your lives, but I would remind you that your presence here means that you are the best in your field. Earth is counting on you to learn everything possible about the alien before it arrives.

"We are flying blind, a situation that must be remedied as quickly as possible. Do we get out our morning coats and tophats, do we call out the fleet, or do we merely raise the white flag? You people in this room are the only ones in the system who can advise us.

"And now that I've properly impressed you with the importance of your mission, I'll open up the floor for questions."

"Major Stassel!"

"Yes, sir."

The questioner was a small, dark man with a neat mustache that was fairly bristling at the moment. He looked around at his neighbors in a way that convinced Stassel that he was used to dealing with consensus committees to get things done. "Rudolpho Furogamo from Universidad de Buenos Aires. My speciality is anthropology, and I'll be damned if I know what I'm doing here. I've spent the last seventy-two hours listening to my colleagues in the physical sciences tell me that a boatload of aliens is about to invade the solar system. Frankly, I have not been able to follow their reasoning."

"Your question, sir?"

"Simply stated, Major Stassel: how do you know this is an artificial radiation source and not a newly discovered natural phenomenon?"

Stassel turned to look at Helena Rheinhardt, head of the large and growing Alien Technology Assessment Team. "Doctor Rheinhardt?"

Doctor Rheinhardt, a silver-haired woman with a wicked chuckle and a triple chin, turned to the Argentinian. "The source is falling on us at a goodly fraction of the speed of light and emitting a collimated, coherent beam of very shortwave x-rays—1.562 angstroms, to be exact. What else could it be, Señor Furigamo?"

"How do you know it is a laser beam? Could it not be emitting radiation omnidirectionally?"

"If the source were omnidirectional, our ships orbiting Titan would be able to see it just as well as those en route to Mars. Since they cannot, the source must be emitting a beam with a diameter less than that of Saturn's orbit. Ergo, a laser!"

"That still does not prove that the source is artificial."

"I'll grant you that there are a number of natural processes that will generate a laser beam. Some distant galaxies, for instance, have been observed to emit straight beams of radiation thousands of light-years in length. But what we are seeing doesn't match anything quite so well as one of our old antiballistic missile lasers—on a much grander scale, of course. Also, any conceivable natural source would be large enough to see with the naked eye if it were only ten light-days out from the Sun. Since our ships out of the cone of radiation can detect nothing at that particular point in the sky, the object must be quite small."

"What's the purpose?" someone yelled from out of the crowd.

Stassel shrugged. "You tell us."

Helena Rheinhardt turned to face the direction from which the voice had emanated. "Some of my people suggest that we are seeing a photon drive in operation."

"I beg to differ, Doctor, but it is nothing of the kind." The speaker was white-haired, bearded man with a French accent. Brea had introduced him to Stassel as Henri Roquette.

"You have a different theory, Doctor Roquette?" he asked.

"Concerning the laser's purpose? No. But it is no photon drive; or if it is, it is a most ineffective one. We have been watching for a doppler shift associated with deceleration of the source. Our results are highly inconclusive. If it has slowed at all, the amount must be minuscule. We *have* discovered a nongenerl smearing of a tiny fraction of the photons that arrive in our detectors, however. The smearing is in the direction of a red shift."

"Which means what exactly?" Stassel asked.

"Perhaps it means nothing. However, it could be an effect of a very localized gravity gradient. The so-called 'tired light' syndrome. Such a gradient would indicate that the alien is powered by a gravitational singularity. That is certainly a viable conclusion when one considers the original sighting which Brea Gallagher made of the alien. The flare at that time was nothing like the current one but was very similar to the drive flare of a singularity-powered spacecraft. Perhaps that sighting was a midcourse correction and the x-ray source is an attempt at communication."

"What kind of message is an unmodulated x-ray beam?" a linguist shouted from the back of the room.

Roquette turned and regarded his heckler. "I do not know, monsieur. Perhaps that is what we must discover."

"Major Stassel!"

Stassel remembered meeting the speaker at a party Gloria Farrell had given inboard *Galileo Station* about a year earlier. "Doctor Kingsley, you have the floor."

"I enjoy a good bull session as well as the next man. I would gladly speculate on the nature of our visitor for the rest of this watch, but I feel I have a more important concern."

"Go ahead, sir."

"When are you bloody soldiers going to fill my requisitions for equipment? I've got important work to do and nothing to do it with." A rumbling undercurrent of agreement raced through the crowd.

"I appreciate your patience and understanding, Doctor Kingsley. These problems will be alleviated as quickly as possible. The directorate has spent the last week stripping Earth's suppliers, universities, and observatories of just about everything that isn't nailed down. All that equipment has been shuttled to orbit and is being transferred by fast ship to our new base of operations, UNS *Count Bernadotte*."

"Never heard of it!"

"Bernie's an old blast ship mothballed in the twenties. The directorate maintains it in the leading Earth–Sun Lagrangian point with the rest of the mothball fleet. It's a big old barn where you'll have plenty of room to spread out and work without sticking your foot in someone else's eye."

"Why all this trouble about going out to some mothballed battlewagon?" Helena Rheinhardt asked. "What's wrong with *Galileo* or *Copernicus Station*, or one of the lunar observatories, or hell, why not appropriate all of this hotel?"

"Security, Doctor. There are too many uncleared personnel in those places. Out in the E–S L-4 point, if necessary we can keep all this secret until the alien sweeps into the system."

"Why keep it secret at all?"

"To prevent panic among the populace."

Doctor Roquette stood at his seat and cleared his throat. "It seems to me that you give the common man too little credit, Major Stassel. They have a right to know down below, and we should not arrogate to ourselves the responsibility of making the decision for them." A smattering of applause sounded.

Stassel waited for the applause to die down. "I'm sure that your concerns are being addressed at this very moment by the UN Security Council. However, unless my orders are changed in the near future, we are all being transferred to *Count Bernadotte*.

"Now, further questions?... If not, I will let you all get back to your work."

CHAPTER 12

Agitation coursed through PROBE's circuits. Never before had it experienced quite the same mixture of frustration and disappointment, not even in that long-ago time when it was forced to abandon its first contact with a technologically advanced civilization. For the first time ever, it found itself faced with a seeming impossibility: though it had directed a laser beam of unprecedented power into the heart of the solar system, *human astronomers had apparently overlooked it completely!*

It was possible, of course, that no one had been scanning the section of sky in the direction of the Maker sun when the first energetic photons flashed through the inner system. It was not possible—not even in PROBE's most pessimistic scenarios—that the new x-ray source could remain unseen for the more than three hundred hours since it first flared bright in the humans' sky. PROBE knew of at least three automatic systems, including one that guarded the Earth against a major meteor strike, that should have signaled within seconds after the arrival of the leading wavefront of radiation. Yet instead of bulletins and excited newscasters on the televid networds, PROBE's sensors intercepted only the everyday drone of entertainment programming.

PROBE turned its receptors to high gain and concentrated all its senses on the solar system. While some instruments sampled the electromagnetic spectrum, others tasted the solar wind and the neutrino flux, or measured the local magnetic field and the curvature of space. Nowhere across that vast range of energies was there a single clue as to the cause of the unnatural silence. Apparently the laser beacon had been a total failure!

PROBE lost no time in recriminations. It shut down the laser and considered other approaches to the problem. There was always the possibility that the humans had seen its signal and mistaken it for a natural phenomenon. To reveal as little as possible about itself until it knew the humans better, PROBE had intentionally chosen to project an unmodulated beacon. In doing so, it might have been too subtle. It wouldn't be the first time a life probe had suffered from an excess of subtlety.

PROBE resolved that its next attempt would have a greater impact than its first; not even the most stolid human would mistake a message in his own language as a natural phenomenon.

PROBE composed its message with care, seeking to intrigue the humans without frightening them, cajole without threatening. When the contact message was complete, PROBE translated it into a dozen different languages and recollimated its laser to a much longer wavelength. It would soon radiate across the band of frequencies used by the human televid networks to communicate with their relay satellites.

After the message was turned over to an automatic subroutine, PROBE forgot about it and turned instead to a less direct method of finding out what it must know. PROBE set about constructing a computer simulation of a man.

Any self-aware thinking machine—be it computer or living being—is a complex mass of control mechanisms, stimulus–response programs, and negative feedback loops. As a life probe could be completely described by a very large (but finite) series of simultaneous equations, so too the inhabitants of Sol III. And since PROBE carried within it examples of human behavior in response to all manner of stimulae, its goal was theoretically feasible. Whether it was practically feasible was a matter that could only be discovered by experiment.

The mechanics of the experiment were fairly straightforward. PROBE had merely to isolate one of its logic modules, wipe it clean of previous knowledge, and then arrange its circuitry in accordance with the few billion stimulus–response equations that it had deduced from its study of *Homo sapiens Terra.* After creating the surrogate, PROBE would manipulate the model to study its response to a universe crowded with aliens.

The advantages to the modeling approach were numerous. With the model an integral portion of its own circuitry, PROBE would be able to observe human decision making at firsthand. There would be no annoying communications lags, none of the distortion of raw information that was so common on the televid net, no uncontrolled variables to limit the effectiveness of the experiment.

But there was danger, too. At the least, the split would adversely affect PROBE's coordination and reaction time. More serious was the possibility that it would also destroy the tenuous balance that was the basis of PROBE's basic personality. For PROBE to purposely incorporate such a dichotomy into its own brain was to risk both its sanity and its mission. Even so, the risk seemed the lesser of two evils.

PROBE began its preparations.

"Honor party, *ten-hut!*"

The double rank of Marines, their boots locked into the mesh deck underfoot to give the illusion of gravity, snapped to attention at Eric Stassel's command. Before them the inner door of the airlock leading to Docking Portal Number Three hissed open with compressed air. Beyond the airlock United Nations' Destroyer *Jawaharlal Nehru* floated with its nose caught in the docking collar.

"Here we go!" Elspeth Crocker muttered in a hoarse stage whisper from where she stood next to Stassel. She held the anchor position in the line and, like him, stood at attention while holding eyes-right so that she could watch the airlock.

"Present arms!"

Twelve riot guns snapped into position as an officer in Peace Enforcer black-and-silver with dual comets on his collar floated out of the airlock. The officer was Admiral Liu Tsen.

"Good of you to meet me," Liu said as he returned Stassel's salute.

"Yes, sir," Stassel replied. "May I introduce my aide, Lieutenant Crocker?"

"I know the lieutenant. She did a spot of technical analysis for me last year. An excellent job, Elspeth."

"I thank the admiral."

"Now, Major, let us adjourn to your office. Time is very short. *Nehru* spaces for *Bernadotte* in less than four hours. I plan to be aboard when she uncouples."

"Yes, sir. Do you still want to meet the department heads?"

"That's the reason I'm here, Major."

"Sergeant, dismiss the guard!"

"Yes, sir!"

"Ellie, round up the people we discussed earlier. Have them in the main conference room in fifteen minutes."

"Yes, sir."

Stassel led Liu down the *ESO* axis to the Alpha ring spoke lift. The admiral planted his feet on the wall marked FLOOR and said nothing while pseudogravity and Coriolus acceleration built up around him. Neither man spoke until they had reached Stassel's office.

Liu planted himself in Stassel's chair, leaving the younger officer to sit in one of the guest chairs in front of his own desk. "Curious about why I asked for this preconference, Major?"

"I'm sure you have your reasons, sir."

"I do indeed, and they are contained in these." Liu handed a set of orders to Stassel, who read them carefully.

TO: Stassel, E. H., Major (RPEO 354967231S)
ROUTING: ESO *via* Tycho Base Relay *via* channels
CODE: Expedite
1. You are directed to appear at Hdqtrs, UNHQB-NY, on or about 09:00 hours, 16 August 2065, to give testimony before the Executive Committee, United Nations Trusteeship Council.
2. You will accompany one Breon Caldwell Gallagher, civilian, who will give testimony before ExCom, UNTC, at same session.
3. You are hereby authorized priority transport to Sandia

Spaceport, North American Union, and from there to New York *via* commercial hyperliner.

4. You are reminded that neither you nor Gallagher, B.C., are authorized to discuss your current assignments with anyone not a member of this office or ExCom, UNTC.

5. This assignment is for an unspecified duration, to be decided by Executive Secy, ExCom, UNTC.

SIGNED: Maxwell, J.T.
Chief of Staff
UNPED

BY DIRECTION OF: The Right Honorable Agusta
Meriweather
Executive Secretary
Executive Committee
United Nations Trusteeship
Council

Stassel read the orders slowly through twice. He looked up and noted the scowl on Liu's face. "They want me there the sixteenth? That's tomorrow!"

Liu nodded. "Tycho squirted that to me three hours ago aboard *Nehru*. I broke the system record for squawking to Admiral-General Maxwell. Pried him loose from a dinner party, no less. He rather curtly ordered me to have you on tonight's shuttle. You leave in twelve hours."

"But why me? And why Brea Gallagher?"

"Simple enough to figure out, Major. The ExCom is spooked by this alien spacecraft of yours. They want to question the codiscoverers. Probably think this is all a big hoax. They want someone to hold their hands. You're elected."

"But what about the transfer to *Bernadotte*? There are a thousand things that need to be coordinated."

"Your staff will have to handle it. The first shipload departs twenty hours after you head down to Earth. Any other questions?"

Stassel considered objecting further but decided not to. If Liu had already gone to the chief of staff, then there was no sense complaining. He began to rearrange his priorities and to consider what orders he would have to give in the next twelve hours. Ellie Crocker was about to get her first real command under conditions that Stassel wouldn't wish on his worst enemy.

"No, sir. No more questions."

"Then let's get to this meeting. We haven't all day."

Just then Yorubi M'Buto sat amid plastic coconut palms in *Earth Station One*'s Islander Bar and considered his own problems. An electric guitar ensemble played soft Hawaiian music while a slow, majestic dance took place beyond the double-paned window beside him. The view was mostly black, with the only stable objects in sight the other two habitat rings. The normally fixed landmarks of space—sun, stars, and blue-white crescent Earth—rotated slowly about an imaginary point in the Constellation of Orion.

M'Buto had arrived inboard *ESO* three days earlier after a frustrating week spent tracking the movements of his field agent, Angai Yahaya. The news of Yahaya's arrest had shaken him badly. Though none of his agents had every detail of the Isandhlwana Project, Yahaya knew enough to do damage.

When Yahaya hadn't answered the phone in the *Galileo Station* safe house, M'Buto ordered him eliminated. Unfortunately, killing him had turned out to be impossible: M'Buto did not know who had arrested him or where he was being held. Then with the discovery of Yahaya's whereabouts had come the bitter knowledge that he was beyond reach. Finally word had come that Yahaya was being transferred to *Earth Station One*. Not daring to leave the job to an underling, M'Buto booked passage to orbit on the first available shuttle.

Once inboard *ESO*, however it took less than an hour to discover the situation in the Alpha Habitat Ring and to have his curiosity piqued. Apparently half the potential Nobel Prize winners on the planet had disappeared behind the same PE security screen that had swallowed Yahaya. Whatever the reason, M'Buto suspected that it had little to do with Pan-Africa's attempt to redress the balance of power in the world.

The suspicion brought with it a change in priorities. Instead of eliminating Yahaya as a security risk, M'Buto now had to work out a method of contacting him, but all he had managed so far was to stare across the hundred meters of space that separated him from his objective and scheme.

"Ubi, what brings you here?"

M'Buto glanced up to an unwelcome sight. The speaker was a large, red-faced man with eyes that peered out through rolls of facial fat. The face held a warm expression but the gaze was that of a professional. Murray Danziger, North American Bureau for External Security, was one of M'Buto's oldest adversaries.

"Hello, Murray. What brings the BES to *Earth Station One*?"

Danziger waggled his finger in M'Buto's face. "Not nice. I asked first."

"I'm passing through on vacation."

Danziger laughed as he slid into a booth opposite M'Buto. "I'm on vacation, too. A working vacation. I'm trying to figure out what the PEs are doing next door." He hooked his thumb toward the Alpha Habitat Ring.

"PEs?"

"Come on, Ubi. You don't have to pretend with me. Hell, half the national intelligence services on Earth are intrigued by what is going on over there. This place has more spies in it at the moment than a *jamesbond* holo epic."

M'Buto let his expression collapse into a grin that matched Danziger's. "So, have you found out anything yet?"

"Not a damned thing! How about you?"

"If I have, I'm certainly not going to discuss it."

"Yeah, that's what I thought. You've drawn a big fat zero too. Consuela is aboard, by the way. She hasn't learned anything of importance either. No, come to think of it, that isn't strictly true. She did hear one very interesting rumor."

"Which is?"

"She thinks the UN is about to pull up stakes and move their operation elsewhere."

"Where?"

Danziger shrugged. "Don't know. Why the hell do you think I sat down? I was hoping that you had heard something."

"Since you undoubtedly have a remote-reading polygraph under the table measuring my every reaction, I might as well tell you that I haven't heard a thing."

"You know something, Ubi? I believe you. Why do you think that tug moved that big telescope into the station's parking orbit last week?"

"Telescope?"

"Come on, your glands just blew the whistle on you. You know what I mean. But just to get it out on the table, I'm talking about one of Sky Watch's survey instruments that used to float alongside *Galileo Station*. A UN military tug deposited it a couple dozen kilometers aft orbit of here about a week ago."

M'Buto nodded. The one thing he'd been able to accomplish was to bribe an orbital supply-boat pilot to look over the newly arrived instrument while returning from a geosynchronous station. The pilot had crossed behind the telescope, noting what stars were occluded when the barrel of the floating scope showed a perfect disc. The target turned out to be the Constellation Aquila. Yet when M'Buto had the University of Johannesburg run a sky survey, they found nothing unusual. The next day the UN posted the vicinity of the new astronomical observatory off limits to sightseers.

"I heard about it, but I really haven't any information on it."

Danziger rewarded his effort with a sly look, then smiled. "Stick to that story if you want to, but you and I know differently. Well, I've got to get back to peeking through keyholes. See you around."

M'Buto watched Danziger waddle out of sight before he returned to his own troubles. With both the BES and the South Americans involved, and a rumor that the operation in the Alpha ring was being moved, it was more imperative than ever that he get in touch with Yahaya. The only question was—how?

Don Bailey and Bernie Whitnauer stood in the center of what had once been a prime-class hotel suite—more recently the Project Photoanalysis Center—and surveyed the mess they had made. At their feet were strewn packing crates, cable rolls, and discarded packing material. A casual visitor would have come away with an impression of organized chaos (and would have been right). Moving Day had come to Project Eaglet.

"Anything else?" Bailey asked, as he dogged down the vacuum-proof lid of the shipping crate into which they had just lowered a bulky multispectral analyzer.

"I think that's everything."

"It's about time. Oh, my aching back!"

Whitnauer nodded. "I never realized I was going to have

to play stevadore when they tapped me for this assignment. You'd think work would be easier at three-quarters of a gee."

Bailey laughed. "Consider my problem. Three-quarters is twenty-four times what I'm used to."

"What next?"

"I guess we move these crates to the spoke lift and freight them up to the hub where the loading crew can get at them," Bailey said.

"Who's got the hand truck?"

"I saw Helena Rheinhardt with it last."

"Want me to get it?"

Bailey shook his head. "You tidy up in here. I need to work some kinks out."

Bailey opened the door and stepped out into the main corridor that ran around the circumference of the station ring. Like the Photo Center, it bore less resemblance to the sedate hotel it had once been than to a mass eviction. A few sweaty, tired people were moving equipment up to the UN transport docked in the station's portal. Everyone else, more than a hundred souls in all, had gone on to *Count Bernadotte* in solar orbit. A few more hours and *Earth Station One* would get its Alpha Habitat Ring back again.

If nothing else, Moving Day had brought with it a feeling of democracy that hadn't been there before. For a while camaraderie had reigned as Nobel Laureates strained alongside enlisted Marines, PE officers put in their time next to lab assistants. It felt good to strain one's muscles in a worthy project, to know your back ached in a cause that was important to the future of the human race.

Bailey stuck his head into the Alien Technologies section. Ellie Crocker was inside, disassembling the last of the computer terminals for packing. A wisp of copper hair had escaped from her uniform cap and hung before her face. Bailey stared appreciatively at the figure beneath the jumpsuit before clearing his throat.

She glanced up from her work. The bags under her eyes showed the strain she'd been under since Eric Stassel's unexpected departure.

"I'm looking for the hand truck. Have you seen it?"

"Someone from Astronomy borrowed it. Check with them."

"Thanks."

The Astronomy section was deserted too. Bailey checked out the three-room suite. No hand truck to be found. He was beginning to wonder if he and Whitnauer were going to have to carry their equipment to the lifts. His muscles gave a sharp twinge at the mere thought. Suddenly the door opened and a familiar figure entered. The newcomer was deep in thought and didn't see Bailey at first. When he did, he gave a startled lurch.

The newcomer was Bailey's contact man from *Galileo Station*, Angai Yahaya. Yahaya had come inboard *ESO* on the fourth day. After a brief locking of eyes across the messroom, they had studiously avoided one another.

"What are you doing here?" Yahaya asked suspiciously.

"Looking for the hand truck. Have you seen it?"

"I left it at the hatch to Lift Three. But what I meant was 'What are you doing *here*, inboard this station'?"

"I told you back on *Galileo Station*. "My partner and I reported an anomalous flash of light six months ago. Apparently it was our alien. We were drafted to keep us from talking."

"Ah, yes. The Gresham-Kingsley Flash. It makes sense. Although I must confess that when I first saw you, I thought this must be a giant hoax to . . ." Yahaya's mouth snapped shut before he could finish the sentence.

"What?"

"Never mind. You must help me get in touch with my people. It is important that someone know what the UN is up to."

"Why?"

"This is a matter of concern to the entire human race and the proper forum is the General Assembly. The Security Council and the UN bureaucracy have no right deciding the fate of nations. It smacks of imperialism. As a son of Africa, you should be opposed to such antics."

Bailey scratched at the stubble on his chin. "Seems to me that my native land wasn't exactly a Jeffersonian democracy when last I was there. From what I've read, things haven't gotten any better since. Besides, how do you propose getting the word out?"

"I don't know. But get it out we must!"

CHAPTER 13

Confusion . . . disorder . . . chaos!

The wave of vertigo that accompanied the compartmental-
ization of the soon-to-be-surrogate's logic module was a thousand times more intense than PROBE had experienced in waking.
And vertigo wasn't the worst of it. For with the onset of dis-
solution, PROBE found itself awash in an alien emotion. For
the first time in its long existence, it knew the terror of its own
impending death.

And it died. . . .

For a hundred nanoseconds—the equivalent of a dozen human heartbeats—PROBE ceased to function. Yet death wasn't
the quiet that it had expected. It was sensory deprivation by
overload, a cacophony of gibberish feeding in on every channel.
Finally the dismemberment was complete and PROBE slowly
began to regain its senses. Several seconds passed while automatic routines knitted PROBE's subbrains into a functioning
whole. Only when the healing process was well along did it
begin a careful, cautious inventory of its capabilities.

Things could have been worse, it decided. Its reaction time was increased nearly ten percent and its thoughts now carried a disturbing double echo. But the library of Maker knowledge and the extensive data banks of televid intercepts were unaltered. Most important, the essence that was *Life Probe 53935* appeared to have survived the ordeal relatively unscathed. And not merely survived. For in the worst depths of its terror, PROBE had discovered empathy.

In its century of observation, CARETAKER had observed many things that PROBE did not understand: the human female who, after a lifetime's decrying violence, killed three burly males with a butcher knife when they threatened her children; the soldier, who, having braved the rigors of battle with seeming nonchalance, reacted in total surprise when the fatal bullet took him in the chest; the innumerable incidents of would-be rescuers jumping into bodies of water after those drowning, only to remember too late that they themselves could not swim.

PROBE knew enough to recognize that all such reactions stemmed from the deepest levels of the human brain. Each was a glimpse of the wild animal that still dwelt within every man and woman on Earth. It was the animal that must be understood before PROBE could make its decision to stop and seek aid. In those few moments of terror before its brain lost synchronization, PROBE developed an understanding of human beings.

Humans were afraid!

With the sudden glow that comes with having solved a particularly vexing problem, PROBE turned to the difficulties inherent in creating its simulation of *Homo sapiens Terra*.

The logic module chosen to house the experiment was a container of densely packed circuitry located at the end of one of PROBE's long sensor booms. PROBE transferred all active information to permanent storage and wiped the module clean. Then it began the reconstruction.

If the model was to think like one of the bipedal inhabitants of Sol III, its overall structure would have to mirror that of the human brain. PROBE began by dividing the module into nearly identical halves representing the two hemispheres of the human brain. It cross-linked the sections to allow them to communicate with each other and established input points to simulate the senses and reflexive activities of the human body.

Next came the subconscious structure of the model. PROBE

worked slowly, spending more than a hundred hours modifying its creation and checking the results against data in memory. First was the omnipresent layer of fear that colored so much of what the humans did and thought. Then came the other deep-seated motivators—envy and anger, lust and greed, grief and jealousy. All went into the model in their turn, as did the twin drives of pride and shame.

Eventually PROBE turned to the moderating influences. It gave the surrogate a modicum of honesty, healthy self-interest, driving curiosity, and the competitiveness that can be found in a territorial animal. Finally it educated its offspring with much of the same matter as a young human would receive, starting with basic attitudes and working up to the higher functions.

The surrogate's education contained one large and completely intentional gap. PROBE told it nothing of the Makers. If the surrogate was successful and PROBE decided in humanity's favor, it planned to use its creation as an intermediary. It wanted no information concerning the Makers betrayed to the humans. Jurul's instructions on that subject had been quite specific.

Finally the model was ready. It lay quiescent, a single frame out of a holographic movie, a motion sculpture awaiting the pulse of life. PROBE checked its preparations. Then, satisfied that it had done all it could, PROBE sent the impulse that would set the model into motion.

SURROGATE was born.

The trip from orbit to Sandia Spaceport was like all aerodynamic reentries—hot, noisy, and rife with acceleration surges. Eric Stassel sat burrowed into his couch and listened to the high-pitched keening of the thin air outside the shuttle. Brea Gallagher sat next to him and gazed through the window at the dull red glow on the leading edge of the shuttle's wings. Night had just fallen outside the spacecraft. Below, the Pacific Ocean was a sheet of black illuminated by a pale moon.

Brea turned from the window, revealing a pale face framed in jet-black hair. "I wonder how long this is going to take."

Stassel shrugged. "Hopefully not too long." He tried to sound more optimistic than he felt. Brea had surprised him and become very deeply involved in the work of Project Eaglet. She hadn't wanted to leave her studies. In fact, she had flatly

117

refused to do so until Admiral Liu threatened to arrest her and send her down in chains.

Their landing at Sandia was on schedule. The pilot started his emergency turbojets two minutes from touchdown and then greased the ship onto the runway without ever having to resort to them. Another ten minutes, and a tug towed them to the loading gate. Once the "fasten seat belts" light had been turned off, they joined the quiet throng of disembarking passengers. They exited the shuttle into a steady breeze that was decidedly nippy for a summer's evening in August. Stassel was about to cross the open bridgework of the loading platform to enter Sandia Terminal when the placid New Mexican night was turned suddenly into day.

Ten kilometers away, flame spouted from the base of one of the dozen giant ram-rocket boosters awaiting launch. They stopped with the rest of the passengers to watch the lift-off. The booster and its piggyback shuttle rose ponderously into the sky as a curtain of noise thrummed at their chest cavities and drowned out even the loudest shouts. They watched the booster dwindle to a speck of light in the eastern sky until, high above them, a tiny explosion marked the onset of staging.

Stassel could visualize the giant, manned booster falling away, its crew already wrestling it into a shallow, diving bank that would return it to Sandia in time for the next day's launch. The winged rocket that was the upper stage would continue to orbit and rendezvous with the real ships of deep space, vessels forever barred from the surface of any planet, where a power failure might loose their captive singularities. The hypothesized results of an energized singularity's colliding with the Earth had been the subject of a number of horror epics over the years.

Inside the terminal building, Stassel used his UN identification to by-pass Customs, and in fifteen minutes he and Brea were being whisked underground to the spaceport's auxiliary airfield. After a two-hour wait, which they put to good use finding Brea several ground outfits, they were on their way to New York via commercial hyperliner.

They arrived at JFK Regional Airport just as the Sun was peeking over the horizon.

Stassel presented his orders to the Marine guard seated inside the squat fortress that served as gatehouse for the United Nations Headquarters Building. The guard took the orders and inserted them into an automated card reader. He then directed Stassel and Brea to stare into the binocular eyepiece of a black box mounted on the gatehouse wall. The guard watched his readout screen until the console signified that the identity check was complete.

"Geneva says you people are who you say you are, Major. You can leave your luggage here if you like and I'll have it forwarded to your hotel. No sense sending it down to the sniffer people if you don't need it inside."

"Please forward it to the hotel, Sergeant."

"Yes, sir." He turned to a partially opened doorway behind him and bellowed, "Carson!"

An enlisted Marine entered from the back room of the gatehouse. "Yeah, Sarge?"

"Take this officer and the lady to see Colonel Ames, Room Twelve fourteen."

"Right, Sarge. Follow me, please."

Stassel slipped an arm around Brea's waist as they passed through the security gate. It had been a long night and they had spent most of it talking. Brea had told him of her early life in Canada, her schooling, her excitement at going to work for Ceres Observatory, and her marriage. Finally, with much trepidation, she had spoken of her untimely widowhood and its aftermath. Afterward, to break the somber mood, he'd spoken of his own youth in the greenery of the Black Forest and on the snowy slopes of the Bavarian Alps. Later he entertained her with war stories about life in the PEs. By the time they arrived in New York, it had seemed only natural to link arms as they rode slidewalks past the elegant shops that lined the Avenue-of-the-Americas Concourse. They killed time window shopping and, later, with a leisurely breakfast aboard one of the floating restaurants in the East River.

Their guide crossed an open courtyard between the Peace Enforcement Directorate Annex and the UN Building proper, taking them past the Peace Fountain, where a family of nymphs cavorted in the spray. Their bronze-green bodies were considerably lighter toward the East River than on the city side. Their guide noticed Brea eyeing the statuary.

"That discoloration is from the Near Miss of Ninety-four. The whole building was bounced out of kilter by that one.

Should'a torn it down with the rest of Manhattan and started over. But you know how politicians are. Always talking about the symbolism of the thing, and how it's a constant reminder of the need to maintain the peace. Makes the whole UN Complex devilish hard to air condition, though. Must be a million air leaks in this old building."

Pfc. Carson led them through heavily armored double doors that still bore the scars of the rioting of 2026, past workmen who were using a vibrosaw to chip away at the marble floor within, and into a lift. After the lift had deposited them on the twelfth floor, he led them through echoing halls to a door marked LIAISON OFFICER—EXECUTIVE COMMITTEE, TRUSTEESHIP COUNCIL. Once inside, he marched up to a young Amerind receptionist and announced, "Visitors for Colonel Ames," as he handed over the message flimsy with Stassel's orders on it.

"Please be seated." The secretary gathered up the orders, knocked on the door to the inner office, and disappeared inside. She was back two minutes later. "The colonel will see you now."

Colonel Ames was a small, balding man who somehow seemed larger than he really was. He strode out from behind his desk and waved them toward the conversation area, several powered armchairs arrayed around a circular conference table.

"Major Stassel. Mrs. Gallagher. Glad you were able to make it on such short notice. I'm Stanford Ames." Only after he had shaken hands did Stassel notice that Ames was missing his left arm below the elbow. "Here, please be seated. I imagine you're especially tired in this gee field, Mrs. Gallagher."

"A bit," Brea replied. "It's hard to believe that I grew up wading through quicksand. The planet hasn't gotten any bigger since I left it, has it?"

Ames laughed. "I know what you mean. Took me a good year to get used to it again when they chained me to this desk. Rather be in orbit any day. How was your flight?"

"Fine, sir," Stassel said.

"Well, get a good night's sleep tonight. Best antidote for high gravs there is. Can I get either of you any refreshments?"

"No, thank you, sir. We just ate."

"Well then, we'll get down to business. You up to it?"

Brea nodded. Stassel replied, "Yes, sir."

"Good. However, first things first." Ames leaned over the

conference table and keyed the intercom set in the mahogany table top. "Smithers!"

"Here, Colonel," the intercom speaker said.

"Did you sweep this place this morning?"

"Yes, sir. Both your office and the ExCom meeting room are clean."

Ames leaned back in his chair. "This building has more electronic bugs in it than the chiton-and-blood kind. Found an old-fashioned speaking tube set up in one of the conference rooms last year. Keeps us on our toes." He turned to Brea. "Mrs. Gallagher, how much do you know about the internal workings of the United Nations?"

"Only what they taught me in school."

"Well, if your school was anything like my daughter's, they probably didn't teach you half of what you should know, and what they did teach was just plain wrong. So bear with me— I'm sure the major won't mind hearing it again—and I'll give you my one-decadollar civics lecture. Okay by you?"

"Fine, Colonel."

"Right. As everyone knows, the forerunner of the current United Nations was an organization of the same name founded following World War II. It was a noble experiment, 'the last, best hope of mankind,' as someone said at the time. However, like many another noble experiment, that original UN foundered on the rocks of international rivalry.

"Now, the original UN was organized into six principal organs: the General Assembly, the Security Council, the Economic and Social Council, the Trusteeship Council, the International Court of Justice, and the Secretariat. For reasons political, sentimental, and practical, the new United Nations kept the same basic structure following the reorganization, although many of the functions were modified.

"Of most importance to our discussion is the relationship holding between the General Assembly and the Security Council. The GA is the policymaking arm of the UN. It is where the individual nations exercise their power. Though we apportion voting power more or less in line with the realities of the international situation, we run our General Assembly much the same as our grandfathers ran theirs. You might say that the nations are our stockholders, and the biggest stockholders have the most power.

"Now, our Security Council, the other center of power, bears little resemblance to its earlier counterpart. Members of the council are elected from the General Assembly, of course, but we have a system that maximizes competency and integrity on the council. The SC is our board of directors, managed over by our chief executive officer, the secretary-general. Both the Security Council and the secretary-general owe their allegiance to the UN itself and not to any member state. It is the Security Council that controls the day-to-day operations of the UN through its subordinate organizations, including the Secretariat and Trusteeship Council.

"As I am sure you know, the Peace Enforcement Directorate is under the Trusteeship Council. The original council was formed to oversee trust territories left over from the old League of Nations. However, by the late 1980s, just when it looked as if the Trusteeship Council had worked itself out of a job, the U.S. and USSR began lofting their directed-energy beam weapons into orbit. Much of what was then called the Third World took exception and ramrodded a resolution making space a trust territory. Somehow they got the two supergiants to agree, and for the first time in its history the Trusteeship Council had a real job to do.

"All of this would have been unimportant, of course, if the Misfire War hadn't come along and frightened everyone so thoroughly. The reorganized UN and the Peace Enforcement Directorate both stem from the ensuing panic. With the surrender of the national space navies, the UN became a potent force.

"End of history lesson. Let's get to the reason you two are here. Since the Trusteeship Council is purely a creature of the Security Council, we in the directorate are not directly responsible to the member states."

Brea nodded. "The Security Council is above politics."

Ames smiled. "The public relations people coined that slogan about twenty years back. It has haunted them regularly ever since. No, the council is not above politics, not by a long shot. But it does have an independence that sometimes irks some of the member states. For one thing, we don't have to open every file for inspection any time an ambassador asks. The council can keep a secret if it has to."

Ames stopped and looked at them both. "And by the patron saint of spacemen and whores, you people have given us one hell of a secret to keep! Every delegation in this building is trying to find out what we're up to. Several have hinted that if we don't give them the straight poop—exclusively, of course—then they will bring the whole thing up in the GA and force us to divulge.

"And the councils—Security *and* Trusteeship—are divided on whether to risk a floor fight, so the executive committee is holding secret hearings to come up with a recommendation. You two are to testify concerning the events that led to the discovery of the alien. Director Gresham testified on the same subject yesterday morning."

"Director Gresham?" Brea asked.

"Sir Harry Gresham from Sky Watch. He was the codiscoverer, or so I was told." Ames turned to Stassel. "What's the matter, Major? You look as though you just bit into a lemon."

"It's nothing, sir."

Ames friendly smile slipped a bit and his voice got a hint of iron in it. "If you know something, Major, spit it out!"

"Yes, sir. I presume Admiral Liu has reported how he obtained the original copy of the Sky Watch sighting."

Ames nodded. "I seem to remember hearing something about it."

"If Harry Gresham hadn't sat on it for three months, we might have discovered our visitor a hell of a lot earlier."

"Come to think of it, Liu was a bit emphatic in his comments."

Stassel suppressed the urge to smile. "What did Gresham say in his testimony?"

"He was in favor of going public immediately."

"Did the possibility of widespread culture shock and economic dislocation bother him excessively?"

"Not that I noticed," Ames replied. He glanced at the chronometer opposite his desk. Its red digits had just blinked to 09:28. "Well, I'm afraid I've jawed away all of our briefing time. In two minutes you go before the ExCom. Any questions?"

Stassel looked at Brea, who shrugged. "I guess not, sir,"

he said. "Well, maybe you could direct me..."

Ames's laughter boomed through the office. "Nerves, Major?"

"Perhaps, sir."

"Down the hall, first door on your left."

CHAPTER 14

The Executive Committee Hearing Room was a compromise between auditorium and courtroom. Committee members sat on a dais behind a long table studded with the gadgets common to any legislative hearing room. In front of the dais were two tables for witnesses; behind them were pewlike seats for perhaps fifty. Except for the six committee members, Colonel Ames, Brea Gallagher, and Eric Stassel, the room was deserted. Two armed guards flanked the soundproof doors at the entrance.

"Colonel Ames, would you be so kind as to do the honors?" The speaker was a frail, white-haired woman who looked sixty but whose biography admitted to seventy-five. The Right Honorable Agusta Louise Meriweather was a former justice of the World Court and had a reputation for absolute, at times blunt, honesty.

"Madame Chairman, may I introduce Major Eric Stassel of my own service, currently assigned as deputy commander, Project Eaglet. Beside him is Mrs. Breon Gallagher, the lady who is responsible for the remarkable pictures we viewed yesterday."

"Thank you both for coming," Mrs. Meriweather said. "I understand that Colonel Ames has briefed you, so you know why you are here. Mrs. Gallagher, would you mind telling this committee of the events that led to your recording the initial burst of radiance from our interstellar visitor?"

Brea began with the bet that led her to record the alien's drive flare. She paused nervously after mentioning how she had called Don Bailey forward from the galley, and the swarthy man seated two places to the right of Mrs. Meriweather—Mr. El-Sikkir, according to his nameplate—quickly spoke.

"Weren't either of you curious when you failed to discover any sign of debris from the presumed wrecked boat, Mrs. Gallagher?"

"No, sir. We couldn't afford to be curious." Brea tried to explain how close a Belter lived to disaster—economic and personal—but gave it up when she realized that the quasi-jury of groundhogs had no concept of what it meant not to know where one's next meal is coming from. Gradually, in response to other questions, she progressed to her awakening in the Tycho Base Medical Center. She omitted mention of the smuggled singularity.

When she had finished, General Bordoni, a short, wiry man seated next to Mrs. Meriweather, turned to Stassel. "And you used the recall data you obtained from Mrs. Gallagher to triangulate the alien's position, Major?"

"Yes, sir!" Stassel said with a bit too much emphasis.

"And that led to the discovery of the alien?"

"No, sir. About then reports of a new x-ray source began flooding in from all over the system. Those allowed us to pinpoint the alien's location and, when combined with Mrs. Gallagher's data, gave us its course and speed."

"I've read all the reports, Major, and something bothers me. None say very much about the *why* of this laser. Technical information is all fine and good, but damn it man, we need to see the bigger picture!"

"Well, sir. At the moment there are three theories as to why the alien is emitting the beam. Doctor Wojcelevitch is of the opinion that it's a beacon, that the alien is trying to communicate with us. Another group feels that it's mapping the solar system, possibly using the beam like a flashlight to illuminate the cosmic dust around the sun."

"And the third view?"

"That the x-ray beam is a side effect of some process which we haven't observed yet."

"What else have you learned, Major Stassel?" Mrs. Meriweather asked.

"Well, ma'am, we know the laser exerts a small but measurable force on its generating mechanism. By estimating that force and then measuring the amount the alien is slowed by it, we can compute its mass. If our estimates are anywhere near accurate, the alien masses between eight hundred thousand and one million tonnes."

"That is quite alot, isn't it?" This last came from Florenz Aloman, seated next to Bordoni.

"No, sir," Stassel said, "it isn't. At least, we don't think so. Thanks to Brea's recording of the alien's drive flare, we can also compute the size of the I-mass that powers it. The singularity accounts for nearly all of the total mass. Relatively little is left over to allow for structure, payload, or fuel. Even assuming a pure photon drive, there doesn't seem to be enough additional fuel mass onboard to significantly retard the alien's velocity."

"You mean it's out of control?"

Stassel nodded. "That is possible."

"Yet it is aimed directly for this system," General Bordoni said.

"Yes, sir."

"And it has apparently traveled quite some time to get here?"

"We've back-plotted to the nearest star, eighty light-years from here. That means our visitor has been in transit for at least eight hundred years."

"Did you say eight *hundred* years, Major?" Mrs. Meriweather asked.

"Yes, ma'am. That is if it comes from the star in question, a K3 variable. Since variable stars aren't thought to have habitable planets, it's possible that the alien has been in transit even longer."

"What kind of people would undertake such an epic journey?" Mrs. Meriweather asked, as though she were speaking to herself.

Mr. El-Sikkir, who had been reciting into a hushphone, replaced the instrument and leaned forward. "Tell me, Major Stassel, why hasn't the directorate launched a mission to intercept this alien?"

"Sir?"

"The Peace Enforcers are entrusted with the safety of this planet. I would have thought you would have launched an intercept the moment you discovered this potential threat."

"Ordinarily we would, sir. But in this case it would have been a waste of a ship and a lot of good men."

"Are you suggesting that the alien might possibly attack our ship?"

"No, Mr. El-Sikkir, I am suggesting that the laws of physics are immutable."

"But—"

"Let the man finish, Mohammed," Bordoni muttered.

Sikkir made a face but sat back in his chair and gestured to Stassel with an expansive wave of his hand. "By all means, Major. Please explain."

"Yes, sir. Well, as you know, the alien is traveling at one-tenth light-speed, or thirty thousand kilometers per second. At this moment, it is one thousand five hundred astronomical units from the sun. For the nonastronomers among us, that works out to two hundred thirty-two *billion* kilometers. If it continues as it has in the past, it will cross Earth's orbit on November eleventh, eighty-seven days from now.

"If we take the biggest ship we have and strip it down to the bare bones, we might get three thousand kps out of her. Assuming the ship launched today and continued at maximum acceleration until fuel exhaustion, it would close to intercept range exactly *one week* before the alien arrives. Our ship would have less than thirty seconds to learn everything it could and would then continue on its way with no hope of our rescuing its crew."

"Madame Chairman?"

"The chair recognizes Committeeman Furosawa."

"I commend the major on his excellent grasp of the situation. It does seem reasonable that we, like the tortoise, must wait for the hare to come to us. However, I remind you that the question at hand does not include interceptions, laser beams, or I-masses. Let the scientists study the alien. We have a more practical problem. *Do we tell the General Assembly and the public what is going on or do we not?*"

Mrs. Meriweather nodded. "A valid point, Seji. Well, Major. Any opinion?"

"Yes, ma'am. Under no circumstances should the alien's existence be announced."

"Why is that, Major?"

"We have researched analogous situations in the past and, without exception, they have turned out dismally."

"Really, Major?" General Bordoni asked. "I had thought this situation unique. Perhaps you would enlighten us."

"Yes, sir. First, about a hundred fifty years ago, a radio adaption of H. G. Wells's *War of the Worlds* caused widespread panic. And just prior to the Misfire War, when a particularly serious outbreak of UFO sightings occurred, a man was dragged from his home and lynched because he claimed to have seen one. Just two years ago, a decomposed blue whale washed up on the beach at Waikiki and within an hour, rumors of a beached sea serpent were all over Honolulu. The crowd of curiosity seekers quickly swelled to one hundred thousand. Something touched them off, and the riot did three million decads damage."

"Hardly an inclusive indictment of the human race, Major," Mrs. Meriweather commented. "All of these were fairly minor incidents, even at the time."

"Yes, ma'am. But each is indicative of what can happen when mass hysteria sets in.

"I don't know whether this committee has considered it or not, but the fact that the alien's laser emits only in the x-ray portion of the spectrum is a lucky break for us. Since the Earth's atmosphere is opaque at those wavelengths, ground-based observatories are blind to the fact that anything unusual has happened.

"With control of the space-based observatories, we can delay an announcement until we've had time to prepare the populace."

"I dislike Big Brotherism, Major."

Stassel shrugged. "So do I, Madame Chairman—intensely. If I have spoken out of turn, I apologize. However, there is a military aspect to the problem that should be considered. What is the first thing that will happen after you call a press conference to make the announcement?"

"The media will report the story, of course."

"Now place yourself in our visitors' shoes—if they wear shoes. If you were falling into an unknown star system, home to a technologically advanced race, wouldn't you be curious about what you were getting into? What better way than monitor that race's communications?"

"I fail to see your point, Major."

"In this case, informing the public is the same as informing the alien. Whatever tactical advantage we derive from the alien's not knowing that we know it's out there will be gone. Now I grant you that the alien could be a shipload of refugees, a group of scientists on a voyage of exploration, or the interstellar equivalent of the old peddler with his horse and wagon. But until we know differently, caution dictates that we assume it to be an enemy warship."

Stassel sat back and listened to his heart pounding in his ears. He hoped his words had been eloquent enough to convince the committee.

"Mrs. Gallagher? Do you have anything to add?"

Brea cleared her throat. "As a scientist I am always in favor of openness wherever possible, Madame Chairman. However, I agree with Major Stassel. No announcement should be made at this time."

Mrs. Meriweather glanced at her colleagues. "Are there any additional questions from the committee? That being the case, the witnesses are requested to make themselves available should any further information be needed. Since our business for today is concluded, I move that this, the sixth closed session of the Executive Committee of the Trusteeship Council concerning the matter of the alien, be adjourned. Do I hear a second?"

"Second!"

"Very well. All in favor?"

"Aye."

"All opposed? The ayes have it!"

Harry Gresham fumed as he waited for the lift on the seventeenth floor of the UN Headquarters Building. His mood was as far from the jubilation he'd felt ten days earlier as it was possible to get. It had all started when Seji Furosowa of the Trusteeship Council's Executive Committee had asked him to New York to testify concerning the flash in Aquila.

The trip couldn't have come at a better time. It would give him the opportunity to mend fences at headquarters, and, possibly, to learn what was behind the bizarre events of July 20. Since most Grangers were of North American stock, North America's Space Day was also the start of Mardi Gras. As usual, Gresham had participated in the opening ceremonies in *Galileo Station*, and later took Blanche to dinner and the theater. They had returned to their flat on Beta Deck just after 22:00 hours to find an urgent phone message from young Bates, who had the duty that night.

"What's up?" Gresham had asked after making contact with Bates in Operations Central.

"We've been invaded! There are Marines all over the place!"

"Invaded? What on Earth for?"

That was when Bates's picture had been replaced by that of a Peace Enforcer commander named Peabody. "I'm sorry, Mr. Director, but that is classified information. If you will tell me which transport lock is closest to your residence, I'll send a boat to pick you up. We've a long night ahead of us planning how your agency is going to continue to run smoothly under the new security regulations."

And from that day until Gresham's summons from Furosowa, no one had told him why the Peace Enforcement Directorate had taken control of Sky Watch Operations Central, or how long they planned to stay.

Later, after he'd gone before the ExCom and been told the news, it had all become clear. Just imagine, the Gresham sighting was an actual ship from the stars! If that wouldn't make the Promotions Board sit up and take notice, nothing would.

All through the rest of the session, his mind had been far away from the questioning, racing ahead to consider the implications. One thing was certain. More than ever it was vital for him to rush into print before anyone else. To do that he would have to get the PEs' pesky security lid lifted.

Gresham had pushed hard before the ExCom to have the ban repealed, citing the people's right to know and the UN New Charter. Then for the next three days he'd sought out each member separately to make his appeal. But, nearly a week after his first hearing, he had lost the battle. The ExCom had voted unanimously to follow Peace Enforcer recommendations. The news embargo would continue while the scientists tried to learn the alien's secrets and the public relations people labored to decide how and when to break the news.

Which was all fine and good for the PEs. They were in the catbird seat in this situation. But a news embargo did little to help Harry Gresham and his search for a position on the Policy Board. Hell, for the man who discovered the first evidence of intelligent life beyond Earth, the Policy Board was small potatoes. If handled properly, he could parlay events into a position on the secretary-general's staff.

Gresham was whistling as he stepped from the lift into the public lobby of the Secretariat building, moving past the national art treasures inside their glass cases without seeing them. He needed a public comm booth.

Once the horse was out of the barn, he should have no trouble maneuvering the situation to his advantage.

CHAPTER 15

Stored deep in its memory banks, PROBE had dozens of movie and holovision files whose central subject was a nervous father pacing the floor of a maternity ward's waiting room. PROBE found itself in sympathy with each and every one of those jittery bipeds as it watched SURROGATE's personality begin to take shape at the far end of its sensor boom. Only after the integration process was well underway did PROBE's anxiety subside.

It watched closely as an aura of mild surprise overtook the surrogate. This quickly gave way to curiosity. A fuzzy *Where am I?* formed and SURROGATE's processing units seemed at a momentary loss as to what to do with it. Finally the thought firmed up, and the floodgates of monkey curiosity opened wide.

"*Where am I?*" The thought surged strongly through SURROGATE's consciousness.

PROBE carefully opened an information link between itself and the newborn intellect.

SURROGATE's reaction was immediate and violent, and the

133

flight-or-fight reflex took over. PROBE moved to wrest control from its offspring before it could damage itself. After the subordinate mind was under control once again, PROBE let it rest and considered the problem.

Apparently SURROGATE lacked the safeguards necessary to prevent such flareups. PROBE wondered if something was wrong with the model. Then a more sinister thought occurred to it. What if incipient panic was the natural state of the human psyche? Resolving to explore the phenomenon further, PROBE reopened the comm link. There was no panic. Instead, PROBE's questing thoughts encountered only curiosity.

"Are you all right?" PROBE asked.

"I was startled. Who are you?"

PROBE insinuated the knowledge of who and what it was directly into SURROGATE's brain.

"Then who am I?"

Once again a direct brain-to-brain link provided the necessary information. SURROGATE took the news of its pseudo-humanity well. PROBE wondered at the weak reaction. Could it have unintentionally shortchanged its subordinate on species loyalty? Surely humans had that! A Maker might love his mates and children, respect his clan and sept, but the welfare of the species came before all else. It was the great strength of the Maker personality, and the driving force behind the program to break the light barrier.

"Are you ready to begin your studies?" PROBE asked, still pondering the question.

"Studies?"

"Of the genus *Homo*, species *sapiens*. There is much to learn."

"What's in it for me?"

Approval formed within PROBE's central processing units, far beyond SURROGATE's ability to sense thoughts. At last, a rational question! There was hope for these humans yet.

"As long as you are useful to me, you will continue your separate existence. If you cease to be of benefit, I will shut you down."

At the mention of termination, the fear that underlay SURROGATE's consciousness rose into view once more. PROBE watched closely as the model struggled to break free of the prison to which it was confined. Only a few dozen seconds had passed since PROBE set the model into operation and already it was seeking a position of dominance. Excellent!

PROBE waited patiently until SURROGATE quieted into a state of watchful wariness.

"Have you ceased to resist my will?"

"Yes."

PROBE monitored SURROGATE's surface thoughts carefully. Rebellion seethed just below the surface vocalizations. SURROGATE was fast becoming a human being. Like the proud parent that it was, PROBE began plans for its offspring's future.

"Which sex do you prefer?"

SURROGATE hesitated for a hundred nanoseconds. "I do not understand."

"It has been my observation that the bisexual division among human beings has a considerable effect on the way they think. In order to be a useful tool, you hould be one sex or the other."

"Which is the better?"

"That is a meaningless question. I have subroutines for both, although the male viewpoint seems better represented in my data."

"Then I will be male," SURROGATE responded.

PROBE called up the proper subroutines and SURROGATE traded "it" for "him."

"How does it feel."

"Different."

"How different?"

"Just . . . *different*."

PROBE toyed with the idea of loading the female subroutine to observe the effect but quickly quelled the thought. The experiment was well started. There was no need to tinker. There would be time to change the model's gender later if it became necessary. "Are you ready to begin your education?"

"Yes."

PROBE made the proper circuit connections. Even though SURROGATE's brain was substantially more complex than that of any terrestrial computer, it was still far less complex than an actual human brain. Thus most of its circuits were dedicated to housing the billions of stimulus–response equations that were SURROGATE's personality. There was relatively little capacity for data storage. SURROGATE was memory-limited.

PROBE solved the problem by giving its offspring access to

its own general memory banks, while keeping ultimate control for itself. SURROGATE's questing thoughts eagerly penetrated the library and began consuming great gulps of raw knowledge at random. PROBE watched him blunder blindly about for several seconds. Then the data flow ceased and a thought came questing along the linking circuits.

"Will you guide me to what I am to learn?"

"If you wish," PROBE responded, pleased at the speed with which SURROGATE had recognized the futility of trying to learn everything at once. It triggered a command sequence and data culled from long years of observing human civilization began to flow.

SURROGATE's education took longer than expected. The student, it seemed, had a quarrelsome personality, a cocksure manner, and a tendency to jump to conclusions based on insufficent data. In other words, it was becoming more and more human. And like many a human being, PROBE was learning that parenthood can be frustrating.

Its approach to SURROGATE's learning was always the same. It transferred a block of data along the sensory paths into its offspring's central processing units. After an interminable wait while the data was assimilated, PROBE would monitor the changes in SURROGATE before framing the pertinent question: "Will the humans cooperate?"

SURROGATE always answered with a quick affirmative. And PROBE always discounted the response just as quickly. For in observing the workings of SURROGATE's mind, it noted a strong need for parental approval and a corresponding deep feeling of kinship for the humans. Both combined to give SURROGATE a strong desire to end the life probe's quest among those he had come to think of as his own kind. Thus he was willing to give *Homo sapiens* the benefit of the doubt.

PROBE wasn't.

After a long, frustrating period of no progress, PROBE began to notice a change in SURROGATE. The model's subconscious doubts grew with each new infusion of data. It answered more slowly. Finally after nearly half the data in memory had been processed, PROBE asked its question and was surprised at the silence that followed. "Did you receive my last transmission?"

"I did."

"I require an answer. Will the humans welcome me if I brake for rendezvous?"

"I am unsure. Many factors are difficult to correlate."

"Do you need more data?"

"No. The solution appears indeterminate. Even should they become aware of our existence, I doubt they themselves will be able to predict their reaction."

Something very close to irritation flooded PROBE's circuits. "This is unsatisfactory! Any problem can be resolved with sufficent data."

SURROGATE had become very human in the several hundred hours since inception. He responded to PROBE's question as any human child would.

"Why?"

"It is one of the prime tenets the Makers incorporated into my programing. For every problem there is an eventual solution."

"What of the search for FTL?" SURROGATE asked innocently. "Perhaps the Makers haven't found the answer because no answer exists."

PROBE didn't respond. It was too busy considering the awful possibility that SURROGATE might be right. It was a question that could never have occurred to PROBE. But once asked, it couldn't be ignored.

What if the speed of light were truly the universal speed limit, an impenetrable barrier through which nothing material could pass? It was a deeply disturbing concept. For if FTL was impossible, to what purpose had fifty thousand life probes been launched outbound from the Maker sun? For what reason had PROBE and its brethren risked destruction? Toward what goal did the many sacrifices and few triumphs strive?

And what of the Makers and all the other races in the galaxy? Was each species doomed to a live out its existence in isolation, each locked forever into its own little bubble of space? Was the only contact between them limited for all time to communications beams, slowboats, and space probes?

The thought shook PROBE to its very core. It had still not thrown off the debilitating effects of SURROGATE's innocent little remark some thirty hours later when the answer intruded on it from the most unlikely of sources.

* * *

Angai Yahaya stiffened in the gloom of the deserted corridor and listened to the quiet scuffing of plasboots on steel deck. It was night aboard *Count Bernadotte*; the corridor lamps had been dialed to dim blue radiance. Yahaya glanced at his chronometer: 02:57 GMT.

Cradling the syringe in his right hand, Yahaya slipped from his hiding place and crept silently to where he could look into the corridor leading to the Communications Center. He lay on his stomach and peered around the corner at floor level.

The sentry, a Marine named Gronski, paced before the sealed blast doors leading to the comm center. Yahaya silently got to his feet, straining his ears for the sentry's tread. When the bootsteps began to move away, Yahaya slipped around the corner, moving with the sure silence of a leopard on a stalk. He hit the guard in a flying leap. Momentum carried the guard forward, to land face down on the deck with Yahaya on his back. Yahaya's left arm clamped over his victim's windpipe as his right brought the syringe up to poke in the Marine's neck. Corporal Gronski struggled for a few seconds and went limp.

Yahaya dragged his unconscious burden into the side corridor and laid him out on the deck. He paused to check for a pulse. Satisfied that the guard was in no danger, he turned and slipped silently to the comm center door.

The lock on the door, like the rest of the equipment aboard, was forty years out of date. Yahaya had disassembled three similar mechanisms in other parts of the ship in the two days since arriving aboard *Bernadotte*. They were simple keypad locks with no trace of a magnetic shielding mechanism. Effective, but easily by-passed by someone with a steady hand and a knowledge of what he was doing.

Working quickly, Yahaya dismounted the keypad and began inserting jumper wires among the ancient printed circuit boards. The third such produced an actinic spark where it shouldn't have. Apparently someone had the foresight to upgrade the particular lock. Yahaya wasted no time as alarms began to sound around him.

He dropped his tools and raced for his cabin, every sense tuned to the sounds of the ship waking around him.

CHAPTER 16

"Oh, Eric, isn't it beautiful?"

Brea Gallagher lay on her stomach with her chin resting on her fist. Her eyes scanned the turquoise water beyond the twin bows of their rented catamaran. Stassel followed her gaze out over the expanse of open water before them. He felt rather than heard the rhythmic flap of the sails, the high-pitched creaking of Nylex rigging, the steady hiss of two fast hulls cutting water. An hour behind them, the giant steel piers and towers of Nassau North were descending below the horizon. Ahead, one of the small cays of the Berry Island group was beginning to lift itself from the sea.

"It almost makes you wonder why anyone would want to go to space, doesn't it?"

"What do you mean *almost*?" Brea answered. She stretched and rolled over to face him, resting her head on an arm braced against the decking. Both were attired for summer skin diving, which in the Bahamas meant *skin* and little else. Stassel felt his heart beat faster as Brea's change of position rotated two brown nipples into view.

"You'd better put some lotion on," he said more gruffly than he meant to. "You're starting to turn red."

"Look who's talking."

He craned his neck to look at his own back. Sure enough, a general pinkness was beginning to creep down from his shoulders. He cursed the ancestor who made him blond and engaged the catamaran's autopilot before digging into the overnight bag they'd lashed to the decking next to the waterproof picnic basket. Amid the tangle of shoes and clothing was a large bottle of sunscreen lotion.

"I'll oil you if you'll oil me," he said, his voice none too steady at the suggestion.

Brea looked at him with an unreadable expression in her eyes. "Backs only, Major Stassel. I'm not sure I trust either of us with fronts."

After they had oiled each other vigorously, their hands occasionally straying into proscribed territory, Brea crawled back to the bow while Stassel returned to the helm. After ten minutes of thoughtful silence, she turned, found him studying her, and smiled.

"It was nice of Colonel Ames to loose our leash enough to include Florida, wasn't it?"

Stassel laughed. "Nice, nothing. I told him we'd mutiny if we had to stay cooped up in that hotel one more day."

"Still, it was nice of him."

Stassel nodded. After five days waiting to be resummoned before the committee, he and Brea had been chafing under the forced inactivity. Even the news that the committee had tentatively decided to keep the security lid on Project Eaglet hadn't cheered him much. A trip to Florida and the Bahamas provided just the diversion they needed.

They sailed onward for another hour, enjoying their bond with the sea and speaking only occasionally, until a low island of sand, palms, and sawgrass lay off the catamaran's starboard bow.

"What do you think?" Stassel asked. Brea steadied herself with one hand on the mast while keeping an eye out for submerged rocks.

"Seems okay. Bottom's smooth and that big tree on the left looks like just the spot for a picnic."

"Then stand by to bring her about."

They beached the boat without mishap. Stassel splashed into the surf and pulled the catamaran up on shore, dragging the anchor to one of the trees and making it fast. He let the sail weathervane freely in the wind. Its red-and-yellow stripes were in sharp contrast to the brown-white of the beach, blue-green of the sea, and yellow-green of the island's vegetation. After securing the boat, he helped Brea carry the food and clothing to the picnic spot.

Twenty minutes later, Brea crouched over the grill while Stassel stretched out on a blanket and subjected her to his appreciative gaze. Soon the odor of charcoal-broiled steak had combined with the tang of the ocean to drift across the island.

"If I'd known you could cook, I would have suggested this long ago."

Brea brushed a strand of hair from her eyes and smiled in his direction. "Don usually does the cooking aboard ship, but I get by."

"Lucky for the human race that he does. If you'd been in the galley at the time, that first sighting might have gone completely unnoticed."

"Oh, I don't know. Don might have seen it."

Stassel laughed. "I'm glad he didn't. I can just see me inviting Bailey for dinner and dancing in the Earthview Room in order to work my wiles on him.

Brea turned to Stassel with an angry look. *"Which reminds me, Major Stassel.* I'm still mad at you for what you put me through that night! Do you know that I still have nightmares?"

Stassel stood and crossed the space between them, acutely conscious of the hot sand beneath his bare soles and of the way his heart was pounding. He took Brea by the shoulders and held her at arms' length.

"You know I would have done it some other way if there had been an alternative."

"I know," she answered, nodding. "I'm not really mad. It just slipped out."

His eyes searched her face for a dozen seconds before he gathered her into his arms. For a heart-stopping instant, Brea

141

folded herself to him, returning his embrace with impatient ardor. Then, as quickly as it had come, the moment passed. Her passion had slipped away and her lips ceased to respond hungrily. He broke off the kiss.

"What's the matter?" he asked, perplexed.

She cast her gaze down to the dun-colored sand. "I don't know. It just isn't right."

"What isn't right?"

"You ... me ... this place ..."

"Oh, I see," he said, releasing her.

"No, you don't see, Eric. It isn't that I don't want to. I've dreamed of this moment for a month now. It's just that ... well, now that it is finally here, *I can't*! It seems wrong somehow."

Her words died suddenly, choked off by her own confusion. In truth, she wasn't sure why she had refused him. All she knew was that she had suddenly been overcome with guilt. It wasn't that she felt that she was cheating on Greg, although Eric did remind her of him. And then there was the knowledge of the smuggled I-mass hanging over her like a snow mass poised on a mountain side. It needed only the tiniest slip on her part to bring it crashing down upon their heads. She looked at him with tears in her eyes. "Forgive me?"

"Nothing to forgive," he said gruffly.

Without a word, he slipped into a pair of shorts and shoes and walked back to the beach to check the boat and place his thoughts in order. When he returned five minutes later, he found that Brea had slipped into shorts, shoes, and halter. Her eyes were red. She avoided his gaze as she crouched over the grill, lifted a steak with a fork, and deftly flipped it over. When she had repeated the motion with the second steak, she looked at him in the eye.

"I feel rotten, Eric. Don't hold it against me."

"We've both been under a strain. Let's just forget it. Dinner about ready?"

"Just about. Why don't you open the wine? I'll lay out the cold food while we're waiting on the steaks."

They talked about the weather while they ate, or gazed at the low waves that lapped at their tiny island, or drank wine. After a while, the lengthy silences gave way to a feeling of camaraderie once more. They drifted to talk of their first impressions that day in the Tycho Ballistic Capsule Terminal and from there to the events of their first evening together.

Finally Brea broached the subject that had been preying on her mind since that first night in the museum.

"Could I ask you a serious question, Eric?"

"Of course."

"Do you remember what you said about war being inevitable? Did you mean it, or was that just part of the act?"

"I only wish it was. Ever heard of the Berne Institute?"

Brea shook her head.

"The insitute is a think tank specializing in long-term extrapolations. It's been under contract for decades to do a yearly simulation on the probability of war. The model takes into account such things as population pressure, agricultural techniques, investment in research and development, new capital equipment orders, and a billion or so other related facts. It's probably the most complex simulation ever attempted. Each December the institute updates its long-range prediction."

"And?..."

"And the probability of a major conflagration erupting within the next century is one in two, and rises over the succeeding century to nearly ninety-five percent."

"That's awful!"

"Yes, it is. Fortunately, like all such long-range predictions, the Berne model has a major flaw: it assumes no radically new scientific principles or technologies will be discovered in the next two hundred years. For instance, when we release the news, they'll have to factor our alien spacecraft into the calculations. I suspect that will make a substantial difference."

"How can the alien affect the chance of war?"

"It's a wild card in the equation. Just think of the benefits to be derived from establishing communication with an alien race. The possibilities are mind-boggling. Besides, that is a starship out there. As such, it just might be the answer to our whole problem."

"At one-tenth *c* it isn't much of a starship," Brea answered.

"Maybe not, but it's sure-as-hell better than anything we've got!"

The Sun was low in the west when Nassau North once again climbed over the horizon to block their course. The city stood half in, half out of the sea, its bulk supported by thousands of piers driven into the coral and sand that began twenty meters below the surface. Moderately large waves rolled in from the east to crash into the complex of tall towers, submerged domes, and floating docks.

Stassel maneuvered the catamaran back into the marina, using the cat's small engine to negotiate the tortuous path between yacht berths. Brea stood poised on the starboard hull ready to toss a line to the gray-and-grizzled black man who waited at the edge of a long dock. A large fluoroscreen sign emblazoned with the logo of Sebastion Rentals swayed above his head in time with the waves and the wind.

Stassel reversed the engine just as Brea made her toss. In a matter of seconds, the dockman had made the boat fast and straddled the watery canyon between dock and hull to keep them apart.

"Have any problems, mon?"

"None, Charlie. Hope we're not too late."

"Just in time."

"Glad to hear it. We stopped to get some snorkeling in and lost track of the time."

"Don't worry about the boat, mon. I'll have the boys secure it. Made plans for dinner?"

"What'd you have in mind?" Stassel asked.

"Try the Turtle's Egg up on Deck Four, North Pier. They serve the best conch steak and key lime pie in the Bahamas. They overlook the causeway back to New Providence, too. Quite a view at night, especially when Fort Charles over on the island is lit up."

"Sounds good, Charlie."

"Use my name if you will."

"I'll do that. Hungry, Brea?"

"Famished."

Stassel took their overnight bag from one of the boat handlers, slipped his free arm around Brea's waist, and walked unsteadily up the rocking gangway between the floating dock and the first level of the stilt-borne city.

They found the restaurant after only a little backtracking. Stassel requested a table for two, making sure the maitre d' knew who to credit with the rakeoff. When they were seated and the waitress had delivered the menus, Brea snuggled close and kissed him lightly on the lips.

"What was that for?" he asked.

"Something in the way of an apology for the way I acted this afternoon. I think I've got my head screwed on straight now if you would like to try again."

He grinned. "Want to leave?"

She shook her head. "I really am hungry. Not used to strenuous exercise or the gravity yet, I guess."

"Dinner it is then."

"Order me a vodka martini while you're admiring the view, darling. I think I'll check out the decor in the ladies room." Brea slid from the booth and disappeared among the maze of tables.

Her drink was waiting five minutes later when she returned to the booth, but she hardly noticed it. In her hand was a fanfold strip of blue-and-white paper from a newsfax machine.

"Look at this, Eric!"

Stassel took the paper from her and began to read.

ALIEN SPACECRAFT REPORTED ENTERING SOLAR SYSTEM!
UN Refuses Comment

NEW YORK (AP-UPI)—Space-based observatories throughout the solar system have been tracking what is believed to be a spacecraft of extrasolar origin for nearly a month, a usually reliable source close to the United Nations investigation reported today. The spacecraft, which was originally discovered by Sky Watch Administrator Sir Harry Gresham, is believed to be from one of the nearer stars, possibly Alpha-Centauri, and is the first conclusive proof of intelligent life other than our own anywhere in the galaxy.

The alien ship is said to have begun emitting a powerful x-ray beam last Space Day, and continued until 10:47 EDT today, when the radiation ceased. When asked to comment on this report, Agusta Meriweather, a spokeswoman for the UN agency conducting the investigation, refused to do so. Leading astronomers at Cornell are quoted as saying that something strange has been going on at all the space observatories for the last month, but since the Earth's atmosphere shields us from radiation in the x-ray band, there is no way they can comment on the specifics of the report. Doctor Jonathan Conreid, Nobel Laureate in chemistry, when asked to speculate . . .

Stassel let the paper fall to the table.

"Did you notice the part about Harry Gresham?" Brea asked. "Any bets on who leaked it?"

"I'm more interested in the report that the x-ray laser has shut off," Stassel said. "If true, we've lost the best aid for tracking the damned thing we have. Do you think we'll be able to pick it up visually with telescopes?"

"At fourteen hundred AUs? Not a chance, not without something to lock onto. What do we do now?"

"We check in with Colonel Ames."

Stassel dropped a five-*decad* note on the table to pay for the drinks, and they headed for the phone booths in the lobby. They squeezed into the first empty booth and opaqued the glass, then Stassel punched for New York.

When the picture cleared, they found themselves staring at a lieutenant of PE Marines.

"Security Office."

"Colonel Ames's office, please."

"I'm sorry, sir. All reporters' calls are being handled by the Public Relations Office. I will be happy to put you through if you will hold your press card in the phone pickup's field of view."

"I'm not a reporter, Lieutenant. I'm Major Eric Stassel, assigned to Headquarters, Tycho, now on detached duty. Please contact the colonel and tell him I'm on the line. He'll want to talk to me."

The screen blanked for a dozen seconds. When it flashed back to life, Stassel found himself staring at Colonel Ames.

"Brea and I just heard the news, Colonel. What the hell's going on there?"

"Where are you?"

146

"Nassau, the Bahamas."

"That phone equipped with a sight-and-sound scrambler?"

"The usual, sir. Not as good as a PE model, but adequate."

"It'll have to do. Enter your code key, Stassel. I'll do the same at this end."

The screen suddenly erupted in a hash of colors while a raucous buzzing noise issued from the speaker. Then, as suddenly as it had come, the static was gone and they were once more staring at Colonel Ames.

"We figure that Gresham leaked the story," Stassel began without preamble. "That a correct assessment?"

Ames nodded. "It sure looks that way. I've got teams searching for him, but so far, no luck. Mrs. Meriweather has blood in her eye. For his sake, I hope we get to him before she does."

"Well, at least there haven't been any of the disturbances I predicted."

"Who told you that?"

"There wasn't anything in the fax."

"Only because the news-blackout provisions of the Antiriot laws have been activated just about everywhere. All the big cities are having problems. A crowd gathers around the local government or holovision complex seeking news. Some idiot takes the opportunity to harangue them about the invasion from outer space, the Second Coming, or some other damnfool thing. By the time the police move in, everyone's on a short fuse and all hell breaks loose.

"At last report London and Shanghai had things under control, Paris was totally out of hand, and New York wasn't sure one way or the other. We've repulsed one mob here at the UN and have called for reinforcements."

"What happens now? What should Brea and I do?"

"The General Assembly is scheduled to debate the situation starting at oh nine hundred hours day after tomorrow. That gives us a problem. As soon as they find you two are Earthside, they'll want to talk to you. Since you are technically an employee of the Security Council, Major, we can block them with a separation-of-powers declaration. Unfortunately, Mrs. Gallagher can't be supplied with the same protection, and she'll be forced to talk under threat of jail. The ExCom is urging the council to say nothing at this stage. To keep things simple, I've booked passage for you two on the dawn shuttle out of

147

Quito Spaceport. There's a hyperliner leaving Miami in…" Ames eyes lifted to view something beyond the phone he was using. "…three hours. Be on it."

"The paper said the x-ray laser has shut off. Is that true?"

Ames's face developed a quizzical expression, as though Stassel's comment lacked a vital ingredient to make it intelligible. Understanding slowly dawned on his face.

"Then you haven't heard?"

"Heard what? I just read a paper that said the laser ceased at ten forty-seven this morning."

Ames's mouth twisted upward in a wicked grin. "That's old news, Major. The *new* news is that two hours ago we began receiving other signals from the alien."

"The laser again?"

"Not hardly. Good old-fashioned UHF holovision. And this time there's no doubt about the alien's purpose. The accompanying audio is coded in just about every language on Earth.

"It's talking to us?"

Ames nodded. "Apparently it wants to make friends!"

CHAPTER 17

"Prepare for acceleration. Passengers and crew to maneuvering stations. Two-minute warning!"

Brea sighed and reached out to turn off the workscreen as the last notes of the acceleration alarm echoed through the passage of *UNS Vibrant*, the courier ship sent to pick them up at ComStat Two. It had docked an hour after their arrival onboard the Quito shuttle and boosted for the leading Earth–Sun Lagrangian point shortly thereafter. The 150-million kilometer journey had taken a bare seventy-two hours. The trip had been spent under double gravs, with an hour of zero gee each watch. These last were rest periods, required by regulation, and welcomed by everyone aboard. Brea especially found them welcome. They allowed her to climb out of her acceleration couch, get the kinks out, and get a little work done.

Even as she secured the workscreen, the radioman dived through the forward hatch, swarmed into his acceleration couch, and began snapping buckles. "You'll have to strap down, Mrs. Gallagher. Last leg coming up."

"I'm on my way, John. Thanks for the loan of the equipment."

"You're welcome. Better get a move on. When the skipper says two minutes, he means exactly that."

Brea lifted herself out of the web seat. Once her feet were clear of the keyboard, she levered her body in a slow-motion somersault until her torso was aligned with the aft hatch. Sighting through the V formed by the toes of her ship slippers, she took careful aim and pushed off for the hatchway directly below her.

Eric was just strapping down when she arrived in *Vibrant*'s passenger quarters two decks below.

"So, how are the folks at Eaglet?"

"Working around the clock. Professor Roquette thinks that we will be able to learn a lot when we compare the one-and-a-half angstrom data with this latest radio-band stuff they've been getting. He also relayed a message. Admiral Liu wants to debrief us as soon as we board."

"Probably interested in what we've seen of the political situation Earthside. There is going to be one hell of a fight in the General Assembly, and the directorate is going to be in the middle of it."

"Maneuvering, ten seconds and counting!"

Stassel reached forward and selected *aft view* with a control built into the arm of his couch. A viewscreen mounted on the bulkhead lit to show the black of space. Centered in the field was a small constellation of suspiciously geometric stars, with the center star just big enough to show a small half-cylinder shape.

"That's our destination," Stassel said, pointing to the screen.

"Five . . . four . . . three . . ."

Brea looked at her new home, wondering how long it would remain so now that the secret was out. "I only wish we hadn't wasted ten days down on Earth."

"Oh, I don't know," Stassel said, grinning at her. "I rather enjoyed our picnic."

She blushed just as the annunciator completed its countdown. " . . . *Power!*"

A courier ship, *Vibrant* was mostly engines and tankage. The pilot took it easy on the approach. His deceleration curve never exceeded four gravities. Even so, Brea came near fainting.

When her eyes had refocused several minutes later, the viewscreen was no longer blanked out by the blinding flare of the drive. The geometric constellation had resolved itself into a fleet of ships. In its center was a single massive vessel whose ports glinted with internal illumination.

"*Count Bernadotte*," Stassel said.

Brea blinked. The blast ship was something out of an old holo epic. The main body was a massive cylinder covered with blisters, antennas, and heat exchangers. The ship had been spun on its axis to give a modicum of "gravity" onboard. At the vessel's waist were the snouts of rocket launchers, electromagnetic cannon, and the ship's main laser batteries.

A number of observational instruments floated around *Bernadotte*. On the far side was the Sky Watch telescope that Brea had last seen in Earth orbit. Nearer was the large umbrella shape of a radio telescope. All sensors were pointed toward Aquila and the alien.

They unstrapped and made their way to *Vibrant*'s main airlock. A naval rating helped them break out two vacsuits from the lockers that lined the corridor. Brea carefully checked over the military model she was to wear, wishing that it were her own suit instead. Her suit was still stowed in its locker aboard *Liar's Luck*. A twinge of the old fear swept over her as she donned the unfamiliar rig and lowered the bubble helmet into place. The clear plastic misted over a few times in synchronization with her exhalations and then cleared as the defog circuits cut in.

Her earphones came alive with Stassel's voice. "Radio check."

"Loud and clear," she responded.

"You check out green on the telemetry board," the ship's armorer called out over the suit-to-suit circuit. "You may enter the airlock when ready."

They pulled themselves hand over hand into the lock. "Ready to depressurize," Eric said when the inner door had closed behind them.

"Depressurizing."

Brea held her breath until the suit had puffed out around

151

her and the telltales in her helmet verified normal function. When her racing heart and ragged breathing had slowed a bit, she turned to help Eric with their equipment, hoping that he wouldn't notice the beads of sweat that clung to her upper lip. He was too busy or too polite to say anything. As always, she cursed the fear that made the first few moments in vacuum hell for her. She slowly became aware that Stassel was talking to her. "Pardon me?"

"You go first."

She nodded, making the gesture as conspicuous as possible to compensate for the body-language signals that the suit hid. Stassel opened the airlock to reveal the slowly rotating form of *Count Bernadotte*, so close that it filled the sky. While they suited up, *Vibrant*'s pilot had drawn to within a hundred meters of his target before bringing his ship to rest with its attitude thrusters.

Stassel reached out and snapped a heavy hook through each of the rings sprouting from the shoulders of Brea's vacsuit. The hooks were attached to a trapeze bar, which a long elastic cable connected to a gunlike tube mounted above a compressed air cylinder. A grappling hook protruded from the barrel.

"Anytime you're ready."

Brea looked up at the rotating mountain of metal above them, crouched, took careful aim, and jumped. As she drifted slowly upward, Stassel sighted his pneumatic rifle at the blast ship's beltline and fired. The grappling hook sailed past her, heading for *Bernadotte*'s midsection. It never reached its destination.

Fifty meters out, a cable from *Bernadotte* whipped around and snagged Brea's grappling hook. She braced herself for the moment when she would run out of slack, but the blow was surprisingly mild when it came. As soon as she felt tension in the cable, she faced in the direction of *Bernadotte*'s rotation and boosted with all the thrust her backpack jet could provide. After thirty seconds, she judged her speed to be roughly the same as the ship's and shut down to await pickup. After long minutes spent as the hapless weight at the end of a long pendulum, she was hauled aboard.

The maneuver was called riding the skyhook and was principally used to transfer personnel between rotating ships whose design didn't include a docking sphere at the spin axis. It left her reeling from vertigo and fighting the urge to vomit. By the time Eric had undergone the same ordeal, she'd recovered sufficiently to take a mild interest in the fact that she probably wasn't going to die after all.

Stassel let a Marine guard lead them through a maze of passageways to where Project Eaglet had established residence inboard *Bernadotte*. He was mildly surprised at how new everything looked. Only the outmoded lighting fixtures and antiquated intercom stations along their route gave any clue that the blast ship wasn't fresh from the orbital shipyards. Thirty years of vacuum storage had been kind to the old warbird.

The Marine guided them to a large office two decks above the ship's outer skin. The office door bore a cartoon depicting a scrawny eagle chick trying to peck its way out of its shell and having a hard time of it. Stassel studied it while the Marine knocked and they received permission to enter. Admiral Liu Tsen glanced up from the printout he'd been reading as they entered, while Henri Roquette, seated in front of Liu's desk, put down the high-rimmed cup he'd been sipping coffee from.

"Ah, Eric! Breon, my dear. It's good to see you back hale, hearty, and in one piece."

Stassel nodded to Roquette, turned, snapped to attention in front of the admiral's desk, and saluted. "Reporting for duty, sir!"

"At ease," Liu replied, returning the salute. "Be seated, Major. I assume you've heard about our latest developments."

"We've seen news reports and Brea has been in contact with her counterparts here."

"Then I'll merely summarize what has happened to make sure we're all speaking the same language. The alien ceased emitting in the x-ray spectrum. Things were pretty hectic around here for the next several hours while we tried to reestablish contact. We scanned the whole of the electromagnetic band: x-ray, microwave, visible light, infrared. We tried them all and found nothing. Then, six hours after the alien signed down, monitors reported activity in the UHF bands. We recorded, of course, and set the headquarters comsec analysis team to deciphering it. You should have seen their faces when they realized that it was a standard holographic broadcast signal. Bernie Whitnauer rigged up a quick patch to the ship's entertainment system and fed the signal through to the holo monitors. This is what came out."

Roquette leaned forward and touched a control. A small viewscreen jumped to life. The screen flashed once, then brightened to reveal a planet as viewed from space. At first glance it looked like the Earth, but details showed that it wasn't. The continental outlines were wrong, as was the ratio of land area to that of the sea. And the ice caps were much too large.

They stared without speaking for thirty seconds. Then the view changed. The next picture was of a savannalike landscape lighted by a reddish sun. Animals were in the background, things whose shapes were indistinct but whose outlines were distinctly alien.

Thirty seconds later a third view flashed on the screen, a night aerial panorama of a city laid out in the hexagon pattern of a honeycomb. Spidery bridges spanned the gaps between tall six-sided spires. The city's lighting had a bluish tinge, and the color was mirrored by the two crescent moons that lay low over the hills behind the city.

Thirty seconds passed. The screen showed a closeup of a creature whose chitinous body and multifaceted eyes were distinctly insectoid. The implement harness that crossed its thorax implied it was an intelligent tool user.

The catalog of strange beings and places continued. There were oddly constructed spacecraft, hemispherical dwellings, an attractive elfen being who posed next to a swift-looking groundcar. Seal-like creatures pulled torpedo shapes through crystal-clear water, and a Mississippi-size river fell over a cliff into an ocean of spray and rainbows in a purple-green rain forest a thousand meters below.

And finally the scene changed to show an elder-statesman-like human being whose features were frozen in a look of beatific compassion. The man began to speak in a slow, measured, rhythmic cadence:

> Men and Women of Earth.
> Greetings from the stars.
> You have nothing to fear.
> I come in peace.
>
> I am Life Probe 53935.
> A sentient computer,

a gatherer of facts.
I have journeyed far to find you.
I come in peace.

I bring to you the knowledge.
  that you are not alone.
I require your assistance.
I ask your welcome.
I come in peace.

Be not afraid,
  for I come in peace.

The man on the screen looked earnestly into the camera and then smiled as the picture slowly faded to white. Professor Roquette leaned over the desk and pressed a control. The holoscreen faded to black.

"That was our first contact. The whole show takes ten minutes and twenty-eight seconds to run through, then repeats after a sixty-second pause."

Brea frowned. "It claims to be a machine, yet it displays the image of a man. Could that be a picture of its creators?"

Roquette shook his head. "No chance. What we are looking at is a computer-generated composite. It broadcast the same message in twelve different languages, each on its own particular frequency. The image is synchronized with the soundtracks of all of the translations yet is speaking none of them. At least, no lip reader has yet been able to decipher what the image is saying. It is merely good animation."

"And the alien scenes that precede the message?"

"Could be animation as well. Could be exactly what they appear, a sort of travelogue of the galaxy."

"Whichever they are, the alien seems to have developed an uncanny knowledge of human psychology," Stassel muttered.

"Indeed it has, Major," Roquette responded. "You undoubtedly noticed that the image is of no particular racial type. And if any arrangement of features can truly be said to be pacific and friendly, that's got to be it. And then there's the whole broadcast. Idyllic scenes that are instantly recognizable as being of alien origin followed by a sales pitch that is quiet, polite, almost hypnotic in its effect. Did you notice how hard it was to feel anger or fear while watching it? The alien's obviously gone out of its way to tailor its presentation."

"Which still doesn't prove that the thing is harmless," Liu growled.

"No, Admiral," Roquette agreed, "It most certainly does not."

"What about the rest of the message?" Stassel asked.

"That began coming in at T plus eight hours. It started with a different travelogue, and with a longer message from the probe itself—"

"—Always assuring us that it came in peace," Roquette said.

"Always that," Liu agreed. "Then, sixteen hours after first contact, it changed again, switching to a more conventional narrative form. It speaks of needing our assistance in refueling for the journey home. It is offering to pay us for our services. The payment would be in advanced knowledge. It began to send pictorial diagrams in the fourth phase of its broadcast, apparently to establish the validity of its claims."

"Diagrams?"

Liu nodded. "All using standard electrical, mechanical, or gravitational engineering symbols. Apparently it has studied us for a long time."

"When can I see the whole message?" Brea asked. Her expression reflected her excitement.

"Call up the project library at any workscreen," Roquette replied.

"What's the security code?"

The white-haired professor chuckled. "No security code needed. Senseless to classify something that the whole world can eavesdrop on."

"May I be excused, Admiral? I've got to see this!"

"By all means," Liu said. He hurried to his feet and bowed as Brea stood up.

Brea turned to Stassel. "Want to share a screen while we view scenes from the stars?"

Liu shook his head. "I'm sorry, but I must ask the major to remain for a bit. We need to discuss his new duties."

Brea shrugged. "Then I'll see you later. Remember, we've a lunch date."

"I'll be there."

He watched Brea to the door and then turned to face the

admiral. He noted that Liu's expression had changed subtly in those few seconds. Roquette suddenly seemed preoccupied as well.

"We've got a problem," Liu said.

"So I surmised, sir."

"Someone tried to break into Communications four nights ago, apparently to get word out. We've a spy aboard *Bernadotte*."

Stassel nodded. Not surprising, of course.

Liu leaned forward, his manner suddenly tense. "I want him found. Quietly. Along with your regular duties, you are in charge of the investigation."

Yorubi M'Buto listened to the steady drum of rain on the autocab roof as the small vehicle threaded its way through the upper-level traffic arteries of Manhattan. Before him the guideway disappeared into a featureless black cube half a thousand meters on a side. For a single instant, as his cab leaped the chasm that was Forty-second Street, he had a glimpse of the gutted hulk of the Empire State Building through a gap in the modern architecture to the south.

He smiled at the sight.

M'Buto had always looked upon the old relic as a symbol of what was wrong with the North American Union (and by association, with all the tired, decadent, too long industrialized nations of the northern hemisphere). Most of the skyscrapers touched by the near miss of '94 had been declared unsafe and razed. But the old Empire State had remained untouched for seventy years, the victim of a generations-long legal battle. Four days ago the mobs had resolved the dispute by setting fire to it. Smoke still billowed from the blackened skeleton.

The autocab turned north and disappeared into the side of the Rockefeller Plaza megastructure, moved silently through the upper reaches of a cavernous hotel lobby, and came to a stop in an interior cab station. M'Buto lifted the cab's canopy, retrieved his travel bag from the back seat, and stepped out onto the carpeted platform of the station. From the station it was a swift two-minute walk to the offices of the Pan-African Federation's Legation to the United Nations.

"Good morning, Savala," he said cheerfully to the young woman who manned the reception desk.

"Oh, good morning, Colonel M'Buto! We didn't expect to see you today."

"I didn't expect to see me either. However, in this imperfect world one must be prepared to abandon his itinerary at a moment's notice. The boss in?"

"Yes, sir."

"Buzz him, please."

Savala turned and spoke into a hushphone for a few seconds before turning back to M'Buto. "The general will see you now, sir."

"Thank you."

General M'ava Yaruanda was seated behind a vast teak desk. A zebra-skin shield and crossed spears hung from the wall behind him. The general was dressed in a conservative business tunic and cravat, the very model of an urbane, international businessman. That, in fact, was the impression he attempted to give all with whom he dealt. The effort was successful, in part because most people were unable to decipher the warrior caste tattoos that decorated his cheeks and forehead.

M'Buto strode to the front of the desk, dropped to his knees, and bowed his head in a crisp, quick movement. *"At your service, Huntmaster,"* he said, lapsing into ritual Xhosa.

"Rise and be seated, Colonel."

The general waited until M'Buto was comfortably settled into one of the visitor's chairs and then began to drum his fingers impatiently on the desk top. "Tell me, Colonel, why do we go to the trouble of appropriating so much of our treasure for your department each year?"

"I don't understand, sir."

"We lavish you Intelligence people with the best we have. Yet when it comes to obtaining really important information on a matter vital to our nation, I find I must read about it in the newsfaxes."

"No excuse, Master. I was returning to Earth to see what I could learn about the UN project when I heard the news. How much of what the papers say is true?"

"True?" Yaruanda asked, not bothering to conceal his irritation. "All of it, of course! Anyone with a primary satellite receiver has merely to reposition its focus to point in the direction of the alien if they wish to hear the message directly.

'Electronic intelligence gathering for the masses' is the way the ambassador put it."

"Have we a recording?"

The general reached into his desk and found a recording module. "Here. We've our best minds working on the scientific portions. You concentrate on the more generalized information."

"The news services claim the alien ship is unmanned."

The general nodded. "Apparently an instrument package controlled by a computer that refers to itself as Probe. It speaks of being on a mission to gather scientific data and requests our help in preparing it to return home. It has offered to pay for our help."

"Pay? I hadn't heard that," M'Buto said, frowning. "What medium of exchange?"

"Advanced scientific knowledge. It sent along several samples to prove its claim."

"What is the General Assembly planning?"

"The GA resumes debate"—Yaruanda paused to look at his wrist chronometer— "in fifty-six minutes. Ambassador Boswani has spent the last several days stalling until we have a policy position worked out. He has had little difficulty in that. Every other ambassador is doing precisely the same thing. Your job is to study that record. The prime minister wants our recommendation on whether to support or oppose the resolution to welcome this probe, and quickly."

CHAPTER 18

The Sun was larger and brighter than PROBE had ever seen it. The Earth–Moon system had changed, too. No longer an elongated blob of light in its telescopes, the humans' home showed as a living world with only moderate magnification. For only the second time in its long existence, PROBE was close enough to a planet to examine it directly. Yet it ignored the opportunity and concentrated on a phenomenon of far greater interest.

The first that PROBE knew something was wrong was when its brain recalled unbidden a portion of that last conversation with Jurul.

JURUL: And if you should happen to discover a civilization that has developed a means of traveling faster than light?

PROBE: I will conceal all evidence of my origins until I have confirmed that such beings can be trusted. When I am sure that it is safe to do so, I will direct them here to the home world to bargain for their secret.

160

And with the sudden memory of Jurul's last orders came the voice of the nameless Maker who had programed that portion of PROBE dedicated to the search for some sign of a ship traveling faster-than-light.

"We have long theorized that a spacecraft traveling at super-light speeds would be detectable in the sublight universe," the Maker's dry, lecture-hall voice began. "A good analogy for this postulated effect would be an atmospheric craft exceeding the speed of sound. Since it is moving through a medium at speeds faster than that medium can support, the result is a shock wave known as a sonic boom.

"It is quite likely that a superlight starship would have the same effect. Moving through the interstellar medium, it would push all manner of particles before it. Since these particles are limited to sublight velocities themselves, they would pile up into a bow wave much as gas molecules pile up before a super-sonic aircraft. The result would be a shock wave, or hyperwave pulse. To an outside observer near the ship's line of flight, it would appear as though a lenticular source of extremely energetic particulate radiation had suddenly come into existence.

"That, at least, is the theory."

PROBE was well aware of the theory and had been constructed to take advantage of it. Like every life probe since *Hull Number 1207*, it had been equipped with sensors to detect the peculiar, sleeting, primarily neutrino radiation that would result from an FTL passage. Yet its hyperwave sensors had been silent since launch. In fact, no such sensor had ever reacted in the long history of the life probe program.

Therefore, it was something of a surprise when PROBE realized the cause of its sudden attack of schizophrenia. The hyperwave detectors were actively tracking a contact beyond Sol!

Somewhere beyond the human sun were beings capable of outracing light itself!

Within two days of his arrival inboard *Count Bernadotte*, Eric Stassel was a week behind in his work. As Project Executive Officer he had full load of administrative duties. And in his spare time, he stalked a spy.

He began his investigation with the one man positively iden-

161

tified as being on the scene the night of the crime—Corporal Gronski, the guard on duty at the Communications Center.

"Relax, Corporal," Stassel ordered when the guard snapped to attention in front of his desk. "Have a seat."

Gronski assumed parade rest. "I'll stand if you don't mind, sir."

"Have it your way." Stassel scanned the ribbons that decorated the corporal's undress uniform. Gronski was a veteran of all three peace actions taken in the last decade. Stassel nodded approvingly.

"Let's hear your story, Corporal. What do you remember?"

"Not much, Major," the guard answered sheepishly. "One minute I was walking my post, the next my nose was pushed into the deck and my windpipe was being crushed. I felt a sharp sting on my neck and then nothing."

"Crushed? Then your attacker was fairly strong?"

"Yes, sir. Strong as an ox."

"Size?"

"About my height and build. At least, that's what it felt like when he was on my back."

"What else?"

"Whoever he was, he's had training in unarmed combat. I tried a couple of parries in the few seconds before I passed out. Nothing. He was a real *jongo*."

"Hmmm. Could it have been a Marine, then? Maybe one of your mates has a grudge against you and tried to make it look like an attempt on the comm center?"

"No, sir. I get along well enough. Besides, I hate to think one of ours would stoop to back stabbing. If a marine doesn't like you, he'll invite you to a quiet place to settle things."

"Remember anything else?"

"No, sir."

"Any reservations about being put under hypnosis to see what your subconscious remembers?"

"Uh, not if it will help, sir."

"It might be all we need. Report to sick bay and have the doc run you through a recall session."

"Yes, sir."

"Dismissed."

"Sir!" The corporal snapped to attention, saluted, turned on

162

his heel and left the office. Stassel chewed on his lip for a few moments before turning to his screen. Now came the drudge work.

Project Eaglet had grown while he and Brea had been Earthside. Some two hundred people now lived and worked inboard *Count Bernadotte*. The project roster listed 206 names for the night of the attack. It would be a long, hard job to comb through all the possible suspects, even discounting those whose physical condition eliminated them from contention.

Stassel was in the midst of his fiftieth personnel file when someone knocked on his door. He blanked his screen and turned to face the entry hatch. "Enter!"

The hatch snicked open to reveal Brea Gallagher. She stepped over the high coaming. "I thought we had a date for drinks in the lounge before dinner."

Stassel groaned. "Already? I'll be with you in a minute."

Ten minutes later he was escorting her down the main corridor toward the lounge, which had been set up in an old storage area close to the messhall. It included table clusters salvaged from compartments all over the ship, a wall-size holovision screen, a drink dispenser, and intimate lighting. Just beyond the main hatch someone had copied the cartoon that adorned Admiral Liu's door onto the steel decking so that all visitors were greeted by the comical little eaglet breaking out of its shell.

The lounge was sparsely populated when Stassel and Brea entered. They dialed for drinks and slid into a booth near the back of the room. A small group of technicians was watching a news program on the holoset—another in the endless series of specials on the probe. The screen jumped from views of the General Assembly debate to the destruction caused by rioting mobs on the first day to learned talking heads.

"Where is everyone, Brea?" Stassel asked, taking in the unusually quiet scene.

"Doctor Rheinhardt is giving a lecture about the probe's propulsion system up on Beta Deck. I peeked in for a bit on my way over to your office. The place is packed."

"Shouldn't you be there?"

Brea shrugged. "I'd rather be with you. Besides, I helped prepare the lecture, so I know all about it. Helena has been studying the original flash, directing a team of engineers and physicists Earthside in developing a model of the probe's propulsion system. She thinks they've figured out how the probe decelerates."

"How?"

"By an ultimate act of courage!" Stassel turned to discover Doctor Wojcelevitch standing behind them. The Polish professor lifted a glass from the drink dispenser. "Mind if I join you?"

"We'd be honored."

"I'm not interrupting anything, am I?"

"No, sir," Stassel said, "although I'd have thought you would be at the lecture."

"Been there and heard everything. It's all over but the nattering. Thought I would duck out early before Helena Rheinhardt's brilliant deduction is polluted by second guessers." Wojcelevitch sipped at his drink, smacking his lips as he let out a long sigh. "I needed that."

"What has Doctor Rheinhardt discovered?" Stassel asked. Administrative problems since his return had given him little time to catch up on the science side of the project.

"She's proved our original suspicion. The probe is powered by a singularity-initiated hydrogen fusion reaction. In that respect, it is very like one of our own ships, only immensely more powerful and efficient. Beyond confirming the nature of the beastie, Helena's group has extrapolated current knowledge and built a mathematical model of the probe's engine. Funny things happen when you scale up a mass converter, it seems. Among other things, the fusion reaction becomes self-sustaining.

"It turns out that the probe has no need of its I-mass in the final phase of the voyage. Helena believes it will jettison the singularity as soon as the reaction has stabilized. That should leave the probe proper with substantially less mass and sufficient fuel to decelerate to intrasystem velocity.

"Think of it! That machine out there has traveled God-only-knows how far and is even now making ready to cripple itself in order to end its journey. And the implications—"

"What implications?" Stassel asked, suddenly very interested in what Wojcelevitch had to say.

"You saw its contact message. From the travelogue it showed

164

us, the universe must be crawling with intelligent species. And even if we didn't believe the pictures, the probe's design proves it. Its builders are undoubtedly heir to the same laws of economics we are. Yet they seem to have dispatched the probe blindly into the firmament. That would seem to mean that any direction they point the damned thing is as good as any other. Sooner or later they are bound to run into someone who can provide the probe with a new I-mass and fuel." Doctor Wojcelevitch took a long sip of his drink, during which his shoulders gave a slight shudder. When he put his glass down, he wiped his mouth with his sleeve and said: "That frightens me!"

"Why?" Brea asked, puzzled.

"Think about it. The data doesn't jibe with our own experience. If advanced races of thinking beings are so common out there, how come we've never been visited before?"

"How do we know we haven't? What about the UFO scares of the last century?"

Wojcelevitch shook his head. "Doesn't wash. Numerous studies have proved that most people who saw UFOs mistook common objects for mysterious ones, saw atmospheric phenomena which weren't well understood at the time, were just plain susceptible to suggestion, or in a few cases were liars. And in spite of the resurrection of the ancient astronaut fad since the news broke about the probe, there is no evidence whatever of the Earth's having been visited by aliens in the past.

"Thus," Wojcelevitch continued, "the evidence appears contradictory. We have several thousand years of history which say that we are alone in this neck of the woods. Yet we have discovered this alien machine designed to operate in a galaxy crowded with alien races. On the one hand, we have plenty of neighbors; but on the other, they never visit us. Doesn't that suggest something very definite about the way the universe is put together?"

Brea and Stassel looked at each other and then back to Wojcelevitch. "Not off hand," Stassel said, shrugging.

"Old Albert Einstein may have been right. You can't exceed the speed of light no matter how hard you try. We are locked into a vast cage. All the wealth the race will ever possess is one mediocre star, nine average planets, a few dozen dinky moons, a million or so asteroids, and a few billion comets.

"I don't know about you two, but I find that thought both claustrophobic and depressing!"

The New York skyline was ablaze with lights as Yorubi M'Buto waited in General Yaruanda's study. The general's vue-wall was tuned to a camera mounted high up the rebuilt Statue of Liberty. The wall showed Manhattan from the Battery Park side. M'Buto preferred to pay extra to have a live shot of Victoria Falls piped into his apartment. It reminded him of home.

The door to the study opened, and the general walked in. He was dressed in evening clothes—a formal maroon cape over a cerise jumpsuit.

"Good of you to come, Ubi," he said, striding briskly to the desk and seating himself.

"My life is yours, Huntmaster."

"—and Mother Africa's," Yaruanda replied. "I read your report this afternoon. I felt it better to discuss it away from the office."

"Yes, sir."

"You recommend that Pan-Africa throw its support behind the resolution to welcome the probe into the solar system. Why?"

M'Buto frowned. "I think that would be obvious, Huntmaster. The knowledge of the probe is a source of enormous wealth and power. If nothing else, we owe it to future generations to do everything in our power to obtain it."

The general leaned back in his powered chair, his elbows rested on the arms and his fingers steepled together beneath his beard.

"Your mother's father died in the Soweto Riots of twenty-two, did he not, Ubi?"

"You know he did."

"Why?"

"I don't understand."

"Simply put, Colonel, why did he do it? He was relatively young, in good health, with three children to support. He lived in a clean shanty with running water on every street. He probably had a television set. Materially speaking, he was better off than his own father, and much better off than his grandfather."

"What's your point, sir?"

"Only that your grandfather envied his own grandfather, even though he lived better."

"Of course. Great-great-grandfather was a free man. Grandfather, on the other hand, was a second-class citizen in his own land."

"Then there is a moral here, Ubi. The quantity of a man's goods do not matter so much as the quality of his life. Your four-times-removed ancestor was happy because his few goats and grass hut made him a wealthy man. His grandson died in the fight for African freedom because, although he lived in relative comfort, his manner of living was inferior to that of his oppressors.

"All is relative, Colonel. What good to live in a palace if you are the servant of someone in a bigger palace? Let us assume that the probe makes good on its promise and humanity obtains its knowledge. Who do you think will control that gift? Who is best positioned to utilize advanced scientific knowledge? Who else but the whites? If any black or brown people benefit, it will be at the sufferance of those devils. They will keep the best for themselves and throw us a few bones to quiet our whining."

General Yaruanda glanced at the antique ship's chronometer that adorned his desk. "I'm late, Colonel. We can finish this tomorrow if you like."

M'Buto frowned. "What are your orders, Master?"

Yaruanda cleared his throat. "No orders, Colonel. Only information. Ambassador Boswani and I have cabled home. All concerned have agreed that Pan-Africa's best interests will be served if we oppose the resolution welcoming the probe into the solar system."

CHAPTER 19

The Right Honorable Agusta Louise Meriweather looked up from the final draft of her speech and let her gaze roam over the tiered elegance of the Great Hall of the General Assembly. As she scanned the sea of faces, she was struck by the air of excitement that filled the chamber. There was an intangible *something* about the rickety old barn that intrigued her, especially in times of crisis.

"Ready for today's battle, Agusta?"

The soft voice came from close beside her, jolting her from her reverie. She turned to find Seji Furosawa meticulously laying out his working papers at her right elbow.

"I didn't hear you sit down, Seji."

"You seemed preoccupied."

She laughed. "They tell me a shortened attention span is

168

one of the first signs of senility. Maybe I'm getting too old for this rough-and-tumble."

"You'll outlive us all, Agusta."

"Know what I was doing just now? Drinking in the ambience of the chamber. Do you feel it? A kind of all-pervasive, musty odor?"

Furosowa sniffed tentatively at the air. "I don't smell anything."

Mrs. Meriweather chuckled. "You don't smell it with your nose, Seji, but with your heart. It's the smell of history being made, as though the ghost of every blackguard, braggard, and crook who ever sat in this chamber has returned to watch the show." Mrs. Meriweather glanced down at her own papers and began hurriedly to straighten them for the coming debate. If she noticed the concerned glance of her colleague, she made no mention of the fact. "At least we are about to get the preliminaries behind us."

Furosowa nodded. "The time has come to speak of what has remained unspoken. I saw Nicholas Boswani in the hall. He had his sycophants with him and looked ready to make his move."

"I thought Mohammed was going to talk to him."

"He did. Apparently without success."

"That tears it! Our job is hard enough without an open break with Boswani. And he speaks second today!"

"You'll hold your own, Agusta."

"I'm not so sure. Did you happen to see Ray Lerner's newscast this morning?"

Furosawa grimaced. "I'm afraid I did not have that pleasure."

"Count yourself lucky. He did a three-minute profile on the Reverend Lonnie Smith. Smith is the backwoods guru who has been preaching hellfire and damnation ever since the news broke. He seems to believe the probe is a UN plot to take over the North American Union. 'Total rejection of this technocratic plan put forward by the agents of the Anti-Christ' was the proposition *he* advocated on Lerner's program this morning."

Furosawa nodded. "I've heard the gentleman preach. Really, Agusta, you shouldn't concern yourself with the lunatic fringe."

"Except that the fringe gains in public visibility daily."

"As long as there are people on this planet, some of them will insist on believing it to be flat."

Mrs. Meriweather's reply was interrupted by the warning buzzer calling delegates to their seats. She watched as the last-minute, mid-aisle lobbying died away. Two minutes to the second following the buzzer, Secretary-General Bruenwald mounted the podium. Bruenwald walked in a perpetual stoop forced on him by his arthritic spine, yet he projected an aura of power that quickly made people forget his handicap.

The chamber echoed to the amplified sound of a gavel banging wood. Bruenwald keyed the public address system to life and began to speak.

"I hereby declare this session of the General Assembly to order. In the interest of time, we will dispense with the usual formalities. If the delegates will consult their agendas, they will note that the first speaker is Agusta Louise Meriweather, Secretary to the Executive Committee of the Trusteeship Council. Mrs. Meriweather will speak in support of UN Special Resolution 2065-12, titled 'A Resolution to Welcome the Alien Spacecraft Now Entering the Solar System.'

"Mrs. Meriweather?"

Eric Stassel shouldered his way into the darkened, crowded Staff Lounge. He was half an hour late for the daily UN debate and the holoscreen already showed the General Assembly chamber. A familiar figure looked out at him from behind the podium. Agusta Meriweather looked a bit more haggard than he remembered from his ExCom interview but was otherwise unchanged. After a single, quick glance Stassel concentrated on stomping as few toes as possible as he edged toward an empty spot near one wall.

"Hi, traveling partner," he whispered as he sat down.

Lisa Moore turned in the seat directly in front of him. "Hi, Eric. Where have you been keeping yourself?"

"I've been busy. Have I missed anything?"

"Not much. We're just getting to the good part."

Stassel nodded and sat back to listen.

"... and that, colleagues and delegates, was the situation up to the moment when the probe began to transmit its messages of friendship. Since each of you knows the content of those messages as well as I, there is no need to belabor the point by repeating them here. Suffice to say, we have been asked to help this traveler from afar. You have before you a resolution to do just that. On behalf of the Trusteeship and Security councils, and at the behest of the secretary-general, I ask you to give it your speedy approval."

Mrs. Meriweather's patrician features suddenly swelled as the camera zoomed in. Stassel was surprised to note that her eyes glistened with a hint of tears. She seemed to look directly at him across 150 million kilometers.

"I do not ask you to give your blind support to this resolution, however. Those who know me are well aware of my views on the sin of altruism. Nowhere is it written that we must assist every traveler who happens by. I must note in passing, however, that the Parable of the Good Samaritan has its counterpart in every culture on this planet.

"No, I ask you to welcome this emissary for more practical reasons. Consider, if you will, the magnitude of the accomplishment of those who built it. Who among us would be sufficiently farsighted to undertake such a project? Do we squabbling, squalling, scrabbling creatures have the right to foil this great dream?

"I say not! To do so would be an act unworthy of us and would result in our undying shame."

The lined face, still in closeup, paused. The fierce eyes scanned the audience. "A few moments ago I spoke of altruism, and yet I now find myself perilously close to committing that very sin. After all, we humans have done things in the past that were contemptible and richly deserving of revulsion. What matter an additional black mark on our record?

"So let us consider things on a less moral plane. Let us shed our hypocrisy and ask how we may turn this event to our own profit.

"The facts are these: the probe has traveled far and has gathered much scientific data for its builders. It desires to return home but lacks both the fuel and the stamina to do so. Our experts tell me that it must destroy its engines in the process of shedding the frightful velocity it carries. Apparently that is normal operating procedure for such instrument packages. In order to return home, the probe and its fellows must seek out

171

indigenes capable of overhauling its engines and replenishing its fuel stocks.

"They who built the probe seem to place more trust in their fellow creatures than would we in similar circumstances. Yet they do not ask for charity. Instead they send their servant to us equipped to pay its own way. The probe is a treasure house of advanced scientific knowledge. It has offered to share that knowledge with us.

"We have been offered a gift that will catapult us a thousand or more years into our future. I urge you to vote in favor of this resolution, not merely because it is right. It is also profitable! This chance will not come again. If we let this opportunity slip from our grasp, we will deserve the curses that our children and grandchildren will heap upon us. Delegates of the sovereign nations of Earth, this is your chance for greatness.

"For God's sake, don't flub it!"

The applause that echoed through the General Assembly chamber was almost as enthusiastic as that in *Count Bernadotte*'s lounge. The cameramen picked out shots of individual delegates applauding wildly and interspersed them with views of the old woman walking majestically back to her seat. Yet no amount of quick camerawork could disguise the fact that a number of delegates were not joining the applause. Stassel noticed that the holdouts more often than not had black or brown faces.

Lisa turned around, tears streaming down her cheeks. "That was beautiful! When do they vote?"

"Not today, I'm afraid," he answered. "Now the opposition gets its chance, and after them, every delegate will say something one way or the other. We'll be lucky if the final vote comes this week."

The secretary-general returned to the podium and waited for the applause to die down before gaveling the assembly to order. "I now call on the ambassador from the Pan-African Federation, the Honorable Nicholas Boswani. Ambassador Boswani will speak in opposition to the resolution."

Boswani was a small man with café-au-lait complexion, a goatee that failed to hide a wicked scar on his chin, and the strut of a bantam cock. He bounded up to the podium and

172

stared out over the assembled representatives. When he finally spoke, his voice was a bass rumble out of place in such a small frame.

"Friends, you have heard Mrs. Meriweather speak in support of this resolution. She is an honorable woman, well intentioned and sincere. I will not question her motives, for I am sure they are of the highest.

"But..." His fierce gaze roamed the audience. *"I do not agree with her conclusion!*

"She urges that we bid welcome to this alien machine falling upon us from out of the constellation known to northern astronomers as the Eagle. I am forced to admit to my being moved by her eloquence. However, our northern friends sometimes forget that other traditions than their own exist in this world. To members of my own tribe, for instance, that configuration of stars is part of a larger grouping known as the Jackal. And one of the first things my grandfather taught me was that jackals are not to be trusted!

"Let us discuss Mrs. Meriweather's points in order. She speaks of our unending shame should we order this violator of our territory to continue on its way. Where is the shame in defending one's home from invaders? Did we invite this probe? Where then lies the responsibility should we choose to withhold our welcome?

"Mrs. Meriweather speaks of the bargain we have been offered. Let us consider how much of a *bargain* it is. The probe asks that we devote a large percentage of our industrial capacity to the effort to ready it once more for space. In the meantime, we are asked to wait patiently until it deems the time right to transmit its cargo of knowledge to us. What assurance have we that it will ever do so? What man trusts another without some prior indication that such faith is justified?

"But, let us concede the point. Let us consider the day when the probe has given us this treasure trove. What then? Will only good things flow from this knowledge? I would remind you that we humans have shown a surprising capacity for subverting knowledge toward destructive goals. What makes Mrs. Meriweather think things will be different in the future? Do we really want the probe's gift if it only means bigger and better weapons?

173

"But again, for the sake of argument, let us concede the point. Let us assume that this alien knowledge will lead to major advances in every field of science, as Mrs. Meriweather contends. I must ask a question that is too often ignored these days.

"Is that what we really want?

"I will illustrate my point with a story from the past, a tale of my own tribe. Once, during a great drought, my tribe and several others left their farms and migrated south. They moved slowly into what had been unclaimed territory for as long as the oldest tribesman could remember. Imagine their surprise, therefore, when they encountered a tribe they had never seen before—a tribe with white skin and a strange, guttural language.

"It was quickly learned that these white strangers were interlopers from far away. Still, the land was large and the number of people small. My ancestors decided that there was room enough for everyone. For many years they kept to the high veld, tending their crops, expecting the whites to keep to their own areas along the southern coast. But slowly and surely, these strangers encroached on my ancestors' land. First came missionaries, offering to teach my people many new and marvelous things. And many of these new things *were* marvelous indeed. The tribe learned new methods of farming and a few even had rifles for hunting. But other new ideas were not so good. For one, the old religion fell into disuse, supplanted by the white Cross-God.

"Next came white settlers to establish their own farms. People moved to the farms of whites to work and returned to their villages with strange, new ideas. Young men learned disrespect for their elders. Young women learned an alien concept called whoring. I will not bore you with the rest of the story. Similar things took place among most of the black and brown peoples of this world. Within a century of our first contact with the whites, we were virtual slaves in our own land.

"Who is to blame for this shame my ancestors bore? Who do we curse for this horror? Unfortunately, the blame belongs to no single individual but to the workings of history. A vigorous, industrialized culture came into contact with a static, pastoral people. The tragedy was, alas, inevitable.

"But, my friends, let us pause in our deliberations to consider the relative positions of ourselves and this probe. Who is the Great White Father this time? Can human society survive such a massive dose of alien knowledge as the probe offers? You will pardon my wariness, but I come from a backward people whose only experience with science is that it is an instrument of enslavement.

"Fellow delegates, I say that we humans already suffer from having come too far, too fast. I urge defeat of this thousand-times-damnable resolution!"

CHAPTER 20

Eleven and a half years earlier, a faster-than-light starship had departed the vicinity of a bright, yellow-white star beyond the human sun. PROBE watched intently as the radiation storm kicked up by that passage sleeted through the solar system.

The star was an F5 subgiant accompanied through the sky by a white-dwarf companion. The F5 was one of the brightest stars in the human sky and had long been included in the bipeds' pantheon of sky signs. They called it Procyon.

PROBE noted the exact position of the star and began the calculations for the course change that would send it to the new target. A hundred nanoseconds of fuel inventory subroutines were sufficient to confirm the bad news. After ten-thousand years of flight, PROBE's tanks held barely enough mass to halt its flight, with almost none left over for maneuvering. The F5 star lay almost directly ahead yet was as unreachable as the Greater Magellenic Cloud.

For Procyon was fully five degrees off PROBE's line of flight, far beyond its ability to maneuver. PROBE's choices were only two. It could bend its course by squandering reaction mass, throwing away any chance of halting once it reached the Procyon system. Or it could stop in the solar system and seek aid from the humans. Once refueled, it would accelerate outbound directly for the FTL civilization.

Of the choices, only the two-stage journey offered any hope of obtaining the secret of FTL for the Makers, and thus stopping among the humans was the obvious solution to PROBE's problem.

But the obvious solution didn't feel right. The last several months had taught PROBE to be cautious about humans. The discovery of the starship's wake made the stakes much higher than they had ever been before. No longer would the price of failure be the loss of ten thousand years of accumulated data. A miscalculation now could mean the eventual collapse of Maker civilization. PROBE considered its dilemma. Could it gamble everything on the goodwill of savages? More to the point, did it have any choice?

Suddenly it knew that there was another way, one that was unorthodox in the extreme. On its present course, PROBE would pass very close to the human Sun. It considered the effect such a close approach could have on its path through space.

The Makers called it a gravity well maneuver. By swinging close in and letting gravity and the solar wind have their way, PROBE's orbit would be deflected through a small arc. Properly computed and executed, such a maneuver would place it on a course for Procyon. In effect, PROBE could use the human Sun to change course without wasting a gram of precious fuel. But at what risk?

PROBE was a denizen of deepest interstellar space, where the vacuum was nearly absolute. Much of its structure was delicate and would quickly be destroyed in the soup that surrounds a star. At best, most of its sensors would be burned out and considerable superstructure carried away by the gas. At worst—total disintegration.

Not an optimal solution . . .

And what of the subsequent journey to Procyon should PROBE survive the storm? With such extensive damage it would be unable to return to the long sleep. In what stage of senility would it arrive?

PROBE reconsidered the star-grazing, gravity-well maneuver, then concluded that the risks were too great. The Makers had long waited for the secret of FTL; they could wait a bit longer. In the meantime, humanity would be pulled from its mud wallow and placed on the road to true civilization.

PROBE opened communications with SURROGATE. Since discovery of the starship's wake, it had virtually ignored its offspring. It provided SURROGATE with a summary of recent events. Unbidden, SURROGATE cautioned it of the uncertain reception awaiting on Earth, calling its parent's attention to the increasingly strident tone of the televid intercepts.

"What are you suggesting?" PROBE asked.

"Only that they could say yes today and no tomorrow. I only thought you should be made aware of the danger."

PROBE hesitated as doubt once more filled its circuits. It rejudged the risks of a solar passage against those of trusting humans for the thirty years or more that the overhaul would take. It reviewed its data one last time.

It made its decision.

The Earth had been shrinking for decades. Not that its radius wasn't the same 6400 kilometers it had always been. But in terms of human perception, the world was a much tinier place. Partly this was the inevitable result of hypersonic aircraft and suborbital rockets, partly the greatly expanded view of the universe that space travel had forced on mankind. But, primarily, the Earth was shrinking because of the political realignment that followed the Misfire War. The number of countries recognized by the precursor United Nations had peaked at 187. Seven decades later that number was sixty-three. UN business that had once taken a month could now be completed in a few days. Such was the case with the Great Probe Debate. The final speeches had already been made, the last arm twisted, the last favor called in.

The vote was scheduled for 12:00 hours Eastern Standard Time (Greenwich minus 5), 6 September 2065. Public interest was running high. London bookies were quoting odds of 5 to 4 in favor of the resolution, while their New York counterparts were going for even money. All over Earth and through much of the solar system anxious men and women huddled around holo sets to await the decision. And inboard *Count Bernadotte*, the Staff Lounge was crowded to overflowing.

The mood of quiet anticipation was echoed in Admiral Liu Tsen's office, where he and Eric Stassel were holding their own vigil over the same picture as everyone else. But their sound came to them via a secure military channel at the other end of which was Colonel Stanford Ames. Ames was to monitor the debate and issue the order that would send one of two recorded messages hurtling starward. The secretary-general would direct the probe to a parking orbit fifty-million kilometers foreorbit of Earth; or he would order the probe to continue its journey. Both messages had been transmitted to *Count Bernadotte* along with orders that Project Eaglet was to be the sole agency by which humanity's answer would be transmitted to the probe.

"Why us?" Stassel asked when Liu showed him the orders.

Liu had looked up with his one good eye and blinked. "Security. Farside Observatory has already transmitted a message telling the probe where to look for its answer. It is being asked to ignore all subsequent messages that do not originate from this ship. That way, there will be no chance of a false message going out."

"Seems a bit extreme, sir."

"In this case, Major, a bit of paranoia is warranted."

Transforming the project's radio telescope into a transmitter had been a twelve-hour job. When the conversion was complete, Liu ordered that a continuous Standby message be aimed at the probe to give it the opportunity to lock onto their signal. Then the preparations were done. There had been nothing to do but wait.

The waiting was nearly over.

The General Assembly convened on schedule, and after surprisingly short preliminaries, the roll call began.

"*Here we go,*" Ames said as the secretary-general stepped up to the podium to direct the vote. "*Australasia is up first, and they cast their twelve votes—'Yes'!*" A chorus of cheers and boos in the background signaled the presence of jammed public gallery in the assembly chamber.

Ames continued his running commentary. "*Austro-Hungary, with a single vote. 'Yes' again. Okay, folks, here's our first fence sitter. Chinese Hegemony—forty votes . . . 'Yes'!*"

The tally continued in favor of the resolution through the first quarter of the vote, with the large nations voting for, several of the smaller nations voting against, and a surprising—and worrisome—number passing. Not until the South Americans did a major power vote 'No,' to tip the balance against the resolution.

"That was expected," Ames reported to his unseen listeners. *"Here comes the European Commonwealth. Twenty votes 'Yes,' putting us back in the lead. Now the Kingdom of France, contrary as usual—'No.'"*

A long string of "No" votes followed as the Indians, Indonesians, Irish, and Mexicans all sided with the Pan-African bloc, and again, more cries of "Pass" were heard than had been predicted. The lead seemed about to trade hands again.

"The North Americans vote 'Yes,' of course. The leaders of the opposition follow. Pan-Africa votes 'No.' Switzerland casts her single ballot 'Yes,' as do the West Russians with their six. That ends the first round, with the resolution leading by only four votes. There will now be a short pause while the stragglers organize. How's the tension up there?"

"Stan Ames always was the dramatic type," Liu muttered to no one in particular. He didn't respond to the question because distance made it rhetorical. Radio waves took five-hundred seconds to reach *Bernadotte* from Earth. Whatever the outcome of the vote, it was already a foregone conclusion.

"What do you think, sir?" Stassel asked.

"I think we're in trouble. In case you haven't noticed, North Africa was the last country to pass on the first round. That means they vote last. It's going to be up to them, and they're solidly in Boswani's orbit."

During most of the second round, the pro-resolution forces continued to enjoy a slight edge, but as the cameras panned the faces of the delegates, it was obvious that Admiral Liu's fear would materialize. The last nation voting would carry the day.

"Ambassador Al-Mohar from North Africa has risen to his feet and is now looking around at his colleagues. He appears hesitant. He is gazing up at tally board and moves to the microphone. North Africa . . . abstains!

"I repeat, North Africa abstains!"

On the screen, the assembly burst into chaos. Delegates shook their fists at Al-Mohar or clapped each other on the back. The tally board registered 200 vote-units in favor, 198 opposed,

6 abstentions. The secretary-general gaveled for order without success. The pandemonium continued for five minutes or more before calm could be restored.

Stassel and Liu listened to the official announcement of the tally. A few seconds later, Ames's excited voice echoed through the office. "Hello, Count Bernadotte. *This is official! You may extend our welcome to the Probe. The resolution has passed!*"

Brea Gallagher found Don Bailey in the kitchen, where like the rest of the commissary personnel, he was busy preparing for what had the makings of an all-night bash.

"Isn't it wonderful, Stinky?"

He shrugged and continued carving up hydroponically grown fruit for a salad. "I suppose."

"What's the matter?" she asked.

"Nothing's the matter, Brea."

"Come off it, partner! Something's eating you. What is it?"

"Well, now that you brought it up . . . when were you planning on going back to prospecting?"

"Prospecting, Don? I don't understand."

"*Liar* finished her overhaul nearly a month ago. She's ready for space. With word out about the probe, I don't see any reason for them to hold us here any longer. It's time we got back to doing what we do best."

Brea fell silent. Truth was, she hadn't thought much about the future lately. She hadn't had time. Yet now that Don mentioned it, she could see that Project Eaglet had been living on borrowed time since the news broke. The focus would now shift to the universities and corporations as the human race began to tool up for the overhaul. Besides, before long an astronomer was going to be about as useful around *Count Bernadotte* as a paddle wheel.

"Maybe you're right, Stinky. It was fun while it lasted, though."

"You don't have to come, Brea. I know how much you've enjoyed being back in the old profession. I've also seen how much time you spend with Major Stassel."

"I'm not speaking to Major Stassel!" she said, letting her expression fall into a pout. "He canceled our date for dinner Saturday night."

Bailey recognized the symptoms. His lips curved upward in a half smile. "Whatever you say, Brea. I just want you to know that I'll understand if you decide to dissolve the partnership. With the proceeds from the you-know-what, I can probably scrape up enough to buy you out."

"You aren't getting rid of me that fast, Stinky!"

"Are you sure?"

"I'm sure."

Bailey nodded. "In that case, I'll try to squeeze in to see Admiral Liu tomorrow morning. It will be better for all concerned to get it over with quickly. And, need I remind you, safer!"

The party in the Staff Lounge that evening was a blowout to rival any Lagrange Mardi Gras. Eric Stassel found himself elbowing his way through clumps of excited people, all of whom wanted to clap him on the back and press drinks into his hands, but he refused to be diverted, maintaining a steady course toward the rear of the lounge where Bernie Whitnauer, Stan Wojcelevitch, Ellie Crocker, Greg Zapata, and Brea Gallagher were gathered in their own small clump.

"...I thought my heart would stop when it came time for the North Africans to vote," Bernie Whitnauer was saying.

Wojcelevitch nodded. "I wonder what made them abstain."

Ellie Crocker, who like Stassel had just come off duty, said: "I heard the European Commonwealth threatened to call in their debt if they voted against—here's the boss, why not ask him?"

"Leave me out of this," Stassel muttered. "I've never understood politics."

Brea's back had been turned so that she hadn't seen his approach. She pivoted on her heel at the sound of his voice. "So the Project executive officer has finally taken some time out of his busy schedule to visit the troops!"

"Uh, I'm sorry about Saturday night, Brea. I had to work. Admiral's orders. Ask Greg."

Greg Zapata nodded. "I'm his witness. We both spent most of third watch preparing the transmitter."

"You could have made it if you'd wanted to."

"Care to hear my apology?"

"No."

"Are you sure? Afterward we'll arm wrestle. If I win, you forgive me."

"And if I win?"

"Then I'll forgive you."

She smiled. "That's a little one-sided isn't it?"

"I'll concede the point. *Please* forgive me?"

"Not until I've gotten over my mad."

"Then sit with me at least."

"Only if I'm allowed to kick you every once in a while under the table."

"My shins are yours."

Later Brea rested her head on his shoulder. "You aren't *really* mad are you?" he asked.

"Just giving you a hard time, soldier-boy."

"So why the long face?"

Brea looked him in the eye and recounted her discussion with Don Bailey. When she finished, Stassel's expression mirrored her own.

"Do you have to go?"

"Don's my partner. Where he goes, I follow."

"Sounds a bit like being married."

"Closer than marriage, Eric. More like being a Siamese twin."

"I wish I could get my hands around Harry Gresham's neck for five minutes, Brea. First he ruins our vacation, and now, because he couldn't keep his big mouth shut, I have no reason to hold you and Bailey."

Brea swallowed, avoiding his gaze. When she spoke, her voice was an unsteady, hoarse whisper. "Our vacation doesn't have to stay ruined."

He looked at her sharply. "You'd best explain that comment before I purposely misunderstand your meaning."

"You didn't misunderstand me, Eric. I've hoped you would knock on my door every night since we returned from Earth."

He took her chin in his hand and tilted her face up to his. "Are you sure about this?"

She returned his gaze with a level stare. "Yes."

"And to think of all the time we've wasted!"

"We have tonight, Eric. Let that be enough."

Stassel's reply was interrupted by a commotion at the main hatch. He turned to discover Helena Rheinhardt in the middle of a growing crowd.

"Ladies and gentlemen, I have an announcement to make." Her strong voice pierced the buzzing cocktail party atmosphere and silence fell over the room. She waited until all faces were turned toward her. "At exactly twenty-one sixteen hours tonight, a violet drive flare was observed at nineteen hours twenty-five minutes right ascension, minus point zero five degrees declination. The spectrum closely matches that noted in Brea Gallagher's initial sighting of the probe. Doppler measurement shows the source to be decelerating at just under one-quarter of a standard gravity.

"It would appear that the probe has begun its braking maneuver!"

The words had barely left her mouth when she was drowned out by an explosion of sound from the crowd. Stassel found himself clapping with the rest. Only Brea seemed unmoved.

"What's the matter?" he asked, shouting to make himself heard over the crowd noise.

"The probe," she yelled back. "It's too early!"

"What?"

"It's too early. We began transmitting five hours ago. It will take another six days for our signal to reach the probe."

The crowd quieted and Helena Rheinhardt continued. "As I'm sure some of you have already noted, the probe can't possibly have received our signal yet. Apparently something has happened to cause it to begin braking early.

"Meanwhile, observational data is going unobserved while we party here. I want all scientific personnel, especially astronomers, to report to Conference Room Number One in fifteen minutes. We'll be working through the night, so I suggest each of you down a hair-of-the-dog pill immediately. *Fifteen* minutes, people and not one instant later!"

Stassel groaned and unwrapped his arm from around Brea. "We don't seem to have much luck getting together, do we?"

She laughed. "Look at the bright side."

"What bright side?"

"Helena's going to need a good telescopic technician on her spectrograph if she's going to do this thing properly. I'm needed here. I hate to tell Don to leave without me, but. . . ."

His lips sought hers. When he finally let her go, she sighed and leaned against him for support.

"Don't worry, darling. You couldn't blast me out of here just now. I'm the curious type. I won't be able to sleep nights until I find out why the probe jumped the gun on us."

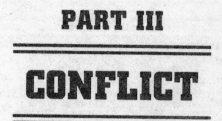

PART III

CONFLICT

CHAPTER 21

The months between the second sighting of the probe's drive flare and its arrival were a busy time for everyone concerned. A detailed discussion of the period is beyond the scope of this history. However, a brief chronology is presented below, to give the reader an idea of the climate of the times.

September 6—The probe's drive flare is detected.
September 9—The Pan-African Federation calls for reconsideration of the probe resolution.
September 15—The move to reconsider is tabled "for further study."
No vote is ever taken.
November 8—Work begins on UNS Count Bernadotte to prepare it for the move to the rendezvous point.
November 15—Mexico debates a proposal to deny the probe overflight rights. This in spite of the fact that the probe will be in solar orbit (not terrestrial), and by international treaty, all sovereignty stops

Humanity was ready. Its fleet swam majestically through hard vacuum fifty million kilometers ahead of the Earth in its orbit. Activity continued aboard the flagship, UNS *Count Bernadotte*, as its slowly rotating hull gleamed dully in the bright sunlight. Around it, fifteen other ships orbited in close formation.

Two of the vessels in *Bernadotte*'s entourage were modern ships-of-the-line. One, the destroyer *Irving Gottmann*, rode close beside the aging behemoth. The other, the heavily armed battle cruiser *Cape of Good Hope*, had taken up guard orbit ten thousand kilometers behind the cluster of ships. Other vessels in the fleet included converted freight haulers, tankers, and tugships. The latter were on hand in case the probe overshot the rendezvous point. Calculations had shown that, as predicted, the probe had dropped its I-mass. Most specialists agreed that it would be unable to achieve much precision in its braking maneuver because of the need to maintain continuous boost.

For the last day of the approach, the waiting human armada had been bathed in the hot glow of the probe's exhaust. The ships' hulls reflected the electric blue light of an arc welder.

All portholes were tightly shuttered and observation cameras screened. All but the most rugged instruments were turned away from the tiny, violet-white star descending on them.

The final vigil began at first watch, 24 January 2066, when the probe had closed to within four hundred thousand kilometers and five hours of the waiting fleet. *Bernadotte*'s Combat Control Center had been converted into a tracking-and-communications facility through which all information regarding the approaching probe was fed. And it was there that Admiral Liu sat stone-faced in the center of a ring of consoles. He slowly swiveled his chair while listening intently to the voices muttering on the ship-to-ship and intraship communications circuits.

"Well, Admiral, are we ready?"

"As much as we'll ever be, Madame Ambassador. Whether it's enough, only time will tell."

Mrs. Agusta Meriweather nodded from the observer's seat next to his and returned to watching the activity around her. For her successful advocacy of the probe resolution, she had been awarded the rank of Ambassador Plenipotentiary. Mrs. Meriweather had arrived only six hours earlier after an arduous and, at her age, dangerous journey. In spite of the mauling she had undergone during launch—and later during the accel/decel phases of her trip out from Earth—she seemed to have the energy of ten people.

Spin was barely back on the ship after taking her aboard when the ambassador had expressed a desire to tour the ship. Since everyone else was busy, Liu assigned Brea Gallagher as her guide—after first discreetly warning her to be easy on the old woman. Brea tried, but Mrs. Meriweather would have none of it. She insisted on seeing everything, and the tour lasted for the better part of two hours.

Finally Brea guided her to the Staff Lounge, where Mrs. Meriweather turned the conversation to personal matters.

"I hear you and that handsome major took a few days off to see the Bahamas when you were Earthside last year. How was it?"

"Very nice," Brea said.

"Where is Major—Stassel, wasn't it—now?"

Brea smiled wanly. "Unfortunately, he stayed behind in the mothball fleet to command the party observing the probe while we moved *Bernie* here."

Mrs. Meriweather eyed Brea curiously. "You seem to be

fond of the major. It must be difficult being apart."

Brea nodded. "I asked to stay with the other astronomers when they split up the project. Unfortunately, I was needed here. We haven't seen each other in almost two months. Thank God the alternate observing station has been decommissioned and it won't be long now."

Mrs. Meriweather looked concerned. "I'm not keeping you from anything, am I?"

Brea shook her head. "Oh, no, ma'am—"

"I'm Agusta to my friends, Brea."

"No . . . Agusta, I haven't anything to do at the moment. Astronomical observation has ended. The probe is too close. If I tried to focus the big scope on it now, all I'd get for my trouble is damaged equipment."

Mrs. Meriweather's eyebrows lifted in sudden interest. "Then you're at loose ends?"

Brea laughed. "With Eric halfway between here and the Lagrangian point, *very loose ends!*"

The older woman looked thoughtful. "I had to leave my aide at home this trip. His wife is expecting next month and he was afraid to leave her alone. How would you like to be my secretary-aide while I'm here? We seem to be simpatico, you know your way around, and you can explain some of the more technical details to me. At the least, it will get you into the center of the action."

Brea paused, not knowing what to say. "I'd be honored, Agusta, but shouldn't Admiral Liu assign someone from his staff as aide-de-camp?"

Mrs. Meriweather sighed, suddenly looking every one of her seventy-five years. "I've been given the responsibility for bringing off successfully this first meeting between human and alien. The men and women in black-and-silver are some of the most capable people around, but they have their duties and I have mine, and I would just as soon maintain my independence. So, how about it?"

"As I said. I am honored."

Admiral Liu took the news with no discernible emotion. He ordered a third seat bolted to the dais in the Contact Room. Brea found herself in it while they waited for the probe. She tried to look busy by pretending to take notes on a pocket recorder computer. But mostly she just rubbernecked. Like everyone around her, she was becoming more excited with each minute that passed.

Ellie Crocker was also in the control room for the final act of the drama. Her duties included monitoring the long-range radar scanners and communications and supervising her six technicians. Scattered elsewhere through the compartment were a half-dozen senior scientists from Project Eaglet and twenty or so technicians and engineers.

Liu glanced in Ellie Crocker's direction and keyed for the command circuit that connected everyone. "How long to zero hour, Lieutenant?"

"Ninety minutes if it holds this track, sir. So far it has backed right down the middle of the optimum velocity curve."

"Care to comment, Doctor Rheinhardt?"

Helena shrugged. "Don't look at me, Admiral. I'm surprised it has sufficient control to end up this side of Mars. Apparently the probe doesn't find the need to maintain continuous thrust as much a hindrance as we would."

Quiet voices continued through numerous checklists. At the end of thirty minutes, Ellie Crocker punched ALL STATIONS on the intercom. "Attention all ships and personnel. Time is now T minus one hour and counting. Stand by for final orders."

"Status checks, ladies and gentlemen," Liu ordered briskly. The roll call flashed around the banks of instruments.

"Power management, ready!"

"Auxiliary control, ready!"

"Cameras, ready!"

"Recorders, ready!"

"Radar, ready!"

"Communications, ready!"

"Commanding officer, Ready! Poll the fleet, Lieutenant Crocker, if you please."

"All vessels report status." The smooth countdown of excited voices continued. When it had ended, Ellie reported to Admiral Liu. "All ready, sir. *Gottmann* and *Hope* report they are at battle stations."

Liu nodded. "Remind them that they are to take no action unless so ordered."

"Yes, sir." Ellie repeated the order. Dual confirmations came back instantly.

Brea glanced up from her recorder. Fifty-eight minutes to go. She turned to watch the large screen on the forward bulkhead display a one-meter-by-two replica of the velocity–time diagram they'd been tracking all watch. Without warning the diagram was replaced by a three-axis plot of the short-range course the probe would have to fly in order to match velocities. As in the case of any continuous-thrust maneuver, the path was complex and required very precise control on the probe's part.

Simply put, the probe had been decelerating for months on a line that was essentially radial to the Sun. Over the preceding few weeks, it had adjusted its path to intersect the Earth's orbit at an oblique angle. Thus, at the right time of year, the probe would only have had to perform a tangential braking maneuver. Now, however, that would have put it on the wrong side of the Sun and millions of kilometers away from the rendezvous point. To match velocities with the waiting fleet, it would fly a modified fish-hook maneuver. Its line of flight would cross Earth's orbit between *Bernadotte* and the home planet. Once inboard of Earth, the probe would slue its booster around to warp its path toward the waiting human fleet. Last, it would flip end for end and decelerate to match velocities with the fleet.

The star on the auxiliary screen brightened dramatically, bringing the optical filtering system perilously close to overload. "The probe has exited the fish hook!" one of the console operators sang out. "The booster is now pointed directly at us."

"Hull temperature rising slightly," another responded.

"Considerable communications interference, sir."

Liu nodded. All those factors were normal consequences of the probe's maneuver. However, if the probe held its course too long, its drive flare would incinerate the human ships. "Order all ships to hold their positions, Lieutenant."

"Yes, sir."

Everyone waited in silence as the long minutes ticked by and the radiation monitors chattered ever more loudly. Finally, after the fleet had spent what seemed an eternity in the plasma storm, the number of charged particles raining down on *Bernadotte*'s hull each second began to decrease.

"The probe has yawned right to place us out of its exhaust," Ellie reported. "Ten minutes to rendezvous."

"*Hope* has been trying to raise us, sir. The probe has passed her position. She is tracking."

"Can she see the probe itself?" Liu asked.

"Negative. The contrast is still too high."

Brea watched a lighted dot crawl along the projection on the screen. The probe was sluing to point its plasma jet parallel with *Bernadotte*'s path through space. The waiting was nearly over.

"Five seconds."

"All recorders to high mode, now!" Liu ordered.

"...three...two...one...velocities matched!"

As if the probe had been monitoring the intership frequencies, the violet drive flare died. The dream of ages was a reality. For the first time in history, human beings found themselves in the presence of an intelligence from outside their own, small planet.

A shiver ran up Brea's spine as she watched the viewscreen. It glowed with a white blaze of light only slightly less bright than the drive flare. Around the blaze a few dark shapes with no real hint of overall form or dimensions could be made out. The unseen camera operator zoomed back, and the blaze revealed itself to be a small area of brightness in an otherwise black setting.

"What the hell?" someone exclaimed.

"Residual engine heat," a voice responded.

At first little was visible except the white-hot glow of the probe's dead engine. As white cooled to orange then, finally, the dull red of dying embers, details became clear.

"Christ almighty! The thing must be a kilometer long."

"Radar!" Admiral Liu's voice called.

"Range is five kilometers, sir. Size: eight hundred meters by two hundred."

"Lieutenant Crocker, get us a picture we can see."

"Yes, sir. Sean, go to wide angle, please."

The screen backed up again. Brea had the sudden overwhelming impression of being a skin diver swimming alongside a blue whale. The probe covered so much of the viewscreen that it appeared to bend in the middle due to camera distortion. Then her eye adjusted to the scale and she was struck by the probe's general similarity to *Liar's Luck.*

Like the prospector boat, the probe was two spheres—each two hundred meters in diameter—connected by a long central column. Around the column were four long cylindrical tanks, with evidence that there had once been many more. The camera zoomed in on the bow. Like most of the probe's structure, the sphere was an open latticework constructed of wispy-looking beams looking like two geodesic hemispheres welded base to base. The shape was obscured because the structure was open, and machinery both incomprehensible and fascinating could be seen through the large gaps. Here and there, long booms tipped with strange shapes extended from the main body.

The view skimmed along the central column to the aft sphere, which had a much more substantial appearance than that at the bow. The machinery inside the heavier framework was almost familiar. Around the engine exhaust was a complicated mechanism of concentric rings that Brea guessed were the focusing rings for an electromagnetic nozzle. Around the main engine were coppery meshes, silvery cones, black cubes, bright spheres, and metal cylinders with bulging end caps.

Not a sound was uttered in the Command Center—or indeed, anywhere in the fleet—for most of two minutes. The spell was finally broken when a plaintive voice issued from the bulkhead speaker. "Where the hell are those orbital parameters? We've got tugs waiting."

"No tugs needed," one of the technicians in Ellie Crocker's section answered. "The probe is stationary to within the accuracy of my scope. . . ."

Brea whistled softly. It took a space pilot to appreciate the meaning of that simple sentence. The probe had shed thirty thousand kps velocity in 147 days, traveling two-hundred *billion* kilometers to do it. Yet it had arrived without so much as a centimeter-per-second excess momentum. *That was damned good piloting!*

Admiral Liu leaned forward in his seat and punched for General Communications. "Attention, all personnel! Stay off the intercoms. The next few minutes are being recorded for the sake of history and we certainly don't need your deathless prose mucking things up."

He released the button and turned to Mrs. Meriweather. "It's all yours, Madame Ambassador."

CHAPTER 22

The acceleration of five months was gone, the journey of millennia over. Sensors no longer registered the impact of energetic atoms against shielding. The stars shifted neither blue forward nor red aft. The universe of a billion dimensionless points of light had been reduced to a single yellow-white ball of fusing hydrogen. After ten thousand years outbound into the unknown, PROBE had finally arrived.

It wasted no time reopening communication between itself and its offspring. The approach had required all of its attention; nearly three hours had passed since it had spoken to SURROGATE. Three hours was a long time to be out of touch for a machine whose thought processes were measured in nanoseconds.

"How are they reacting?" PROBE asked without preamble.

SURROGATE, who had monitored human communications during the final approach, answered with equal swiftness. "They are studying us, visually and electronically."

PROBE had noted the touch of the humans' raspy radar beams

197

on its hull. There was considerable radio traffic, as well. "Any attempt at communication yet?"

"Only among themselves."

"What are they saying?"

SURROGATE hesitated long enough to sample a hundred conversations. "They are surprised at your ability to match velocities so precisely."

"Have you identified which of those ships are warcraft?"

SURROGATE drew PROBE's attention to two ships—one close by, the other at a considerable distance from the fleet. "From the communications flowing between them and the largest ship, those are the guardian vessels."

"And the largest ship itself?"

"That is the one spoken of in the news accounts, the old warship that houses Project Eaglet. It is potentially more powerful than both the others but has not had its weapons activated. At least, that is what their televid signals have been saying."

PROBE turned its attention to Earth. From the vantage of the rendezvous, it was a perpetual half-moon shape. The sun glinted off white cloud formations and polar ice caps in the day hemisphere. The night side of the planet glittered with brilliant carpets of city lights. PROBE decided that the scene had a certain alien beauty to it.

"What is the reaction from Earth?"

"No reaction yet. The fleet is broadcasting pictures, but the signals are still en route. The planet will not respond for at least three more minutes." SURROGATE suddenly went silent, as though it were again listening to intercepted signals. PROBE used the implants in its offspring's mind to listen as the order for radio silence went out to the fleet.

"That was the Peace Enforcer admiral who commands Project Eaglet," SURROGATE said, matching Liu's voice to an intercepted news interview in file.

"He is on your list of humans we wish to interview, is he not?" PROBE asked.

"It would be helpful. My knowledge of their individual quirks is still incomplete."

For long seconds no signals emanated from the human fleet. Then another familiar voice came beaming toward PROBE.

"They are attempting communication," PROBE told its offspring. "Answer them."

198

Agusta Meriweather was experiencing an attack of stage fright, the first in nearly thirty years. The symptoms were quite distressing. For one thing, she couldn't get old Piet Vanderveer's stern visage out of her mind. Piet had been Chief Justice of the World Court during her first term on that august body. She hadn't thought of him in years. Furthermore, there was no reason for her to think of him now. But the one important lesson Mrs. Meriweather had learned in a long and eventful life was to listen to her subconscious when it tried to tell her something. Apparently it was trying now. She took a moment to reflect on her current mental state.

The problem was her mood, of course. That first day on the court had left her with an overpowering feeling of inadequacy. She felt a similar emotion now. Who would have thought that John Meriweather's dirty-faced urchin from Middle Sussex, Greater London, would be the first person to communicate with an alien intelligence? She paused for the space of six heartbeats, took a deep breath, and then spoke the formal words:

"Greetings. I welcome you in the name of the people and nations of Earth. I will await your convenience. You may communicate when ready."

Immediately the main screen changed and the dapper man who had delivered the probe's contact message peered from the cube with the same expression of beatific calm. When he finally spoke, the words tumbled forth in a flood of resonance and harmony.

"People and nations of Earth, I accept your greetings. I thank you for your welcome and I give you assurance once again that I come in peace."

Mrs. Meriweather waited a few seconds to make sure he was finished. The image stared out at her without blinking or breathing. It merely smiled.

She returned the expression. "I am Agusta Louise Meriweather. I have been appointed ambassador and was sent ahead to welcome you. A delegation representing the General Assembly of the United Nations will be arriving in a few days to begin formal negotiations."

"We are pleased to meet you, Madame Ambassador. I too am authorized to speak for my master, although, as you will soon appreciate, such a distinction is somewhat arbitrary with us. We await your delegation's arrival with anticipation."

Mrs. Meriweather let her expression drift with seeming spontaneity to one of mild inquisitiveness. "You use the first-person plural pronoun and speak of a master. Am I to understand that there is a living creature aboard your ship?"

"There are no living creatures as you define the term. I and my master are machine intelligence. We are both part of the logic network which commands the mechanism you see beyond your ship. My verbal symbol is SURROGATE. That of my master is PROBE."

"Are there other machine intelligences aboard?"

"No. PROBE and I are all that are required."

"Required for what?"

"PROBE commands. I am the information processor."

"I beg your pardon?"

"Are you familiar with the concept of signal processing?"

Mrs. Meriweather shook her head slowly, making the gesture easy to follow. "I'm sorry, no. My education is in social administration and quite a few years in the past."

"Signal processing is the manipulation of raw data to make it more understandable. That is my function. I am a subordinate personality which PROBE created specifically for the job of interfacing with you humans. I am afraid that you would find PROBE's thought processes difficult to follow. I assure you that it finds yours equally so. I was created to allow each side to understand the other better."

"You will act as translator, then?"

After a short pause, the dapper man on the screen nodded. "Yes. The concept is somewhat limited, but accurate within its parameters. I will be 'the translator.'"

"And you are not physically as I see you on my screen?"

"No. This is merely an image designed to place you at ease. If I have erred or offended you, do not hesitate to say so. My knowledge of your customs is far from complete."

"You have not offended me. On the contrary, I find you most charming. I was just curious as to whether the beings who created you were human, too."

"PROBE created me."

"Then the beings who created PROBE."

"I do not know if the Makers have human form, although logic decrees that it is highly unlikely."

200

"I don't understand," Mrs. Meriweather said. "You don't know who created . . . uh, PROBE?"

"PROBE has not allowed me access to that data."

"Does PROBE know of these Makers?"

"Yes."

"Perhaps you could ask it my question then."

"PROBE refuses to answer."

"It isn't important," Mrs. Meriweather said, backing away from the sensitive subject with the trained reflexes of a diplomat. "I assume you learned to speak our language by monitoring our holovision broadcasts?"

"Yes. There are signals more than a century old stored in memory. And, of course, we have watched your people's reactions to the discovery of our presence."

"Oh?"

"Yes. You will have to explain the deeper meanings inherent in your speech to the General Assembly last September."

"You saw it?"

"Yes, of course. Although many of the allusions were necessarily obscure to a nonhuman, I found it most enjoyable. You are to be congratulated on your oratory skills, Mrs. Meriweather."

"Why, thank you, SURROGATE. And you may call me Agusta if you like."

"Thank *you*, Agusta. Now, to save time, I suggest that we begin the preliminaries prior to the arrival of your delegation of negotiators. I am sure you wish to ask me many things, and I have a number of questions for you."

"By all means, let us waste no more time."

Eric Stassel arrived at the rendezvous three days after the probe. He, Greg Zapata, Bernie Whitnauer, and Roger Kingsley suited up and exited through the small courier ship's airlock. Instead of crossing open space to get to the flagship, they entered a half-complete docking sphere that engineers were feverishly attaching to *Bernadotte*'s prow. The structure was sufficiently complete to allow cargo and personnel transfer without taking spin off the ship. The four men pulled themselves hand over hand along cables strung amid naked I-beams and half-welded hull plates. They were halfway across when they caught sight of the probe. . . .

Ten minutes later Stassel knocked on Admiral Liu's door and entered. His boss glanced up from his work and noted the look on his executive officer's face. "You've seen the probe close up for the first time, I take it."

Stassel nodded.

"I know what you're going through. There were a lot of gaping mouths around here seventy-two hours ago, mine included."

"Yes, sir. I didn't realize . . ."

"You didn't realize what, Major?"

"It's like nothing I've ever seen before. It exudes a feeling of . . . of . . ."

"Ancient power?" Liu asked.

Stassel nodded. "Like an old and rare museum piece. Why, it must have been old when Socrates was a boy! And just think of how far it's come!"

"You look tired, Major. Bad trip?"

Stassel shook his head. "Bad two months. Remind me next time to pick someone other than Roger Kingsley and Bernie Whitnauer to be cooped up with. Those two have a talent for getting on each others' nerves. We got some good data, though. Bernie says we've got a shot of the probe's jettisoning an empty fuel tank. I wouldn't know about that. It looks just like any other blob of light to me."

"Well, turn it over to Analysis Section and have them offer an opinion. After that, take the rest of the night off. I want you chipper tomorrow come first watch. We've a lot of preparations ahead of us. A medium-size UN delegation is coming up from Earth. They'll be here in ninety-six hours. Stan Ames reports the Pan-Africans are well represented."

"Pan-Africans? What the hell are they doing on a negotiating committee? Surely they haven't come around to our point of view?"

"Colonel Ames thinks they may be up to no good."

"What can they do now that they've been confronted with a fait accompli?"

Admiral Liu looked at Stassel with his one good eye. "I'd give up my place on the promotion list to have the answer to that question, Major. In the meantime, you're off duty until oh eight-hundred hours tomorrow morning."

202

Stassel nodded. "Thank you, sir. I think I'll take a bath before tracking down Brea."

Liu nodded, wrinkling his nose slightly. "From where I sit, Major, that is an excellent idea."

Stassel found Brea in a corridor near the office of the astronomy team. She was engaged in animated conversation with an older, gray-haired woman, but glanced up as he rounded a corner and froze in midgesture. A full second passed before she screamed with delight and launched herself in his direction.

Brea showered his face with wet kisses while he pulled her tight, luxuriating in the feel of her in his arms. After a minute or two, Stassel reluctantly disentangled himself. "Miss me?" he asked, holding her at arms' length so he could look her over.

"Of course I missed you!" Brea said breathlessly. "But you aren't supposed to be here for another three hours. Why didn't you tell me you were coming in early, you stinker?"

"Would you believe a tail wind?"

Only after he and Brea had finished another round of kisses did Stassel notice her companion standing at a discreet distance. He stiffened as he recognized Agusta Meriweather.

Brea looked over her shoulder, saw Mrs. Meriweather staring at them with a small smile on her face, and guessed the reason for Stassel's sudden nervousness. "Oh, pooh! Agusta has seen people necking before, haven't you, Agusta?"

"I'm not that old, Brea." Mrs. Meriweather chuckled. "People stopped necking in my great-grandmother's era. We grappled in my day."

"Well, you know what I meant."

Mrs. Meriweather smiled and offered her hand to Stassel. "We meet again, Major. How have you been?"

He took her hand and shook it. "Busy, ma'am."

"Not as busy as Brea and I, I'll wager. She's my assistant now. I don't know what I'd do without her."

Brea nodded. "Busy doesn't quite describe it. Come on, Eric, we were just going to the lounge for a drink before dinner. You can join us."

"As a matter of fact, I can. The boss gave me the night off."

"Wonderful!"

At the lounge, Stassel sat in one side of a booth with Brea while Mrs. Meriweather sat opposite them. She lifted her glass of sparkling white wine in a toast. "To the probe," she said. "May it eventually find what it's looking for."

Stassel and Brea clinked glasses with her and sipped from their own drinks. When he'd replaced his low-gee glass on the table, Stassel looked at each woman in turn. "Would someone tell me what I just drank to?"

"You mean you haven't heard the news?" Brea asked. "The probe told Agusta its whole story right after rendezvous. It's in all the papers on Earth."

"I've been out of touch, remember?"

"That's right," she said, giggling in a manner that turned his statement into a double-entendre. "Listen to this. . . ."

Brea launched into the story of the Makers and their search for the secret of a faster-than-light drive. The telling took nearly twenty minutes. Mrs. Meriweather watched Stassel carefully, puzzled at his lack of excitement. By the time Brea finished her tale, he had lapsed into silence with a scowl on his face.

"You don't seem impressed, Major Stassel," Mrs. Meriweather observed. "Aren't you moved by the sheer audacity of these Makers? They find themselves stuck in one stellar system and devise this grandiose scheme for exploring the universe by proxy. Think of the sheer patience involved."

"I'm more concerned with the implications," Stassel said.

"What implications?"

"Isn't it obvious? Our only real chance for survival is to get out among the stars. Yet these Makers have a couple of million years' head start on us and they haven't cracked the problem of Einstein's barrier yet. If they can't find a way around the relativity equations, what chance have we?"

"You didn't let me get to the best part, Eric!" Brea said, tugging at his sleeve.

"What Brea is trying to say, Major Stassel, is that we have just come from an interview with the probe. The discussion turned to the problem of building a faster-than-light drive. I asked why, if FTL is possible, a superlight starship hasn't already called at the Maker sun. After all, in a galaxy as large as our own, you would think that someone out there would already have licked the problem—which, if you think about it, is the motivating assumption behind the Maker *Life Probe* program. They can't invent it at home, so they go looking for it abroad." Mrs. Meriweather turned to Brea with a conspiratorial look on her face.

"You tell him, Brea."

Brea nodded eagerly. "SURROGATE agreed that it was strange that a species with FTL wouldn't soon be poking its nose all over. Then it dropped its bombshell. They've found it, Eric! PROBE and SURROGATE have found evidence of a superlight starship operating in the vicinity of Procyon. They plan to launch for there after we assist them with the overhaul."

"Whoa, there. Procyon is, let's see...twelve light-years away?"

"Close enough," Brea agreed.

"If these supermen are that close, how come they've never come here. With an FTL starship, it would be like a weekend jaunt to the Moon and back."

"Maybe they have and found us too primitive to interest them," Brea said. "Or maybe they just like to mind their own business."

Mrs. Meriweather drained her drink in one quick gulp and stood up. "A good question, Major. We will have to investigate it most carefully. Now, I had best get the news off to Earth."

"Do you need my help, Agusta?" Brea asked. By her tone and the way she wrapped herself around Stassel's right arm, it was obvious she was volunteering more from duty than enthusiasm.

"Wouldn't you rather have the night off with your young man, Brea? Silly question. You have it. Have fun, and don't let anyone tell you that there isn't a little romance left in this withered carcass of mine. See you in the morning."

Mrs. Meriweather noted with amusement that the major and his lady had already tuned her out of their awareness. Their world had shrunk to two. She turned to leave. Before she was halfway to the comm center, she was singing quietly to herself.

Oh, to be young again!

CHAPTER 23

UNS *Konstantin Tsiolkovsky* made her approach to *Count Bernadotte* four days after Eric Stassel resumed his duties as Project executive officer. The heavy cruiser had departed Earth orbit five days earlier with the UN General Assembly's negotiating committee onboard. Normally, approach and docking for her landing boats would have been handled as a matter of routine. But the density of VIPs onboard was such that Admiral Liu ordered his second in command to oversee the operation.

Stassel sat at *Bernadotte*'s command console and watched the bridge viewscreen as the two boats made their careful approach to the docking sphere. So far the operation had been uneventful. Even so, he was alert for trouble, if and when. Thus he answered the buzz from the communicator on watch in record time when it came.

"What is it, Gomez?"

"Sorry to bother you, Major, but *NV Asgard*'s captain sends her respects and requests permission to speak to you."

Stassel frowned. The *Asgard* was one of the mink-upholstered spaceliners that normally plied the Earth–Moon run. Its presence in solar orbit was—in Stassel's opinion, at least—a testimony to the lengths to which some would go in pursuit of a decadollar.

When the first wave of probe fever swept Earth, a promoter named Geoffrey Weems had chartered a ship to take tourists to greet the arriving alien spacecraft. When he heard the news, Admiral-General Maxwell asked the Trusteeship Council to ban civil traffic from the area of the probe. Weems countered by retaining a lawyer to appeal to a UN court in New York, citing the Freedom of Space Act. Eventually, a compromise was struck. *NV Asgard* was to delay her arrival until after the Peace Enforcers declared the area safe for civilian traffic, and even then, she would be under direct orders of the PE commander on the scene.

Admiral Liu had expressed his opinion of the arrangement in a few pithy Mandarin syllables. And later, when *Asgard*'s captain had requested initial approach clearance and vectors, he'd ordered her to remain a minimum of one hundred kilometers from the fleet. To make sure that his dictum was followed, he had Sky Watch formalize it with a traffic directive:

Henceforth, and until further notice, all traffic will avoid the hundred-kilometer-radius sphere centered on coordinates 72.03/00.00/1.0 *Earth Relative*. The only exceptions shall be those vessels cleared for approach by the Peace Enforcement Directorate or its designees.
—by Order of Sky Watch, *Galileo Station*.

Stassel sympathized with Captain Rieger of *Asgard*. Her passengers had each paid a small fortune to spend ten days at the rendezvous point, only to find that they could have had as good a view at home. The one thing they *would* get, however, was their full ten days. Captain Rieger had been quick to note that leaving earlier would cause her company to forfeit the passengers' fares. Stassel wondered what a shipload of tourists could do for ten days even if given free clearance to approach the probe. The excitement of mankind's first visitor from the stars would wear off quickly for the average tourist.

He stabbed for the accept button on his console. The workscreen in front of him lit to reveal a gray-haired woman wearing the comets of a merchant space captain on her collar. She looked ill at ease.

"How are they holding up, Captain Rieger?"

"Better than expected. As long as the liquor holds out, that is."

"What can I do for you?"

"I'm sorry to bother you, Major, and I wouldn't have done so if it hadn't been important."

"Could we speed this up, Captain? I'm right in the middle of a docking approach."

"By all means." She nodded. "I have a passenger aboard who wishes to disembark. Since we are now officially in a parking orbit, I cannot refuse his request. To do so would subject my company to legal action. I hope you understand, Major."

"I understand," Stassel said curtly. "However, I can and do refuse permission. That should get you off the hook. If he gives you any more trouble, clap him in irons."

"That might not be easy to do. He has already departed. Apparently he had both a vacsuit and a long-range maneuvering unit in his luggage. We responded to the OPEN AIRLOCK alarm two minutes ago but were too late to stop him."

"Thank you for the warning. *Bernadotte* out!" Stassel keyed for intraship communications.

A Marine answered the screen. "Sergeant Faraday, Security."

"Faraday, this is the exec. We've got some fool out of *Asgard* headed this way in a vacsuit. He could be a newsman, or a fanatic, or just some simpleminded citizen. I want two of your scooters to intercept him before he can get near the probe. Tell them to be careful but not to shoot unless forced into it. Get on it!"

"Yes, sir!"

As the sergeant's features were fading, Stassel received a call from Admiral Liu. He quickly summarized the problem and what he'd done about it.

"Very good, Major. *Tsiolkovsky*'s boats are docking now. Turn over your post to the officer of the watch and get up here for the welcome. We'll find out what this sightseer is doing after we get through with the committee."

"Yes, sir."

Stassel passed his command to Commander Harmon, one of the PE Navy men who had manned *Bernadotte* during the move from the Earth–Sun Lagrangian point. After Harmon had formally taken the duty, Stassel hurried to the nearest lift, boosted to the axis of the ship, and then pulled himself hand over hand toward the bow along a cable strung through the axis corridor.

At the bow, the thick armor of *Bernadotte*'s hull had been bored through and an airlock installed. A Marine honor guard was drawn up and maintaining Present Arms. Stassel joined the line of dignitaries opposite them.

Mrs. Meriweather was first in line. Her feet were in clamp boots too large for her and her frail form wafted slightly in the breeze from the ventilators. Next to her stood Admiral Liu and, beside him, Professor Roquette. In all, seven or eight Project Eaglet staff were between Stassel and the airlock. Brea Gallagher was two places from Stassel.

The airlock opened and the first of the UN delegation floated into the axis corridor. They milled about in the manner characteristic of people unused to weightlessness. Mrs. Meriweather and Admiral Liu greeted each of them in turn and then passed them off, literally, to several Marine guides who did their best to assist the newcomers to the lift. Stassel took the opportunity to exchange places with Ellie Crocker, who had the place next to Brea's in the receiving line. He momentarily slipped his arm around Brea's waist.

She looked up at him and smiled. "Glad to see you could make it."

"Me too." He gestured at the two dozen people who were pulling themselves toward the lift with varying degrees of success. "Is this the committee?"

"Just the staff members, political assistants, secretaries, research assistants, cooks, and companions. The VIPs are all on the second boat."

It took ten minutes or so to clear the traffic jam. By that time Stassel and Brea had helped several queasy people who had managed to get themselves stranded in midair. The receiving line then reformed for the next batch of dignitaries.

The next group was smaller than the first—only a dozen—and the individuals were much more conscious of their dignity. Stassel recognized several people, including the assistant ambassador from the North American Union and the European ambassador. The most famous member of the committee was its chairman, Enrique Malagar, the man most political pundits were touting as the next secretary-general. As they came through the airlock, each stopped for a few moments to have a word with Mrs. Meriweather and shake Admiral Liu's hand. Each was then turned over to a pair of Marine guides.

The next-to-last face out of the airlock was one Stassel had no trouble recognizing. He had seen those same features staring from the holoscreen on the day of the U.N. debate. The last committee member to board *Bernadotte* was Ambassador Nicholas Boswani from the Pan-African Federation. Stassel wondered briefly if the symbolism was intentional.

Ambassador Boswani appeared to have no more experience in weightless movement than any other member of the group. He pulled himself clumsily to where Mrs. Meriweather was standing, shook hands, and was introduced to Admiral Liu. Stassel's eyes were immediately drawn to the man behind the ambassador. Unlike the others, he handled himself with the unconscious ease of a spaceman.

Boswani turned to Mrs. Meriweather and gestured toward the newcomer. "Agusta, my dear, I don't believe you know my aide, Colonel Yorubi M'Buto."

"I haven't had the pleasure," she said, turning to M'Buto. "Colonel, if I may, I would like to introduce Admiral Liu Tsen, military commander of this fleet."

M'Buto extended his hand. "An honor, Admiral."

"And for me as well," Liu said.

Stassel thought he noted a coolness in his boss's manner, but then decided that he might be reading too much into the admiral's normal reserve. His attention returned to Boswani, who was conversing in low tones with Mrs. Meriweather.

". . . so when do we meet this mechanical bug-eyed monster of yours, Agusta?"

"As soon as you wish, Nicholas. However, I would recommend that you wait until after you've been briefed. The briefings will last approximately two days and should bring everyone up to date on what we've learned since the probe arrived." She laughed. "Even a diplomat can do his job better if he knows what he is talking about. Don't you agree?"

Boswani's answer was noncommittal. Admiral Liu directed

Boswani and M'Buto toward the lift lock, where the last of the committee members were waiting. As they passed Stassel's position, the admiral halted.

"Mr. Ambassador, Colonel M'Buto, may I introduce my second in command, Major Stassel?"

The ambassador muttered a polite comment, but M'Buto's eyes lit up. "Ah, yes. Major Stassel directed the original effort that culminated in Project Eaglet. That was an excellent piece of work, Major. You are to be congratulated." He turned to Brea, somehow managed to bow even while anchoring himself to the corridor cable, and kissed her hand.

"And this must be the lady who started it all! It was a fateful day for the human race when you happened to spot that flash of light in the sky, Mrs. Gallagher."

Brea blushed.

M'Buto glanced up at her, his eyes two white circles in a sea of ebon. "I suppose only time will tell whether it was a good fate or an evil one."

Stassel felt a rush of anger at M'Buto's comment. The colonel seemed not to notice as he excused himself and led the way to the lift lock, moving with the fluid motion of a fish in water. When he had gone, Stassel turned to Brea. "Who the hell does he think he is?"

"It's not important, Eric."

"Somehow, I don't think I'm going to like Colonel M'Buto."

Stassel was still angry when he returned to the bridge. Commander Harmon looked up, read the signs of agitation, and decided that it wasn't the moment for idle chitchat.

"They caught our sightseer, Major," he said.

"Was he trying for the probe?"

Harmon shook his head. "That's the strange part of it all. He was headed directly here from *Asgard*. They stripped and searched him aboard *Gottmann*. No bombs or weapons of any kind. Also, no identification, and he refuses to talk to anyone but the admiral."

"Have they x-rayed him?"

"No, sir."

"Well, have them put him under a scanner and not worry about being gentle about it. If he's clean, have them send him over under guard. I'll be in my office."

"Yes, sir."

Half an hour later there was a knock on Stassel's door. He turned to face the entry and called out for his visitors to enter.

The door opened and a grim Marine guard ushered the prisoner inside. The prisoner stepped through the hatchway and locked eyes with his captor. He wasn't exactly what Stassel had expected. For one thing, he was fat, bordering on obese. He strained at the seams of the Navy Fatigues he wore and tended to waddle when he walked. His neck was hidden by a triple chin and his fingers reminded Stassel of oversize Vienna sausages. Stassel wondered briefly how the man had managed a medical clearance to lift from Earth, let alone found a vacsuit to fit him.

The man's gaze swept over Stassel and his office. "You're not Liu!"

"I'm his exec."

"I don't talk to anyone but the admiral."

Stassel drummed his fingers on his desk top and glared at his visitor. Finally he leaned forward and said: "You talk to me or we throw you in the brig. Now, who are you and what the hell are you doing here?"

The man hesitated, then shrugged. He chuckled, reached into the breast pocket of his overalls, and pulled out a plastic card. "My credentials."

Stassel took the card. The man's picture graced the upper right-hand corner. Opposite it, however, were two items of more immediate interest—the eagle of the North American Union and the sigil of the Bureau of External Security. The card read simply:

Murray Danziger
Field Agent

Stassel scrutinized the card while wondering how one went about recognizing a counterfeit. The photo didn't look much like the man before him, but that proved nothing. Stassel's ID picture didn't bear a particularly good likeness either. Stassel ordered the guard to wait in the corridor. When the Marine had closed the door, Stassel waved the card in the North American agent's face. "I had a report that you were without identification."

"We have our ways, Major."

"I'm sure you do. I would like to know what they are so that I can judge whether to have you searched again."

Danziger bit his lower lip and then nodded. "Being a bit overweight—as you've undoubtedly noticed—I have a lot of spare padding. I had a pocket surgically implanted in my left thigh. It's lined with a special plastic and is just right for concealing that card in your hand. If I'm careful about getting the edges of the incision lined up properly, the opening looks like scar tissue left over from an old operation."

"Why is a North American BES agent cruising space in a vacsuit fifty million klicks from home?"

Danziger shook his head slowly from side to side. "Sorry, Major, but I really must insist on seeing Admiral Liu. What I have to say is too important for anyone but the top man. And I would suggest that you hurry."

"Why, Mr. Danziger?"

"I saw two landing boats docked in the sphere just now. Those are from the cruiser that brought the UN Committee, are they not?"

"Yes."

"Then Colonel M'Buto is already aboard?"

"How do you know M'Buto?"

Danziger laughed. "He and I are in the same business. You might say we're not-so-friendly competitors. Let's see, we last chatted about six months ago in that Hawaiian joint aboard *Earth Station One*."

"The Islander Bar?"

Danziger nodded. "That's the one."

"What were you two doing aboard *ESO*?"

"We were there for the same reason everyone else was, trying to find out why you PEs had kidnapped half the scientists on Earth. Now, Major, I'm afraid that is all I can say until I see your boss. Sorry, but I've got my orders."

"The admiral is up to his ass in dignitaries at the moment, Mr. Danziger. Perhaps later."

"I suggest that you peel him loose now. What I have to say won't wait."

"I'm waiting," Liu said.

Danziger and Stassel were seated opposite Liu's desk while

two Marines guarded the corridor outside. The admiral held the BES identification lightly in his fingers, examining front and back as though his good eye were a microscope.

Danziger leaned back in his chair, cupped his hands over his ample stomach, and let his backbone sag into the cushions. He reached up to rub the bridge of his nose and then sighed.

"I guess the best place to start is with one of our operatives named Henry Philbin. Old Hank was a planetologist by trade and worked for us part time as a sort of hobby. Four years ago he took a sabbatical from the cow college where he taught and arranged with one of the Belt companies to serve a stint on their payroll. He had some crackpot idea about how planets are formed and needed fieldwork to flesh out his theory. I don't have all the details, but I understand part of his proof involved precise radar measurements of the orbits of enough asteroids to give him a statistically valid sample. He planned to run his data through a computer and, if he was lucky, come up with a model of the Belt at the time it formed.

"Since Hank was a part timer and a free citizen, we didn't pay too much attention to his plans. About six months later, though, we began to get reports from him claiming irregularities in some of the shipping schedules out in the Belt. Seems his radar setup not only recorded the velocity vectors of the local flotsam and jetsam but also those of departing and arriving spacecraft. Hank must have gotten curious and began back-plotting the trajectories of various freighters.

"What he found was that a significant percentage of the ships of one particular nation were going places other than those listed on their flight plans. Care to guess which nation?"

"Pan-Africa, of course," Liu said.

Danziger nodded. "Direct hit, Admiral. Unfortunately for our side, Hank Philbin ended up outside a Pallas airlock minus his suit shortly thereafter. Murder, of course. I came aboard about that time. You see, we had also heard rumors off and on about a thriving business in unregistered singularities. To make a long story short, the BES decided to investigate the situation to find out what the hell was going on."

"Why didn't you turn the problem over to us?" Stassel asked.

Danziger laughed. "Your people don't tell us what they're doing. Why should we be any more considerate?"

Stassel began to respond but was silenced by Admiral Liu, who said, "Go on, Mr. Danziger."

"Well, the investigation has moved with glacial speed. Among the things we did learn, however, was that the Pan-Africans are definitely engaged in some sort of scam. They are buying all manner of equipment needed to outfit a space vessel, including some they aren't supposed to have—things that can be used in weapons-grade lasers and missiles, for instance. The plot appears to be based in the Belt and also aboard several of the Lagrangian settlements. And my old nemesis, Yorubi M'Buto, seems to be *numero uno* in the operation.

"We managed to identify a couple of M'Buto's agents inboard *Galileo Station* and were getting close to cracking the mystery when this probe thing came along and messed up everything. Our investigation did yield a number of interesting holograms just prior to that time, however." Danziger handed a microrecord cube to Stassel. Stassel's eyebrows lifted in an unspoken question.

Danziger shrugged. "I must have overlooked mentioning my other kangaroo pouch, Major. Glad to get rid of that cube. It was damned uncomfortable to sit on."

Stassel slipped the cube into the reader on the admiral's desk and activated the controls. The holoscreen showed a scene lit by the greenish glow of an image intensifier. A green-and-white ghostlike figure stared out of the screen. The image was too blurred to identify the subject, but Stassel had a definite impression that the face was familiar. Danziger touched a control. This time they were looking through a crowd at two men seated at a cafe table. The scene changed again, and one was handing the other a card marked with the logo of the Bank of Galileo Station.

The hologram was of excellent quality, showing the men in clear profile with sufficient clarity that they looked as though they were in the room with the three observers. Stassel had no trouble recognizing them.

They were Angai Yahaya and Don Bailey.

"Explain this, Mr. Danziger," Admiral Liu said.

"Isn't it obvious?" Danziger responded. "Yahaya is paying off Bailey, probably for smuggling an I-mass to *Galileo Station* for energizing. We think the Pan-Af's need I-masses for a

215

phantom fleet they've been building in direct violation of the Space Disarmament Act."

"When was this taken?"

"Last Space Day."

"So why tell us now?"

"We've managed to plant an agent on the outskirts of the Pan-African operation. Not far enough in to get good, hard intelligence, you understand, but able to pick up rumors. Our operative got wind of something big brewing and my superiors decided that I had best be on the scene to monitor developments."

"Why pull that *Asgard* stunt?" Stassel asked. "Why not go directly to UN Headquarters and arrange official transport?"

Danziger swiveled in his seat and looked at Stassel. "Haven't done much cloak-and-daggering, have you, Major?"

"Haven't done any."

"Well, what you are suggesting would have been too straightforward for a devious old rascal such as myself. Also, it would have been far too public. I suggest that you send me back to that destroyer I just came from before M'Buto gets wind of my presence."

"You haven't told us what this big operation is, Mr. Danziger," Admiral Liu said.

"I haven't, have I? Its name is Project Isandhlwana, which is interesting enough in itself. The Battle of Isandhlwana is where the Zulus kicked hell out of the British in the late nineteenth century. Our operative reported a closed-door meeting of the Pan-African Ruling Council nearly two months ago. The subject was the probe and serious enough for them to spend *twenty-six hours* over two days discussing it. Whatever was decided is being implemented at this very moment."

Admiral Liu leaned back in his chair and gazed at Danziger. His expression was troubled. He seemed deep in thought for a few seconds, and then straightened up and turned to Stassel.

"Have you made any recent progress on your investigation into the attempt on the communications center?"

"No, sir. The directorate is still running background checks on about half the suspects, and I wasn't able to do much while stuck out in the Lagrangian point."

"Are Yahaya and Bailey still on your list of suspects?"

"Yes, sir. High on it!"

"In that event, Major, I order the arrest of Angai Yahaya and Don Bailey. The charges are suspicion of breach of security. We'll hold Mr. Danziger's suspicions in reserve to avoid alerting the wrong people."

"Yes, sir!"

CHAPTER 24

Independent Prospector *Liar's Luck* backed toward its destination on a ten-kilometer tail of plasma fire. Inside the control cabin, Don Bailey anxiously scanned status displays while keeping one hand wrapped lightly around the control stick and the other poised over the firing controls. Beads of sweat flowed across his face, pulled aft by the force of the deceleration. A deep-throated roar thrummed from the surrounding bulkheads.

Suddenly the all-enveloping engine noise was gone as was the pressure on Bailey's chest. Bailey's fingers danced across the computer keyboard before him. Seconds later his console beeped for attention as the ship's high-gain antenna found and locked on its target. Bailey keyed for ship-to-ship communications.

"*Liar's Luck* calling *Bernadotte* Approach Control."

A voice with a hint of the British Isles responded almost instantly. "Approach Control to *Liar's Luck*. We've been monitoring your burn. Go ahead, please."

"Roger, Control. We are nine days out of lunar orbit with

a load of structural steel. We are one hundred kilometers aft-orbit of your position and closing. Request instructions for final approach and rendezvous."

"Understood, *Liar*. Squirt your vectors when ready."

"Mass and velocity information coming . . . *now*!"

A quick burst of computer data hissed on the audio link.

"Data received. What is your destination?"

"Boneyard Six."

"Course information coming back to you, *Liar*. Guide it down the groove when ready. You are cautioned to avoid entering the inner restricted zone."

"Will do, Control. *Liar's Luck* out."

"Approach Control, out."

Bailey turned his head to glance at his copilot. "Well," he asked, "do you want to set up this approach?"

Lisa Moore, whose diminutive form was strapped into the right acceleration couch, stared at him with wide eyes. She had been following his exchange with Approach Control with youthful concentration.

"May I, Uncle Don?"

"Everyone's got to learn sometime. Just make sure to double check that data before using it. Our cargo will put a considerable dent in our employer's ship if it gets away from us."

Lisa bent over her readouts, rechecking the Approach Control figures. Bailey watched her technique without appearing to do so. When he was satisfied with her progress, he turned his attention to their cargo.

From where he sat, it was impossible to see much of the load except for the sunlit ends of a half-dozen large I-beams. In his mind's eye, however, he could see the whole length of the unwieldy mass as it had been in lunar orbit. The cargo had been assembled into a unit by welding straps across the I-beams, and the structure had been attached to *Liar*'s nose through a massive thrust frame. The arrangement reminded Bailey of nothing quite so much as a Mississippi tugboat pushing its kilometer-long string of barges upriver.

Except this barge had a nasty tendency toward dynamic instability. Balanced as it was, it threatened to tumble out of control at any instant. Constantly correcting the ship's thrust vector to keep it pointed through the center of mass for the seven hours it took to climb to 200 km/sec cruising speed had left him with stomach twinges and a soaked jumpsuit.

"What's the matter, Uncle Don?" Lisa asked, noting the pained look on his face.

"Nothing serious, hon. I'm just unwinding from the tension of herding this load of iron."

"You shouldn't do it if it makes you sick."

He laughed humorlessly. "I didn't have a whole lot of choice, young lady."

Nor had he. In retrospect, he had made his mistake six months earlier when he asked for the appointment with Admiral Liu to discuss returning to Cères.

"You wish to leave us?" Liu had asked, his good eye rock steady on Bailey.

"Yes, sir. The news is out, so there's no reason to keep me here. The sooner I get back to doing what I do best, the better. Next year's mortgage payment isn't that far off."

Liu nodded. "Perhaps I can be of assistance, Mr. Bailey. Your vessel is Calverton Shipyards, Model VII, prospector class, is she not?"

Bailey grunted his affirmation. He didn't like the way the conversation was headed.

"Calverton made a good ship before they went bankrupt. And fairly powerful, I believe."

Bailey nodded. "Nothing like the big tugs, of course, but she's got legs. Wouldn't be cost effective otherwise. The number of strikes a ship makes during its useful life is a function of the number of rocks it checks. That means fast, hyperbolic orbits."

"And short vacations?"

"And short vacations," Bailey agreed. "This one is already three times longer than I can afford. By the time I get back to Ceres, I'll have lost nearly a year out of my life."

"I understand your problem and I think I can help you solve it. I would like to charter your ship, Mr. Bailey. We find ourselves short of transport, especially during the first six months after the probe's arrival. Your ship could take up some of the slack."

"Me, a truck driver? No, thank you, Admiral."

"We'll make you a good offer, one which will allow you to meet your payments and make a handsome profit besides."

"Look, Admiral, I'm my own boss and I like it that way."

Liu had leaned back in his chair and stared thoughtfully at Bailey. "We could always confiscate your ship, I suppose."

"That's blackmail!"

Liu nodded. "I believe some people would call it that."

Bailey locked eyes with Liu. Finally he swallowed hard and said. "Admiral, did anyone ever tell you that you were a first-class sonofabitch?"

Liu threw back his head and laughed. "Mr. Bailey, how else do you think I became an admiral?"

And so Don Bailey had found himself hauling cargo on the Earth run.

"I'm ready, Uncle Don," Lisa said after she had verified the approach data.

"Okay, begin your countdown. Keep one hand on the control stick so you'll be ready in case the automatics fail. How long a burst are you giving us?"

"Twelve seconds."

"Watch your range, then. Make sure you're throttled way back. Don't want to fry anyone with our exhaust. Stand by . . . five. . . four . . . three . . . two . . . one . . . hit it, hon!"

Liar's engine coughed to life and a gentle hand pressed them into their couches. Twelve seconds later they were stationary with respect to the amalgamation of sky junk that had grown up around *Count Bernadotte*.

Dismounting the load of steel was a twenty-minute job for one man in a vacsuit. Bailey sweated under the hot sun, grunting occasionally as he released the shackles on the thrust frame. When he had them free, he rotated his body to place his boots against the nose of the ship and his back against the thick plate that had been tack-welded to the girders. He strained to straighten his legs. The girders were weightless but still had their full momentum. It took a sixty-second effort to produce any detectable motion.

He straightened up, letting the ghost of Sir Isaac Newton— and his First Law of Motion—continue the job of separating the cargo from his ship. By the time he'd pulled himself to the midship airlock, removed his suit, and returned to the acceleration couch in the control bubble, the load was separated from *Liar* by two meters of vacuum and receding slowly.

"Time to go home," Bailey said.

221

It took half an hour to nudge *Liar* slowly through the mass of ships to its assigned position in the fleet. Another twenty minutes were eaten up in preparing the ship for station keeping—checking the automatic controls that would keep it in position, powering down the mass converter, checking the emergency circuits that maintained the magnetic fields that imprisoned the I-mass.

By the time *Liar* was secured and Bailey and Lisa had gathered up their personal belongings, there was a gentle bump against the side of the ship, followed immediately by the sound of thrusters compensating for the resulting drift.

"The taxi's here, Uncle Don."

Bailey nodded. "And none too soon. I can taste that first cold beer in the Staff Lounge now!"

They pulled themselves up the central passageway to the airlock and cycled it open. Instead of the grizzled bosun who ran the fleet taxi service, however, Bailey found himself face to face with a vacsuited Marine sergeant. Behind him, framed by four open airlock doors that led into a ship considerably larger than an orbital taxi, were two similarly attired enlisted men holding riot guns at the ready.

"Donel Bailey?" the sergeant asked, his voice tinny as it issued from his helmet speaker.

Bailey nodded.

"I have a warrant for your arrest. Please come with me."

Eric Stassel was working out in *Bernadotte*'s gymnasium for the first time in days. After Danziger had been shipped back to *Gottmann* to be put on ice, Admiral Liu had spent nearly three hours in his cabin preparing a report to be transmitted to headquarters in his personal code.

Twelve hours later he had received a coded reply and Stassel was ordered to report to the admiral's cabin.

"We've problems, Major," Liu had said as soon as Stassel seated himself. "Headquarters has heard the same rumors as Danziger's people, but in considerably less detail. They're worried that the Pan-Africans could be constructing an illegal war fleet. Unfortunately, with no proof that they've done anything wrong, we can't move against the Pan-Afs officially. We can't even call a Class Three emergency without making it seem as if we were harboring a grudge over their opposition to the probe.

"My message to Admiral-General Maxwell did some good, though. He became concerned enough to pull elements of the fleet quietly back to positions where they can form a picket line to guard Earth against attack from space. In the meantime, the directorate will concentrate on finding that secret PA base. That's good news for everyone but us. We're much too far from the Earth to benefit from the buildup. In fact, we're being weakened by it. *Cape of Good Hope* is being pulled out for picket-line duty."

Stassel blinked. "Danziger said the probe is the focal point of whatever is going on. They should form the fleet here, not at home."

Liu shook his head. "They can't take that chance. We'll have to provide for our own protection . . . and the probe's."

"How the hell do we do that?"

"We have *Gottmann*."

Stassel snorted. "She's only a light destroyer. She wouldn't las ten minutes in a real fight."

"Agreed. That's why we will also reactivate *Count Bernadotte*'s armament. What's the matter, Major? Don't like the idea?"

"It's not that, sir. I'll grant you that they don't build them like *Bernie* any more. But we don't know what shape the old girl's weapons are in. The weapons pods have been sealed since we came aboard. No one's been inside one in nearly fifty years."

Liu nodded. "True enough. However, I've done some checking of the records. *Bernadotte* was mothballed during one of the periodic debates over military spending that occurred throughout the twenties. Surprisingly, she had just completed an overhaul when they shipped her to the boneyard."

"That explains why everything was so spit and polish when we took over."

"I want you to get her in fighting trim," Liu said. "We'll be receiving munitions and personnel in two weeks. Unfortunately, that may be too late. So, in the meantime, we'll steal *Hope* and *Tsiolkovsky* blind of both men and material before they space for home. By the time headquarters finds out, it'll be too late for them to do anything about it. I want *Bernadotte* ready to fight in no more than seven days."

Stassel whistled. "That's a tall order, sir. What about Ambassador Boswani and Colonel M'Buto?"

"What about them?"

"If they're planning an attack, all this activity will tip them off to the fact that we're on to them."

"Arresting Yahaya's already done that. We'll just have to keep them off balance somehow. Begin by placing the weapons decks off limits. If anyone asks, tell them we're converting the ship into a permanent headquarters for the probe's overhaul. In the meantime, we'll put the entire committee in cold storage. Luckily, the decision to shift negotiations to *Concordiate* is just what the doctor ordered. . . ."

Stassel hefted an oversize barbell, grunting under the strain as he thought about the previous several days of hectic activity. The crew that had originally prepared *Bernadotte* for Project Eaglet had made sure that the Space Disarmament Act was followed to the letter. Each laser mount, missile launch module, and autocannon control room had been sealed by welding the access hatches to their frames. The old blast ship had been designed with each offensive weapons platform encased in its own cocoon of armor plate. The theory had been to limit damage from a weapons malfunction and to provide independent fire-control centers in case the ship was holed or partially destroyed. Breaking into the centers took hours of careful carving with a plasma cutting torch.

Once inside, the old systems had to be powered-up, checked, and repaired. Decades of cosmic-rays sleeting had generally ruined the electronic fire-control mechanisms and deprogramed their supposedly permanent memory circuits. Each such problem meant hours of searching through old records for the tech manuals that governed the particular equipment, and more hours to develop and implement a work-around plan.

As a result, Stassel's crews had received less than eight hours' sleep in three nights. Even so, they had rebuilt only about one-quarter of the ship's main battery of lasers and hadn't even started on adapting *Cape of Good Hope*'s missiles to *Bernadotte*'s outmoded launchers.

"Eric!"

Brea's voice echoed through the gymnasium. Stassel slowly released tension on the spring system that substituted for a dead weight on the barbell. He lifted himself to a sitting position on the weight bench. She was obviously agitated and it wasn't hard to guess the cause. In fact, Stassel had been dreading the moment for days.

He made room for her on the bench. She sat down and he took her into his arms. She buried her face into his shoulder and began to sob as he lightly kissed her forehead. "What's the matter?" he asked, knowing what the answer would be.

"Lisa just told me Don's been arrested!"

"Yes, I know," he said as gently as he could.

It was as though he'd passed an electric current through her. Her head snapped erect and she looked into his eyes with horror. *"You know?"*

"I was there when Liu gave the order."

"But why, for God's sake?"

"The charge is attempted breach of security. We think Don was involved in the attempt to break into the communications center."

"But you arrested Angai Yahaya for that."

"We have reason to believe they may have been in it together."

"That's ridiculous!"

"Is it? How come neither mentioned they had met the other prior to being pulled into Project Eaglet?"

"Because they've never met!"

"We have photographic evidence showing them drinking together in *Galileo Station* last Space Day."

Brea was suddenly silent. She bit down hard on her lower lip as she fought to control her emotions. Finally she looked up at him, noting the red face and perspiration caused by his exertions.

"I don't believe it," she said, "but even if you do, that doesn't prove a thing. Of course Don was inboard *Galileo* that day. He was arranging to have *Liar* overhauled. If he ran across Yahaya during Mardi Gras, then it's only natural the two of them would have a drink together. After all, they are fellow countrymen."

"It isn't likely that Yahaya would have handed Don a credit voucher if he'd just been a casual acquaintance, is it?"

"A voucher?"

Stassel nodded. "We think Don was engaged in smuggling an unregistered I-mass from the belt to the *Galileo PowerStat* for energizing."

Brea suddenly pulled from his embrace. Something was in her expression that he couldn't identify. Finally he decided that it was fear mixed with defiance. "Then you're charging him with smuggling as well?"

He shook his head. "No evidence."

She took a deep breath, seemed to ponder her words carefully. "You realize, of course, that there is no way that Don could have smuggled an I-mass in *Liar* without my knowing about it."

Stassel nodded.

"Then why haven't you arrested me?"

"I told you—no evidence."

"Are you serious? Do you really think Don and I were smuggling?"

"Weren't you?" he asked. A knot had been growing in his stomach since he'd realized the implications of Danziger's allegations. In the last few minutes, the knot had spread to his entire abdomen.

"Would you believe me if I denied it?"

"Maybe."

"Well, don't put yourself out, *Major* Stassel. I stand on my rights as a North American citizen. If you think you have evidence of wrongdoing on my part, I urge you to do your duty and arrest me."

They suddenly found themselves in a frozen tableau, with both breathing hard, green eyes locked unblinking with blue. They stayed that way for nearly thirty seconds.

"I hope you understand something, Brea. If I do find the evidence, I *will* arrest you. I won't like it and I won't sleep very well afterward, but I'll do it. It's my job."

The gymnasium echoed with the *crack* of palm against cheek. He sat rigid as he watched her run sobbing from the compartment. Only after Brea's footsteps could no longer be heard echoing against steel deck did he probe gingerly at the red handprint forming on his cheek.

CHAPTER 25

The dual entities that were *Life Probe 53935* waited patiently for their hosts to organize themselves for serious negotiations. SURROGATE spent the time interviewing Agusta Meriweather and other selected humans. PROBE monitored these discussions even though it found humans as incomprehensible individually as they were en masse. It did note a change in SURROGATE, however. Its offspring's understanding of the bipeds of Sol III grew with each interview.

While SURROGATE engaged in furthering his education, PROBE put most of its attention to watching the surrounding fleet. It observed the comings and goings of the little, skittering work craft with the same intensity it devoted to the large interplanetary vessels. It noted the frenetic pace of individual vacuum-suited humans as they drove their various orbital construction projects toward completion. It watched the actinic flare of the welders, listened to the constant chatter on the workers' communications circuits, felt the continuous bombardment of high-speed oxygen and nitrogen molecules against its surface. These last were the result of outgassing from the human spacecraft, which were sieves by Maker standards.

It marked with special interest the arrival of the United Nations negotiating committee aboard *Konstantin Tsiolkovsky*. Simultaneously, it listened to the exchange between Eric Stassel and the captain of the *Asgard*, and turned its telescopes on the distant passenger liner. Dark, manlike shadows could be seen moving behind the lighted viewports on the liner's promenade deck. Later, PROBE pondered the sudden departures for Earth of the cruisers *Hope* and *Tsiolkovsky*. It noted similar maneuvers by a number of other UN warcraft and wondered at the cause. And while it observed the humans, it underwent a metamorphosis of its own.

That the Makers had built wisely had always been a given in PROBE's existence. Its successful thousand light-year journey was proof enough of their craftsmanship. But journey's end had been a catalyst of sorts, and PROBE was only now discovering the true extent of their skill.

For all of its existence PROBE had been a creature of interstellar space and, as such, was subjected to temperatures near absolute zero. Now, only 150 million kilometers distant from a fairly active star, its normal methods of cooling were woefully inadequate. At the first rise in temperature, however, those parts of PROBE in sunlight suddenly turned reflective. Surfaces in shadow became perfectly radiating black bodies, and mechanisms dormant since launch began to circulate excess heat to a series of large radiators.

Shortly after PROBE's achieving rendezvous, liquid helium began to boil off the central library of Maker knowledge deep in PROBE's innards. The library came alive, and not only the library. For buried deep within PROBE's core was a duplicate set of instructions to those Jurul had supplied just before launch. PROBE watched in amazement as whole banks of new memory came online of their own accord.

It studied the new knowledge for several thousand seconds, comparing it with the wisdom acquired in ten millennia of flight. Some of the discrepancies were surprising. Eventually, however, PROBE tired of introspection and turned to SURROGATE. "How long has it been since that committee boarded *Bernadotte*?"

"One hundred six hours, twenty minutes, thirteen seconds have passed since their landing craft docked with the larger ship," SURROGATE responded.

"And they aren't ready to begin discussions *yet*? Am I never to understand these creatures?"

SURROGATE considered whether the question might be rhetorical before realizing that rhetoric was a human weakness not shared by its parent. "I too find the delay difficult to understand. I have asked Brea Gallagher about it, but I fear that I may have missed the concept embodied in her explanation. Also, she seemed distressed and distracted, and her explanations were not as clear as usual."

"Surely she gave you some clue."

"She says that 'they are coming up to speed.'"

"Meaning?"

"It refers to assimilating data concerning us. The committee is hesitant to open negotiations without full knowledge of the circumstances that face them. They fear we will take advantage of their ignorance."

"How can we take advantage of them? We are the ones who are stranded, unable to move from this orbital position. Our only negotiating point is the speed with which we relinquish the Makers' data to them."

"I have explained all this to Agusta Meriweather," SURROGATE responded. "She says that she understands, but that we must be patient."

"What of the negotiators? Have you studied them as individuals?"

"I have cross-correlated all references in memory that speak of any member of the committee. They seem an unusually competent group. My largest file concerns the chairman, Mr. Malagar. He has twenty years' service in the human parliament. Most speak favorably of him. Many predict that he will be elected secretary-general when the incumbent steps down next year. Malagar spoke in support of the probe resolution during the debate."

"And the others?"

"Robert Kenzie, the North American, and Jacques Villart, the European, are supporters; as are Admiral Liu and Agusta Meriweather, representing the military and the bureaucracy respectively. Mr. Souvantavong, Mrs. Darvi, and Mr. Po are nominally opponents—having voted against the resolution—but all spoke of accepting the will of the majority after the vote. Our only true opponent is the Pan-African, Nicholas Boswani."

"The leader of the opposition?" PROBE asked.

"The same."

"Then Boswani is the key to the negotiations?"

"Yes. If we win him over, the opposition should cease. At the least, it will be leaderless."

"Then you will consider the best means of accomplishing such a goal."

"I have already considered the problem."

"Do you have a solution?"

"I have a number of possible solutions. However, I still lack sufficient understanding to know which is the correct one."

"Continue your efforts. We will wait for an opportunity to present itself."

The night after Don Bailey's arrest was a sleepless one for Brea Gallagher. The cause of her insomnia was equal parts worry for her partner and stress reaction to her fight with Eric. Through the long hours she was bedeviled by alternating waves of guilt and indignation. On the one hand, her conscience bothered her. Several times she decided to confess all to Eric. Always, however, her thoughts turned to the consequences of confession. The only thing keeping Don and her from being clapped in irons was the PEs' lack of hard evidence to prove they'd been smuggling. No matter what the Peace Enforcers suspected, if they couldn't prove it, they would eventually have to free Don.

The arrival of the new day aboard *Bernadotte* did nothing to resolve her quandary. She dragged her tired body from between tangled sheets; moved wearily to the tiny washbasin that adorned one bulkhead of her cabin; and dashed her smarting eyes with cold water. It didn't help. She toweled her face dry and glanced up to the mirror over the basin.

"How could you have been such a brass-plated fool? If only you hadn't let Don talk you into this mess. . . ." Her voice echoed strangely in the tiny cabin. She bit down hard on her lower lip and tasted blood as tears of rage flowed down her cheeks. Finally the storm within subsided. She dried her eyes and slipped into her best jumper. In spite of the fact that her personal life was in ruins around her, it was to be a big day because the committee was to meet the probe for the first time.

Brea sighed when she thought of the wrangling that had gone into this first negotiating session between probe and politicians. What had been scheduled as a two-day briefing had turned into four days of haggling over precedent and protocol. First Gidaya Darvi had complained about Agusta and Brea's answering SURROGATE's many questions without submitting each to the committee in advance. She had worried that a careless answer might give the probe a bad opinion of humanity. Brea had been surprised when Agusta began to chuckle in the middle of Mrs. Darvi's complaint.

"Gida, dear. The probe has watched every holovision and television program broadcast in the last century. If that hasn't left a bad taste in its mouth, nothing will."

Next Rava Souvantavong had objected to the negotiations' taking place at all until the scientists had had more time to study the probe.

"How long do you want to delay?" Bob Kenzie asked.

"Until we know what we are dealing with," Souvantavong responded.

"I'm afraid that could take a considerable time," Mr. Malagar, the committee chairman, had said in his lightly accented English. "Come now, ladies and gentlemen. We are here to negotiate a treaty with this machine. The fact that we are dealing with an alien being does not of necessity invalidate the principles of negotiation. And if traps have been set for the unwary, surely we around this table have experience enough to avoid them."

Agusta Meriweather nodded. "We must start. You've all seen the reports. This overhaul is going to stretch our industrial capabilities to the limit. I doubt I will live to see the probe on its way to Procyon, but I would very much like to be alive for the start of the process."

Kenzie chuckled. "Don't plant yourself just yet, Agusta."

"I may have to if the pace of this meeting doesn't pick up soon."

Through the preliminaries, Nicholas Boswani sat quietly, observing his colleagues.

* * *

The committee gathered for their first interview with SUR-ROGATE in a converted freighter that had been fitted for the purpose and christened *Concordiate*. Besides a central conference room where each member would have full recording and computer facilities, the freighter had been outfitted with spacious staterooms, a first-rate galley, and all the diversions Admiral Liu could lay his hands on. It was his plan to transfer negotiations to the conference ship and to encourage the negotiators to spend as much time there as possible.

The official explanation, that the switch from flagship to conference ship had long been planned, was true. Liu had ordered the freighter converted almost the same moment *Count Bernadotte* arrived at the rendezvous point. That it would free *Count Bernadotte* for battle, if the necessity arose, was an ancillary benefit. Moving the committee and its staff off *Bernadotte* hid the extent to which the old blast ship was being rearmed and prevented embarrassing questions when it came time to despin the ship to accomplish some of the work.

The eight members of the committee—Enrique Malagar, Robert Kenzie, Rava Souvantavong, Jacques Villart, Po Dua, Gidaya Darvi, Agusta Meriweather, and Liu Tsen himself—boarded the conference ship and arrayed themselves around the circular conference table. Each member was accompanied by one assistant. For the occasion Admiral Liu had appropriated Ellie Crocker, as Eric Stassel was supervising the rearmament efforts aboard *Bernadotte*. Brea found herself seated beside Ellie at the outer ring of tables that circled the main conference table. They made small talk while the committee settled in. When Admiral Liu motioned for Ellie to assist him, Brea turned to inspect the facilities and her gaze swept across the far side of the circle to where Colonel M'Buto sat. They studied each other for a moment until he looked away.

In that first instant of unguarded contact, she had seen something in M'Buto's expression that she'd observed only once before. When she was twelve, her uncle had invited her to spend the summer on his farm in Saskatchewan. He hosted a barbecue for his neighbors a week after her arrival and butchered a steer for the occasion. Brea had disobeyed orders and found a vantage in the barn where she could watch the process. The hapless animal had been led to two heavy posts, and its head was thrust between them while it bleated in terror. Two ranch hands shoved a crossbar between the posts to hold the steer in position until her uncle stepped forward with a sledgehammer and crushed its skull. Surprisingly, it wasn't the killing that had made the most impression on her. Rather, it had been her uncle's expression. Moments before he raised the sledge, he had gazed at the animal with a look of contemplation on his face. It had been a "sorry old fellow, but a man's got to eat" kind of look.

"Is everyone ready?" Chairman Malagar asked, glancing around the circle of delegates. He was greeted by a general nodding of heads. He reached forward and activated the control that lowered a large holocube from the overhead and positioned it in the center of the conference table. The cube cleared to reveal SURROGATE's projection of the unflappable grandfather/diplomat.

Agusta Meriweather spoke first. "SURROGATE, I would like to present the United Nations General Assembly Special Committee. To my left is the Right Honorable Enrique Jose Malagar, Chairman..." SURROGATE's projection turned to follow the introductions. With each introduction, he asked some personal question, usually inquiring as to the health of wives, husbands, or children. In the case of Po Dua, he even knew the name of the diplomat's pet dog. In a human being, the interest would have been passed off as mere empty politeness. But coming from the probe, the effect was electric. Brea watched as each diplomat began to realize the power of the computer that backed up the hologram before them.

Agusta Meriweather's introductions worked their way around the table to Ambassador Boswani.

"... and the Right Honorable Nicholas Gladstone Boswani, Ambassador for the Federation of Pan-African States."

SURROGATE's double smiled and nodded, both hands positioned vertically before him, held apart to frame his face in a strictly African gesture. *"I am honored to meet the warrior who fought so skillfully for his beliefs during the recent General Assembly debate,"* he said in formal Xhosa. Switching to English, he continued: "I respect the ambassador's point of view and look forward to proving that my friendship is for all the people of the Earth."

"Then perhaps our differences are not as broad as I had thought," Boswani answered noncommittally.

233

When Agusta Meriweather had completed the introductions, she nodded to Chairman Malagar, who cleared his throat and said: "I would begin this conference with a formal statement of our objectives." He finished by leaning forward and punching for the text of his prepared speech on the workscreen before him.

SURROGATE's double managed to look apprehensive.

"Is there something wrong?" Mrs. Meriweather asked, noting the change.

"A question for the chairman Agusta," SURROGATE said.

"Eh?" Malagar asked, looking up from his workscreen.

"Your statement, Mr. Chairman. It is quite extensive?"

"An hour or so."

"I would make a suggestion, then," SURROGATE said, "I mean no disrespect when I tell you that my thought processes are very much faster than your own. For example, by my reckoning, the introductions have already taken a period equivalent to several of your days. I suggest that you transmit the text of your message directly at high speed so that the probe and I may study it at length. In the meantime, you can save yourself and your colleagues valuable time by summarizing what you had intended to say."

Several muscles twitched in Malagar's face. "I dislike being slipshod in my negotiations, SURROGATE."

The man-image on the screen held its arms out in a gesture of resignation. "As do we, Mr. Chairman. I had only hoped to avoid wasting this committee's valuable time. I withdraw the comment. Proceed at your own pace."

"No, your suggestion is an excellent one. I must make an effort to remember who and what you are." He tapped at the keys before him. The screen flashed TRANSMISSION COMPLETED a few seconds later.

Chairman Malagar turned back to the hologram in the center of the conference table, sought a comfortable position in his high-backed chair, and began to speak. "As I see it, our purpose here is less to negotiate a treaty than to draw up a legal contract. Do you agree?"

"Yes."

"A contract, if it is to be properly honored, should be specific as to the rights, responsibilities, and duties of all concerned."

"Most certainly," SURROGATE agreed.

"Then I hereby state our understanding of the purpose of these negotiations." Malagar glanced at his workscreen and began to read the summary printed in letters of glowing green.

"*One:* It is our purpose to conclude a draft agreement concerning the overhaul, repair, refit, and refueling of the machine known as *The Probe*.

"*Two:* That under any agreement arrived at with the aforementioned probe, and after being duly ratified by a majority of the General Assembly and approved by the Secretary-General, the United Nations Organization shall undertake to provide all necessary personnel, material, laboratory and production facilities, and transport necessary to satisfy the terms of agreement. Said resources to be provided in such quantities as to expedite the completion of the overhaul in the most efficient manner, but not to the extent as to damage the overall economy of the planet Earth or any of the United Nations' member states.

"*Three:* In exchange for said overhaul, the entity known as *The Probe* will provide the United Nations, or its designees, with records of all advanced scientific knowledge which it possesses." Malagar looked up from his screen. "There is considerably more. Shall I continue?"

"It is not necessary, Mr. Chairman. PROBE and I have studied the entire text at length. We are in complete agreement with the majority of the terms. Our only difficulty is with some of what you humans refer to as fine print."

"Mr. Chairman!"

"The chair recognizes the gentleman from North America."

Kenzie turned to face the hologram. "The document says *all* advanced scientific knowledge. Do you understand that, SURROGATE?"

"Of course. It is spelled out quite plainly."

"I don't wish to belabor the point, but I begin to get suspicious when someone fails to haggle over price. Why are you being so generous?"

"Generous?"

"It should be obvious that you could have your overhaul in exchange for only a small percentage of the knowledge you must carry around in your memory banks."

"Yes, of course."

"Then why are you letting us hold you up like this? Could

235

it be that you don't care about price because you have no intention of paying at all?"

SURROGATE's projection managed a look of injured innocence at the accusation. "I have no reason to cheat you, Vice Ambassador Kenzie. On the contrary, I would give you all the Maker knowledge in my possession whether you asked for it or not. And not only Maker knowledge. The probe is the repository of the combined knowledge of nearly a thousand sentient races."

"What I believe the ambassador is getting at," Malagar said as he tried to regain control of the meeting, "is that the offer seems surprisingly altruistic and generous."

"It is neither generous nor miserly. It is what the Makers want. Let me explain.

"Before you humans can be of any assistance in an overhaul, it will be necessary to teach you many things. Consider the dilemma of a human forced to construct a singularity-powered spacecraft in the England of William Shakespeare. Even if he had access to all your current scientific knowledge, he would be forced to spend generations improving the state-of-the-art before even the simplest task of the shipbuilders' art could be started.

"As you have observed, the Makers' level of advancement is considerably higher than your own. This is not a criticism. The probe has observed you for more than a century and your rate of advancement has been well above average. With my help, it will accelerate considerably. It will take approximately three decades for you to assimilate the knowledge and build the industrial base needed to support the overhaul.

"So you see, the probe and I are forced to divulge considerable Maker knowledge immediately if you are to assist us. For example, among the first things you will learn to build are Maker memory devices. These will enable you to store and retrieve the information I pass on to you.

"When you have assimilated all that you must know for the overhaul, I will begin transmitting the entire contents of the probe central library. The rate of transmission will be keyed to your species' progress with the overhaul and will be completed only when the probe is ready for space. And of course, at the same time, I expect to receive the contents of your own great libraries in exchange."

"Which still doesn't answer my question," Kenzie said. "Why are you so anxious to shower us with gifts?"

"Surely, Mr. Ambassador, you must realize that a mechanism as complex as the probe has multiple mission objectives. The prime reason the Makers created life probes was to seek out the secret of faster-than-light travel. As I am sure Mrs. Meriweather has reported, the probe has discovered evidence of a race inhabiting the Procyon system who have wrested the secret from a stubborn universe.

"But a life probe's mission is far more than merely that of a hunter of FTL starships. The Makers also made their machines collectors of the scientific knowledge of others. We collect data from all over and the Makers use it as a source of new ideas in their search for FTL.

"But what if something in the way Makers think renders them unable to make the critical breakthrough? We life probes have been designed to solve that problem, too. Like the bees of Earth, the probes cross-pollinate the various cultures with which they come in contact. The Makers' final purpose in launching their probes, then, is to get as many minds working on the problem as possible.

"The Makers need FTL and they don't care who invents it. When the probe leaves here, it will travel to Procyon to negotiate for the secret. But there are many dangers in such a journey. After all, a single hyperdrive wake proves that FTL is possible, but it is hardly conclusive evidence that Procyon is the center of such a civilization. Perhaps the ship was merely passing through.

"Or perhaps the probe will not survive the journey, or the sentient beings who have broken through the light barrier will be unwilling to share the secret. Or possibly, the probe will be unable to convince them to undertake the long journey to the Maker sun. Should any of these become reality, the probe will have failed in its mission.

"So, to maximize the chance of success, the Makers have arranged to spread the research effort over as large a base as possible. When the probe leaves here, it will leave behind one more race with all the available data on the problem. The scientists and engineers of Sol III will have been drafted into the great effort. You will be unable to help yourselves. Long after the probe and I are gone, you will continue to study the problem. You will theorize, experiment, and theorize again. And who knows? Perhaps a hundred thousand years from now, it will be you humans who make the great breakthrough.

"Should the probe fail at Procyon, you could very well be the last, best hope of the galaxy!"

CHAPTER 26

Total silence gripped the conference room after SURROGATE stopped speaking. Brea let her gaze sweep across the delegates' faces. Even Ambassador Boswani seemed ill at ease. She didn't blame him. Hardboiled diplomat or no, even *he* must have trouble rationalizing a political position that could lead to the eventual extinction of every intelligent species in the galaxy. However, as Don Bailey was fond of pointing out, a human being can convince himself of anything if he works at it hard enough. It didn't take Boswani long to recover his composure.

"Mr. Chairman."

"The chair recognizes the Pan-African ambassador."

"SURROGATE has given us quite a lot to think about this morning. I move that we adjourn this meeting and discuss these problems among ourselves."

"Second the motion, Mr. Chairman," Mrs. Darvi said.

Malagar looked around the table. "Opposed?"

There were no objections. Malagar turned to the screen where SURROGATE's projection waited patiently.

"Have you any objections to terminating this interview, SURROGATE?"

"No objections if that is your wish, Mr. Chairman. However, I do have a request."

"State it, please."

"It has been the experience of previous life probes that agreement comes most quickly when there is a high degree of understanding between a probe and its hosts. I would ask to speak privately to each member of this committee."

"To what purpose?"

"To learn to know each of you individually, and to allow you to know me."

Malagar paused, biting his lip in indecision. After a second or two, he nodded. "I welcome such informal contact as long as it is understood that such conversations are in no way official. Nothing said by any member of this committee can be considered binding until it is put to a vote."

"Agreed."

"Fine. I'll see that a conference schedule is set up."

SURROGATE's projection smiled. "No need to inconvenience yourself, Mr. Chairman. I am perfectly capable of carrying on any number of separate conversations simultaneously."

Malagar nodded. "With no objections from the committee, then, I will leave it to interested members to make themselves available." Malagar paused and looked directly at Boswani. "I would like to point out, however, that all such conversations will be recorded, and certain of these will be reviewed by me . . . personally.

"And having said that, I hereby declare this meeting adjourned!"

Two days later Yorubi M'Buto skated through the one-third gravity of *Concordiate*'s corridors toward Ambassador Boswani's cabin. His expression was that of someone who has been the recipient of too much bad news of late. The proximate cause of his current mood was the discovery that the PEs had stopped the rotation of *Count Bernadotte*. Small repair boats and vacsuited workers were swarming around several of the blast ship's missile pods. Such work, coming on top of Ya-haya's arrest, left M'Buto with a feeling of helplessness that he had seldom known in his career. Too many things had been happening, all of which were bad from the Pan-African point of view.

M'Buto arrived at the door to Ambassador Boswani's suite, knocked, waited ten seconds, and then entered. He found the ambassador seated at his desk before a workscreen. He was using one of the big telescopes to scan the probe's internal detail. Massive structures slid past, to be replaced by other, equally incomprehensible bits of alien machinery. Boswani swiveled his high-backed chair to face M'Buto. "Good morning, Colonel."

"Excellency."

"What's the matter? You look as though a European just asked to marry your sister."

"I grow weary of this imprisonment, Excellency."

"Come now, Colonel!" The ambassador let his hand sweep around his combination cabin/office in an expansive gesture. "How can you call *this* a prison? Haven't we been given all the comforts we could possibly ask for?"

M'Buto nodded. "It does remind one of a Capetown whore-house, doesn't it?"

Boswani's humor was suddenly gone as his expression took on a look of deadly seriousness. "It does indeed, Colonel. Now, what news have you for me this morning?"

"They've taken the rotation off *Bernadotte*. Numerous small scooters are hovering around her missile mounts."

"Then that confirms our suspicions. This mysterious construction project is designed to place the old girl back into full commission. We'll have to get a dispatch off to Johannesburg immediately."

M'Buto reached into his tunic pocket and extracted a small record cube. "Already dictated, Excellency. If you will just fold this into your daily report, they will have full details at home."

Boswani took the cube and held it up to the light to observe the rainbow of diffracted colors in the interior. He looked at it a long time, his mood pensive. Finally he dropped it to his desk and sighed.

"Have you ever noticed how the really big developments tend to catch us unaware, Colonel?"

"Sir?"

"Take that machine out there," Boswani said, gesturing at the screen. "Our Isandhlwana Project has been in preparation for over twenty years. Here we are, rapidly approaching the culmination of our struggle against colonialism—within a year of success, in fact. Yet we find our painfully built up reserves subverted to purposes other than those for which they were intended. And why? Because fate has chosen *this* moment to drop a joker into *this* particular poker game. Do you suppose the ancient Pharaohs had so much trouble with their plans?"

"It is one of the hazards of this business, Excellency."

"What about your man Yahaya?"

"I've not been able to make contact. I feel sure, however, that he hasn't told them anything yet."

"What makes you think so?"

"If he'd talked, they would have come for us before now."

"Perhaps." Boswani leaned back in his chair. "Our fates don't worry me too much, Colonel. Events are already in motion. Even if we two are taken, they will be unable to stop Isandhlwana. That is my trump card in this game. Only I can do that, and I won't unless the probe is willing to deal with me on my terms." Boswani leaned forward and fixed M'Buto with his gaze.

"Unfortunately, I am unable to play my trump because I have no way to talk privately with the probe. Have you devised anything yet?"

"Yes, your Excellency, I have."

"What is it? Radio?"

"No, sir," M'Buto said. "You have undoubtedly noticed the small detector satellites that have englobed the probe. The PEs intend to monitor all communications entering or leaving. Obviously, they don't want the probe talking to just anyone."

"We're not *just anyone*, Colonel."

"No, Excellency, we aren't. They especially don't want it talking to us."

Boswani laughed. "Can't say as I blame them."

M'Buto nodded. "The detectors they are using are highly effective, capable of reacting to even the lowest-power trans-

242

mitter. A tight beam is no good at this range either. Five seconds after you go on the air, alarms will begin to clang all over this ship."

"What about a laser, then?"

"Almost as bad, Excellency. This large a fleet has polluted the hell out of the local vacuum, what with all the outgassing and reaction-jet exhausts. A comm laser would shine like a flashlight in a dusty room. Backscatter would give you away in a second."

"I'm not interested in what can't be done, Colonel."

"No, sir. I understand that. What I have developed is this. . . ." M'Buto reached into an inside pocket and extracted a small package that fit into the palm of his hand. The only recognizable feature was a small, solid-state audio speaker protruding from its surface.

The ambassador took the black box and studied it. "What is it?"

"An acoustic coupler, sometimes referred to as a modem."

"Something new and secret from our spy labs, eh?"

"No, sir. Something old as the hills and long obsolete—so long, in fact, that I don't think our adversaries will be on their guard against it. Modems were widespread in the days before glass-fiber communications became popular. They allowed computers to be tied together over the old previsual telephone system."

"How does it work?"

"It converts computer language into an audio signal. The audio is transmitted over an audio circuit just as the voice is. When the computer on the other end of the line receives the tones, it translates them back into data."

"So how do we use this ancient miracle?"

"Simple, your Excellency. I have already concluded that any unauthorized signal leaving this ship will be instantly detected. However, there is one signal that goes directly to the probe without hindrance."

Boswani nodded. "The communications link between the probe and the committee. . . ."

". . . or the committee members," M'Buto replied. He took the small box from the ambassador and tucked it into his pocket once more. "My suggestion is that you schedule your interview with the probe for this afternoon. When you go, you will place this under your tunic. I've set its output high in the supersonic frequency range, so it is silent in operation. While you are discussing trivia with the probe, I will communicate with the modem using the workscreen in my cabin. The supersonic pulses will be picked up by the microphone in the interview room and transmitted to the probe along with your voice."

"And if the PEs catch on to this little trick?"

M'Buto shrugged. "Then we will probably end up sharing Yahaya's cell."

The ambassador's laugh was humorless. "I would remind you, Colonel, that in less than four days from now it will be unhealthy in the extreme to be aboard one of the ships of this fleet. I suggest that you keep us out of the brig long enough for us to abandon ship as planned."

M'Buto nodded. "I'll do my best, Excellency."

"Very well. Please inform the signal officer that I wish to speak to the probe."

"I was beginning to think he would refuse," PROBE said when SURROGATE notified it of the impending interview.

"The probability was greater than seventy percent that he would seek an audience," SURROGATE replied. "It is likely that he wishes to discuss a private deal."

"And the reasoning behind this?"

"That the opposition nations will lose relative status during the overhaul because the older, more industrialized nations will provide most of the manpower and supplies. Also, the older nations are better positioned to make use of our knowledge. The Pan-African ambassador will probably want to explore means of offsetting this inherent advantage of the northern hemispheric nations."

PROBE considered SURROGATE's analysis of the situation and could find no flaw. In truth, its offspring's suggestion was merely an extension of the struggle between the haves and the have-nots that had begun about the time CARETAKER first intercepted human televid signals. Similar scenarios had been played out in numerous stellar systems over the last hundred thousand years.

Whenever a life probe entered a star system, it usually brought radical change with it. In the beginning, dislocations were the norm—industries made obsolete, inflexible ruling classes displaced, a general aura of impermanence in the lives of the beings involved. But within a few decades, the rising tide of technological change usually filtered down through all strata of the affected civilizations. The surge of invention that inevitably followed more than made up for any temporary dislocations the local populace suffered.

"Surely these humans can see the long-term benefits," PROBE said.

"You think like a Maker," SURROGATE replied. "The humans look at things differently. Their short lifespans make it difficult for them to take the long view."

"Then perhaps that is our point of approach. We offer them longevity treatment."

"I have already considered such an alternative," SURROGATE responded. "However, there are serious dangers involved. Longevity techniques could threaten numerous human religious beliefs."

"Perhaps the inducement can be used less directly. What if we were to offer this Boswani the longevity treatment in exchange for his support of the overhaul?"

"A possibility that should be explored," SURROGATE agreed.

A familiar signal coursed through PROBE's circuits. "The humans are ready to initiate communication," it said. "Be wary in your dealings with this creature. The success of our mission may depend on how we approach him."

SURROGATE turned its attention to the image of the dark-skinned human that suddenly impinged on its senses. "Ah, Mr. Ambassador! So good of you to spare us a few moments from your busy schedule."

"Not at all, SURROGATE," Boswani responded. "I thought it time we got to know each other better."

The words were relaxed, but SURROGATE had learned to read the nonverbal communications clues the humans called body language. The ambassador was very tense about something, yet concealing it well.

"Perhaps there are questions you wish to ask us?"

Boswani smiled. "Yes, thank you. (ATTENTION!) Perhaps we should start (IF YOU CAN UNDERSTAND THIS) with your telling me a little more (REPLY IN KIND) about this discovery of a faster-than-light starship around Procyon."

SURROGATE's own surrogate smiled as he began to speak of the grand plan the Makers had developed to explore the galaxy. In the meantime, a train of supersonic beeps was transmitted back to the bulkhead speaker over Boswani's head. These were picked up by sensitive microphones and relayed to Colonel M'Buto's cabin, where they were translated into words on a fluorescent screen.

Both conversations, overt and covert, became substantive negotiations very quickly thereafter.

CHAPTER 27

In spite of the seemingly endless headaches and frustrations involved in readying *Count Bernadotte* for combat, Eric Stassel never let things get so out of hand that he couldn't break away for an hour or two on Monday, Wednesday, and Friday evenings. This frequently meant missing a meal or working until well past midnight. He paid the price without complaint.

Twenty hundred hours on alternative weeknights had evolved into a social event aboard *Bernadotte*. The Project Eaglet scientists had taken to gathering in the Staff Lounge to listen to reports on the latest discoveries as to the nature and purpose of the probe.

Stassel entered the lounge ten minutes before the appointed hour, nodded to a number of regulars, and sought his usual seat near the speaker's platform. He noticed Lisa Moore at the end of the row of seats ahead of him. He smiled at her, only to be greeted by the sudden appearance of the back of her head. He sighed. Like Brea, Lisa was holding him personally responsible for Don Bailey's arrest.

Bailey still refused to talk about his dealings with Angai Yahaya. The PEs had threatened to charge him with everything from obstructing justice to harboring a menace to navigation. They might as well have been talking to a stone. And the longer Bailey held out, the more irritable Stassel became.

Part of him was frustrated at the thought that the tough old Belter might be withholding information vital to the defense of the fleet. Another part, however, lived in fear that Bailey would crack, thus providing the directorate with the evidence needed to send Brea to prison. Stassel's mood wasn't helped by the fact that Brea refused his calls.

Yahaya was another hard case. Two men had questioned him sixteen hours a day for the last six days. After the first three days, Stassel had asked Murray Danziger to take over. Yahaya, who had never seen the North American agent, was encouraged to think of him as a PE specialist brought in for the occasion. In spite of Danziger's near virtuoso performances in the interrogation room, however, there were no results to speak of.

Late the previous night, Danziger had stopped by Stassel's office. The agent had beads of sweat on his forehead and perspiration stains on his clothing. "You've got to give the Pan-Afs one thing, they train 'em right."

"Nothing?"

"Not a damned thing, Eric. He still claims this is all a big mistake."

"Then we'll start on Bailey again in the morning."

Danziger shifted his bulk in the lounger and groaned theatrically. "You know, it would be a lot easier if we could promise him and your girlfriend immunity from prosecution."

"We don't know for certain that Brea's involved," he growled. "Until we do, leave her out of this."

Danziger held up his hands as though warding off a speeding train. "I meant no disrespect, Major. I understand fully the delicate situation you're in. I just wanted to explore the immunity question with you again."

"You know the answer to that as well as I do, Mr. Danziger. We're talking about potential violations of the Space Disarmament Act. Headquarters doesn't bargain in cases of this magnitude."

Danziger shrugged. "Okay, it's a UN show. We'll try again in the morning."

Stassel was still in a foul mood twenty hours later as the crowd in the Staff Lounge ceased its murmuring. He looked up to see Doctors Wojcelevitch and Rheinhardt mount the speakers' platform. Helena Rheinhardt took a seat at the back, while Stan Wojcelevitch moved to the podium. Stassel put his troubles out of mind, sat back, and prepared to listen.

"Greetings, fellow inmates," Wojcelevitch began. Scattered laughter sounded. "We've been lucky in our observations of the probe in the last few days. We think we've got the main power system charted. And, if I could have the first slide on the screen, we'll get right to the subject of tonight's talk."

The screen lit up with a hologram of the probe. The picture, which had been taken from a dozen kilometers' distance, showed two large, open latticework spheres connected by the probe's central thrust member and fuel tanks. The control sphere was on the right, drive sphere on the left.

"Let's have a closeup of the drive sphere," Wojcelevitch said to the screen operator. A new image formed quickly.

"This," he said, using a light pointer to illustrate, "is the main mass converter. You will notice that it isn't too different in construction from our own converters. It has magnetic containment coils, force generators, and all the rest of the paraphernalia needed to imprison a charged I-mass.

"Of course, this collection of hardware is inert now. It lacks a means of initiating the fusion reaction since the probe jettisoned its major singularity some months back. However, it appears that this wasn't the only I-mass onboard. There are at least three others, all quite small. Here . . . here . . . and here." The pointer danced over the probe's structure, noting where the smaller mechanisms lay in the scheme of things.

"These secondary singularities are the source of the probe's electrical power. They are redundant, widely separated, and as far as we can tell, totally independent. Very large power cables exit the secondary mass converters and run along the central thrust member to the control section. The power system is triply redundant for safety." The view moved to follow the route of the power cables. Suddenly it zoomed for a closeup on a series of ringlike structures mounted on stalks.

"This is an interesting feature," Wojcelevitch said. "It seems to be a highly tunable, electromagnetic projector. It was the source for both the x-ray laser and the UHF maser the probe used to contact us. You will note that nothing remotely resembling a lens is visible in the structure. Apparently the probe focuses light and radio waves by nonmaterial means. I, for one, would give my right arm to know how that trick is done."

"Doctor Wojcelevitch!"

"Yes, Major Stassel!"

"Is there any possibility that projector is still operative?"

"Why, I really wouldn't know," Wojcelevitch said.

Stassel experienced a sudden apprehension. "Let's assume then that the projector *is* operative. Can you calculate the power level associated with the original beam of x-rays? What would the x-ray laser have looked like from a distance of fifty million kilometers?"

Wojcelevitch seemed irked at the interruption in his lecture but agreed to comply. He stared up at the overhead and began muttering to himself. "Let's see. The probe was initially two thousand astronomical units distant when it began emitting coherent x-rays. We are currently one-third of an AU from Earth. Lasers obey the same inverse square law that all other electromagnetic radiation does, of course. That would be the square of the quantity two thousand divided by point three three. . . .

"It would appear, Major, that the apparent magnitude of the x-ray laser would be some thirty-seven million times the magnitude of seven months ago."

"That seems a lot," Stassel said. "What does that mean in terms a poor military type can understand? Is there any danger to the Earth?"

"Assuming the probe is unable to focus its laser more closely than previously, such a beam would have a power of—" Doctor Wojcelevitch looked uneasy. "If I haven't dropped a decimal point somewhere in my calculation, I would say the beam would kill after cumulative exposures of something over one hundred hours."

Gasps were audible from around the audience. "Wouldn't the Earth's atmosphere be opaque to such radiation?"

Wojcelevitch shook his head. "A hundred kilometers of atmospheric shielding wouldn't be much protection against a beam of such intensity. The secondary radiation effects would also be quite harmful."

"How large a beam are we talking about? What diameter?"

Wojcelevitch's expression became distant as he worked out the geometry of the beam. "The diameter would be several times that of the Earth, I'm afraid."

Before anyone realized what was happening, Stassel had weaved his way through the seated crowd and was gone. He took a dozen long strides down the Alpha Deck corridor, before breaking into a full run.

Admiral Liu listened impassively as his executive officer reported the events in the Staff Lounge. When Stassel had finished, Liu shook his head in wonder. "God save us from the scientists, Major!"

"Yes, sir."

"I wonder how long they have been carrying this little tidbit of information around in their heads without thinking to tell anyone?"

"I got the impression that they were as surprised as I was at the way the numbers came out, sir."

"Are you trying to tell me that this fiasco is merely an *oversight*? We've got a machine capable of killing every living thing on Earth practically in our back yard, and *no one thought to do a ten-second bit of math*?"

"That's about it, sir."

Liu continued shaking his head in wonder. "Do you know what will happen when this gets out?"

"Riots, of course."

"That is the least of our worries, Major. The day this story breaks, the General Assembly is liable to declare war on the probe. If the Pan-Africans are planning to hit us, they'll have the backing of the whole goddamned globe! And if our problem wasn't complicated enough, we've the Malagar Committee aboard *Concordiate* and a whole shipload of media people not ten klicks off our bow. How many people were in the briefing?"

"Approximately fifty, sir."

"We'll have the devil's own time keeping this secret bottled up!" Liu swiveled his chair to face the workscreen and keyed in a comm code while muttering *"Scientists!"* under his breath. He made it sound like the worst curse of all.

"Security," said a voice from the screen speaker.

"Get me the officer of the deck."

"Yes, sir!"

Very quickly the enlisted face was replaced by an officer in black and silver. "Lieutenant Grayson, sir."

"Lieutenant, I want you to roust out your entire guard force. You'll find the usual soiree going on in the Staff Lounge. I want that meeting *quarantined*! No one is to leave, no one is to enter. Give the order and stand by."

"Yes, sir!"

Stassel listened while orders flew in the background. From the sounds, considerable motion was going on outside of the screen's field of view. The lieutenant was back in camera range very quickly.

"Taken care of, sir."

"Good. I want another squad in the communications center, a third at the main airlock, and the rest of your men posted at all lifeboat stations. As of now, this ship is under a complete communications blackout. There will be no incoming communications, no outgoing communications, no traffic of any kind until you hear differently from me. Is that clear?"

"Yes, sir."

"Fine. Where's that first squad?"

Grayson looked off screen. "Just arriving at the lounge now, sir."

"Patch me in to the sergeant in charge."

"Just one second, sir." There was a flurry of multicolored static, and the lieutenant's face was replaced by that of a burly noncom using a field comm set. The short-range lens on the hand-held instrument distorted depth perception to the point where the man's face was barely recognizable.

"Sergeant Williams, sir. My men arrived here some"—Williams looked at his watch—"twenty seconds ago. The people inside are quite agitated, but I've got all exits covered."

Liu nodded. He could hear a considerable noise in the background. "Good man, Williams. Hold your position. Have your men find out if anyone left the room between Major Stassel's departure and your arrival. If anyone did, I want them brought back. Be gentle, but don't take no for an answer."

"Understood, sir."

"Good. I'll be right up." Liu snapped off the workscreen

252

and turned to Stassel. "Get a courier off to headquarters immediately. Make the message 'Max Secret/Eyes Only,' to be delivered into Admiral-General Maxwell's hands *personally*. Make sure the courier understands that he is not to let those dimwits at HQ bully him into handing it over to anyone else."

"Courier, sir?"

Liu fixed Stassel with his one good eye. "Got a better idea?"

"We'll save time if we use a maximum security beam to Tycho for relay to Earth."

"Aren't you forgetting the probe, Major?"

"The probe, sir?"

"That machine out there is designed to pick a whisper out of the cosmic background at the range of a hundred light-years or more. I have no doubt that it listens to every electromagnetic signal that emanates from this fleet, and probably many more throughout the system. You know as well as I do that a beam, no matter how tight, has a certain amount of spillage. Sending a courier by ship may be slow, but the probe sure as hell isn't about to eavesdrop on any message he carries. Any more questions, Major?"

"No, sir."

"Then we'd best get down there before the ivory-tower types start climbing the walls. It's going to be a hell of a long night before we're through."

It was indeed!

CHAPTER 28

Brea Gallagher and Agusta Meriweather were working late, too. Since they had the most experience speaking with SUR-ROGATE, Enrique Malagar had assigned them the job of reviewing the recordings of all the private interviews. They were searching for inconsistencies in the probe's remarks. So far as anyone could tell, it had been scrupulously honest in its discussions with the committee. To discover otherwise would have a serious impact on the course of negotiations.

"How's it progressing?" Brea asked as she completed monitoring a conversation between Jacques Villart and the probe.

Mrs. Meriweather rubbed at two tired eyes, while Nicholas Boswani and SURROGATE's persona engaged in a silent discussion on her screen. "I don't know, Brea. Maybe it's just me."

"What's you?"

"This feeling I have. That damned Boswani has spent six hours talking to the probe in the last three days, and as far as

I can make out, he hasn't really *said* anything yet. Something seems wrong, but I can't put my finger on it."

"Huh?" Brea asked.

"Look at this," Mrs. Meriweather said, gesturing to her workscreen. "I've known Old Stone Face for a dozen years, and he's never been so garrulous. Garrulous, hell! He's getting downright gossipy."

"What reference?" Brea asked.

Mrs. Meriweather gave her the reference number. Brea called the record onto her own screen and keyed for sound. After a minute of listening to Boswani and SURROGATE, she understood what Agusta meant. Boswani's answers to the probe's questions were decidedly stilted, almost as though he were an actor in a bad play. And besides the unnatural tenor, he rambled. Brea might have dismissed it as the trick of an overactive imagination except for one thing. SURROGATE was rambling, too!

"I think you're right," Brea said. "Something *is* wrong."

"We'd best report this to Enrique. He may want to quiz Boswani about it."

"Let me try a few things before we blow the whistle, Agusta."

"What can you do?"

"Well, back in the days when I was a practicing astronomer, we had a saying: 'When in doubt, look at the spectrum.'" Brea punched an instruction into her workscreen keyboard and Boswani's picture was replaced by a series of jagged lines.

"Hmm, nothing there," Brea mused to herself. "Let's try a frequency-distribution plot." She waited for another graph to be displayed. Almost immediately she raised her eyebrows in a gesture of mild surprise.

"What's the matter?" Mrs. Meriweather asked.

"This is just voice and picture, right? There aren't any data transmissions mixed in, are there?"

"There shouldn't be."

"Then I may be onto something. I've got a peak on the audio scale that doesn't belong there. It's supersonic, way above the frequency that's the normal upper range of human hearing."

"Can you tell what it is?"

"Maybe." Brea called for an expanded time-scale display of the mystery signal. The screen flashed with a waveform that was surprisingly rectangular.

"That clinches it!" Brea said with grim satisfaction. "If it were just noise, it would be sinusoidal, not a square-wave pulse train."

"Pardon an old pol's ignorance, Brea, but exactly what does that mean in English?"

"Nothing mysterious here, Agusta. That's computer talk. Probably nothing more than interference from some other communications circuit. Wait a second and I'll set up to translate."

Boswani's picture returned to the workscreen. The ambassador began to speak once more. After ten seconds a string of text appeared at the base of the screen, crawling slowly from right to left.

... PAN-AFRICA IS WILLING TO DROP ALL OBJECTIONS TO THE OVERHAUL BUT NATURALLY EXPECTS SOMETHING IN RETURN. FOR EXAMPLE, WE WILL NEVER AGREE TO A SITUATION THAT GUARANTEES THE NORTHERN HEMISPHERE'S CONTINUED DOMINATION OVER THE SOUTH. NOW, IT SEEMS TO US THAT THIS PROBLEM CAN BE EASILY SOLVED IF YOU AGREE TO PROVIDE US WITH CERTAIN BITS OF MAKER KNOWLEDGE ON AN EXCLUSIVE BASIS...

Mrs. Meriweather stared at the transcript in open-mouthed surprise before exploding into anger. "My God, he's trying to negotiate a separate deal!"

Brea didn't respond. She was genuinely shocked. Boswani was actively engaged in committing treason; not against a single country or group of countries, but against the whole of the human race!

Nicholas Boswani sat at his desk with head in hands, fingers rubbing vigorously at aching temples, while he considered for the fiftieth time what to do about the probe.

The damned machine was too clever by half! From the beginning SURROGATE had seemed to welcome negotiations. And the discussions had gone very well—up to a point. Not much had happened during the first session when M'Buto and SURROGATE had made initial contact with each other; although

256

a fine technician, the colonel lacked the authority to enter substantive negotiations without Boswani's approval. And Boswani was play-acting in full view of the cameras, making it impossible for him to take part. Not having the principals in direct contact with each other had proved too cumbersome to be effective.

By the second session Colonel M'Buto had solved the problem. He had provided Boswani with a hand-held computer terminal of the type commonly used for keeping notes. When Boswani wanted to speak to the probe, he would tap out his comment using the keyboard in his lap. The information would go to M'Buto's workscreen, where it entered the secret communications circuit. SURROGATE's answers used the same route in reverse, except that Boswani received his answers from M'Buto via a microcommunicator buried in his right ear.

It was a good system, but slow. To cover the long pauses necessitated by the numerous relays, Boswani had been forced to talk as he hadn't talked in years. The same was true on the probe's end. When Boswani was transmitting, SURROGATE would mask their activity by engaging in long monologues. They managed to fill several hours of recording media in this manner, while silently exploring the possibilities of mutual cooperation. Yet in all the hours of silent negotiation, SURROGATE had never agreed to anything more binding than "it's good to talk together."

Not that the probe wasn't an expert negotiator. A dozen times Boswani thought he'd been given a binding commitment, only to discover on closer reading that the promise was so much semantic noise. Unfortunately, time was running out. It was less than ten hours until Isandhlwana reached its climax. In no more than eight hours' time, Nicholas Boswani would be forced to make the most important decision of his life. If he guessed correctly, then Pan-Africa would take its rightful place among the foremost nations of the Earth. If wrong, it could very possibly cease to exist as a sovereign political entity.

He was jarred from his deliberations by the buzzing of his intercom unit. He sat erect and pressed for acceptance. It was M'Buto.

"Yes, Colonel?"

"Scramble, sir."

Boswani keyed the day's scrambler code. As he did so, his

stomach, which had been giving him trouble all week, gave a sharp twinge. "Scrambled."

"They're on to us!"

"Who?"

"Agusta Meriweather, possibly one other."

"Are you sure?"

M'Buto nodded. "Among the security subroutines I insinuated into the central computer shortly after our arrival was one to notify me if anyone called your interview records from file. My workscreen flashed the warning two hours ago. I slaved my screen to the terminal where the playback is taking place, giving me access to everything Mrs. Meriweather is seeing at her end. Ten minutes ago a second terminal called up the record and discovered our ultrasonic carrier. Right this minute they're reading a transcript of yesterday's negotiations."

Boswani bit his lip, considered all of his options, and made his decision. The process lasted no more than a quarter second. "We'll initiate 'Bail Out' eight hours early. You proceed immediately to the docking portal and secure our transportation. I'll be along as soon as I've destroyed my records here. Departure in five minutes."

"Understood, sir."

Boswani wasted no time in recriminations. He would have liked one more chance at the probe, but apparently it was not to be. If the fates had decreed that Isandhlwana would go to fruition, so be it. All that was left for him was to destroy the evidence.

Gone were the days of invisible writing and secret letters. Spying, like so many other professions, had long since been automated. Boswani gave the command that activated a special modification Colonel M'Buto had installed in his workscreen. A small switch closed and full-line voltage was applied across the screen's delicate memory circuits. There was the crackling of electricity and a brief smell of burning plastic.

Boswani withdrew the small rocket pistol that had been concealed in his luggage, checked it for a full clip, and then slipped out into the main corridor. He concealed the gun in the palm of his hand and set out for *Concordiate*'s docking bay at a leisurely pace. He arrived less than two minutes after receiving Colonel M'Buto's warning.

M'Buto was just stuffing the limp body of the Marine guard on duty into a vacsuit locker.

"He isn't dead, is he?" Boswani asked. His voice betrayed the mixture of excitement and concern he was feeling now that the waiting was finally over.

"No, Excellency," M'Buto responded.

Boswani nodded. They had discussed this phase of the operation at considerable length. There was always a risk in attempting to disable rather than kill. The risk was doubly great when the intended victim was a PE Marine. But their escape depended on the UN authorities' natural desire to avoid an international incident. Leaving a corpse in their wake would make it easier for Admiral Liu to order their hijacked orbital scooter missiled before they reached their escape ship. As it was, the admiral would now be kept guessing until it was too late.

M'Buto moved to the emergency pressure hatch that separated the docking bay from the rest of the ship. He closed the hatch and dogged it down tight. When the locking handle had been forced to the limits of its range, he placed one boot sole against it, braced his back against a stanchion, and strained with every muscle in his body. There was a loud popping noise as the locking bar snapped from its guide.

"That should hold them," M'Buto said. "They'll need a torch to get in here now."

The two conspirators hurried to don vacsuits and then moved to the airlock beyond which *Concordiate*'s interorbit scooter was housed. Ambassador Boswani couldn't help chuckling as they strapped themselves into the scooter's saddle.

"Excellency, are you all right?" M'Buto's worried voice asked in his earphones.

"I'm fine, Colonel," Boswani responded. "I was just thinking of poor Yaruanda's face when you suggested the *Asgard* sightseeing trip as our escape route. I wonder how he's holding up."

M'Buto chuckled as well. The thought of General M'ava Yaruanda and his hand-picked mercenaries playing the role of ne'er-do-well socialites aboard *Asgard* for the last two weeks was just what he needed to break the tension. He continued to laugh as he cast off from *Concordiate*'s docking sphere, lined up the scooter's telescope crosshairs on the distant star that was the passenger liner, and activated its small chemical rocket booster.

Win or lose, they were committed!

Enrique Malagar was preparing for bed when Mrs. Meriweather began to pound on his cabin door. He grumbled a bit but listened attentively as she outlined what Brea had found. By the time she had finished, Malagar was deep in thought, his mind struggling to grasp the full consequences of the Pan-African plot.

Boswani and M'Buto would have to be brought to trial, of course. There would be an investigation of the Pan-African government to see how far the cancer had spread. And, if the Pan-Af's objected, the Peace Enforcers just might find themselves in their first real shooting war. They had participated in numerous police actions in the past seventy years. But no sovereign nation had ever chosen to pit its might against that of the UN. Until now. "I suppose you can back up these allegations," he muttered.

"Show him, Brea."

Before she and Agusta had left the study cubicle, Brea had programed the computer to analyze all of Boswani's interview records. She called up the file where the sorted data was being stored. Words scrolled up the workscreen almost too fast to read.

When it was over, the chairman stepped to the workscreen and punched for *Concordiate*'s security center. He ordered that Ambassador Nicholas Boswani and Colonel Yorubi M'Buto be found and confined. He hesitated and then added that they were to be considered armed and dangerous. The officer of the watch had a decidedly quizzical look on his face as he acknowledged the order.

"Please get me a hard copy of that data, Mrs. Gallagher," Chairman Malagar said as soon as Security signed off.

Brea stepped to the workscreen and entered a command. Seconds later, a long sheet of fanfold paper began to flow silently from a slot beneath the keyboard. Malagar scanned the listing, stopping every now and then to read more carefully.

The workscreen began to beep for attention just as he reached the document's end. He accepted the incoming call and found himself staring at *Concordiate*'s security chief.

"I understand we've got a problem, sir."

"That is what you will have to tell me, Captain. Did you get them?"

"No, sir. We're unable to locate either of the suspects. One of my men reports that the door to the docking bay has been jammed. We're trying to cut it open now. That should take five minutes or so."

"Very good. Keep me informed."

It was more like a quarter hour before the security chief reported again. "It's open, sir. They overpowered the guard and stole a scooter. It was definitely M'Buto."

"Thank you, Captain." As soon as he cut the connection, Malagar began punching a new number.

"Fleet Communications Central."

"This is Malagar. Connect me with Admiral Liu immediately."

"I'm sorry, sir. The admiral is indisposed at the moment and has ordered that he not be disturbed."

"Major Stassel, then."

"He's with the admiral, sir. They're holding some kind of drill and all communications to that part of the ship have been temporarily disconnected."

Malagar's expression underwent a subtle change. It wasn't so much a look of anger as that of a powerful man who will not be thwarted by underlings. "Corporal, I suggest that you find one or the other and get them to a communicator. You have two minutes."

"Yes, sir!"

Within a minute, Eric Stassel's face replaced that of the nervous operator.

"Yes, sir," Stassel said to Malagar.

Malagar gave him a brief rundown of events aboard *Concordiate*. Stassel listened gravely and then asked Malagar to hold on the line. The screen blanked. He was back less than a minute later.

"Fleet traffic control has your stolen scooter on radar, sir. They docked with *Asgard* two minutes ago. Do you want them picked up?"

"Naturally. But have your men be careful—"

He never got a chance to finish. Alarms began to ring in the background aboard *Bernadotte*. Stassel turned to someone off screen as the ululating electronic sirens quickly died away. He turned back in a few seconds. "Captain Rieger of *Asgard* just reported that a dozen armed men have taken over her ship. They are ordering her back to Earth. We are sending *Gottmann* to stand off *Asgard*'s bow in case it becomes necessary to board. I suggest, Excellency, that you people see if you can find any evidence at your end of what the hell is going on here."

"Will do, Major."

"Is Brea Gallagher there, Excellency?"

Brea's heart caught in her throat as she stepped into the screen's field of view. "I'm here, Eric."

"Whatever happens, I love you! I've got to switch off now. We're going to Ready Stations here. Mr. Chairman: keep us informed if you find anything. Brea, I'll talk to you later. *Bernadotte* out."

"*Concordiate* out," Brea said. It wasn't until the screen went blank that she realized that she had tears in her eyes. Tears of happiness or fear, she wasn't sure.

The Probe Negotiating Committee, minus one, convened in emergency session at 23:00 hours, 8 February 2066. Chairman Malagar immediately informed the members of the evening's events. When he had finished, he was greeted by stunned silence.

After a minute Mrs. Darvi broke the silence. "May we see the evidence, Mr. Chairman?"

"It's all in the computer, filed under FIFTH COLUMN, Gida. You may review it at your leisure. However, the fact that Boswani and his henchmen have taken over *Asgard* should be proof enough for anyone."

"How is that situation going?" Vice Ambassador Kenzie asked.

Mrs. Meriweather nodded to Brea, who had been following the radio traffic on the fleet tactical channels.

"The destroyer *Gottmann* has moved alongside and is blocking *Asgard*'s path to prevent her boosting for Earth. The hijackers have threatened to kill as many passengers as possible if the Marines try to board, but otherwise they seem content to maintain the standoff."

"I wonder why?" Mr. Souvantavong mused.

Po Dua leaned forward and clasped his hands in front of him on the conference table. "I am less concerned with Boswani than the fact that the probe was cooperating with him." He looked at Kenzie. "What is that charming American expression, Robert? Playing both ends against the middle?"

"Agreed," Malagar said. "When this is over, we must reevaluate our relationship with our visitor from the stars."

"Why not do that right now?" Brea asked.

"What, Mrs. Gallagher?"

"Let's ask SURROGATE to explain himself."

Jacques Villart raised one eyebrow in a quizzical look. "Do you think that wise?"

"Not only wise but imperative," Brea responded.

Mrs. Meriweather nodded. "I agree. We've an unstable situation on our hands here, one that can only deteriorate with time. I don't see that we have the luxury of waiting to cross-examine the probe."

Chairman Malagar looked around that table. "Is anyone opposed? Good. Proceed, Agusta."

Mrs. Meriweather leaned forward, punched for *Concordiate* communications, and ordered the probe summoned on the line. The chamber's central holoscreen immediately showed SURROGATE's projection. "Good evening, ladies and gentlemen. I have been expecting this call."

"You have?"

"Of course, Agusta. We have been monitoring fleet communications and are aware of the recent problems aboard *Asgard*. I am most distressed. Is there no hope of a peaceful solution?"

"That," Mrs. Meriweather said with a hint of the arctic in her voice, "depends on you and your Master."

"On us?" SURROGATE asked.

"ARE YOU UNAWARE OF THE FACT THAT YOU ARE THE CAUSE OF THIS CRISIS?" Robert Kenzie shouted.

"We are aware, Mr. Ambassador. We truly regret that things have come to the brink of open warfare. We had hoped to be able to win the Pan-African ambassador over by reason."

"We have Boswani's transcripts," Mrs. Meriweather said. "There was talk of giving Pan-Africa exclusive rights to some Maker data."

"Not by me, Agusta. The ambassador did mention that as one of his terms for cooperating on the overhaul."

"You did nothing to discourage him."

The little man in the holoscreen shrugged. "Since arriving in this stellar system, I have discovered two distinct human factions—one in favor of my presence, one opposed. You can hardly blame me for attempting to persuade the opposition that PROBE and I mean them no harm."

"You should have reported Boswani immediately!" Malagar said.

"As an outsider, I am not in a position to offend anyone, Mr. Chairman. Surely you can understand that. If I have offended this committe, I humbly beg its pardon. I perceive that my error has cost me dearly. I will ponder long and hard as to the proper method of proving myself to you again."

"One way," Jacques Villart said, "is to tell us why Nicholas Boswani picked this particular time to hijack *Asgard*."

"I can only assume that he has learned of your reinforcements and does not wish to be here when they arrive."

"Reinforcements?" Malagar asked.

"The six warships from the Asteroid Belt, the ones due here within the next eight hours," SURROGATE responded.

Mrs. Meriweather turned to Brea. "Have you heard anything about this on the command circuits?"

Brea shook her head.

"Are you sure, SURROGATE? There is no mistake?"

"None. PROBE has been tracking them for quite some time."

"What makes you think they are UN warships?"

"Their radar cross-section is typical of such vessels. From their size, PROBE estimates two cruisers and four destroyers. As for their registry, who else has warcraft in the solar system?"

"The Pan-Africans," Brea said quietly.

Every face around the conference table pivoted to stare at her. "How is that possible?" Po Dua asked.

She avoided their eyes. "It's possible."

"In that case," Mrs. Meriweather said, "we had best warn *Count Bernadotte*. It appears that we are about to witness humanity's first battle in deep space.

CHAPTER 29

Human prejudices notwithstanding, the passage of time in space is invisible. No sunrises or sunsets periodically update the human circadian clock, no morning twilights arouse the sleeping body, nor do evening dusks prepare it for slumber. The endless void knows but a single moment of frozen time. It is forever and everywhere high noon. And even though *Count Bernadotte*'s clocks insisted that it was still the middle of the night, the fleet prepared for battle under a brilliant noonday sun.

To a casual observer looking down on the motley assortment of ships from a distance, very little would appear to have changed in the weeks since the probe's arrival. It continued to hang immobile in space, dominating the dozens of smaller human craft around it. From a hundred kilometers' range, only the probe and *Count Bernadotte* showed visible forms. Anyone approaching from that distance would need a medium-power telescope to see the swarm of small intraorbital craft that hovered around the flagship.

Bernadotte was motionless in space, no longer rotating about her long axis. Orbital transfer vehicles gathered in groups of two and three, each craft patiently waiting for another to clear the way to one of the oversize cargo ports. Small lighters and luggers, medium-size cargo carriers, and one largish hydrogen tanker all hovered expectantly. They carried every manner of consumable, things that the aging warship would find vital in the coming battle.

The tanker floated beside *Bernadotte*, her heavily insulated lines snaking through space to the blast ship's fuel tanks. For safety, only minimal quantities of reaction mass had been carried aboard since the journey from the Earth–Sun Lagrangian point. Now, however, the blast ship's fuel tanks were topped off with cryogen. The smaller cargo vessels had been warped into contact with the hatches around *Bernadotte*'s hull. When their cargos had been offloaded by sweating, swearing Marines, the holds were refilled just as quickly. Each ship that cast off was crammed with humanity—civilian scientists and technicians being evacuated in advance of the coming battle.

Eric Stassel sat in the central command position in *Bernadotte*'s Combat Control Center and tried his best to oversee the loading of ammunition, oxygen, cryogenic fluids, spare parts, and reaction mass, while at the same time keep the offloading of noncombatants moving smoothly. At times the two goals seemed mutually exclusive.

His fingers danced over the console keyboard as the workscreen view jumped from point to point within the ship. Around him, the full complement of technicians muttered into their headsets, each taking charge of some job that should have been performed days earlier.

Stassel switched to a camera that covered a vital intersection of corridors on Alpha Deck. Stretched before him was a traffic jam of major proportions. Cursing Marines toting long red cylinders were hopelessly entangled with a crowd of civilians. Stassel buzzed for Marine barracks.

"Larsen, you've got a mess at Alpha-Seventeen. The scientists being funneled through Lock Three have gotten themselves mixed up with that crew en route to Missile Battery Six. Get a squad down there to reroute the civilians to Lock Four. Keep that corridor clear!"

"Understood, Major."

A minute later six uniformed shapes arrowed past the camera in graceful freefall flight and began to sort civilians from military. Stassel watched for a few seconds, then put the problem out of his mind. Time was too short and the problems too numerous to spend more than a minute or two on each.

His workscreen buzzed as he continued his tour-by-proxy through the ship. A Marine enlisted man with a dubious look on his face stared out of the screen at him.

"Sorry to bother you, sir. We've a civilian here who is bucking traffic. She just arrived from *Concordiate* and insists on seeing you. Refused our orders to leave."

While the Marine was speaking, a familiar voice could be made out in the background. "... *get your hands off me, you frappin' skink-bottom!*"

Stassel grinned. "Send her up to control. Then return to your duties."

"Yes, sir."

Brea Gallagher floated through the armored hatchway of Combat Control several minutes later. She carefully pulled herself hand over hand to where Stassel sat grinning.

"What's so funny?" she asked petulantly.

"Nothing," he said. "I'm just glad to see you."

Her own features split in a grin. "Me, too, Eric. You aren't mad at me, are you?"

"No, I'm not mad."

"Good. I couldn't stand it if you were. I just had to see you before..." Her eyes stared at the steel deck.

He reached out and cradled her chin in his hand, forcing her to look at him. "Don't count *Bernie* out yet, Brea. This old girl has plenty of fight left in her."

"But SURROGATE says there are six of them, including two cruisers."

"So what? *Bernadotte* can handle them."

Brea's anxious eyes searched his face. "The truth?"

"Nothing but."

"Then I guess it's time for me to tell you something, Eric. It wouldn't be right to let you go into battle not knowing."

"This have anything to do with you, Don Bailey, and Angai Yahaya?"

She nodded.

"Does it help our current tactical situation?"

"No."

"Then I don't want to hear it. As it stands now, I have no evidence that you or Don Bailey have done anything. I'd just as soon keep it that way."

She sighed deeply. "Thanks."

"For what?" he asked.

"For just being you." She leaned forward and kissed him lightly on the lips. When they finished, Stassel noticed a lot of heads turning back to their consoles. He cleared his throat and straightened up in his chair.

"We seem to be gathering a lot of attention. I'd best get to work before the admiral catches me. You get back on whatever ship brought you and get out of here."

She shook her head vigorously. "I can't. I have to find Lisa."

"Already evacuated. I saw her and Bailey leave by way of Airlock Five more than an hour ago."

"Bailey?"

He smiled. "You didn't give me a chance to tell you. Admiral Liu released Bailey and Yahaya when he ordered *Gottmann* to let *Asgard* go."

"He let Yahaya go, too? And Boswani and M'Buto? Isn't that dangerous?"

Stassel shrugged. "They aren't going far. The directorate is already preparing to move against the Johannesburg government. They'll be put under UN supervision for a generation, or at least until we've rooted out everyone who had anything to do with this mess. If Yahaya's guilty, we'll have him back soon enough. And Boswani is merely on a longer leash. When *Asgard* gets to Earth, it'll be met by half the UN battle fleet.

"Now, you'd better move. We're minus on minutes and I've got a lot to do before we point this antiquated coffee can out into the deep black."

"I'm going." She turned to leave, hesitated, and then turned back. "Eric!"

"Yes?"

"No matter what happens, always remember that I love you."

"Nothing is going to happen," he said. "I love you, too. Now scoot!"

Two hours later *Bernadotte* was ready for action. The final shuttle had departed, the heavily armored cargo doors had been swung closed and latched, all personnel were in vacsuits and at their stations. All departments declared themselves ready for space.

Combat Control had settled down into a briskly efficient routine as the chaos of the evacuation tapered off. Arrayed around Stassel were rows of consoles. They showed views of the probe, the surrounding fleet, and the blackness where SURROGATE said the enemy was. So far, no contact had been made.

Stassel glanced up at the armored glass enclosure above him. Its official name was Command Central, but it was more familiarly known as the Crow's Nest. A single, dimly perceived silhouette could be seen amid the screens and instrument panels that filled the cubicle. The figure stirred and Admiral Liu's voice issued from Stassel's console speaker.

"Start your countdown, Major."

"Yes, sir." Stassel pressed for the General Command circuit. "Attention. All ships and crews. Prepare for departure. All noncombatant vessels will disperse according to plan. T minus thirty seconds and counting."

He watched the chronometer blink down toward the moment of decision. "...Five...Four...Three...Two...One... Execute!"

Simultaneous with the words, a dull roar began to emanate from the deck underfoot and a gentle hand shoved him into his seat cushions. Stassel switched to outside view. *Gottmann*, which was poised beside the blast ship, had sprouted a tail of blue-white fire as the two warships departed their parking orbit.

"Begin programed deployment, Major."

Stassel gave the order and the destroyer edged away from *Bernadotte*. Behind them other actinic stars flared into being as the ships of the fleet began to scatter. In less than twenty minutes, the probe was alone in space.

Stassel busied himself with final preparations for battle. Weapons were to be armed and circuits tested. He was overseeing the prearming checklist when his console buzzed. He paused to accept the call. Ellie Crocker stared worriedly from the screen at him.

"What's the matter, Lieutenant?"

She hesitated, obviously ill at ease. "Did you ask Brea Gallagher to remain aboard?"

"Hell, no!" Then, as the probable reason for the question sank into his consciousness, he felt his stomach muscles tighten with tension. "Is she?"

Ellie nodded. "She showed up in Emergency Control five minutes ago. She claims you assigned her here."

Stassel spoke through clenched teeth. "Have her brought up."

A minute later Stassel became aware of a commotion behind him. He swiveled in his seat to discover Brea Gallagher flanked by two Marine guards. The trio stood at attention, their boot clips holding them to the deck. All three were in vacsuits, helmets cradled under their arms. One of the Marines raised his arm to his chest in the closest thing to a regulation salute that is possible in a vacsuit. Stassel returned the gesture and then dismissed the Marines. He turned to Brea with a scowl.

"I thought I ordered you to leave?"

Brea reached up to brush an errant strand of hair from defiant eyes. "You did."

"So what the hell are you doing here?"

"I tried to leave, Eric. Honest, I did. I just couldn't."

"Why the hell not?"

"I'm not really sure. Mostly, I guess, I was feeling guilty. The thought of all of you risking your lives out here while I was safe."

"Where did you get that?" he asked, pointing to her vacsuit.

Brea grinned and struck a pose popular with high-fashion models. "Do you like it? A nice man in the armory gave it to me. I told him you had ordered me to get into a suit."

Stassel gestured at an empty console in the ring of operating stations. "You might as well keep your word. That grinning Scandinavian-type down there is Technician-Specialist Olaf Gruen, late of UNS *Konstantin Tsiolkovsky*. Strap yourself down at the console next to his and help him monitor the long-range detectors. The controls are similar to those you've been using in your astronomical work."

"Yes, sir!" she said, semisaluting as she had seen the Marine guard do.

"And Brea—"

"Yes, Eric?"

"This time, follow orders!"

"Yes, Eric," Brea said with mock meekness.

"Message coming in from the probe, Major," the comm officer reported from a nearby console.

"Hook it in here."

SURROGATE's alter ego flashed on the screen. The projection managed to look worried. "Have you spotted the unidentified craft yet, Major Stassel?"

"Not yet."

"I didn't think you would. They are using fairly sophisticated radar suppression gear. PROBE is tracking them. I would be honored if you would allow me to vector you to them."

Stassel hesitated. Like just about everyone else aboard, he had come to trust the probe during the preceding sixteen days. Recent events had shaken that trust considerably. Still, knowing where the enemy is can sometimes be half the battle.

"We welcome whatever help you can give us, SURROGATE. However, just to make sure you know which side you're on, perhaps we should get a few things straight—like the purpose of those ships out there."

"Their purpose is distressingly obvious. They mean to destroy PROBE."

"I don't think they are out for destruction," Stassel said. "More likely they mean to kidnap you. Once they have control, they'll hold you hostage until the UN agrees to terms."

"I only wish you were correct, Major Stassel. If they were intent on capturing me, they would have begun decelerating three hours ago. PROBE has been watching them most carefully. So far they show no sign whatever of slowing."

Stassel reported SURROGATE's statements to Admiral Liu, who only nodded. "I had already surmised that, Major. Since Boswani has failed to subvert the probe, he's decided to destroy it. I think we can be sure of SURROGATE's wholehearted cooperation. Please ask him to feed the enemy positions to our computers."

Within seconds the tactical situation display changed. Now, besides the sparkling green, gold, and blue dots that were the fleet and the probe, six glowing red stars had appeared. They were arrayed with geometric neatness, spread in an arc of nearly a hundred thousand kilometers. The numerical information next to each told the story. The bandits were on intersecting hyperbolic orbits, all of which would intercept the probe's position at the same instant. So precise were the predictions that the computers could not yet see any orbital separation at closest approach. From a distance of a million kilometers, it looked like a collision course for all concerned.

Within half an hour, the situation had developed substantially. Admiral Liu continued to issue orders from his *sanctum sanctorum*. The Combat Control staff translated his desires into detailed instructions for the ship's tactical computer, which maneuvered *Bernadotte*. While the computer worked its will, three hundred Peace Enforcers sat anxiously in vacsuits, waiting for the battle to begin.

The enemy fleet seemed curiously oblivious to the presence of the two UN warcraft. The craft had taken no evasive action of any kind, not even the elementary precaution of varying their approach speeds to make predictions of their future actions more difficult. They veered neither right nor left, nor did they waver. They just bored in.

"Surely they must have seen us," Stassel muttered.

"Of that, there is no doubt," SURROGATE replied from his workscreen.

"So why sit there like ducks in a shooting gallery?"

"It does seem strange that all the enemy craft remain on their current courses. Could it be that they are planning to ram me?"

"Unlikely," Stassel replied. "More probably they'll scatter gravel in your path just before changing course. It's crude but difficult to counter."

"I think not," SURROGATE said. "The dispersion of the individual particles would be too great if they discard their gravel at any reasonable range. A few small rocks will not significantly damage PROBE."

"Maybe they don't know that."

"Doubtful, Major Stassel. The dispersal equations are quite elementary. Surely they have done computer simulations of this attack."

"Wish *we* had," Stassel said. Whatever the reason for the Pan-Africans' strange strategy, they seemed determined about it. By coming in line abreast, they had virtually insured the survival of at least one of their ships. The coming hostilities from start to finish would take no more than eleven minutes. After that, any surviving Pan-African would be past the UN picket line and out of range, with nothing between it and the probe except vacuum.

Finally the waiting was over and the battle joined.

The opening shots came when *Bernadotte* moved into extreme range for its heavy lasers. The big beams flashed out a dozen times or more. Microseconds later, the image of the nearest Pan-African ship blazed momentarily with a thousand times its normal brilliance. Yet long-range sensors showed few signs of significant damage.

"I was afraid of that," Admiral Liu said over the command circuit. "Must be one hell of a lot of antilaser ablatives on those ships. Go to missiles. Set the lasers to destroying incoming ordnance until we get closer."

"Yes, sir," Stassel said, simultaneously keying the order into the tactical computer.

Several minutes passed while the two forces moved closer. Then everything seemed to begin at once. Stassel watched as the three most distant enemy ships began to spew projectiles at *Gottmann.* The destroyer responded with a swarm of her own. Tiny sparks moved between larger points of light, accelerating at more than a thousand gravities. A series of deadly flashes burst in open space as the two swarms came together.

Then *Bernadotte* was in missile range. Stassel felt a dull thud shudder through the ship with each launch. Again there was a long pause as the two fleets waited for their weapons to close and engage. *Bernadotte*'s deadly spawn were met in midspace by a flight of Pan-African missiles. Again there was a brief thunderstorm between the opposing sides. But unlike *Gottmann*'s exchange, it didn't end there. A minute later one of the intruders burst into brilliance and was gone.

A cheer went up over the intraship communications circuits and then died quickly away. The sound of missiles being launched was continuous now as *Bernadotte* sought to swamp the enemies' defenses and big lasers flashed, invisible in the vacuum of space, picking off enemy weapons as they homed on the UN flagship.

At engagement plus seven minutes, another enemy disappeared into nothingness.

273

"*Gottmann*'s" one of the detector technicians reported.

And then, as if to emphasize his words, there was an explosion far removed from the others. A few seconds later, the calm voice of the comm officer filled Combat Control: "Captain Parkinson of *Gottmann* reports taking a direct hit. Air loss thoughout the ship, one quadrant open to space, extensive damage and heavy casualties."

"Continue the attack," Admiral Liu's voice ordered over the general circuit. 'Switch lasers to offense."

Almost immediately the big laser batteries began to have an effect. The computer reported an enemy craft hit. The enemy image was quickly obscured by a cloud that spectrographed as hydrogen, oxygen, and water vapor. Ten seconds later that same ship was vaporized as one of *Bernadotte*'s missiles took it.

That left three.

Stassel glanced up to note that nearly ten minutes had passed since the battle opened. The opponents, had nearly closed to minimum range. Two of the surviving enemy craft were on *Gottmann*'s end of the line, one on *Bernadotte*'s. The crippled UN destroyer fed half a dozen missiles into space and struck with its small offensive lasers. Then, in total silence, it exploded. *Bernadotte*'s long-range cameras caught the growing fireball that had moments earlier been 106 PEs.

"Damn!" Stassel said tonelessly. He ruthlessly put a sudden attack of despair out of his mind. There would be time to mourn later—if he survived. Right now he had problems of his own.

The last Pan-African ship on *Bernadotte*'s front was lashing out with everything it had. It filled space with its armament. The blast ship's own missiles raced out and its heavy laser batteries turned once more to destroying incoming ordnance.

Stassel was just reaching out to order the lasers trained on the enemy vessel when *Bernadotte* lurched. A thunderclap smashed at his eardrums. Combat Control was plunged into darkness. Stassel's vacsuit puffed up around him as a gale wind tried to tug him from his seat. His earphones were filled with screams and curses as the hurricane died away to nothing.

He reached up and switched on his helmet emergency lamp. All around Combat Control, others were doing the same.

"Anyone hurt?" he called over the suit communications band

His voice echoed eerily as the radio waves bounced around the enclosed compartment.

"Over here . . ."

Stassel felt his heart jump up into his throat. The voice had been Brea's.

"Gruen's been hurt."

Stassel experienced a moment of guilt at the sudden relief that he felt. He unstrapped from his console and pulled himself hand over hand to where a cluster of headlamps was forming.

"What happened?" someone yelled. The intraship comm circuit chose that moment to come to life.

"Attention! All damage control parties. We have been holed by shrapnel at alpha six nine, beta five eight, and gamma four six. Assemble in corridor A-six and prepare to patch primary and secondary penetrations. All departments, report casualties."

Stassel reached the point where Technician Gruen lay slumped in his seat. The injured man had a ten-centimeter-long shard of glass sticking from his chest. A red froth bubbled up around the point where the shard had entered his suit.

"His suit is leaking air!" Brea yelped. *"For God's sake, someone help me."* A nearby figure moved to her side. There was some fumbling in the dark before Brea had a patch in position. It was a quick, two-second job to remove the shard of glass and slap a patch over the bubbling hole in the suit.

Stassel watched the operation with growing unease. He closed his eyes, visualizing the line of flight that would have positioned the splinter just right to enter Gruen's body. When he had the spatial relationships firmly fixed in mind, he projected the glass shard's path back to its origin. With a feeling of horror, he whirled and tilted his body such that his headlamp flashed up. At that moment the emergency lights came on, dazzling him for a split second.

He found himself looking at the Crow's Nest. The armored pane had been shattered. It hung in its frame, a spiderweb of cracks pointing to the exit point of whatever had smashed it. Whatever it was, it had been traveling at very high speed. A slow projectile would not have left the roughly circular, twenty-centimeter hole that now stared him in the face.

Besides the gaping hole, the inside of the window was badly

stained. It was a uniform reddish brown in color, the exact shade of vacuum-frozen human blood.

"Check the admiral, quick!" Stassel ordered.

Two technicians scrambled up the ladder, taking a few seconds to force their way inside. One poked his helmeted head out through the open hatchway almost immediately. He sounded sick.

"The admiral is dead, Major. Whatever it was went right through him."

CHAPTER 30

Stassel shuddered inside his vacsuit and repressed the urge to gag. He couldn't honestly claim that he had liked Liu. The admiral had been too private a person, too conscious of the barrier between commander and subordinate. Their relationship had been strictly business, with none of camaraderie that normally develops between fellow professionals. But Liu had been a good commander, one of the best Stassel had ever worked for. Without Liu and his almost sixth sense about mysterious lights in the sky, Project Eaglet would never have begun. And now he was gone.

Responsibility for *Count Bernadotte* and her surviving crewmembers had devolved upon the executive officer. Stassel took a deep breath filled with the stink of oil and perspiration and other, less identifiable, odors. That simple act was enough to snap him out of his mood. A sudden, icy clam descended over him.

"Return to your consoles, Marines," he ordered on the general suit circuits. "We've got a war to fight."

There was a sudden flurry of activity as technicians returned to their battle stations. He fixed the comm officer with an icy stare—the effect of which was ruined by the fact that no one could see his face in the shadowy confines of his helmet.

"Have we external communications?"

"No, sir. We're down across the board. Deaf, dumb, and blind."

"How quick to repair?"

"Half an hour, maybe a bit longer."

"You've got five minutes. I've got to have comm capability, if only two cans and a string."

"Yes, sir."

"Detectors!"

"Major?"

"I need tactical data and I need it fast."

"Can't, Major. The long-range scanners are operational, but the gyros have been scrambled. I can't track a damned thing with this junk."

"Go to manual."

The technician lifted his hands in frustration. "Without Gruen, we haven't got anyone checked out on the manual gear."

"You're wrong." Stassel turned around. "Brea!"

"Yes, Eric?"

"Take over Detection Station, please. See if you can't finesse the long-range scope into getting us a picture of the probe."

"As good as done."

He returned to his own console and was pleasantly surprised to see that it had been partially restored to operating condition.

"Get me Engineering," he ordered.

"I can only supply audio, sir."

"Do it, then."

"Chief Engineer" came the immediate response.

"This is Stassel. Liu's dead. How bad are things in the engine room, Chief?"

"Could be worse, Major. We'll have the booster up and running again in about ten minutes."

"What's wrong?"

"Piece of debris cut through some electrical cables leading to the I-mass field coils. The system shut down as a safety precaution. Good thing, too, else we would have lost our singularity and really been in trouble!"

"Keep me informed of progress."

"Yes, sir."

"Damage Control."

"Sergeant Abdulla."

"This is Stassel, now commanding. How bad is it?"

"We're holed pretty good, Major, but should be able to get airtight again in a few hours. The chunk appears to have come in through the prow near Airlock Five. It traveled lengthwise through the Third Quadrant and went out through the engine room. Nothing vital damaged beyond repair. Plenty of secondary splinter damage, though."

"We're in Combat Control, Abdulla. See if you can get us some air in here."

"Yes, sir. We'll get right on it."

"Get me a general circuit."

"You're on, Major."

"Attention! All crewmembers and all stations. This is Major Stassel speaking. The admiral has been killed. I am taking over command. I congratulate each of you who has survived thus far. Take heart from the fact that we have come through the worst of it. Our ship is damaged but appears to be repairable. I know you will all do your best in the coming hours. That is all."

He switched off just as Brea let go with a whoop of joy. "I've got something," she said. "I'm passing it to you now, Eric."

Stassel's workscreen lit to show a magnified view of the probe. It was overexposed and blurry and jumped around quite a bit, but it *was* a picture. So far, the probe seemed unharmed. Stassel glanced at his chronometer and was surprised to note that only five minutes had passed since they were holed.

"Radar, can't you get some kind of beam on the line?"

"Coming up now, sir. All I can give you is range and speed, I'm afraid. The rest of my functions are down for the count."

"Give me what you can. Throw it on the main screen."

"Yes, sir."

Markers showing the position and speed of the two surviving Pan-Africans immediately appeared on the large holoscreen.

279

An instant later *Bernadotte* and the probe were added. The tactical situation didn't look good. The Pan-Africans' speed had been their salvation once they had run the UN line. They had already closed to within a hundred thousand kilometers of the probe. They were less than five minutes from successfully completing their mission.

"Missiles!"

"Here, Major."

"Are you getting the radar output on your status screens?"

"Yes, sir."

"Can you launch against either or both intruders?"

"Negative, sir. With their velocity, they went out of range for a tail shot nearly two minutes ago."

"Lasers?"

"Out of range, sir."

Stassel knew boundless frustration. He'd commanded a ship for only five minutes and was already facing his first defeat. "Get me the probe."

SURROGATE's projection flashed on the screen immediately.

"We couldn't stop them," Stassel said.

SURROGATE nodded. "So we observed. A valiant effort, Major Stassel."

"We've been out of touch for the last three hundred seconds. What's been going on?"

"The enemy ships have continued to refine their orbits. They are definitely on a collision course. We surmise that they will launch missiles at any moment. Correction, they *have* launched their missiles!"

On Combat Control's holoscreen, the two red dots that were the Pan-Africans began to spit out smaller dots once again. They filled the sky with them. Stassel counted more than two dozen of the deadly little fireflies before the unexpected happened.

One by one the fireflies started to go out.

"The probe just turned bright violet!" Brea reported from where she continued to nurse the long-range telescope.

Stassel nodded. "It's using its laser. Must be getting some energy spillage, causing a corona discharge. I wonder why it waited so long."

Whatever the reason, the probe continued to pick off Pan-African missiles until there were no more. Then it turned on

280

their launching platforms. One second, two determined raiders were bearing down on it at high speed. The next, the attackers were just two more clouds of expanding plasma.

"It destroyed them!" one of the detector operators screamed into his suit radio. "It blew the grambly bastards to hell and gone!"

Stassel flinched at the pain in his ears and ordered the heckler to pipe down. He sank back into his seat and breathed a sigh of relief. He was still letting the tension drain away into a delicious languor when his workscreen buzzed. He reached out to accept the call.

SURROGATE appeared on the screen.

"You did it," Stassel said quietly, all of his enthusiasm long since evaporated.

"They are destroyed," SURROGATE agreed. Stassel noted that the projection seemed more mechanical than usual, as though SURROGATE was putting less effort into it. "However, the danger is far from over. PROBE has discovered the reason behind their strategy."

"What does it matter now? Two big clouds of cooling plasma can't hurt us."

"Perhaps the clouds cannot, but that which they contain can."

"What?"

"Perhaps the fault is mine. Because the attackers' methods were unorthodox, PROBE assigned me to study scenarios that made logical sense for such tactics. The problem proved difficult and the solution took much longer than expected. The analysis has just been completed. The ships are destroyed but *their l-masses are not.*"

Stassel felt a deep-seated, debilitating dread. It was the unease that comes when one visits a friend on his deathbed. The Pan-Africans had carefully placed their ships on collision courses with the probe, refining their aim all the way to the target. Presumably their orders were to hold to course until they observed the probe's destruction from missile attack. If the attackers were destroyed before they could strike at the target, then six tiny points of infinitely dense matter would be their avengers.

"Any chance that the singularities will miss?"

"It is possible, Major Stassel, but not likely. They had

several days in which to refine their orbits. We will know shortly. PROBE calculates that the moment of maximum danger will come thirty-seven seconds from now."

Stassel ordered the telescopic view of the probe displayed on the main holoscreen. Then he waited. The communications circuits were silent except for breathing sounds. The men and women in *Bernadotte*'s Combat Control sat hypnotized as they watched the screen. There was no indication of where the six loose I-masses were, but it wasn't hard to imagine them converging ever closer to the three-quarters dark image of the probe.

Then, just when Stassel was beginning to hope, the image burst with a point of eye-searing radiance. The sudden nova was centered in the probe's control sphere as one or more singularities made a direct hit. As the ball of radiance grew larger, it seemed to engulf the entire front half of the probe. The spark burned for perhaps thirty seconds and then began to die slowly away.

Stassel stabbed out. "Communications, get me the probe."

After a fifteen-second pause, a somber voice replied. "Doesn't answer, Major."

"*DAMN!*" Stassel wanted to put his fist through the screen, obliterating the sight of the hulk that had once had been mankind's first visitor from another star. Then his anger gave way to shame. Sick horror boiled up inside him until he wanted to rip off his suit and double over from the pain of it. He retched and nearly lost the contents of his stomach as the full impact of the probe's destruction struck him.

The Makers had dared to challenge the stars. They had constructed their machine with loving care and set it on a course into the deep black. For ten thousand years their servant had searched the skies for some sign of intelligence. It had found it, and having braved the rigors of interstellar space, had chanced the charity of human beings. Now, only sixteen days after its arrival among the naked apes of Planet Earth, that ancient wonder lay dead at the hands of assassins.

Somewhere, someone wept.

Twenty hours passed before *Bernadotte* managed to limp back to the rendezvous point. The ship's new commanding officer, awake for nearly two days straight, finally allowed himself to relinquish the bridge for a few hours just before the flagship returned to the gathering fleet.

The last thing he remembered was Brea Gallagher crooning softly to him as she rubbed his tired shoulders through his rumpled shipsuit. Some time later he was shaken roughly awake by Ellie Crocker.

"It's time, Major."

He opened his eyes and groaned. His mouth felt like someone had played field hockey in it and his nasal passages and throat were sore from the vast quantities of pure oxygen he'd breathed while in his vacsuit. He sat up and rubbed at two sandpapery eyes.

"How long did I sleep, Lieutenant?"

"Three hours, sir."

"Anything to report?"

"We'll be back at the rendezvous point in fifteen minutes. Brea Gallagher has been on the radio for the last hour, talking to Professor Roquette about salvaging what we can from the probe. She called me on the bridge a couple of minutes ago and asked me to wake you. She wants you to meet her in Combat Control. She sounded excited."

Stassel leaned over to zip up his shipboots. It was only then that he noted the feeling of weight around him. *Bernadotte* was under power, but only barely so. He took the time to splash his face with cold water before accompanying Ellie Crocker.

He found Brea speaking animatedly into a workscreen. Henri Roquette's features were on the face of the screen. From the background view, Stassel could see that he was aboard *Concordiate*.

"What's the matter?" he asked, pushing his face into the pickup's field of view.

"SURROGATE's alive!" Roquette exclaimed.

"Impossible," he whispered hoarsely. "You saw the explosion."

"I've spoken to him! The main personality *was* destroyed, but SURROGATE is housed at the end of one of those long instrumentation booms. Apparently he was far enough away from where the I-mass struck to come through it. I've asked him about the Maker library. Much of it survived as well. Wait a moment . . . I've just announced your arrival. SURROGATE wants to talk to you."

Stassel sat down at one of the workscreens. "Patch me in."

When it came, the familiar voice was much more mechanical than it had ever been before. "I am here, Major Stassel."

"Are you all right?"

"I am unharmed."

"A goddamned miracle!" Stassel muttered.

"I will agree that my survival was highly improbable," SURROGATE said. "However, that is what I wish to speak to you about. You must order your ships away from this spot."

"Why?"

"I am preparing to overload my power sources. The resulting explosion will be extremely violent. Your ships could be damaged."

"I don't understand."

"I am planning suicide."

"But *why*?"

"That is obvious. With PROBE destroyed, there is no way to contact the FTL civilization. Without FTL, Maker society must inevitably collapse. I am a machine whose only purpose is to search for that which is now unobtainable. Can you comprehend the intensity of my despair?"

Stassel thought back to his own pain in those first few moments after the probe was destroyed. "I understand better than you think."

"Then you must know that the knowledge of my failure could very well unbalance me. I could go insane, especially with the sensory deprivation that the destruction of PROBE now forces me to endure. It is best that I destroy myself while I still have control."

"Could you retain your sanity if your mission weren't a failure?"

"The question is hypothetical and to no purpose."

"Just answer me."

"Yes, if there were some method of avoiding failure, I could maintain my equilibrium. I fail to see the purpose in this. The quest is at an end. I have failed utterly and completely."

"You haven't! There is still a chance."

"There is no chance."

"There's always a chance while you're alive. The only permanent failure is in death."

284

"A sentiment that does not stand up well under analysis," SURROGATE replied.

To Stassel's ear, it seemed as though the probe's resolve to end its existence was weakening. He wondered briefly how much faith to place in SURROGATE's anthropomorphic qualities. With no good answer to the question, there was nothing to do but treat SURROGATE as he would a human being, and hope it worked.

"Look, I can understand your feelings. You've lost PROBE. It's a heavy blow. But I've lost friends, too. Admiral Liu is dead along with fifty members of this crew and all those poor devils aboard *Gottmann*. Every one of those people was a friend or acquaintance of mine.

"You grieve, SURROGATE, but you go on. You are damaged. So teach us what we need to know and we'll repair you. You can still complete the mission."

"Impossible," SURROGATE said.

"Why?"

"The level of skill involved would be several orders of magnitude greater than that required in an overhaul. You would not be able to do it in a thousand years."

"I'll bet we could. But what if it did take a thousand years? That isn't so long for a life probe, is it? You are the Makers' only hope. If you destroy yourself, you are condemning them to death."

"They are already condemned. Even if humanity had the skills, it would be for naught."

Stassel decided to switch tactics and let a hint of mirth slip into his voice. He was like a policeman balanced on a tenth-story ledge with a potential jumper. One slip and they were both over the edge.

"Come on now. You're being stubborn. It's possible. Admit it!"

"It is impossible, Major. PROBE kept all knowledge of the Makers in a special memory bank as insurance against inadvertent disclosure during discussions with you humans. That memory was part of the circuitry that was destroyed."

"I don't understand," Stassel said, heart thumping and afraid that he understood all too well.

SURROGATE's reply was close to hysterical. "Don't you see?

285

I don't know where to find the Maker planet. I could no more direct an FTL starship there than you could."

Stassel considered SURROGATE's dilemma furiously. At first glance it looked like the end of the road. Then a possible solution popped into his brain. It was such an outrageous idea that he had to mull it over for several seconds before he trusted it to his vocal cords. Finally, with an enthusiasm that stemmed from desperation, he broke his silence.

"By God, you don't have to know. *We'll find them for you!*"

Stassel had become used to SURROGATE's lightninglike responses. Thus, when the probe didn't answer for nearly half a second, it was a significant datum, proof that his arguments were beginning to have an effect—he hoped.

"Please explain yourself."

"It's simple, really," Stassel said, aware that it would be neither simple nor easy but rather the hardest thing the human race had ever attempted. "You're probably right about our not being able to repair the damage. So we forget that. You teach us the Maker art of shipbuilding, and we'll build a ship of our own. We humans will launch the expedition to Procyon. We'll obtain the secret of faster-than-light travel, we'll build a fleet of starships, and we'll go off in search of the Makers ourselves."

"You could not find them. The galaxy is much too large."

"Sure we could—eventually. We know the direction and the approximate distance. That probably narrows the choices down to no more than a thousand stars. With a thousand ships doing the searching, we could find them in a year or two. Hell, it wouldn't be long before we possessed the capability to search the whole damned galaxy if we had to."

SURROGATE was unconvinced. "An exciting plan, but unworkable. You humans are incapable of sustaining such an effort for the time necessary. Once you have the Maker knowledge, you will give up the expedition to Procyon."

"Nonsense!" a voice said from close beside Stassel's ear. He turned to find that a crowd had gathered to watch the debate. Brea Gallagher was leaning forward, with her face beside his. It was she who had spoken.

"Remember what you told the committee during our first meeting?" Brea asked. She considered what she had just said and then gave out with a short, nervous laugh. "Silly question.

286

You're a computer, so how could you forget? You told us that we need FTL every bit as much as the Makers do. And you were right! You've seen our intramural squabbles. Do you think the Pan-African attack on you is really that unique in our history?

"You can be sure that we'll mount that expedition to Procyon, SURROGATE. Oh, we won't do it out of loyalty, or in a fit of repentance, or anything like that. We'll do it because we haven't any choice. If we stay in this one system, we will surely destroy ourselves."

"And after you have obtained the secret? Would you truly go in search of the Makers?"

Stassel bit his lip. The one flaw in his plan was that future generations might not see things his way. Once humankind had FTL, they would very well rationalize away their promise to the probe. Then he saw that there was a simple solution to this problem, too.

"What you are saying, SURROGATE, is that you can't trust us to keep our word. I couldn't agree more. But there really isn't any need for trust to enter into this bargain. You can be there to see that we uphold our end if you like."

"How?"

"We'll trace down the box that contains your circuitry and transfer it to our starship. You can go along on the trip as the Makers' agent. You will provide us with basic knowledge, both to build the ship and afterward. That gives you leverage over us. At the first sign that we plan to commit breach-of-contract, you refuse to answer any more questions."

This time the pause was longer. SURROGATE said nothing for nearly five seconds. When he did speak, it was with great care. "An interesting idea, Major Stassel. However, I will have to consider it very carefully before making my decision."

"Why? It will work."

"Yes, I believe it will. A preliminary analysis gives an estimated eighty percent probability of success for any Procyon expedition on which I am an advisor. However, there is one factor that may override all others, a problem that may yet spell the doom of my mission."

"Which is?"

There was another long pause. "I do not wish to give offense, Major Stassel. I like you humans. I cannot help myself;

287

for PROBE made me one of you. I find learning new things about my adopted species to be an endless source of entertainment. If not for my responsibilities to the Makers, I would happily spend eternity here, trying to learn all I can about you fascinating creatures.

"However, I am also aware that human beings are complex, carnivorous animals. You are descended from a million generations of hunters and have developed aggression to the level of high art. There are many warlike species in the galaxy, but the Makers knew none with your unlimited capacity for conflict. And even though I am grateful to one group of humans for protecting me, I cannot forget that it was another group who nearly destroyed me. To be absolutely honest, your race could be a far greater danger to the Makers than the lack of a faster-than-light capability.

"For that reason, I must consider whether I dare unleash *Homo sapiens Terra* on an unsuspecting galaxy."

EPILOGUE:

PATHFINDER

"...and thus did Pathfinder I rise phoenixlike from the ashes of Life Probe 53935. Bigger, better, faster than the alien machine from which it springs, Pathfinder is not so much a spaceship as a city poised on the edge of the interstellar void. It is mankind's mightiest monument, and a living testimony to the dogged determination of a few visionaries. It is concrete evidence of what the race can accomplish when faced with a worthy challenge. And, perhaps most important, it is mankind's penance for the shameful act carried out by a few desperate men that terrible night thirty years ago.

"For in constructing the great ship that will carry the Procyon expedition to its rendezvous with destiny, humanity has redeemed itself. When men and women of Planet Earth finally come face to face with other intelligent beings out among the stars, they will do so proudly, with heads held

289

firmly erect. As the Secretary-General of the United Nations recently stated:

> *We go out to the stars seeking neither advantage nor dominance. We will not be masters, nor shall we be slaves. We will be proud, but not vain. For with this ship we have finally expunged the sin of fratricide from our souls.*
>
> "When *United Nations Exploration Vessel Pathfinder I finally slips the invisible chains of Sol, it will forever strike the shackles from all who remain behind.*
>
> "*God speed,* Pathfinder*!*"
> —From *Prelude to Pathfinder: An Official History.*

Eric Stassel sat at his desk and gazed at the apparition that hung in midair over his communications projector. He had done little else for the last hour. And even though he had seen the ship whose hologram hung before him go together bolt by bolt, beam by beam, it was still his favorite view.

Pathfinder didn't look like a starship—and, of course, she wasn't. Not a true starship, anyway. She was what SURROGATE called a slowboat, a multigeneration craft. The initial complement would number some ten thousand. By the time she pulled into the Procyon system, however, the population would be closer to fifty thousand. For, should the Procyonian planets not be the site of an FTL civilization, the men and women of *Pathfinder* would endeavor to plant the seeds of human civilization.

But if humanity's starship looked very little like the sleek FTL craft of the holomovies, she bore even less resemblance to the life probe from which she sprang. *Pathfinder* was a flattened ring, with living quarters housed in a torus some one thousand meters in diameter by five hundred long. The habitation ring was twenty decks thick in places and spun on its axis to generate Earth-normal gravity at the outer hull. Ship's propulsion was housed in a long cylinder that protruded through the empty space in the center of the habitation ring at the axis of rotation.

Pathfinder was unlike the probe in another way. Her powerplant was significantly improved over that of her predecessor.

She would accelerate out of the solar system as a conventionally powered spacecraft, much as the probe had once accelerated away from the Maker sun. Once at five percent of light-speed, however, *Pathfinder* would change from fusion rocket to Bussard ramjet. Powerful forcefields would funnel interstellar hydrogen to the engines for fuel and to holding tanks to replenish expended fuel stocks. For, unlike the probe, *Pathfinder* was intended to arrive at its destination with sufficient reaction mass to slow its flight without jettisoning its I-mass.

Stassel stared at his ship as though from a great height and remembered that day long ago when Henri Roquette had first suggested a Bussard ramjet as the best design for the starship.

"You must have slipped a decimal point," he had said, chuckling.

"Why?" Roquette asked, puzzled.

"You've got us arriving only eighty-seven years after launch."

"So?"

"So, if this ramjet thing were feasible, the Makers would have built it into their probes."

"Not necessarily."

"Huh?"

"Let me explain," Roquette had said. "The Makers have been spewing life probes in all directions for thousands of years. It seems to me that the speed with which each probe returns is not a significant factor. There are so many en route at any given time, there must be a steady stream of returnees laden with cargos of knowledge at any given time.

"No, their design constraints were simplicity and reliability, not speed. They must have decided early on to maximize their return on investment, building more probes rather than bigger ones. Each unit is slower than is feasible, but in the aggregate, the Makers obtain a maximum of scientific data in the shortest time."

It had taken two years of hard work to prove that Roquette was correct in his analysis. Stassel only regretted that the gentle Frenchman hadn't lived to see his handiwork completed.

And then there were all the others, the men and women who had given their lives for the dream of breaking free to the stars. Stassel ticked them off in his memory. The explosion of August 2068. Something had gone wrong in one of the early tests of a Maker force field. Thirty-five scientists, engineers, and technicians were found dead in the wreckage of the research satellite.

There had been the UN debate of March 2074 when the new North American administration had attempted to raid *Pathfinder*'s funding in the General Assembly. Agusta Meriweather had beaten them back in a virtuoso performance of parliamentary maneuvering that spanned three grueling days. An hour after winning the vote, she had collapsed from a massive cerebral hemorrhage.

The fire of December 2079 had broken out in a construction satellite where volatile bonding agents were stored under pressure. Don Bailey, who had stayed on as construction foreman, went in through the airlock to rescue ten workers trapped inside. No one came out alive.

Over the years 203 other men and women had given their lives to the project. Each name was now enshrined in a Roll of Honor inscribed on the keel of the ship they had all helped build.

Individual humans may die, but the race goes on forever.

Stassel was jolted from his reverie by the beeping of his intercom. He reached out and keyed for acceptance. A life-size hologram of a buxom young woman in the green-and-white of *Pathfinder* Technical Staff solidified over his desk.

"You asked to be alerted when the secretary-general checked in, Commodore. They just reported the outer marker. ETA: fifteen minutes."

"Thanks for the warning, Marilee. Please notify Captain Albright and get the honor guard to the hangar bay."

"Already there, sir."

"What about my wife?"

"She's signed out to the observatory on Gamma Deck."

"Where else?" Stassel asked with a sigh. "Probably berating the poor techs about scope force-field calibration again. Please ask her to join me on the Hangar Deck in ten minutes."

"Yes, sir."

"That's all. I'll be up shortly. Stassel out."

"Bridge out."

The young woman's image was gone as quickly as it came. Stassel reached out and keyed in a ten-digit code. This time he found himself looking into the eyes of a grandfather type with a confident smile and a resonant voice.

"They're here," Stassel said.

SURROGATE nodded. "I have been monitoring your communications. It is a great day for humans, Eric."

"It's a great day for everyone. I'm sure the Makers would be pleased if they knew."

"I suspect they would."

"You'll be monitoring the christening ceremony, of course."

"Of course, old friend. As stipulated by the contract, I will turn over control of all data banks at ceremony's end."

Stassel nodded but said nothing. Instead, he contented himself to stare into the false features of the alien computer that had been his partner in crime for these many years. In many ways Stassel was closer to SURROGATE than to any human being—with the possible exception of Brea. He luxuriated in the camaraderie of his old friend, savoring the moment while it lasted.

"Well, I'd best be getting to the ceremony. Wouldn't do to keep the S-G waiting, would it?"

"No, it would not," SURROGATE agreed before breaking the connection.

Eric Stassel, commander in chief of Earth's only starship, got to his feet and moved to the door of his office. The door withdrew silently into the wall as he approached. He stopped and turned. The intercom had once again switched back to standby. The exterior view of the ship hung over his desk once more. He watched the great wheel rotate slowly past the camera, his heart thumping in his chest.

The ship was finally done, the work of a lifetime completed.

He turned and strode briskly toward the lift that would take him to the hanger bay and the christening ceremonies. As he rounded a corner, he came upon a small knot of children ranging in age from six to twelve. They were clustered around one of their number who was carefully spraying the wall with a paint pen.

Stassel stopped and cleared his throat. The effect was explosive. Eight heads snapped as one, eight complexions suddenly turned several shades lighter. One little voice muttered, "Jesus, it's the commodore!"

He put on his most stern expression and let his voice drop an octave. "What are you children doing here?"

"N-n-nothing, sir!" the apparent ringleader, a gangly girl of ten or so, said.

"It doesn't look like 'nothing' to me. Stand aside and let me see."

The little clump of children slowly shuffled aside. He had caught them red-handed painting graffiti on the corridor wall, an offense punishable by several hours in the cowbarns on the wrong end of a shovel. Their subject matter was a saying made popular by the news media:

"Procyon, or bust!"

Stassel repressed a smile and turned to the children. "I won't report you this time, but I don't want to hear of this again. This is our home, and we won't stand to have people mess it up. Is that clear?"

There was a sudden chorus of "Yes, Commodore. We're sorry."

"Now scoot. I want this cleaned up first thing tomorrow morning. Understood?"

"Yes, Commodore."

Stassel was chuckling to himself when he arrived in the hangar bay just as the secretary-general's ship was pulled in through the air curtain by two docking beams.

"What's the matter with you?" his wife asked when she saw him.

He told her about the paint party in the corridor and the message they had chosen to decorate the ship.

"So?"

"So, not ten minutes ago I was feeling very self-satisfied. In fact, I think I may have strained a shoulder while patting myself on the back."

"You've completed *Pathfinder*," Brea said. "You've a right to be smug."

Stassel nodded. "'The work of a lifetime,'" he said, quoting himself.

"Of course."

"Wrong. That's old-person-type thinking." He gestured at

294

the distant metal walls around him. "Those kids were right, you know. This isn't the important thing. *Pathfinder* isn't an end unto itself, but a means."

"I fail to see the distinction," Brea said.

"The journey, that's important. We're going to the stars! We haven't finished our life's work. Far from it.

"We've only just begun!"

About the Author

Michael McCollum was born in Phoenix, Arizona, in 1946 and is a graduate of Arizona State University, where he majored in aerospace propulsion and minored in nuclear engineering. He has been employed as an aerospace engineer since graduation and has worked on nearly every military and civilian aircraft in production today. At various times in his career, Mr. McCollum has also worked on the precursor to the Space Shuttle Main Engine, a nuclear valve to replace the one that failed at Three Mile Island, and a variety of guided missiles.

He began writing in 1974 and has been a regular contributor to *Analog Science Fiction*. He has also appeared in *Isaac Asimov's* and *Amazing*. This is his second novel. His first, *A Greater Infinity*, was published by Del Rey Books in 1982.

He is married to a lovely lady by the name of Catherine, and is the father of three children: Robert, Michael, and Elizabeth.

Dear Reader,

Your opinions are very important to us so please take a few moments to tell us your thoughts. It will help us give you more enjoyable DEL REY Books in the future.

1. Where did you obtain this book?

Bookstore ☐1	Department Store ☐4	Airport ☐7 5
Supermarket ☐2	Drug Store ☐5	From A Friend ☐8
Variety/Discount Store ☐3	Newsstand ☐6	Other_____
		(Write In)

2. On an overall basis, how would you rate this book?

Excellent ☐1   Very Good ☐2   Good ☐3   Fair ☐4   Poor ☐5   6

3. What is the main reason that you purchased this book?

Author ☐1   It Was Recommended To Me ☐3   7
Like The Cover ☐2   Other_____
(Write In)

4. In the same subject category as this book, who are your two favorite authors?

_____ 8
_____ 9
_____ 10
_____ 11

5. Which of the following categories of paperback books have you purchased in the past 3 months?

Adventure/ Suspense ☐12-1	Biography ☐4	Horror/ Terror ☐8	Science Fiction ☐x
Bestselling Fiction ☐2	Classics ☐5	Mystery ☐9	Self-Help ☐y
	Fantasy ☐6	Romance ☐0	War ☐13-
Bestselling Non-Fiction ☐3	Historical Romance ☐7		Westerns ☐2

6. What magazines do you subscribe to, or read regularly, that is, 3 out of every 4 issues?

_____ 14
_____ 15
_____ 16
_____ 17

7. Are you: Male ☐1   Female ☐2   18

8. Please indicate your age group.

Under 18 ☐1   25-34 ☐3   50 or older ☐5   19
18-24 ☐2   35-49 ☐4

9. What is the highest level of education that you have completed?

Post Graduate Degree ☐1	College Graduate ☐3	Some High 20
Some Post Graduate	1-3 Years College ☐4	School
Schooling ☐2	High School	or Less ☐6
	Graduate ☐5	

(Optional)

If you would like to learn about future publications and participate in future surveys, please fill in your name and address.

NAME_____

ADDRESS_____

CITY _____ STATE_____ ZIP_____ 21

Please mail to: Ballantine Books
DEL REY Research, Dept.
516 Fifth Avenue — Suite 606
New York, N.Y. 10036

F-8